THE BOY KING

BOOK THREE OF THE SEYMOUR SAGA

JANET WERTMAN

First printing 2020 in the United States of America; Los Angeles, California

ISBN 978-0-9971338-6-8 (Kindle edition)
ISBN 978-0-9971338-7-5 (Paperback edition)
ISBN 978-0-9971338-8-2 (EPUB edition)

Library of Congress Control Number 2020911977

Cover designed by Jennifer Quinlan of Historical Editorial
Formatting by Sweet 'N Spicy Designs

CONTENTS

PART ONE

PART TWO

PART THREE

For Liana, Holly and Elon - my children who are children no more

PART ONE

JANUARY 28, 1547

*T*he wind bit at Edward Tudor's tender face, and the saddle hurt his bony rear, but the nine-year-old prince was determined not to complain. They would be dismounting soon; he could rest then. He shifted his weight forward and bit his lip.

His uncle, the formidable Edward Seymour, Earl of Hertford, had arrived earlier in the day at Hertfordshire Castle, the young prince's household. The elder Edward had refused to rest, insisting they leave immediately for court as the King wished to formally invest his son with the title Prince of Wales. They would just stop at Enfield Palace first for his half-sister Elizabeth, so they could bring her too.

It was the fastest pace Edward had ever taken on the sixteen-mile trip. It was also the first time he had ridden after dark, and the first time no one had established a strict rest schedule for him. Yet the exhilaration at finally being treated as an adult was wearing thin.

Sir Anthony Browne, his father's Master of the Horse, turned around and peered at the way Edward's legs gripped his gray courser, then raised his gaze to Edward's hands. "Are you comfortable, Your Highness?"

"Yes," Edward said between clenched teeth, his hands tights on the reins. Browne looked at Hertford and lifted a single, questioning eyebrow.

Instead of answering, Hertford peered through the cold fog and announced absently, "It's right up ahead."

Looking up to find a hint of red bricks emerging from the dark, Edward thrust out his chest: he had made this journey as a man.

The rest of the way felt easier, though he did not relax his grip. He even pretended nonchalance when they arrived. "Brush her down well," he said to the page who took his reins. "She seems tired."

"Make sure she is ready to leave in the morning," Hertford added, his tone sharp. "Make sure they are all ready to leave in the morning." He put a hand on Edward's shoulder. "Let us find your sister."

The Earl's face twisted, and he exchanged glances with Browne. Edward didn't understand, but then he rarely understood what transpired around him. People dissembled, claiming it was for his own good. He had complained about that to his father once, and the great Henry VIII had laughed and turned it around: "People will do far worse. All your life, they will lie to you. Practice discerning their true meaning; you will need to be expert at it."

A round-faced man with blue eyes greeted them at the door with two pages in tow. One was about eleven, the other a few years older. Edward studiously ignored the lads' surreptitious glances – people were always curious about him, and he had learned that aloofness commanded more respect.

"I am Thomas Parry, cofferer. My Lady Elizabeth's chamberlain being away, I welcome you on her behalf. She awaits you in the Great Hall."

Hertford cut him short. "I need a message sent to my brother at Whitehall. Immediately."

The older page leaped forward. "I can be there quick like, my Lord."

Hertford nodded. "Tell him I will be back no later than noon. That I have the...er...packages safe."

"Will you not stay longer, my Lord?" Parry asked, but Hertford kept his eyes fixed sharply on the page.

"There is a special reward if you deliver your message before midnight."

The lad sucked in his breath and bolted for the stables.

Parry swept his arm wide to invite them inside. "Shall we then?"

Edward took a step forward but his uncle stood still, staring at the stable door. Only when the messenger had burst out on his horse and galloped away did Hertford turn back to Parry. "No one else leaves the house tonight. No one leaves the house until we are gone."

Parry's eyes narrowed. "Is there—"

"Do you understand?"

"Aye." Parry looked at the other page. "Make this known," he said, and the boy raced away.

Hertford nodded, a tight smile on his face. "We will see the Lady Elizabeth now." He motioned for Edward to precede them.

Edward wanted to ask what was going on, but the set to his uncle's jaw told him no answer would be forthcoming. Swallowing his curiosity, Edward donned indifference as if he understood.

A hearth fire blazed in the Great Hall, illuminating the Tudor royal crest carved into the wood mantel and making the heraldic lion and dragon seem to dance atop the painted motto, *Service Alone is Virtue: the Rest is a Cheat.* His half-sister Elizabeth stood at the end waiting to receive them, her hands crossed before her. Like Edward, she had inherited the Tudor red hair from their father, though hers was pulled sharply back under her French hood. The rest of her was equally self-possessed: she was a full-grown thirteen, and much more worldly. Edward stood up straighter.

"My dear brother," Elizabeth said, with a curtsy as low as any other courtier would have made.

"Sister," he replied with a bow. Edward longed to get over this part so he could hug her and brag about how well he had completed this journey, but he reined in his impatience.

"My Lord Hertford," Elizabeth said with another curtsy, but a smaller one. "And my Lord Browne," she said with barely a bob.

The two men bowed back, and Edward shifted his feet. Soon, now, he would have his chance.

But instead of inquiring after health and completing the dozens of other normal courtesies, Hertford stepped up with a grave look on his face.

"Now that you are both here, together, I have news for you." He looked around the room, checking the corners. Then he removed his hat and sank to one knee before Edward. Edward took a step back from the blazing eyes that bore into him.

"It pains me to tell you this," Hertford said, "but your father has gone to his heavenly reward."

The words made no sense to Edward. Then Browne and Elizabeth sank to their knees. Panic rose in Edward's throat. Should he, too, kneel at this solemn moment? What should he do? No one had prepared him for this.

Hertford's voice rang out, filling the hall. "The King is dead, long live the King." The guards and pages at the doors repeated the time-honored phrase as they sank to their own knees. As Edward contemplated his next move, Hertford, Browne, and Elizabeth looked up at him, their faces gazing at him with reverence as if he were Christ on the cross.

Or King of England.

Wonder enveloped him, but pain quickly supplanted it. His father dead? The sun and the moon that ruled the kingdom and the world was no more?

Elizabeth sprang to her feet and came to him, arms open. He

hugged her, glad to have something and someone to hold onto. They stayed that way a long time, shaking with tears, lost in thoughts.

Hertford cleared his throat. Edward loosened his grip on Elizabeth, and she released him immediately. The servants rose slowly from their knees, though they kept their heads bowed.

"I wanted the two of you to have each other to share your pain," Hertford said. "We will return to London tomorrow morning. Early."

"I have ordered food," Elizabeth said. "In case you were hungry from your trip."

Edward suddenly realized he was famished. "I would take some gladly."

"And I," Browne said, the first words he'd spoken.

"Thank you for your foresight," Hertford said.

Elizabeth lifted her hand to signal the pages. Almost immediately, four boys brought in trays and laid them on the trestle table before turning to Edward and kneeling. They rose and knelt again, even a third time. They were more deferential than Edward had ever seen, except of course during one of his father's rages.

He felt dazed. Distant from the world. Confused. As if he had a fever. Everything had changed.

Hertford put his hands on Edward's shoulders and gave him a little shake. "I know it must feel too soon for you to come into this great estate. I know how scared you must be."

Edward nodded, his throat tight. Hertford guided him over to sit at the table, talking as they went.

"That was your father's greatest regret, that he was leaving you so soon. But I promised him I would take care of you. Keep you safe, keep your throne safe, keep England safe for the day when you shall rule her as a man." Hertford's eyes glistened. "I will serve you with everything I have."

Relief flooded Edward. "It seems a fearful thing to be King."

Hertford laughed. "I will see to everything, on your behalf, until you are ready. I won't let you down."

Edward pressed his eyes shut in a quick prayer. When he opened them, the sight of the food made him ravenous. He reached for a sweetmeat and popped it in his mouth.

A question nagged, one he now felt he could ask. He was entitled to know everything now, he *needed* to know everything now. He turned to his uncle. "Why is no one to leave here?"

Hertford bit his lip as if trying to decide how to explain. "You know I am a cautious man. I want you in London, surrounded by loyal guards, when this is known. For your safety."

Safety? The word clanged emptily in Edward's mind.

"There's no pretender as could steal the throne," Parry muttered.

"There is no excuse for carelessness," Hertford said, his voice icy.

Silence fell over the group. Hoping to banish the oppressive awkwardness, Edward turned his attention to the food. The sweetmeats shared the trays with venison and rabbit – his sister loved to hunt – and custards.

"If I'd had more warning, I would have had the cook make the wafers you love," Elizabeth said with a forlorn sag to her shoulders.

Wafers were Edward's favorite. Flavored batter pressed between hot irons to make thin biscuits – he could never get enough of them. But as his people were afraid of excess in all things, he was often denied. Now it would be harder for them to refuse.

"Are they permitted you?" Browne asked Elizabeth, his voice sharp. The sumptuary laws restricted the crisp treats to the highest-ranking people. Elizabeth was a king's daughter, but a bastard nonetheless.

"They are permitted my brother," she replied quickly, then paused and donned a deceptively sweet smile. "I did not offer them to you."

Edward hid his glee at his sister's audacity and resolved to copy her wit. It was a comforting thought, and he was glad he was here with her, though he still liked Mary better.

"I am sorry Mary is not here with us to pray for our father," he said.

"She is safely at court, with the Queen," Hertford said. "Or rather, the Queen Dowager."

Queen Dowager. Like the way the Duchess of Suffolk had become the Dowager Duchess after her husband died two years ago and Edward's young friend Henry had inherited the dukedom. Another reminder of the sea change that had taken place. Edward felt a little nauseous.

"Safely?" Parry arched an eyebrow.

"We don't want Spain to consider forcing Mary on us," Hertford said. "Not that they would, not that she would agree. But yes, she is held close. And all the ports have been closed."

Edward's eyebrows knitted. Hertford was worried about Mary? Why? Would anyone support a bastard's claim to the throne? Besides, a woman was no fit ruler, or so his father had always said. Did he really need to fear his eldest sister?

It occurred to Edward that Hertford might have had a second motive for bringing him to Enfield. Perhaps this was a way of seeing that Elizabeth was held close as well, even though she had no faction at all given that her mother had been a bitch and a whore, not a proper princess like Mary's mother, or a well-bred gentlewoman like Edward's.

Always search for men's true motives, his father had taught him. *You will almost always find self-interest.*

But Edward could find no self-interest here, thank goodness. His uncle Hertford was different. His uncle Hertford could be trusted.

"That is indeed wise," Parry pondered, shaking his head slowly. "Did the King – or rather the King-that-was – order this?"

Hertford's eyes narrowed. "You have been away from court

for some time. You would do well not to question the decisions that are necessary for the future of the realm."

Parry glanced at Browne, whose stony gaze offered no quarter. He bowed to Hertford. "I meant only admiration, not criticism."

Hertford nodded. "Good. And after this, I think the new King should be allowed to pray for his father and for his own future. We should all do the same."

"I do that every day," Elizabeth said. "And my chapel is ever at the ready."

"The *prie-dieux* in our chambers will be sufficient," Hertford said. "We need to rest for tomorrow's ride."

Edward nodded. He could not imagine how he would get through it all – the riding *and* the ruling. Again, he was glad his uncle was there to help. It would seem insurmountable otherwise.

January 29, 1547

The mid-afternoon sun was powerless against the day's dark gray clouds. The sense of unreality intensified when Edward dismounted from his horse in the courtyard of Whitehall Palace. This time people didn't bow the way they had at Enfield; no one bowed any more deeply than they ever had: no one at Whitehall knew yet of his father's death. Trays for every meal were still being brought into the King's apartments, trumpets blaring along the way. Everything to keep the secret until Edward arrived and the nobles could all kneel to him. It had something to do with magic, with capturing the transfer of power in a single moment in men's minds. For that, the new King needed to be there.

Edward hurried along with Hertford, Browne, and Elizabeth through the deserted halls where only their footfalls broke the heavy silence. When they reached his father's Presence Chamber, the throne shone from its place at the center of the massive room, dominating the space even with its glow tarnished slightly by the stench of rot. It was his father's smell, from the terrible ulcers in his leg that never healed – the cross his father had to bear. Edward felt a brief chill but pushed it aside, praying for the strength to bear his own crosses in life.

The double door to the bedchamber stood ominously closed. Edward shivered as he realized his father's lifeless body lay just beyond the carved oak panels.

"Would you like to see him now?" Hertford's voice was low.

Edward's answer was both yes and no. This was the first time Edward had been so close to death, other than to a hunt's prey. No one who was even ailing had ever been allowed near his rooms, all to keep him safe. Edward was curious, but did not want to see his father so reduced.

Still, it was his duty, wasn't it?

He glanced over at Elizabeth. Her face mirrored his confusion.

"This would be the time," Hertford said. "The Council will visit after they have bowed to you, and then he will be moved to the Chapel Royal. You should have this chance."

Edward bit his lip. Even before he had nodded, Hertford quietly opened one side of the doors and motioned Edward and Elizabeth in. The ornately carved bed, hung with cloth of silver and gold and trimmed with purple velvet, stood on a dais in the middle of the room.

The two siblings crept toward the great bed's closed curtains, Hertford close behind. Right in front of the bed, Edward stopped. Hertford put his hand on the embroidered edge and opened the curtain.

The mound of Henry VIII's huge belly was covered by a miniver blanket gathered around his chin, revealing a face the same whitish gray as the fur. The mouth gaped slightly, the lips a slash the color of cooked liver. The eyes were open just enough to show a thin milky line. The form was utterly devoid of movement, of soul. An empty shell.

Panic rose in Edward's chest. He sank to his knees and

closed his eyes. He felt Elizabeth and Hertford copy him and hoped it was a sign he had done the right thing, that this was not merely polite indulgence like the time at one of Edward's early court banquets when Katherine Parr had spilled her own wine onto a pearl white tablecloth to pretend that she, too, was clumsy sometimes.

As soon as his heart slowed, Edward rose and backed away. Hertford drew the curtain and followed Edward and Elizabeth out of the room, closing the door behind them.

The dim lights of the Presence Chamber were bright after the dusk of the death room, and Edward gulped in air that now felt fresh. Before him stood two comforting figures, their hands clasped in front of their bodies: Archbishop Thomas Cranmer and Edward's uncle Tom Seymour.

Edward hadn't seen his uncle in a long time: he had been sent to the Netherlands a few years ago to represent England, and visited rarely. Edward longed to hear of his adventures, but the first greeting belonged to the most senior person. "Godfather," Edward said, holding out his arms to the cleric. But instead of enveloping Edward with the comforting embrace he expected, Cranmer sank to his knees, his white cassock billowing around him. Tom followed, doffing his feathered cap with a flourish.

Of course, Edward realized. His throat thickened from the loneliness of his new position.

Cranmer rose and made the sign of the cross over Edward. "May the Lord bless you and succor you. May you long reign over us in strength and faith."

The words warmed and scared Edward at the same time. "Thank you," he said, his voice hoarse. He looked at Tom and saw three more men gathered behind him, his father's closest servants: Sir Anthony Denny, Groom of the Stool; William Paget, Chief Secretary; and John Dudley, Viscount Lisle, a man Edward had only met once or twice. They, too, had to be greeted before Edward could relax.

"Does Gage have the Tower ready for us?" Hertford asked.

"Everything is prepared. Not just the apartments but also the welcome. The ships that accompany the King's barge will fire salutes, which will signal the churches to start ringing their bells. All London will rejoice."

"Perfect," Hertford said. "Then summon the rest of the Council so we can begin."

Edward took a deep breath. This was so quick.

"You should receive them on your throne, Your Majesty," Hertford said, pointing at the massive chair of estate.

Edward swallowed. He hoped no one in the small crowd noticed the quiver in his legs as he mounted the three steps to the chair and climbed into it. The chair had been large even for his father, and Edward found that when he sat back, his feet stuck out. He quickly moved forward so the edge of the seat was right behind his knees. His feet still dangled above the floor, but at least he could sit tall and proud, like a king should.

Hertford smiled and nodded at him. "Good job," he whispered, then came to stand at Edward's right.

His uncle Tom came forward immediately and straddled the three stairs with one foot on the platform and the other on the ground. He looked up at Edward with a soft smile and scratched his red beard. "God save you, Your Majesty," he said. "You will have a faithful servant in me forever."

"Many faithful servants," Paget said, coming up behind Tom and bowing. The others all copied him, professing loyalty and love, all with that strange smile everyone was wearing now, a lifeless grimace topped by eyes brimming with calculation.

It was the look people donned when they wanted something from him. But what could they want right now?

The lords began filing in, all nodding to him with that same smile, then nodding to his uncle Hertford beside him with an inscrutable intensity. No one looked toward Tom or Elizabeth or the others, and Edward threw a glance just to make sure they were still there.

More than a dozen men swarmed before him, strangely

silent. Did they know his father was dead? They must, since they showed no surprise at Edward sitting on the throne. And yet they offered no reaction, made no change in how low they bowed. He wished his uncle had thought to explain this part beforehand, or that Edward had been bold enough to ask more questions.

Hertford stepped forward and put his hand on Edward's shoulder. "The King is dead. Long live the King."

"*Vive le noble roi, Edouard,*" Tom echoed in French.

The lords dropped to their knees as one. The guards at the door followed suit, then the ones down the hallway. Edward imagined a soft echo from falling knees rippling out through the palace and the country like waves in a pond.

All eyes in the room looked up at him expectantly, and his heart raced. Another moment no one had thought to prepare him for. He bowed his head to accept their devotion and hoped that would satisfy.

There was a rustle at the door and the page rapped his stave on the floor. "The Queen Dowager," he announced.

Edward's stepmother, Katherine Parr, stood in the doorway in a severe black mourning gown adorned only with ropes of shockingly white pearls. Her ladies, also in black but with fewer jewels, gathered behind. Katherine dropped to the floor in deep reverence. A half a second later Mary joined her, as was her right, and then the other ladies after her.

"God save you, my son," Katherine said, her eyes moist.

"God save you, my brother," Mary echoed.

"God save you," repeated the ladies, and the rest of the room joined in.

Edward was glad to see them both, relieved they were there. He wanted to run to them for comfort, but this was too serious an occasion. Ritual came first. He glanced at Hertford, who nodded at him reassuringly. But still, he did not want to put a foot wrong.

"Thank you," he said. That was safe enough.

Katherine Parr rose and approached his dais, leaving her ladies behind. As she made another reverence, Hertford spoke. "I know I speak for the King and all the court when I offer my great condolences on the death of your husband."

The prompt was helpful, telling Edward what was expected. "Yes, I am so sorry for us all." He looked around him but could not read people's reactions, and worried that their inscrutability reflected disapproval. He could do better. He had to: he was King now. "Though it must console us that my noble father led a virtuous life and governed the state aright." The lords nodded, and their agreement emboldened him. "He ever promoted piety and banished ignorance, and now he hath a most certain journey into heaven."

"Amen," the room exhaled as one.

Hertford patted Edward's shoulder.

Katherine's eyes crinkled in sad approval. "Thank you for your kind words," she said. "We all grieve for the great King-that-was, though we must turn our focus to the great King-that-is." She turned to Edward, her face lined with love. "I promise to serve Your Majesty well and faithfully, and to guide you as God guides me."

Her words reminded Edward how little he knew of what was involved in ruling, or judging men's souls, or any of this. "I shall value your counsel."

"The King will not lack for counsel," Hertford added. "The late King, your husband, was a wise man when he created the Regency Council to guide his son to the wisdom of maturity. I was honored when, toward the end, he asked me to serve as its head."

"So Paget has told us." The interruption burst from Thomas Wriothesley. "But he has not shown us any document that says this."

Katherine Parr's wide eyes jerked to Wriothesley, then to Hertford. Her mouth gaped.

"I have his will," Hertford said. "Like everything else, he gave it to me for safekeeping."

It occurred to Edward that he was part of this "everything

else" being kept safe by his uncle. He didn't know how he felt about that. Of course, he didn't quite know what to think of any of this conversation. He knew the words hid a different meaning, but he had no idea what.

"I am not to be Regent?" Katherine Parr's voice trembled. "I was Regent when my husband" – she drew out the word *husband* – "went to France; he proclaimed himself happy with my stewardship."

"And he was," Hertford said, his voice smooth. "He often praised the way you kept his country safe from your quiet hearth. But he wanted a man's hand at the helm during these coming years, and so he turned to me. I will be Lord Protector of the King's realm."

"Will I be Protector of the King's person?" she asked.

"The King honored me with that duty as well."

Katherine Parr lowered her eyes. "I know how much my late husband esteemed you, how much he valued your advice. I also know how important family is," she said through clenched teeth. "I hope you will remember the King has a second uncle he can trust," she added with a nod to her own brother, the Earl of Essex. Edward looked, and his uncle William Parr smiled at him before bowing. Edward smiled back.

"And a third," his uncle Tom Seymour said.

Katherine Parr looked up at Tom and her face softened. "Three uncles," she said.

Wriothesley almost spat. "I still think we should discuss this further."

Hertford looked at Paget, who nodded. "We will," Hertford said. "At the meeting of the Council tomorrow. We will meet to confirm the arrangements – the Council members, my protectorship. Once that is settled, we can begin to execute the other details of the late King's will, the gifts and titles he made at the end. Including yours, my soon-to-be Earl of Southampton."

Wriothesley's lips were a thin line as he bowed. Hertford

stood up even straighter. Edward had the feeling his uncle had just won whatever fight he was in.

Right then, Sir John Gage was announced. He entered the room and somehow the crowd knew to part to let him come straight to kneel before Edward. "Your Majesty," Gage said, "I was Constable of the Tower to your father, and it will be my honor to welcome you there in triumph to await your coronation."

The Tower. His coronation.

From his studies, he knew the last Edward who had gone into the Tower to await his coronation had been a minor like himself and was killed by an uncle who coveted the throne. Edward looked at Hertford and shook off the troubling thought. Every English monarch since the Conqueror had followed the hallowed ritual, consolidating his power in the impregnable Tower before emerging to be crowned at the glorious Westminster Abbey. Edward had no choice in this.

He had no choice in anything.

February 1, 1547

In the complex of buildings that made up the Tower of London, the Wakefield Tower was the largest and most impressive. Its thick stones suggested safety – but its history proved otherwise: the Wakefield Tower was where King Henry VI was murdered by the man who became King Edward IV. The King's apartments had been moved after that, but the new location proved fatal as well, so the Wakefield Tower had resumed its original role. It was a vast relief to Edward: he did not want to think of poor Edward V, the last newly enthroned minor, stealthily smothered to clear the path for Richard III.

Edward looked around the Audience Room where he spent most of his time. It had been set up to pay homage to him, *Edouard Grace à Dieu*. The storerooms had yielded rich tapestries for the walls, scenes featuring Josiah of Judah, the ruler who had brought Israel back to God, cleansing the land of all sites of pagan worship. Edward asked no better than to do the same for England.

Edward's chair of estate had been positioned in front of his desk so he would look industrious when men entered. Since he had little to do, he was most grateful for the window that let him watch the Thames and the hundreds of boats, ferries, and people scurrying like ants.

The door creaked open and a page leaned in. "John Cheke asks leave to wait upon you."

Edward's heart leaped. "Have him enter," he said.

Cheke walked in holding his already-doffed hat behind his back and knelt quickly. The sight of his beloved tutor's head never failed to bring a smile to Edward's face, since the man's closely cropped hair contrasted sharply with his bushy beard. Only thirty-five, Cheke had achieved renown for his expertise with Euripides, Herodotus, Homer, Sophocles...every Greek whose writings populated Edward's lessons. But Cheke's seriousness hid a kind heart and infectious enthusiasm.

"You may rise," Edward said, but Cheke merely looked up.

"I am sorry for the loss we have all experienced," he intoned with his usual solemnity. "Your father will remain an inspiration for the ages. Such a passing prompted me to think about history's great eulogies. I thought we could study some of them; they would present a wonderful vehicle for your Greek and Latin lessons."

Edward nodded.

"And theology and politics as well," Cheke continued. "For you have been called to a noble charge and your own legacy begins now. Always be guided by how you want men to remember your reign."

Edward felt tears in his eyes, overwhelmed by the vision of his future and duty that rose before him like a mountain to be scaled.

"But also remember balance. Hard work deserves honest

pastime." Cheke winked and held out his hat. It wiggled. "Take it, Sire, it is for you."

Edward stretched out a cautious hand and lifted the brim by an inch. A black nose and two tiny, wide eyes greeted him.

"Cheke?" Edward asked, uncertain what to say.

"I thought you could use a companion."

Edward took the puppy and held it close against his chest. It wiggled up to lick his face, and a wave of sheer delight lifted Edward's soul. His entire body relaxed as he inhaled the puppy's sweet, intoxicating scent and kissed its nose. Cheke was right: these last few days had been lonely ones. They had also reminded Edward how young he was – it would be nice to have a loving friend, especially one that looked up at him instead of down.

"But you must promise to pay attention to me, not it, during your lessons," Cheke said.

"I am glad they will continue. There is much more I need to learn."

"You and your companions."

Edward's heart soared. "Will I have them too?"

"Of course. The King chooses his gentlemen."

Edward's heart crashed and he shook his head. "My uncle has already selected my attendants. He says my friends are too young to serve me."

"Too young to serve in your Privy Chamber, but fine to learn with you as they always have. He has agreed there will be no change there." Cheke's voice changed from firm to joking. "Besides, what will his own son do if he can no longer share your lessons?"

Edward laughed. "Teddy helps me. They all help me. I learn better with them there."

"Though there will be some subjects you might study alone, like how to rule men's hearts and minds."

Edward thought about that and nodded. "That makes sense."

"This will be an interesting few years," Cheke said.

The words echoed Edward's own thoughts and his melancholy rose. "But I am afraid I will forget them too easily. My father used to say time pressed in and shrouded the details of his younger days. I feel it already, the days blending into each other."

Tiny paws circled Edward's lap to curl up and nap; the sensation calmed and awed him at the same time.

Cheke pointed at the dog. "Take a lesson from that one," he said. "Trust the world enough to relax fully." He paused, then smiled. "You could also chronicle your experiences. Indeed, a dark and imperfect reflection upon affairs floating in the memory is like words dispersed and insignificant, whereas a view of them in a good book is like the same words digested and in good order, and so made significant."

The nobility of the exercise buoyed Edward's spirit. He closed his eyes and took a deep breath.

A metallic clank warned of the door opening, and Edward looked up as a page appeared on the threshold. "Your Council is here to wait upon you, Sire."

The puppy whimpered and Edward scratched the soft fur of its head to quiet it. "Thank you," he said to the page.

Hertford entered first and came straight over to kneel and kiss Edward's hand, while Cheke backed up against the wall to be out of the way. The others followed one by one; Edward's uncle Tom added a smile and a wink when it was his turn.

Once the full Council was assembled before Edward, Hertford nodded to Wriothesley, who drew himself up and cleared his throat self-importantly. "Sire, as your Lord Chancellor, I am honored to inform you of your Council's actions this day."

Wriothesley's pause hinted that a response was expected. "Proceed," Edward said.

"After reading your father's will from beginning to end, we its executors did swear to duly and faithfully observe it."

They had done the same the day before, but Edward supposed that was part of the process.

"And therefore we thought it meet to declare to you what we did touching the naming and placing of the Earl of Hertford, your uncle, to be Protector of your realms and dominions and Governor of your person. And secure your consent to the same."

Again, Edward had already consented to this the day before, but his uncle had explained that the transfer of power was complex. And Edward rather appreciated that they cared so much for his approval.

"I agree," he said with what he hoped was a sonorous tone.

"With your permission, then, Sire, the Lord Protector shall dispatch letters to the Emperor, to the French King, to the Regent of Flanders, and all others who should be informed of the sorrowful news of the death of your father of noble memory."

"Of course."

"And you understand that these letters shall be signed under his hand and seal alone, as will the realm's other business. You give this power to him willingly."

"I do."

The men looked at William Paget, the Chief Secretary, who made a quick notation on his paper before Wriothesley continued. "We have also agreed that on Thursday all the Temporal Lords shall take their oaths to Your Majesty. On Friday, all the bishops shall do the same."

Edward wondered why they needed the days, and tried to remember what his uncle had told him. It had something to do with the titles and other gifts his father had made too late to include in his will. The letters patent had to be issued before the oaths could be administered, or something like that.

The letters patent. Almost every gentleman in the room would soon be known by a new name. His uncle Hertford would become the Duke of Somerset, Paget the Baron Beaudesert, Wriothesley the Earl of Southampton. And so many more changes, some barely visible like his uncle Tom Seymour who would become Baron Seymour of Sudeley. The generosity seemed a little uncharacteristic of his father. Not that his father had been stingy, just that he had always counseled that rewards needed to be contained. They could never be reduced, so they needed to be right. But if Hertford – no, Somerset – said so, it must be the case.

"I will be happy to receive their oaths at the proper time," Edward said.

"Excellent," Hertford-Somerset broke in. "The next order of business is to consider your father's funeral and then your own coronation, which will follow three days after. Do you have any special wishes for either of these occasions?"

"I thought I was not allowed to attend the funeral."

"But you may offer suggestions."

Edward nodded. "Where will it take place?"

"He asked to be buried next to your mother."

"What will I be doing during the ceremony?"

"Your friends will be with you, my Teddy too. Perhaps you could schedule your lessons for that time." Hertford-Somerset looked at Cheke. "It would be the perfect occasion to discuss the great works of the King-that-was."

Cheke gave a quick bow. "I already discussed with His Majesty that I wanted to study the great eulogies of history. This can be the culmination of that exercise."

"Perfect," Hertford-Somerset said. "But will you also assemble for us the texts relating to coronations? The boroughs will surely come to us for advice and ideas."

It was custom for the monarch to parade through the City, stopping every few blocks to receive gifts and tributes from his loyal subjects. The tributes could be plays, or *tableaux*, or songs. Maybe parables. Edward had read the chronicles by the men who had attended his father's and his grandfather's coronations, describing the spectacles. He knew the ordeal would last for hours.

"I would be honored," Cheke said. "Can we plumb the Howard archives for help? Surely they contain guidance."

It occurred to Edward that since his accession he had not

seen the Duke of Norfolk. Edward looked around guiltily: he should have noticed. Perhaps the man was sick... "The archives?" he asked to elicit the news.

"As the premier peer in the land, the Duke of Norfolk traditionally prepares the monarch's coronation," Cheke said.

"I knew that," Edward replied, annoyed.

"We have all we need for the coronation," Hertford-Somerset said between tight lips. "We want nothing from a traitor."

Edward gaped at the words. *Norfolk a traitor?*

Tom leaned over to explain. "Thomas Howard sits in a dungeon right now, for supporting his son's plans to steal your throne. Surrey has paid the penalty, but your father died before Norfolk could be executed."

Edward's stomach flipped at the nearness of danger averted. And at the sudden fear that it might be unleashed again. "But doesn't tradition require that I pardon him now? Aren't all prisoners freed upon an accession?"

"Never." Hertford-Somerset said. "Nor Edward Courtenay."

He said the name without lowering his voice. Edward had only ever heard the name whispered. The last hope of the Yorkists, a sprig of the White Rose that could challenge Tudor rule.

"Is that necessary?" Wriothesley asked. "The King is right – the tradition is important. Releasing Courtenay could be a compromise."

"No."

"He's no threat. He has spent his adult life in prison and is unaware of basic politeness. He is also slow-witted and penniless; he could never rouse a crowd."

"His slow wits won't prevent him from being used by others who might try to seize power in his name. The King-that-was knew this and kept danger confined. I will never fail him on that count, releasing his foes to threaten his son."

"Hear, hear," the Council members shouted. Wriothesley blanched and bowed deeply. "I was wrong to speak before thinking."

Edward's chest tightened again. Everything was momentous now. There were no small moments, no innocent thoughts.

Hertford-Somerset turned to Edward without deigning to respond to Wriothesley. "Did you want to discuss your coronation? Or the funeral?"

Edward scratched the puppy's head. "No, thank you."

"Are you tired, Your Majesty?" asked Lisle-Warwick.

The real answer was no, but that might obligate him to speak more about unpleasant things. He needed to steel himself before that happened. "Yes."

"Then we will retire for now," Hertford-Somerset said. "But before we do…" He drew himself up and looked around. "I would be remiss if I spoke only of ceremonies and did not mention the holy work they presage. I promise that your reign will bring men closer to God."

Edward had to stop himself from hooting in glee. This was his most fervent desire, one that Somerset shared. "Tell me!"

Somerset winked at him and turned to the Councilors. "The first laws attributed to the King will restore the purity of the Gospel. The day after you are crowned, we will repeal the Act of the Six Articles and remove the restrictions preventing men from printing Bibles. No longer will priests be able to keep men in ignorance, separated from God and their consciences."

"What about the superstitions? How will we cleanse them from the Church?" Cranmer asked. "We must stop men from worshipping idols instead of the one true Lord."

"No more images, no more beads, no more candles," Hertford-Somerset said.

"Nothing?" Edward asked, hoping it was true.

"Only on the altar before the sacrament," Hertford-Somserset said.

"You trust people to follow these rules?" Lisle-Warwick asked.

"We will send commissioners, thirty of them, to see that the rules are obeyed throughout the land.

"There is so much more, though," Edward said. "You have addressed the outer shell, but what about—"

"You need to give men time to change their souls and thoughts, else they will rebel as they did when your father closed the monasteries. They need to forget about the candles and incense, then it will be a small step to change their vain opinions of purgatory and masses."

Edward picked at a knot in his doublet.

"I know this is important to you," Somerset said. "I will not fail you."

Edward nodded. "Thank you, Uncle."

Somerset gave the King a half smile before leaving, followed by the lords of the Council. Cheke bowed and followed them. Edward lifted a hand to call him back, but was not sure he should after telling the Council he was tired.

The empty room closed in on Edward. He looked down at the puppy. It was sleeping quietly on his lap, content and safe. A fierce sense of protection surged in Edward's chest, strengthening him.

"I'm going to call you Argos," he whispered, "after Odysseus's faithful dog."

Stroking the rounded puppy with one hand, he reached over with the other for a sheet of parchment that he placed neatly in front of him. He took a quill, marveling at its perfect sharpness, and dipped it in the ink. Inspiration fired his belly, but no words emerged. It seemed wrong just to start recording random events. That was not the way this should be done. This would be a great history of his reign, with all his triumphs. He would even record his struggles so his own heir would be instructed.

A great chronicle must set the stage, give the history and the context to the work.

Again the consciousness of legacy gripped him. He was not just anyone, he was England's king. He had to act like it.

He took a deep breath, and once again dipped his pen in the inkwell.

In the year of our Lord 1537, a prince was born to King Henry the Eighth, by Jane Seymour, then Queen, who died within a few days after the birth of her son and was buried at the Castle of Windsor ...

February 16, 1547

At Windsor Castle, Saint George's Chapel was eerily silent despite the multitude crammed into the sanctuary. Mary Tudor bowed her head and crossed herself as Bishop Stephen Gardiner incensed the massive coffin before the altar. The white-haired cleric, who had always been the tallest man in the room after her father, seemed dwarfed by the dead King's bier.

Gardiner was equally dwarfed by the glowing wax effigy of her father supervising the ceremony. The figure wore golden robes of estate and held a jeweled scepter that captured the only light in the black-draped chapel.

Before the altar, the Privy Councilors and hundreds of other lords crowded to join this historic event. The ladies crowded into the Queen's Closet, the small room above the quire whose balcony overlooked the sanctuary.

The four highest women in the land sat in the front row. Katherine Parr and Anne Seymour were in the center, flanked by Mary and Elizabeth. Bound by family, they were also drawn together by affection; Mary was glad to have them in her life.

Mary felt a gentle hand on her knee: the Queen Dowager looking for or giving comfort. Mary patted her stepmother's hand, and the gold signet ring Mary wore on her pinkie winked against the embroidered purple pattern of her black damask skirt. The ring had been a gift from her blessed mother, and now she could wear it unafraid that her father would recognize it.

Mary smiled wanly, trying to hide the lingering bitterness mixed in with her grief. She had worshipped her father, yet he had allowed two of his wives to harden his heart against her, his own daughter. As he approached his end, he had started to come to his senses, allowing Mary to assume her rightful status as his firstborn princess. Still, he had never completed the journey, never fully done right by her: she still had no proper title, no husband, no child, and no real place in the world.

"He always did love the incense," Katherine Parr whispered. "It was his main complaint against the reform church, that they eliminated too much ritual."

"They've not done that today," Elizabeth responded.

Indeed, just the opposite. Henry had commanded a formal Requiem Mass in Latin to summon the full power of the Catholic Church and its promise to purify men's souls. In the end, Mary's father was not foolish enough to risk his soul for the Lutheran heresies.

Mary looked again at the coffin and at the floor under it, half expecting to see the blood she'd heard about. God's judgment, displayed when the funeral procession from Whitehall to Windsor had stopped for the night. The attendants had installed the coffin in the Chapel Royal but didn't attend it as they should have. They returned the next morning to find the King's blood had leaked onto the stone floor below – where a dog lapped it up, eyes glowing red, just as Friar Peto had warned so many years ago when the King had put aside Mary's sainted mother to wed the Jezebel Anne Boleyn: *You are as Ahab, the dogs will lick your blood.*

If only her father had listened then, the great tragedy of Mary's life would have been averted. Henry could still have married Jane Seymour after Catherine of Aragon's natural death, but he would not have broken with Rome and God's law. And he would not have raised a witch, however temporarily, to England's throne.

Mary put regret aside and glanced at Elizabeth, the daughter of that unholy union. Poor thing. Sober, discreet. It was not her fault her mother was a whore. How terrible to be the living reminder of a sinful mistake.

A twinge gripped the side of Mary's forehead. She rubbed it, hoping to slow the arrival of the approaching migraine. They plagued her far too frequently, numbing the good times and aggravating the bad ones.

She shut her eyes against the light and raised her hands as if in prayer, keeping this posture while sixteen of the strongest Yeomen of the Guard lowered her father's massive coffin into the vault below the center aisle. She lowered her hands to watch Henry's Lord Chamberlain, the Earl of Arundel, step forward; he solemnly broke his white stave of office, the symbol of his service, and dropped it into the grave. He took a step back and the other yeomen came forward as a group to do the same. The staves struck the coffin with a terrible thud, a sound of finality that made Mary cross herself. It hurt that few mourners did likewise – reform had spread too far. It also hurt that traditionalists like Gardiner and Arundel had lost their prominence in the government. Wriothesley would likely be next, despite his new earldom.

The Council exited. Mary stood with the other ladies, ready and relieved to retire to the Queen's apartments.

The corridor had been cleared for them out of respect, so they were left to their own thoughts on the silent walk back. The dim lights felt like a prayer that comforted Mary's aching head, and she half-closed her eyes in thanks.

The Queen's rooms were bright enough to renew Mary's pain. Katherine, Anne, and Elizabeth went to sit in the chairs set up in the corner, framed by the giant windows. Mary hung back, contemplating a quick exit as the ladies-in-waiting arranged themselves on cushions at the feet of their mistresses.

Unfortunately, Frances Brandon Grey, Marchioness of Dorset, hung back with Mary for a private chance to commiserate. Mary could not be so rude as to leave her cousin quickly.

"The last of that generation," Frances said quietly. "My mother was the first."

Frances's mother, for whom Mary was named, had died when Mary and Frances were both around twenty. The elder

Mary had also hated Anne Boleyn, so the two cousins had always been close.

"Mine followed only three years later," Mary said.

The conversation faded and the two women turned their attention to the room. Jane Dudley, who had recently become Countess of Warwick, was holding up a hoop to Katherine Parr. "Would you like your sewing?"

"I would rather listen to devotions," the Queen answered. "It seems more fitting to the moment."

The ladies arranged themselves and began to read. The text was a favorite of reformists. Katherine Parr favored the new religion, a preference barely noticeable when she first married Henry VIII. Indeed, she had been allowed to choose all of Edward's tutors. Now she had no need to hide her views.

Mary turned back. "How is your husband?" she asked Frances. "I have not seen him for a time. I hope you will stay at court awhile so we can visit together."

Frances wrinkled her nose. Henry Grey, Marquess of Dorset, had not been named to the new government as he'd had no part in the last one. "My husband and the Duke of Somerset have never been close. I suspect we will be stuck in the country."

The family title and fortune had stayed with Charles Brandon after Mary Tudor died. He had remarried a much younger woman who'd given him sons that supplanted Frances in the inheritance that should have been hers. Another thing the two cousins shared.

"At least you will be together. I envy you that," Mary said.

Frances had a happy marriage and three beautiful daughters. Mary had wasted all her life waiting for that for herself.

"Think you that diplomacy might see you married soon? To strengthen the throne?"

Mary shook her head. "Just the opposite. I am too much of a threat: any husband they give me might be tempted to press my claim while the King is young and therefore weak. I'll be an old lady before I say any vows."

Frances sighed. "How terrible for you." She looked down. "Though at least you will be spared my mother's fate of being wed to a man you could never love."

"It was a small price to pay for a lifetime of happiness," Mary said, meaning it. The eighteen-year-old Mary Tudor's marriage to the fifty-two-year-old King of France had lasted less than three months. Barely out of mourning, the young widow had married the love of her life, Charles Brandon.

Frances sighed. "You forget how difficult it was for my parents for a long time."

Mary took a deep breath, remembering. Henry had been furious to lose such a valuable chit in the world of diplomacy and had imposed crippling fines to teach them a lesson. And to make sure people understood that treason always had terrible consequences. Still, Frances's mother had avoided being wed to another doddering old monarch.

Mary patted Frances's hand. "I don't mean to complain. I may not understand why God has chosen to deny me the comfort of a husband and child – against His own commandment – but I accept it fully."

Mary's temple throbbed. She pressed her fingers hard against it.

"You should retire," Frances said. "You look unwell."

As Mary lowered her hand to answer, the Council walked in. Somerset entered first, waiting for the other lords to file in before bowing to the Queen. "Again, I am so sorry for your loss. I know how broken your heart must be."

"Thank you."

Tom Seymour, Somerset's younger brother, pushed to the front. God had divided His blessings between the two siblings, giving intelligence and discretion to Somerset and good looks and gallantry to Tom. Mary was still shocked that Tom was impolitic enough to let his dissatisfaction with his new barony lead him to insist on taking the post of Lord High Admiral away from the new Earl of Warwick. Warwick was known to be vengeful.

Before locking eyes with the Queen, Tom stared deeply at Mary, then Elizabeth, like a dog seeking a hidden bone. "At least I hope the ceremony brought you comfort."

"It was the ceremony he wanted," Katherine said simply.

"It made me feel close to God," Mary said. "I find the need to pray further, and I hope you will excuse me."

"Of course, my child," Katherine said.

Mary nodded to Frances and quickly bowed out. As Mary hurried down the hall, praying for just enough relief to make it to her room, Eleanor Kempe, one of Katherine Parr's ladies, called out. "Your Grace, would you allow me a moment?"

Much as Mary simply wanted to lie down, she softened at the worried look on Eleanor's lined face.

"Of course."

"Please forgive me this impertinence," Eleanor said, "but I was hoping you would consider accepting me into your household."

Mary's mouth dropped open. "Surely the Queen Dowager has not dismissed you?"

Yes, Katherine Parr's household was likely to shrink with the change in her status, but Eleanor had been one of her most hardworking ladies.

"No, Your Grace," Eleanor said quickly. "It's just…just…" She wrung her hands as if it would give her strength. "I know that the Queen Dowager favors the reform religion, as does the King and everyone around him. I don't want to lose my Mass and you…" Her voice trailed off and her shoulders slumped.

Mary's heart went out to her, knowing she was surely right. Reformists wanted to do away with everything that was beautiful about the Church and its rituals. They wanted to destroy the magic of God's grace. Mary resolved to save this woman who had always reminded Mary of her mother.

"I would be pleased to accept your service," Mary said. "I

will speak with the Queen Dowager, but I cannot imagine she will object."

Tears sprang to Eleanor's eyes. "Thank you. You will not regret it."

"You can even start now," Mary said. "I need to lie down, and it would be nice to have help removing my overskirt and sleeves."

"And to have someone bring you a cool compress for your forehead," Eleanor said. "Is your stomach aching? I can bring you something for that too."

Mary smiled, deeply comforted. "Thank you. That would be nice."

February 19, 1547

Edward held out his arms so his attendants could fasten the belt around him. It was silver filigree and, like his cloak, studded with rubies, diamonds, and pearls that set off the white velvet of his doublet and cap. It was a struggle to move under such weight; it made him feel weak even though it made him look magnificent.

"His cap has enough diamonds to seem a halo," Tom said in a playful tone. "He'll glisten from a great distance."

"Good," Somerset said with his usual sternness. "Today his people will look upon him and see him closely for the first time. This will remind them of God's will."

Today Edward would ride through London with his whole court: messengers, trumpeters, lords, gentlemen, and diplomats. He would receive his people's homage, and then tomorrow he would be crowned, anointed with the holy oil that would sanctify his reign.

"The King is ready," Somerset announced. "Let us be off."

Immediately Edward's entourage formed a circle around him, and the group surged out of the chamber and down the hallway like a wave to the shore.

There must have been a thousand people in the courtyard waiting for him, the highest-ranking mounted and the rest on foot. Everyone cheered, and Edward happily waved back as he was escorted to this horse. It, too, sparkled, with crimson satin trappings covered in pearls.

Somerset put out his hand to help Edward mount, and right away six noblemen rode forward with a canopy to hold over his head.

"No one will be able to see him with all of you surrounding him," Tom called out.

Warwick walked his horse around the assembly. "He is quite hidden from view."

"The King should ride first, with his Council behind him," Somerset said. "The canopy can cover the women."

A general murmur of agreement spread through the crowd, and Edward found himself nodding along. His people needed to see him; his father had always emphasized that lesson.

Somerset nodded and gracefully mounted his horse. Edward resolved to ask his uncle to teach him that skill. After all, the man had begun his career as Master of the Horse – there would be no one better to learn from. Other than Warwick, of course: he had been Master of the Horse to Anne of Cleves and Catherine Howard.

"I shall ride right behind the King," Somerset announced loudly. "Let us begin."

Warwick quickly walked his horse next to the duke's. "You should be attended."

Near the gate stood four armed guards wearing surcoats of scarlet and green and carrying an enormous flag with the royal heraldry. At Somerset's words, they sprang to attention to lead the charge. The rest of the company rushed to obey.

When he passed through the Tower gates, Edward's stomach quivered at the sight of the throng. The people stood some fifty deep for as far down the road as he could see. His uncle had explained that the first row of spectators were craftsmen, priests, and clerks who had been charged with ensuring that the delirious crowds behind them did not break through to interfere with the procession. A small price to pay for their favorable placement.

The windows and balconies he passed dripped precious arrases and cloths of silver and gold, and every few blocks stood choirs singing sacred music. Edward had never seen London look this clean, this rich – or this spiritual. The procession stopped to acknowledge the bands on the raised platforms, but merely nodded to the groups gathered on corners. Edward felt a little bad, but there was no time to stop for everything: they could only delay for the most elaborate displays – like the staged fight where angels watched his mother's phoenix and his father's crowned lion defeat serpents with belching fire. Or the rockery painted all over with roses and carnations from which dancing children – representing Grace, Nature, Fortune, Charity, Logic, Rhetoric, and more – recited verses of praise. Or yet another lion, this one not a costumed performer but an actual lion with its cub, and more angels and more phoenixes and more small children, all praising Edward for wisdom he had not yet shown and deeds he had not yet done.

As the procession went on, the shouts of "God save the King" got louder and the crowd more rowdy, perhaps because the conduits to every fountain in the City were running either white wine or claret, and the men and women were helping themselves liberally. But after a while it all blurred together in Edward's mind. The sights and smells and sounds hit him in the face like a summer rain, each drop indistinguishable from the others.

While he was hiding a yawn, the procession stopped at the Cross in Cheapside to greet the Mayor of London and his aldermen. The men hadn't bothered with allegory or other costume, their black robes standing out against the colorful crowd. Edward was wondering why they had been honored with a stop when the Mayor stepped forward and knelt, proffering a velvet sack, also black.

"A thousand crowns for the Crown of the country, delivered straight into his own hands," the Mayor called out, and the crowd roared.

"I thank you," Edward said.

Everyone stared at Edward expectantly. His stomach dropped and he turned to Somerset for guidance.

"Take it."

Edward eyed the purse, unsure how he would hold something so large. Would he even be able to hold his reins? "Why do they give this to me?" he asked Somerset.

"It is the City's custom, to honor you and show their tremendous loyalty."

Clearly, then, Edward had no choice. He took the purse and flushed deeply when he almost dropped it from the weight. He could not get it settled on his lap, and panic rose in him.

The Mayor raised a hand as if to take it back, or to catch it, Edward was not sure which.

"Give it to the Captain of the Guard," Somerset said quietly. The Captain advanced and took it, but Edward's relief was cut short when he noticed the scowl on the Mayor's face. Edward had given offense.

Edward opened his mouth to thank the Mayor again, but all attention was captured by a mechanical lion rolling out, his head moving to and fro. Behind him a fair maiden held a lamb on a leash, and then "Saint George" made a speech in English and called upon a small boy to make his speech in Latin. After three or four faltering words, Somerset called for the procession to move on. "I have just been told we are behind schedule. We must get to the next church. We thank you, good people!"

The Mayor still scowled, and Edward tried to shake off his guilt. He had done nothing wrong. If he had kept that ridiculous purse, he would not be able to react to the crowd. That would be the worse evil.

The cavalcade moved past Saint George's Church, past a spectacle that caught Edward's eye and made him rein in his horse: a rope, as great as a ship's cable, had been stretched over the street, between the gate of the Dean's house and the top of the church steeple. A man was standing on the rope, in midair, as casually as if he were on the floor. At Edward's approach, he cast his arms and legs wide. There was a thinner rope hanging from the cable, and the tumbler flipped himself in the air, caught the rope and slid down like an arrow shot from a bow. In the moment it took Edward's mouth to open in amazement, the man was right there before him, kissing his foot.

Edward's heart pounded and he clapped his hands. "Thank you," he said. "It was wondrously fine to watch."

"I will treasure your stopping to watch me." The man's accent was tinged with a foreign sound. "Even more your praise of my skill."

"Where are you from?" Edward asked.

"Aragon, Your Majesty." And I bring the good wishes of all Spain."

The reference to Aragon made Edward look around for his sister Mary, to make sure she knew this man was from her mother's country, but then the acrobat was off, climbing back up the rope, walking on it the way other men walk on solid ground. When he was over the middle of the churchyard, he started to cast himself from one leg to the other. When it looked like he might fall, he tumbled instead and hoisted himself back upright. The crowd *oohed* and *aahed* in amazement, Edward among them.

"Move on," Somerset said to continue the procession.

"No!" The word came out as a shout, and Edward was as surprised as the people around him. "I am enjoying this," he pleaded.

It seemed Somerset might argue with him, but then his uncle nodded. "There will be other displays we can cut short. This is your day. But not too long."

A great lightness spread throughout Edward's limbs, and he turned back greedily to the scene.

As he watched the man perform trick after trick, it occurred to Edward that this was the first time since his accession that he had actually done what he wanted instead of what someone else wanted. The first time he had asserted himself. Successfully, anyway.

It felt good to rule.

February 20, 1547

From a deep sleep, Edward heard his bed-curtains open abruptly. He opened his eyes into the frowning face of his uncle Somerset, who quickly turned around to harangue the six Gentlemen of the Privy Chamber running in. Michael Stanhope and John Fowler were fully dressed, but the others were stuffing their shirts into their breeches. One was Ned Seymour, Somerset's son by his first wife, and he was the one on whom Somerset rained his wrath.

"It is six of the morning and His Majesty is not yet attended," Somerset growled. "On his coronation day."

Fowler spread his arms. "We were waiting for you."

"Then I should have seen you at the ready, in His Majesty's Presence Chamber." Somerset's voice dripped correction, and Edward cringed for the men being scolded, however much they deserved it.

Stanhope stepped forward. He was a patient, kind man – very different from his sister Anne, Somerset's wife. "Our real duties don't begin until tonight, when the full crew will arrive. We are still learning the new ways."

"We will be ready then," Fowler added. He waved his arm and the men came forward, each bearing some different article of clothing.

"Is that when my friends will join me?" Edward asked.

"Are we not your friends, Sire?" asked Ned Seymour.

"You know what I mean," Edward said, embarrassed. The attendants Somerset had chosen for him were good men, wonderful men, but they were at least fifteen years older, some much more.

"Your lessons begin tomorrow, and your friends will be there then," Stanhope said.

"I would have liked to share this day with them," Edward said, trying to keep the wistfulness from his voice.

"You will," Somerset said. "They have been seated in the quire."

Edward smiled. The quire was not so far from the High Altar. Given the enormity of Westminster Abbey, their seats could have been far worse.

"Are you ready for another long day?" Tom's voice boomed from the door as he entered. "Twelve hours start to finish, and no naps in between."

"Seven," Somerset said between clenched teeth. "We have made some changes in deference to the King's age. Just as we did yesterday."

"As long as you left him energy for tomorrow's jousts," Tom said.

"Duty first," Somerset said. "Will you never learn?"

The jousts would continue for the next three days. A coronation was drawn out over time, to lengthen the shining moment during which God Himself would lay His finger on England's brow and smile on her. Tiers and galleries had been added to Westminster Abbey so ten thousand people could cram into the church, but all London – nay, all England – wanted to feel God's smile. Many more thousands could watch the jousting from the surrounding fields, and, with all of the days, most everyone who wanted could share at least a moment in the hallmark of a generation.

"And of course money," Tom said. "Some of the coins from that fat purse yesterday. Did you save any of them?"

Edward didn't understand what he was asking. Was this about the state of the Treasury? He was still new to this; why was he being asked to answer for anything?

"What are you talking about?" Somerset asked, and Edward was relieved that he was not the only one puzzled.

Tom reached into his codpiece for the purse he kept there, winking at Edward as he did so. He handed the purse to him. "You are a king. You need money of your own."

Edward's was not the only mouth that gaped. "Tom, enough," Somerset warned.

"What, you are trying to keep the boy away from his right?"

Somerset narrowed his eyes at his brother. "Every moment of the day has been planned: every person he will meet, every gift he will offer. You think to burnish his image with random coins still warm from your cod?"

Edward was shocked yet impressed. Such anger from Somerset, so well expressed. Edward knew Somerset was right – and yet he wanted the purse. It occurred to him now that the velvet sack yesterday was the first time he had ever actually held a coin of the realm. A coin of *his* realm. Why should he not have a purse in his own codpiece? He was the King!

He became aware that every eye in the room had widened, and most faces were struggling to erase all expression. Were they as surprised as Edward that people would dare to fight in front of him? Or did they agree Somerset was too harsh?

Tom rolled his eyes. "Let him have the fun bits. Giving *largesse* feels good. You want him to grow into his role, fine, but you should not stop him from being generous."

As Somerset opened his mouth to reply, Edward felt a rising eruption of energy, a spur to take the step that terrified him.

"I would like that," he said.

Somerset's mouth snapped shut for a moment before he answered. "You must not start giving gifts until you know how to do it properly. You should know the times when they are expected or deserved. And when they should be withheld."

Edward's shoulders bowed under the weight of responsibility.

"But he can hold onto the purse for now, right?" Tom asked.

Somerset's lips tightened. "Fine."

"Good," Tom said. "Because the King needs funds as I need funds."

Again, Edward saw eyes widen at another topic that had never been broached in front of him. He glanced at Cheke, hoping his face contained a clue, but saw only hard blankness.

"You have your inheritance, your title," Somerset retorted. "You—"

"A pittance. I am the King's uncle as much as you. It is not right for me to live as I do."

"What?"

"A good brother would not have discouraged my suits to Mary and Elizabeth."

"Neither of us is born to be King, or to marry kings' daughters."

"And yet either one of them could wed a husband who would threaten our nephew. Marriage to me would ensure the safety of the realm." Tom turned to Edward. "Isn't that right, Your Majesty?"

Edward's heart shrank in fear. No one had ever fought before him – men were careful to restrain themselves. And now he was being asked to arbitrate.

When he didn't answer, Tom turned back to Somerset. "I ask only your support. I will look to the rest."

Somerset shook his head vigorously. "You overreach, Tom. And you are an idiot. We will speak outside."

Somerset spun around and bowed to Edward. "We will leave you now to prepare. We leave here at nine for Whitehall so you can be formally robed to proceed to Westminster Abbey."

When they were gone, the room shook off the anger like a dog shaking off water. Dressing and a quick breakfast flew by, with nervous silence quickly ceding to jollity. Excitement rose with every minute, and by the time Edward came out to the courtyard the universal goodwill was back to its fever pitch.

Again, crowds lined the river and the streets to wish him

well, though today the crush was greatest between Whitehall and the Abbey: people wanted to see the regalia borne before him, the orb and scepter he would hold reverently in his hands, those quasi-magical symbols of power that reminded people of Edward's uncontested right to rule. His uncle Somerset would hold the sword of Edward the Confessor, its blunted blade symbolizing the mercy that should temper the sharpness of royal justice.

Once inside the hallowed walls of Westminster Abbey, Edward proceeded slowly down the center aisle, feeling as shy and expectant as a bride walking alone to her new life. He took small steps, placing every foot carefully and praying he would not trip over his robes or otherwise ruin the blessed moment.

The High Altar was dominated by the Coronation Chair, the same chair that had blessed every English monarch since Edward the Confessor. Edward sucked in his breath. The oak of the chair enclosed the Stone of Scone, the same one on which Jacob himself had rested his head at Bethel. For five hundred years it had been used to test royalty – for the chair would groan if a man was of royal blood, and keep silent for a pretender.

Edward held his breath when he sat on it, gingerly at first because it was sacred, then adding a tiny wriggle to settle in and let it know he was there. He exhaled in gratitude when he heard the creak. The sound softened the hurt of having to use a special step because he was small yet, another of the constant reminders of the great road he had to travel before he would be truly worthy of his station.

The streaming light from the soaring clerestory windows made the crowd glow. Tiers had been built so the faces were eight high, making Edward feel like he was surrounded by angels.

As if to underscore the holiness of the moment, Thomas Cranmer stepped forward to open the ceremony. Although the pulpit belonged to the Dean of Westminster, the Archbishop of

Canterbury was the highest religious figure in the land. After Edward, of course.

"Sirs," Cranmer called in a voice that surely rang in all corners of the great cathedral. "I present King Edward, rightful and undoubted heir by the laws of God and man to the Royal Dignity and Crown Imperial of this realm. His consecration, enunction, and coronation is appointed by all the nobles and peers of this land to be this day. Will you serve at this time, and give your goodwill and assents to the said consecration, enunction, and coronation as by your duties of allegiance ye be bound to do?"

The entire congregation answered with a loud and enthusiastic series of "Yea" that bounced and echoed off the walls, surrounding Edward and penetrating to his very bones. In an outpouring of love even more overwhelming than the day before, the people called out his name as if he were the Lord himself. A lofty feeling expanded his chest and he sat straighter in his chair.

After a joyous time, he caught his breath and his heart slowed to normal. Despite his determination to imprint every word on his heart, it all blended together like the day before. Not the actual anointing, of course. The warm oil's touch on his forehead was a mystical cord binding him to Christ. For a moment he *was* Christ, all blinding light and pulsating energy. Then the cord pulled him back and from that height he tumbled through time, past the other sanctified prophets and rulers, until he was just himself sitting on the holy chair again, a boy straining to hold the heavy regalia upright.

The loss left him forlorn and confused, and a whiff of unreality dogged him for the rest of the singing and prayers that went on for hours. And even when they repaired to the dining room, the prayers and toasts and wishes went on and on, and he felt alone and young. The crown on his head both helped and made things worse. He was allowed to keep it on the whole time, even after it almost fell off when he twitched from momentary sleep.

Finally they let him return to his room. The room his father had died in. That fact woke him, tightening his throat and chest.

The huge bed was eerily empty now. Only the straw mattress sat on the frame, though it still sported the same silver and gold trappings. It was surrounded by eight Yeomen of the Bedchamber. Edward entered the room, and his six gentlemen followed, fanning out behind him. Somerset stood at his right.

One of the yeomen bowed and walked, bedclothes in hand, toward Edward. The yeoman gave the pile to Edward's Gentleman Usher, who examined every inch of them, holding them up to the light and twisting and bending them before nodding and handing them back and bowing himself to Edward.

A second yeoman held a *flambeau* over the bed while a third stabbed the straw mattress with his dagger to make sure no one was hidden inside. Then they too bowed to Edward.

A fourth and fifth yeoman produced a feather mattress, which was searched by another gentleman before they placed it over the straw mattress and delivered another round of bows.

The last three yeomen were joined by the first one, and the four of them each took a position at a corner of the bed. They stretched the sheet out over it, then, at the command of the Gentleman Usher, laid it down so all parts of it touched the bed at the same time. They bowed and stepped away, and the other four yeomen did the same with two blankets. Finally, they tucked in the coverings, making the sign of the cross and kissing the spots where their hands touched the bed.

"This will be done every day to ensure your security, though from now on it will be done well before you arrive," Somerset said to Edward. "For today, I wanted you to see the process."

Edward was relieved to hear that. This was not something he wanted to endure every evening, though for today it was actually comforting to see that this was well and truly his bed and built from scratch. It had worked to dispel the image of his father.

Anxious just to crawl between the newly made covers and rest and sleep, Edward opened his mouth to thank and dismiss the men, but before he could say anything the noblemen behind him had fanned out around the room, each holding some accessory – a towel, an ewer, a posset cup – or his nightshirt and nightcap. His attendants then approached him and started to undress him, each man performing only one piece of the task – if even that: it took two men to remove his shoes, two men for his hose. This was even more formality than his father had required, and Edward's anxiety rose: how would he stand this interminable ritual day after day?

His uncle must have sensed his frustration. "The King must command respect. Because of your age, a constant outer show becomes all the more important. Disdain is like sin, where a small transgression unchecked will lead to larger ones."

Edward nodded, understanding. He accepted the ministrations with better grace, and without his upset the process became less annoying. He even found his mind flying elsewhere, so he barely noticed anything more until he was in the bed, which had been sprinkled with holy water and blessed by his chaplain. Argos jumped up to be with him, wagging his tail enthusiastically, but Somerset quickly caught him.

"We have a special bed for him, a basket right between the main doors of your bedroom, right before the antechamber where your attendants will sleep on their pallets."

"He will be lonely," Edward said, hoping to change his uncle's mind.

"Nay, he will understand," Somerset laughed. "He will be proud to protect your door."

"What about the King being lonely? Why should the men not sleep in his chamber with him?" Tom asked, and Edward could swear he heard challenge in his uncle's voice. "At least Fowler here could keep him company."

"Fowler is an old man whose wheezing and snoring might disturb His Majesty. When our nephew is old enough to select his own Gentlemen of the Privy Chamber, he can choose to be bothered. For now, he will sleep better on his own."

"You just don't want a friend of mine to develop a position of influence," Tom said, provoking a harsh stare from Somerset but no response. Edward suspected Tom was right, but Edward didn't want anyone snoring near him so he held his tongue.

When they had all left, Edward found himself staring up at the bed's damask tester, surprisingly unable to sleep in the calm after the day's din. He snuck out of his bed to his desk and took out his Chronicle. There was a scratching at the door, and a low whine, and he ran over to let Argos in. The dog frisked around him, and Edward picked him up quickly to hush him. Back at the desk, Edward settled Argos on his lap before picking up his pen to write.

The King, then being but nine years old, passed through the city of London and came to the Palace of Westminster.

He thought about trying to describe the things he had seen, but shrugged. The tightrope walker was the highlight, but there was no way to do the spectacle justice.

The next day he came unto Westminster, and the people were asked whether they would have him to be their King, and they answered, "Yea, yea." Then he was crowned King of England, France and Ireland by the Archbishop of Canterbury and all the rest of the clergy and nobles, and anointed with all such ceremonies as were accustomed, and took his oath, and gave a general pardon, and so was brought to the hall for dinner, where he sat with the crown upon his head.

He sat reliving the feeling that had lasted the entire meal, the weight of Saint Edward's crown and the warmth of the ermine robes. Wonder and exhaustion hit him hard. He closed the book and put it back in its spot, then picked up Argos and carried him back to bed.

March 15, 1547

The thin tapestries between the bookshelves in Edward's library at Whitehall muffled even more sound than the books, so the boys jumped when the page entered to announce Thomas

Seymour, who was not expected until later. Edward looked side-long at Cheke for guidance. No one had ever interrupted the daily lessons, and until now Edward had assumed this was not permitted.

"Have you not done with your work yet?" Tom said with feigned amazement. "I thought to have a moment with Your Majesty."

Edward had no idea what the right answer was and he looked again at Cheke, who nodded reassuringly and took control of the situation. "Ah, my Lord, lessons dominate life," he said. "But today His Majesty grasped the most intricate details immediately, so you may have the King while the others catch up to his prowess."

Tom winked at Ned Seymour and turned to Ned's younger half-brother, wagging a finger. "Careful, Teddy, or I will tell my brother you are lagging."

"I am not far behind, Uncle," Teddy replied. "You would never know me for the youngest of the group."

Teddy was only seven. He had been part of Edward's house-hold for ages – he and Henry Brandon, Henry Maltravers, Barnaby Fitzpatrick, and Henry Paget. Brandon and Barnaby had been with him in his nursery; Teddy and Paget had joined after Edward was breeched.

Barnaby and Brandon had been breeched first, though of course for them it was only about changing from dresses to breeches. When it was Edward's turn, all their lives transformed: they started lessons – Divinity, Greek, Latin, French, Spanish, and Music – and began to ride and hawk. Edward had been the first to get a bird, a marlin, which his father had too quickly replaced with a peregrine. Peregrines were what princes were supposed to fly, but Edward was small and the new bird was harder to handle than his beloved marlin.

Edward brought his thoughts back to the room. Lately, memories like that had been plaguing him more than they used to. Perhaps because his entire life had become harder to handle.

"I know you and you," Tom said to Barnaby and Brandon. "And you two," he pointed to Maltravers and Paget. "But I was away from court for a long while and never met you," he said, waving toward the older boys.

Robin Dudley rose and bowed. "Robert Dudley, my Lord."

"Ah, Warwick's son," Tom said. "They call you Robin, don't they?"

"Yes, Sir."

Tom looked to the next face. "And you?"

"Henry Stanley, my Lord."

"Norfolk's grandson?"

Stanley blushed. "Only on my mother's side."

"And you?"

"George Talbot, Sir."

"Talbot – the son of the Earl of Shrewsbury?" Tom didn't wait for an answer. "The King is surrounded by the scions of powerful men."

"Mostly," Barnaby said and they all laughed. Barnaby was only the son of a baron, but it was an Irish baron who had provided important support at a critical point in some campaign. Or so Somerset had explained to Edward.

"What about you?" Tom asked, pointing at William Cecil. "You are too old to be a part of this group. You are a second teacher?"

Cheke put a hand on Cecil's shoulder. "He could be, but he prefers government to Greek. He is here for a few months more so I can complete his education before he joins your brother's household."

"My brother's household?" Tom put on an affected air, though Edward was not sure why. "You leave the King's service? And you think that progress?"

Again, Cheke replied for his protégé. "He has no position here; he is my guest. He will serve as Secretary to the Lord Protector and learn everything he needs to better serve the King later, when the time comes."

Tom shrugged and looked at Edward pointedly. Edward had no idea what to do.

"But as I said," Cheke continued, "this is a good time for the others to review the lesson the King has grasped. Come, boys, let us retire to finish your work."

Edward's friends stood and bowed and left the room with their teacher. Edward felt a bit forlorn without them, though he was happy to have the chance to speak with his uncle privately.

Tom bowed. "Your Majesty," he said as if he had just come into the room, a sign he sought permission to begin a conversation.

"Uncle," Edward answered, agreeing. The protocol was coming more naturally to him now; he appreciated the ability to avoid discussions even if the people closest to him knew ways around the rules.

"I am glad to see you looking well."

Edward's heart fell. He had hoped his uncle was coming to bring him another purse so he could make gifts to his friends. After that initial conversation right before his coronation, Somerset had arranged for lessons about *largesse*, and which servants, teachers, and friends were most deserving and when were the best times for offering thanks. Somerset did not believe many occasions warranted parting with a coin. Edward felt differently. Edward loved nothing more than to thank people in the kingly fashion he longed to embody. He felt regal giving away money, watching the gleam in men's eyes. His father always said he could take the measure of a man by whether he was swayed by a gold coin. The men who cared less deserved more.

"You look well too, Uncle," Edward said, trying not to grumble.

His uncle Tom put his head back and laughed loudly. "God's Blood! Your Majesty needs to learn to hide your emotions a little better. Fowler told me you needed money." He tossed a purse, and Edward fumbled but didn't drop it.

His uncle Tom had co-opted John Fowler as his go-between for matters like this, and Fowler had quickly become one of Edward's favorite Gentlemen.

"Thank you," Edward said, pretending his fingers were not trying to count the coins through the velvet.

"I know what it is like to have to do Somerset's bidding," Tom said. "I know what it is like to be kept lower than you have earned. You deserve to be more of a king."

Tom leaned in and his face changed. He looked sly. "If I were Lord Protector, I would see to it that you had far more authority than you do. God's Blood, you deserve it. How dare he be miserly with a few coins?"

How dare he indeed? Edward found himself angry.

"He gives you nothing," Tom continued, "as he's given me nothing. He hasn't even found me a suitable wife. I need to be married, and he won't help me."

Edward had never given the matter much thought, but it was true his uncle was almost forty and never wed. What a terrible state of being. "You should be married, Uncle. How could he deny you that?"

Tom raised his hands. "He pretends to want to help me – but he proposes only lowly women because he is jealous and wants to keep me small. Even though advancing me reflects well on you – since we share blood."

Edward nodded pensively, and Tom pushed the point. "Who do you think I might marry?" he asked.

Edward thought for a moment. Who would be a good bride for his uncle? The perfect answer came to him, an echo of another conversation. "My sister Mary."

Tom's eyes widened. "Mary?"

"Mary. You asked for her hand and I agree it would be a good match. You can convert her to Protestantism."

Tom's face twisted, much as he tried to hide it. He did not like his own idea for some reason. "That is certainly a most generous suggestion," he said slowly. "Though the Council has already refused that request – and my brother would never allow it."

"Why not?"

"They would accuse me of being overly ambitious. Of thinking myself better than I am."

"Nonsense," Edward said. "You are my uncle and therefore you are quite noble. At least as noble as my illegitimate sister. I love you both and this way you could both be happy."

Tom shook his head. "You assign me too great a task, Your Majesty. I don't know that I have the strength to be equal to it."

"Nonsense," Edward repeated. "You have great strength. More than anyone I know." It was true. Who else ever stood up to Somerset as Tom did? He was a true champion; married to Mary, he could be England's champion.

"I confess I was thinking someone kinder than Mary. Someone closer to my age. Someone I love and admire with all my heart already."

Elizabeth leaped into Edward's mind, but he quickly discarded the thought: Elizabeth was even further from Tom's age than Mary. And her religion was already true. "I still think Mary is the best choice," he finally said.

"What about the Queen Dowager? Have you given no thought to her?"

Edward pondered. His stepmother was a good lady, kind and pious. She had been a wonderful wife to his father, and she would be a good influence on Tom. But she was deeply in mourning, more than any of them. "I cannot imagine she would entertain your suit right now."

"Not now, certainly. It would not be proper. But when the time comes, would you approve?"

The thought of the two of them together, side by side, gave Edward comfort. "I give you my blessing," he said.

A triumphant smile spread across his uncle's face. "Now who are you planning to share your coins with?"

The question transported Edward into the center of a smiling crowd. In his imagination, he was taller than all of them, handing out little velvet purses, without a care in the world. The tumbler from his coronation was there, prostrated on the floor in thanks.

Tom put a hand on Edward's shoulder. "Let us walk a bit while you consider."

True to his word, Tom did not try to talk. Edward was free to continue to contemplate the pleasures of generosity…

April 7, 1547

Whitehall, the Crown's largest palace, was a vast complex with separate facilities for banqueting, tennis, cockfighting, and of course, hastiludes. Mary was on her way to join her brother, who sat with his attendants watching the men of the court tilt at the quintain in practice for the upcoming tourney. She nodded to Anne Seymour Somerset who was with her; both women wanted to assess the competitors' skills. It would offer an important advantage in the betting.

Mary loved betting. Never too much, of course, but it added a spark of fun to the match. It was a good way to test her judgment. And others'.

She pinched her damask gown between her fingers to hold it above the muck stirred up by the morning's rain. The pole had been raised in the courtyard between the tennis building and the jousting field. A gravel path led to the covered stand that provided a comfortable perch for spectators. The walkway offered a good view of the goings-on, and she and Anne watched as they walked.

At the smack of steel striking wood, they turned to see whether the rider would be swift enough to escape the bag of sand that swung around. He was not, and raucous jeers rose from the stands.

As they approached the platform, a flash of gold told Mary where the King sat, surrounded by the duller clothes worn by his classmates. Cheke's bushy beard stood out immediately behind them, and the Gentlemen of the Privy Chamber formed a tall group just beyond.

Mary squinted to see Edward's face, and rejoiced at his relaxed and happy expression. Usually his brow was furrowed with concentration as he tried to live up to people's vast expectations of him.

Another smack, louder this time, and the boys jumped to their feet and shouted, arms raised in triumph. Mary paused and turned around, shielding her eyes to see and then quickly lowering her hand to applaud. Ned Seymour had just hit the quintain with his lance and was accepting congratulations. Anne pressed her lips together and Mary pretended not to notice. Anne did not like the children of her husband's first wife, and never reveled in their successes.

As the women mounted the platform's three small steps, Cheke nudged his royal pupil. Edward turned and his face brightened. Mary smiled and the two women curtsied to him.

"Your Majesty," they said.

"Greetings, ladies," he replied. "Did you see Ned's strike? That was the best one yet."

"We saw Your Majesty's reaction," Anne said. "An even better joy."

A grunt and galloping hooves told them that the next rider was on the field and charging. Edward immediately turned back to watch. The salutations over, the women continued on to the Queen's section, where Katherine Parr was already seated.

Anne startled when she saw her, but Mary was not surprised: after Henry's death, Katherine Parr had formally retired from court to the Chelsea mansion he had given her as a wedding present, but its location was close enough for her to visit often, especially when the court was at Whitehall.

Katherine smiled and nodded as they approached but did not rise to greet them as expected, instead quickly turning her attention back to the field. Anne stood over her, swaying gently from side to side and biting her lip as though she wanted to say something, but then she turned around and flounced into the second chair. Mary sat in the third.

Tom Seymour held his lance high before lowering his visor. The King and his attendants responded with shouts. They raised their fists to cheer his charge, then stood with frenzied applause when his lance thwacked squarely on its target and he escaped the bag of sand. Even the Queen joined in the merriment, though Mary and Anne remained seated.

What a difference from last year, Mary thought. Then, as for years, her father had avoided watching the practices; it was said he resented being too old to participate in the sports he had loved. But now the young boy who occupied the throne was happy to watch every moment he could.

Edward turned to the women in delight. "Did you see that, Mother? I shall do that soon."

"I don't know about soon, but yes, you shall." Cheke replied in her stead.

"Why should I not? I am King now."

"You are too young," Cheke replied. "You father did not joust until he was eighteen."

"Seventeen," Edward said. "On his accession."

"You forget he was six-foot-two and done with his growing," Cheke said.

"No one jousts at nine," Katherine Parr said.

"Who is jousting at nine?" Thomas Seymour had ridden up without anyone noticing.

"I'm not asking to joust," Edward said. "But the quintain is no more dangerous than riding a horse, and I should be allowed to work at that."

"The quintain has its own dangers," Cheke said. "You are too young."

Edward's lip trembled and his hands balled into fists.

"That's not unfair," Tom said soothingly. "You are still a child, under the law, until thirteen. I can see how you should wait until then."

"I think the Lord Protector might want you to wait longer," Cheke said. "Perhaps until you are fifteen at least."

"His uncle is determined to keep him a child," Tom said. "The lad could be wed at thirteen; his bride will want a man who is skilled."

Edward and his friends laughed at Tom's elaborate wink. Katherine Parr did as well. Anne Somerset did not.

"My husband is determined to protect the King, and rightly so," Anne said. "This is not the time to make such a decision."

Tom looked at Edward and shrugged, then bowed his head and trotted back to the next contestant, fifteen-year-old Robin Dudley. "Hold your reins tighter," Tom called as he rode. "And pick your pole up."

A crowd gathered round Dudley, pointing out the mistakes in his stance and bearing. This was what made these practices so long to watch; the men were always debating techniques in between the actual attempts. Edward and his friends leaned forward but there was no way to hear, and their own guesses as to Dudley's shortcomings quickly ran to other pastimes.

"You're supposed to twist the lance at the very end, with your wrist, like a tennis racket."

"We should play tennis tomorrow, have a tournament. Your Majesty?"

"I like that idea. Cheke? Will we have time in the morning before lessons start?"

Mary's attention was caught by Anne Seymour fidgeting, an unusual occurrence. Mary put a hand on her friend's knee. "Is anything amiss?"

Anne's lips were still pressed together but she shook her head. After another minute fidgeting she hissed at Katherine Parr. "I should be in that seat."

"I beg your pardon?" Katherine said.

"I am the wife of the Lord Protector. The first seat is rightfully mine."

Katherine looked shocked. "You are a duchess; I am a queen."

"Queen to the King-that-was, not the King-that-is."

"A queen dowager still sits above a duchess."

"My husband is the Lord Protector. The King's representative. He outranks everyone in the land but the King, so his wife outranks everyone but the Queen. You are not the Queen, but the Queen Dowager. The seat is mine."

Katherine's lips quivered but no sound came out. "Ridiculous," she finally sputtered. "The Queen Dowager remains the highest-ranking woman in the land until her son takes his own Queen."

Shouts from the King's Box interrupted the women's argument, and they turned to the field and clapped politely, the moment over.

Mary sat, still uncomfortable, turning the arguments over in her head. Anne should be right. And yet, a queen could only be unseated by a new queen.

Tom Seymour stepped into view, surprising them. The King clapped in glee, but Anne flinched; it was well-known she thought her husband's younger brother a liability.

Only Katherine Parr was unsurprised by Seymour's arrival. She leaned forward and smiled, though her face was still tight. "Good tilting, my Lord. You will surely dominate the field."

"For such encouragement, I shall wear your colors. I warrant they will bring me luck."

Anne wrinkled her nose. "Wildly inappropriate," she muttered.

Tom turned to the field. "Go ahead," he called. "And keep your lance high."

Nicholas Throckmorton spurred his horse, and for a moment his lance was even, but then it sagged and he missed the target entirely. They all groaned.

"God's blood, Throckmorton," Edward yelled. "Keep your lance higher."

Mary froze at the blasphemy, and saw with relief Cheke had done the same.

"What did you say, Sire?" he asked.

"I got overexcited," Edward replied with a wave of his hand.

"There is no excuse for that," Cheke said. "Where did you learn such a phrase?"

"They are just words."

"Words that diminish the great estate to which you have been called. Where did you learn them?"

"It is not important," Edward said. At least now he had the grace to flush.

"I cannot tell you how disappointed I am in you," Cheke said.

"But he is the King," Tom said. "Why should he not speak as he pleases?"

"Because it hurts the people around him to hear such filth from one who should be so far above them."

Edward shook his head and Mary could see a small smile play on his lips. She held her breath at the affront.

"Bring me a rod," Cheke called to the guard.

The boys exchanged worried glances. Mary herself wondered what would happen. Five or ten lashes would be a standard punishment for such an infraction, but did the tutor really intend to strike the King of England?

When the branch was in his hand, Cheke took a deep breath and looked directly at Edward. "Barnaby, come here," he said.

The boys froze. Cheke tore his gaze from Edward and bore it into Barnaby. "I said come here."

Barnaby walked forward, his shoulders hunched like a fearful dog, and stood before Cheke.

Cheke looked back at Edward. "I said your words hurt the people around you. This is how I will show it."

"Bend over," he told Barnaby. "You will bear the pain for your king. Hopefully he loves you enough to keep you from further torment."

Mary exhaled, relieved by this solution to the problem and grateful for the tutor's wisdom. He was a good man, even if he leaned too far toward religious reform.

Edward looked at Tom, who was studying his shoes, then at Katherine, who was picking at her cuticles. When her brother's gaze sought support from her, Mary quickly lowered her own eyes.

The first strike provoked a choked scream from Barnaby. Mary peeked up from under her lashes and saw tears filling Edward's eyes.

With each new strike, Edward flinched, and when his friend was released Edward mouthed an apology.

"I pray I will never have to repeat this," Cheke said.

Edward pressed his lips together and turned his gaze back to the field. "You never will."

Awkward silence reigned among the uncomfortable spectators. Only polite applause greeted the next rider's strike of the quintain, and even that died out quickly. "Please excuse me," Tom said. "I go now to prepare my next turn."

The Admiral's departure lessened the tension, and the boys began to stir like chickadees after the disappearance of a hawk. Mary prayed Tom would not return: he was too much an instigator.

May 17, 1547

"If you have finished your work, you may be excused," Cheke said to Ned Seymour, Nicholas Throckmorton, and John Bourchier, who jumped up even before the sentence was complete, clearly delighted to leave the smell of ink and paper and run off to the daily strength training lessons that would make them fit for the midsummer joust.

Ned was the best of them, but then Ned always tried to be the best at everything. He was desperate to make his father proud, always trying to overcome his shame at being born to Somerset's adulterous first wife, and the possibility he was Somerset's half-brother instead of his son.

The boys bowed in unison, each with his own flourish, then exaggerated their movements so their swords clanked noisily as they passed the bookshelves under the library's clerestory windows. Greenwich was a much less solemn place than Whitehall, its library more brightly lit and airy – and more conducive to bravado.

Edward pressed his lips together, jealous. He was stuck with the younger boys doing translations, and trying to swallow his annoyance over being too young for the real fun.

"We shall return," Throckmorton called.

"There is no need to disturb the rest of us," Cheke said. "Else I may reconsider my permission."

The three lads froze. "Nay, sir, I apologize," Throckmorton said.

They waited, chins quivering, until Cheke's gaze shifted from them to Henry Brandon's paper. They jumped to bow at the dismissal and left in careful silence.

Edward fumed and worked more quickly; within a half hour he had come to the end of the page. The small callus on the side of his finger throbbed from the quill, and he sucked on the injured skin to soothe it. "May I go visit my stepmother now?" he asked.

Edward loved when Katherine Parr came to court. Spending time with her comforted him, returning him to a routine that had governed the time he remembered spending at court himself. In her rooms Edward could pretend nothing had changed, that he was still safe in his father's shadow instead of thrust forward as the ultimate authority.

Cheke bent over to inspect his work. "Well, you have earned your fun," he said with a twinkle in his eye.

Robin Dudley and Barnaby looked up hopefully, but Cheke shook his head. "You still have more to do. Besides, this is His Majesty's special time with his stepmother."

"And uncle," added Edward happily. Tom Seymour enjoyed visiting Katherine as well. And he was always ready to commiserate when Edward was treated like a child by Somerset. And to give advice on how to respond, even if that advice was not always sound.

"The Lord Protector joins in your time with the Queen Dowager?" Cheke asked. "I thought he spent his afternoons hearing the people's petitions."

"No, the Lord Admiral," Edward said.

Cheke's eyes narrowed. "How often is he there?"

From Cheke's look, Edward knew he had said the wrong thing, but now he had no choice but to answer. "S-sometimes."

"Is that where the cursing came from?"

Edward hung his head without answering.

Cheke put a gentle hand on Edward's shoulder and patted it. "The penance for that mistake has been paid. Enjoy your reward."

Edward smiled gratefully at his tutor and skipped out of the chamber. He was halfway down the hallway when he remembered his station; he stopped, embarrassed, and looked around sheepishly. The guard at the Council door kept his gaze high and averted, but a small smile played around his mouth. Edward drew himself straight and walked calmly the rest of the way to the Queen's apartments as if nothing was wrong.

When he arrived, Katherine was in her chair, at her sewing. Tom was not yet there, and Edward was glad that his "sometimes" seemed less a lie.

She rose and curtsied, indicating the chair opposite hers. He quickly took it and she sat back down with a contented sigh. "It is a blessing to see Your Majesty smiling," she said. "Tell me what you have learned today."

Edward took a deep breath. She asked that question every time, and he rejoiced in telling her. He felt as professorial as Cheke explaining difficult concepts, and she was always impressed with his logic and knowledge.

"Today we discussed how even though Priscian says Tryphon was the first to set off the participle as a part of speech on its own, the truth is that Aristarchus had already assigned a separate place to it two hundred years before."

"Oh my."

"Of course, at the time he considered its nature combined the properties of two other parts of speech."

The Queen continued to interject little encouragements, and Edward happily kept going, quoting explanations and declining nouns and participles until he reached the end of the lesson. He allowed his voice to trail in the hope he would think of something else.

The Queen put down her sewing and sighed. "Your Majesty's brilliance inspires me. May I borrow it for a passage of the book I am writing?"

Katherine Parr was a learned woman who had published two books already, translations of earlier works. This new one, *Lamentations of a Sinner*, was entirely her own.

"I would be honored," he said, and it was true. To be asked for help like that was even better than sharing his lessons.

"I am glad for that," she said. "Your prose is more graceful than anyone else's."

Edward's chest puffed. His sister was admired for her poetry, but their stepmother preferred Edward's work. He silently prayed she would repeat this to Cheke.

"His Majesty *graceful?*" Tom Seymour's voice boomed from the doorway. "Nimble, elegant perhaps – but he is a man."

Tom bowed low, approached, and bowed again to them both. Katherine Parr smiled and held out her hand for him to kiss. "His Majesty is King to all his subjects; it is only right he exceed us all in every quality."

A look passed between Tom and Katherine, soft like affection but with something more. Ever since his uncle had mentioned his intention to court the Queen Dowager, Edward had watched the two of them closely to see if he could catch growing warmth. Perhaps this was finally a sign. "Thank you," was all he said.

"But he cannot exceed you in feminine beauty," Tom said. "You are a queen, after all."

"I was a queen," Katherine said. "Now I am a...no longer." Edward could not understand the look on her face, so he decided to say something comforting. "When your mourning is over, you will be able to consider a new life."

She bowed her head.

Tom raced over and threw himself at her knees. "Do not cry, sweetheart," he said, reaching his hand up to stroke her face. Instead of recoiling, she put a hand over his and smiled down.

Edward was as puzzled over her utter lack of tears as he was shocked by the breach of etiquette. His face must have shown his reaction, because they blushed and separated quickly.

"You caught us," Tom said. "Her new life has started."

"Tom," Katherine admonished, shaking her head.

Tom turned to Edward. "We have married, Your Majesty. Her grief was so great one day that I thought to comfort her. Then our shared melancholy transformed into something different, something beautiful. We...we married."

Eyes wide, Edward turned to his stepmother. "Is this true?"

Katherine Parr nodded. A small smile played at her lips, a little rueful perhaps. "The Lord in His mercy has given me a chance at new happiness."

Edward nodded, unsure what to say. *Didn't widows wear their black for two years?* "It seems terribly fast."

"Ah," Katherine Parr said, "I married your father with less of a wait after my Lord Latimer died. His Majesty persuaded me that life is for the living, told me that at my age I had to turn quickly from grief lest I propel myself into my tomb. That wise advice guided me then, and it guides me now."

Edward turned the explanation over in his mind. His father had surely said it – and it made perfect sense. "I wish you all happiness," he finally said, meaning it.

"There will be little of it for some time, Your Majesty," Tom said.

Edward's eyes widened. "Why so?"

"My brother will be furious with me. The whole Council will be angry when I tell them. They will fine me dearly."

Edward's stomach roiled. Secrecy so near the throne was never a good thing. "The Council does not know?"

"I know I should have waited for their approval." Tom spread his hands in apology. "But your father's example and words stirred me, and I could wait no longer. It has been almost a month!"

Edward bit his lip.

"Besides, I knew Your Majesty understood our pure hearts," Tom said.

The words hit Edward harder than any lance. Had he given consent? Would he be punished for this? Or, more accurately, would Barnaby be whipped for this?

"I was thinking to tell my brother first," Tom said.

Right then, Edward felt like the rabbit who by some miracle escaped a pursuing goshawk. Tom was not looking to push Edward further than he'd gone. "He will understand," Edward said, knowing Somerset wouldn't. But at least he would accept Tom's characteristic brashness and would sway the Council as well.

"But I don't want to tell him when his wife is around. She doesn't like me, and she'll spur him to greater anger."

"She doesn't like me any better," Katherine said, and her sad eyes hardened. "She thinks herself higher than me – she refused to carry my train the last time we dined in public. Now that I have married her husband's younger brother, she will be insufferable."

Edward waved his hand. "You were married to my father; she is only married to Somerset."

"We need to remind them to love whom the King loves," Tom said. "That was always the rule during the late reign."

It occurred to Edward this rule was still being followed, except that people loved whom the Lord Protector loved, not the King. They bowed to Edward, obsequiously so, but they listened to Somerset.

"And besides—" Tom began before he froze, eyes wide as if he'd just had a sudden thought. He turned to Edward. "Perhaps Your Majesty could write a letter?"

Edward pushed down the queasy feeling those words gave his stomach. "What kind of letter?"

"You could write to the Queen, expressing your great love for her." Tom narrowed his eyes. "And mention how she loved your father more than anyone."

Edward turned the idea over in his mind. That didn't sound very dangerous. And it was true. Edward nodded. "I could do that."

Tom's mouth widened into a broad smile. "How about now? The desk awaits Your Majesty."

Edward walked to the desk, which already had a sheet of paper and a quill ready for him. For a second he wondered whether Tom's sudden idea was less sudden than it seemed, but he pushed the thought out of his mind to concentrate.

"Why am I writing her a letter when I see her often?"

Tom and Katherine exchanged a wide-eyed stare. Katherine broke away. "You can answer the letter I wrote to you back when I was at Saint James," she said. "A letter always deserves a written response."

Tom exhaled as if he had been holding his breath. Edward considered the idea and nodded.

"But put it in your own words," Tom said.

Edward dipped the quill in the ink and began. He wrote of her letter to him, then of her love of God and love for his father.

"Don't forget you have to speak of your love for her," Tom said.

Edward shot him a glance but said nothing. He dipped his pen again and continued. *Wherefore, since you love my father, I cannot but much esteem you; since you love me, I cannot but love you in return; and since you love the word of God, I do love and admire you with my whole heart. Wherefore, if there be anything wherein I may do you a kindness, either in word or deed, I will do it willingly.*

"Perfect," exclaimed Tom from his perch over Edward's shoulder. The ink still glistened, not yet dry.

Edward forced a smile. Not even his stepmother's hug could dismiss his unease.

May 28, 1547

The archery field beckoned through the giant leaded glass windows of the King's Library, making it hard to concentrate on lessons. Edward looked down at the paper in front of him, trying to remember. "*Cantum erit,*" he finally said.

"No, Sire, that is the future perfect passive: 'It will have been sung,'" Cheke said. "Teddy? Can you tell me 'she is about to sing'?"

"*Canendum est.*"

"Better, you used a periphrasic. But you used the wrong one, and you merely told me 'it must be sung.'"

"*Canturus est!*" Edward called out.

Cheke looked heavenward. Edward blushed and corrected himself. "*Cantura est,* since the subject is female."

"Thank you," Cheke said. He sighed. "The beautiful weather tempts you like the sirens tempted Odysseus. I should have drawn the curtains before commencing the lessons."

The rap of a stave interrupted them.

"Your Majesty's Council wishes to speak with Your Majesty," announced the page.

Cheke's smile was twisted. "I pray politics will interest Your Majesty more than Latin. Come, boys."

Edward's advice was needed. His chest swelled and he sat up straighter, lifting his chin while his tutor and friends removed themselves to stand against the wall. He wasn't sure what he was about to rule on, but it probably had something to do with Scotland. That was all anyone wanted to talk about lately.

Somerset was continuing the Henrician policies, following through on the dream to unite England and Scotland under a single crown, England's crown, by having Edward marry the Scottish queen, Mary. The two were still far too young yet – Mary was only five and Edward nine – but this was clearly God-inspired because of the territories involved. Edward wondered again what it would be like to wed a woman he'd never seen.

"Have them enter," he said, waving a lofty hand.

Somerset entered first, his dour face more drawn than usual. The rest followed in the careful line of protocol, but then Somerset stood aside, eyes downcast. Warwick spoke for them.

"Sire, Thomas Seymour has married the Queen Dowager. This is a matter of grave consequences and we intend to censure them both."

Edward quickly looked at Tom, who gave a discreet shrug.

"Transgressions of this magnitude call for confinement in the Tower," Thomas Wriothesley said.

The fire in Wriothesley's eyes scared Edward. Somerset had told him the man was a conservative, a papist who hated the reforms that brought people closer to God. Edward didn't like him, but he had no choice in the matter.

"But why?" he asked. This was far worse than he had expected.

"The Queen Dowager should have been locked away, for safety. What if she fell pregnant by Seymour? She might have pretended it had been sired by your father. That would have tainted the succession."

That was serious. Edward bit his lip for not having thought of it.

"She's had several monthly courses since the death of the King-that-was," Tom said. "She has also formally stated she was not with child by him when he died."

"That doesn't change the fact that you overreach. A royal bride? That is far above your station," Wriothesley said, his lip curling.

Tom sneered and took a step forward. "Is there something wrong with Seymour blood? Say it loud for the King, my nephew, to hear."

Wriothesley turned to the King and dropped to one knee. "That was not my meaning, Sire. But I think it dishonors your father's memory for his widow to cleave to a man who holds only a barony, and *that* only recently."

"But if they love each other?" Edward tried to keep his voice from trembling.

"He sought to wed either Mary or Elizabeth before he settled on the Queen," Wriothesley said, rising. "Is love so changeable?"

"I did not meddle with either of them," Tom said, pointing his finger like a gun at Wriothesley. "I accepted your decision."

"That is not the issue before us," Somerset said. "That one was resolved."

"But it shows his conceit, and should factor into the punishment," Warwick said.

This was the first time Edward had seen his Councilors attack each other, and it scared him. It scared him even more since he had given permission to his uncle to do this.

"That would distress the Queen, whom the King loves dearly," Tom said. "You saw his letter."

"He would not have written such a letter had he known what the woman had done," Warwick said.

Tom looked at Edward but said nothing. Edward's mouth was as dry as ashes. He glanced at Somerset. Why was he not doing more to calm the men?

As if he had heard the unspoken question, Somerset answered it. "Because he is my brother, I will not seek to impose order on the others. I do not believe it is my place to do so and would do more harm than good."

That made sense. But it meant Edward would have to rise to

the occasion. Summoning all his courage, he began. "After I wrote the letter, my uncle came to me to ask my permission. I gave him my blessing."

Silence descended on the room as all mouths but Tom's dropped open.

"You knew of this?" Somerset's voice was almost a hiss.

Edward shuddered. "I did," he whispered.

"And you said nothing?"

"I-I did not think it was as important a plan as you all seem to."

"Anything that concerns Your Majesty is of primary importance to the realm," Somerset said, his narrowed eyes intensifying his gaze. "My brother was well aware of this, even if you were not."

Edward's lips tightened. He had done wrong. He had trusted too well, and had been manipulated like the child he was.

"The Queen, too, should have known better," Somerset continued.

"Really?" Tom stepped forward. "She was denied the chance to serve as Regent, cheated out of her rightful role as Governor of the King's person, and—"

"Silence," Somerset yelled and the whole room cringed. "Silence, you criminal. This is not your time to speak."

"To the Tower with him," Wriothesley said, and nods spread across the room.

Edward's stomach turned over. "But I gave my consent."

"Your Council need not be bound by that," Wriothesley said.

Tom took an angry step toward him, but Warwick extended his arm to hold him back. "Sire," he began, and heaved a sigh, "since Baron Seymour had your permission, we must in all honesty allow him to remain a free man. But in the future, we ask that you confer with us before important decisions. It is why we are here, to guide you in such matters."

Edward nodded, even though he had no idea how he would determine importance in the future. He knew if he asked Somerset, he'd be told that anything Tom did needed to be discussed with the Council. But that didn't tell him why.

Warwick's voice turned to a purr. "Perhaps you did not feel comfortable coming between your uncles. If that ever happens again, you may always come to me."

"He can always come to any of us," Wriothesley sputtered.

"The King has already said it was not discomfort but ignorance," Somerset said. "You are making too much of this."

A sense of impotence and failure swamped Edward, and hot tears threatened his eyes. "Leave me," he said quickly, so the lords would not see his weakness.

After the Council had gone, Edward noticed his friends still frozen in their places against the wall. Their eyes were downcast, their shoulders bowed, Teddy and Robin most of all. Edward blushed at how weak he must seem to them.

"Boys, it is time to hawk," Cheke said. "Go get your horses ready; the King and I will join you soon."

Edward's attendants exchanged glances and quickly sidled off. Cheke, his face long, pulled up a chair next to Edward and sat heavily.

Edward heaved a sigh. "Go ahead, tell me how stupid I was."

"I do not think you were stupid at all," Cheke said. "I think you needed this lesson, and, God be praised, the situation is of little import."

Edward turned to his tutor, curious. "Please explain."

"Your uncle used you in this. He used your love and your trust to get you to do something that the Council would reject."

"You're saying I need to love less? Trust less?"

Cheke sighed. "No, only that you need to be more aware, because like a dog who has learned a new trick, your uncle will try this again. Many men will."

"So, you think the marriage was wrong?"

"There is nothing treasonous in the marriage: it has no bearing on the succession. It may affect the balance of power on the Council; that is why they are concerned."

"Why would the Council be affected?"

"The Queen Dowager is rich and respected and is one of the few people who has Your Majesty's ear."

"Is that so important? To have my ear?"

Cheke gave a wry smile. "Look what it did in this situation."

Edward turned that over in his mind. The sharp edges hurt. "So you are saying there is always a motive behind people's kindness."

Cheke looked pained. "No, that is far too stark. This is only about awareness, nothing more."

"How can I be aware if no one tells me anything?"

"I will mention to the Duke of Somerset," Cheke said, "that he should involve you more. Certainly it was his own omission that allowed this situation to unfold as it did. Now shall we join your friends?"

Edward nodded, and they took off for the stables. As they walked, Edward continued to ponder his tutor's words. He knew he could not let this issue slide – he never wanted to find himself in such a humiliating situation again. He had to press Somerset himself, after Cheke's conversation had opened the door.

He opened his mouth to mention this – and closed it just as quickly. He would keep his own counsel. It was what a grown-up would do.

August 24, 1547

As they walked along the covered colonnade at Hampton Court Palace, raindrops whispered around them while a warm breeze chased away the worst of the heat. Edward wiped his forehead with the back of his hand.

It was just the three of them, Somerset, Tom, and himself. Argos had run off to dig in a garden bed, oblivious to the soft rain. His entire being was focused on the mole that had shown its nose earlier.

A gardener in his green-and-white livery came running to

chase the dog away, scolding it quietly so he would not bother the most powerful men in the land. No – wait – his hose and cap were blue: he worked in the kitchens. Why was he outside?

Edward pressed a fingernail deep into the flesh of his palm to force his attention back to the matters at hand. Was he such a child as that? They were discussing war for goodness' sake, the plans to invade Scotland to force the Scots to let Edward marry their Queen. Somerset and Tom were discussing details – even asking Edward's opinion. They were treating him more like an adult than they ever had, and his mind was wandering.

"I will have only ten thousand, maybe eleven thousand, infantry to support my attack. I need fifteen," Somerset said.

"What about cavalry?" Edward asked, hoping the question sounded wise.

"Only five or six thousand," Somerset said. "I should have ten."

"You will have eighty cannon," Tom said. "They'll do the damage you need."

"Do we not have more men and horses?" Edward asked.

"The Council wants to keep men here in case France attacks from the south," Tom explained. "We can't leave you unprotected, after all."

"There would be plenty of artillery and warships to keep London safe." Somerset sounded peevish, but at least his temper was held in check.

"If France sends a fleet, we'll need them all," Tom said.

"What about mercenaries?" Edward asked, proud his alternative sounded wise and considered. "Could we make up the difference with them? Hired harquebusiers would provide more firepower than our English longbows."

Before Somerset had a chance to answer, Tom changed the subject. "Ah, Your Majesty, did you ever think men would work so hard to get you a royal pillow on which to lay your head?"

It was a comment typical of Tom, who always brought conversations back to immediate personal needs. It wasn't appropriate during a serious conversation, especially since Edward's age precluded all thoughts of bedding. Not for another eight years or so, anyway. Edward's cheeks burned at the reminder of his youth and inexperience.

Too, the contrast was disturbing. They were warring on Scotland to achieve the peace of marriage. No wonder the Scots called it a "rough wooing."

"This is about far more than a pillow for His Majesty," Somerset said between clenched teeth. "This is for the safety and future of the realm, and you would do well to remember it."

"And yet the cost of the venture seems high," Edward said, repeating the line that was always on Tom's lips.

Somerset stopped walking and turned to him, eyes wild. Edward cringed.

"What choice do we have?" Somerset snarled. "We need to prevent Scotland from marrying the young Mary off to a Frenchman. This was your father's policy, his dream. It will be my honor to lead the military effort for you as I did for him."

Somerset had made quite a name for himself when Henry VIII had sent him north years ago, subduing the Scots by torching their land. They would likely quake in their boots to hear he'd returned, just as Edward was quaking now. Maybe that would be enough to persuade them. Hopefully that would be enough.

"Who will guide me here while you are gone?" Edward asked.

"Me, of course," Tom said. "And your stepmother."

"You should be coming to Scotland," Somerset said to Tom. "The King doesn't need you. My wife's brother will remain Chief Gentleman of his Privy Chamber for all his personal needs."

"My place is here," Tom said. "The King's person needs more lords around him than just Sir Michael Stanhope."

"And so you refuse an active command?" Somerset's tone was clipped. "Against my wishes and those of the Council?"

"As Lord High Admiral, I belong in London, or Portsmouth if need be. 'Tis the French who have ships, not the Scots."

Edward had no doubt Tom would stay and insist on more authority once Somerset was gone. He pondered briefly what that would mean for himself. Tom was more relaxed than Somerset, with far less of a temper. On the other hand, he was more impulsive, more erratic – that would be stressful.

Still, he was likely to give Edward more freedom. And if he did, and Edward proved he used it well, perhaps Somerset might continue once he returned. Edward prayed that would be the case, that it would not be a question of exchanging one jailer for the other. He just wanted to be older. It was hard to wait.

"Your Highness!"

Barnaby's voice came from inside the Palace seconds before he emerged, running. When he saw Somerset and Tom, he skidded to a stop and bowed. "Sorry, your Lordships, I was looking for the King."

"Is there an emergency?" Somerset's voice dripped sarcasm.

"Robin Dudley suggested a tennis tournament, and, and…"

"You knew he was with us, did you not?" Somerset asked.

Edward felt bad for Barnaby, but his friend did not seem to mind the scolding.

"One of the servants brought Argos back to His Majesty's apartments, and we thought your meeting was over."

"Do you not remember what it was like to be young?" Tom asked his brother. "There was a time when you would have understood impetuosity. A very short time, admittedly."

Somerset sniffed. "I did not have the luxury of leisure."

"Says a former Master of the Horse," Tom answered with a wink to Edward.

"Yes, exactly," Somerset said. "I take even my pastimes seriously."

Tom rolled his eyes. "And shame those of us who choose to live life as God gives it to us."

"God and your hard-working family, you mean."

Edward glanced at Barnaby, who was shifting from foot to foot, as uncomfortable as Edward before this display.

"Go, enjoy yourselves," Tom said. "This need not concern you."

Somerset paused but nodded. "We are done here. Go."

Edward did not need to be told twice. He immediately set off for the building that housed the royal tennis court.

When they were out of earshot, Barnaby let out a slow whistle. "Your uncle Tom feels quite a rivalry there. I wonder if my own brother is as jealous of me?"

Edward felt a jolt that Barnaby had chosen to address Tom's needling rather than Somerset's wrath. He pressed further. "You think my uncle Tom is jealous of Somerset?"

"Look at his face. It devours him."

Edward pondered this new idea. "Perhaps," he said to avoid committing himself to anything.

"Not that there is anything wrong with that," Barnaby hastened to add. "Of course siblings are jealous, it's just the degree."

Edward wondered in passing whether his sisters were jealous of him, of the fact that he sat on the throne instead of them. Impossible. This was just the right order. God's decision.

It was different.

November 13, 1547

Mist shrouded the parklands in the thin morning light as the small group stepped their horses into the clearing. Edward and his four friends had been joined by three of the men of his Privy Chamber and his uncle Tom.

Edward locked eyes with the peregrine perched on his arm. Another new hawk for him, this one only recently trained. Thankfully it did not bate. Edward hated that, hated the desperate beating of the wings and the inevitable headlong dives, hated feeling like he could not control his hawk. And resentment made it even harder to display the gentleness and patience needed to coax the bird back onto his fist. It would be different if the moment were private, but Edward's moments were never private. There were always witnesses to his failures.

Edward shook off the doubts. *As with your hawk, so with your life. Focus on the bird and the pure truth he teaches you.* That was his father's most oft-repeated lesson to him, echoed by Somerset. You could only control a bird if she trusted you, and she would never trust you if you were weak. You needed to be firm and fair and brave. Absolute. And Edward, God's anointed, needed to be better at this than anyone.

He took a deep breath to squelch his rising fear. He had to, or she would sense it. For her, he had to be bold, maintain a still presence.

It worked. She stared deep into his eyes, and he slowly slipped the jeweled hood back onto her head.

"Such perfect control, Your Majesty," Tom said. He turned to the others. "The rest of you would do well to emulate him…but later. For now, he needs room. The bird is new; let him fly it alone. With me."

A flash of suspicion warned Edward this was a ploy. The others reined in, doubt on their faces as well, but Tom reached down and grabbed the bridle of Edward's horse to lead it away a bit. "We will take this field."

"You are the expert, my Lord," Fowler said. "We will hunt the woods."

Once they were comfortably away from the others, Tom relaxed in his saddle. "Much better," he said.

The bird relaxed as well, apparently happy to lose the crowd, and Edward felt ashamed for doubting his uncle.

"Ah, this is glorious, is it not, Your Majesty?"

Edward nodded.

"Would that it could continue forever, me guiding you like this."

Something in his voice made it sound like he was getting at

something. "Mmmm," Edward said noncommittally.

"But my brother is returning from Scotland for your first Parliament, and he will surely sour things. He sours everything."

There it was. Over these past few months, all Tom had done was complain about Somerset. His bad temper, his bad judgment, his twisted views. It only made it worse that many of Tom's gripes were legitimate.

Still, Edward was too scared to add fuel to the fire with open agreement. Especially not when Somerset would be there so soon. "Mmmm," he repeated.

"I need for you to write a letter to the Lords of the Council for me."

The peremptory tone of Tom's voice was shocking. And upsetting. "What?" Edward said.

"It is none ill thing," Tom said hastily. "They have just been reluctant to support me."

"Support you in what?"

"It is for the Queen's Majesty."

Edward was not sure what he was talking about. The conversation had started out about Somerset and now Tom was invoking the Queen.

The echo of Tom's arguments earlier in the year, the manipulation of Edward's trust, came rushing over him. *Like a dog who has learned a new trick, your uncle will try this again.*

"If it is good, the Lords will allow it," Edward said.

"The Lords will take it in better part if you write it."

Edward looked his uncle full in the face and let his exhaustion show. "Unless they think it ill."

Tom started to sputter a response but Edward turned away and spurred his horse to walk.

Tom fell in behind, silent.

A partridge flew overhead. Edward quickly raised his arm and removed his bird's hood. The peregrine shook her feathers, then fixed her eyes on the movement above. Edward jolted her into flight and she soared into the air. When it seemed she could go no higher, she turned and swooped down. The partridge raced for cover but nothing could stop her losing at the game of life and death.

"Well done," Tom cried.

Edward knew it was true. His skill changed the way he felt, changed the very color of the day. He straightened his back and smiled.

"That is the way I like to see you," Tom said. "The way a ruler looks."

Edward sat even taller in his saddle and looked around to see where the rest of the group was. Unfortunately, they were too far away to witness his prowess.

"You must take upon yourself to rule more," Tom added. "You soon should be allowed. Ah, that will be a glorious day, when you can be more generous with your friends. Right now, you have no money to even dice with, or give to your servants."

The reference to money struck a chord in Edward's heart. Still, he tried to resist its lure. "Somerset had Stanhope leave me some coins."

Tom laughed. "Surely not enough. I will give Fowler money for you."

Much as he wanted the purse, Edward did not want to write the letter his uncle wanted. He didn't know what the purpose was, but if Tom was reluctant to tell him, it had to be wrong. "I am well enough."

Tom lifted a single eyebrow. This time he was the one who spurred his horse to walk and Edward had to fall in behind. After several paces, his uncle resumed in a neutral tone. "For whom would you want money?"

The question unleashed something within Edward, and his mind supplied name after name. Cheke. Barnaby. Latimer. Belmaine the book-binder. And on and on. With each name, his humiliation and resentment increased. Somerset had made him a beggarly king.

"Here," Tom said, holding out a purse. "Take this. And if

anything is said against me, do not believe it until I speak to you myself."

December 15, 1547

Edward groaned when his fingers picked the wrong string and his lute emitted a discordant twang. This was the fourth time in a row he had gotten the passage wrong, and each time made him angrier. "It's too cold in here," he said, looking around.

It wasn't quite true, of course. The fire in the nearby hearth blazed, and the books in the shelves reflected the heat back into the room. The warmth was why they were seated in the library to begin with.

Still, his music teacher jumped up. He threw another log onto the pile and poked at it with the hoe until the flames crackled. "You should go on, before you reinforce the mistake," said Philip van Wilder when he resumed his place.

"I must stay with this measure until I do it properly," Edward said between clenched teeth. That's what Somerset always insisted.

Noise at the door drew his attention. The guard was arguing with someone in the hall. Edward could pick out Tom's voice but not his words – until he began to shout. "God's blood, did he say he didn't want to be disturbed or did he not? The door is open, for sweet Jesu's sake. Ask him."

Edward sighed. His uncle's fuss would carry over to the Council room and inflame Somerset, who would likely take his annoyance out on Edward. "Let him enter," he called.

After a smug "Ha," Tom Seymour stalked into the room and bowed. "You may retire," he said to the musician.

Edward was a bit annoyed, but his uncle was tapping his foot with impatience. This might have something to do with the letter, and it would be better if they were alone.

Heat rose in Edward's face. He had succumbed to Tom's request. In the dead of night, he had hastily scrawled a note and hidden it under the carpet for Fowler to retrieve discreetly. As if that would keep the secret.

Tom began the second van Wilder was out the door. "Your letter won't do." He took it from his pocket and unfolded it. In the light of day, the scrap looked sad and dirty. A visual representation of the mistake it was. Edward closed his eyes.

"All it says is, 'I recommend me unto you and the Queen, thanking you always for my remembrance.' That is too vague."

"What more do you need?"

"I need you to address the Council, not me, and ask them to favor my suit. I will take care of the rest."

"What is your suit?" Edward asked.

Tom took a deep breath. He lifted his chin and planted a hand on his sword. "I would be Lord Protector in my brother's place."

The words chilled Edward to his bones. This was not about money or a title. This was a coup to give his uncle power he was not capable of wielding.

"You know I would make you happier than Somerset. I would see you married and jousting and enjoying life. I would make you a true king."

"I don't think I can write that."

"Have I not been your friend? Have I not supplied you with money, to act as the King you are?"

"My father set rules to protect me during my youth. It is not my place to meddle with them."

"The Lords will do it, not you. They just need to know you prefer me, for my brother tells them the opposite."

"I can't."

"You must."

Edward shook his head. "I don't know."

"To be a king is to rule. All this year, I have encouraged you to do that – and I have backed up my encouragement with more than a hundred gold sovereigns. It is time for you to pay me back."

"I can't do it now."

"Later, then."

"I…"

"Promise me."

Edward nodded and immediately ran to his bedchamber, shutting the door behind him. Thank heavens Tom did not try to follow him.

Edward pressed an ear against the door, listening for the clink of his uncle's sword as he left the room. When all was silent, Edward sank to his knees, ready to weep.

"Your Majesty?"

The words came from inside the room; he jumped and looked around wildly. It was Cheke. He'd been reading by the window; now he looked worried. Edward was caught.

"What is amiss?"

The fear and love shining from his tutor's eyes was more than Edward could bear, and he quickly confessed everything.

"He wants to be Lord Protector."

Cheke paled. "What makes you think this?"

"He tried to trick me into signing a request that the Council favor his suit."

"You were right not to sign."

The confirmation should have comforted Edward, but it only worried him more. "But I said I would."

Cheke shook his head. "He cannot force you."

"I…I…" Edward swallowed. "I took money from him. A lot of money."

Cheke sighed. "To my eternal shame, I took money from him too. Until now, I did not see the harm."

"So you are stuck, too?"

"Not at all," Cheke said firmly. "I owe him nothing and you owe him even less. Give him one of your jewels. That is more than he deserves. And don't take anything more."

"But he will pressure me, he will—"

"He can't unless he gets you alone, and we will see to it he cannot."

The tightness in Edward's chest loosened and he found himself able to breathe normally. "How?"

"Only your gentlemen ever have a reliable chance to speak with you alone. That is why Seymour uses Fowler as his go-between."

Edward considered it. "He will not give up."

"He will if we tell Somerset."

Edward's stomach turned over and tears stung his eyes. "Tell Somerset?"

"He will be grateful for the warning."

Much as Edward wanted to believe that, it was too much to hope. "He will rage, and it will be a horrible thing."

"His rage will be directed at his brother and at me, not at you."

Edward looked at Cheke, worried for his tutor. "What if he sends you away?"

"Fear of punishment should never stop us from doing the right thing. Whatever happens to me, this will protect you. Once Somerset formally takes up the fight, Seymour will have no reason to pursue you any further."

"You think?"

"I know."

Despite the confidence on his tutor's face, Edward still trembled. "You don't have to tell him about you. I could not bear it if he sent you away."

"Only by confessing can I be worthy of being near you. I believe the good Duke is wise enough to accept that."

Edward thought a moment and then sighed. "I pray you are right."

"And this might even be enough to get Somerset to change his ways and give you coins himself."

A tiny spark of hope kindled. "He did have Stanhope give me a purse when he went to Scotland." The spark died. "But it wasn't much."

Cheke put a hand on his shoulder; the touch softened the

harsh spike of Edward's fear.

"This too shall pass," Cheke said.

January 6, 1548

Mary stepped into the Great Hall at Hampton Court Palace and made a deep reverence to her brother, ensconced on his throne at the far end. The chair sat atop a platform with a height that required the nobles standing around him to look up slightly. The sight of the Duke and Duchess of Somerset and Elizabeth to his right made Mary exhale in relief. Katherine Parr had not yet arrived.

Mary bowed her head a second time before she rose. The room would assume it was another gesture for the King, but in truth this was gratitude for the God-granted respite. Mary had left court immediately upon hearing the shocking news of the Queen Dowager's hasty remarriage, and time and distance had not softened Mary's anger over the insult to all England.

Mary had come to court for Twelfth Night, after months of absence, and felt the change. The lavish holiday decorations, the heady scent of pine and Eastern spices, soothing music everywhere – these were the same as always. But under the glittering façades, faces were more sinister: they wore the look of men who controlled the King rather than the other way around.

After every five paces she stopped and curtsied again, as she'd been instructed. Somerset had increased the level of ritual surrounding the King, as if the outer show of respect would penetrate men's hearts. Mary thought it was just the opposite – a stark reminder the King was a powerless boy.

When she was directly in front of the dais, she knelt and looked up at her brother, waiting. Heavily worked gold thread crowded the dark red satin of his doublet. The design continued on his black velvet cap, in a *trompe l'oeil* pattern of gold pins. His pale face stood out from the finery, more angular than Mary remembered. His chin was sharper, his lips thinner and more tightly pressed. He no longer looked like the soft, trusting boy of the year before. He looked disappointed somehow, or perhaps resigned or even nervous. What must his life be?

Edward glanced at Somerset, who was dressed as his larger twin. Receiving an almost imperceptible nod, Edward began.

"Greetings, sister." His thin voice boomed loud enough to reach the far corners of the room, commanding the attention an important guest deserved. "You are welcome to court."

Mary made her voice equally loud. "Your Majesty, it is a delight to see you after all this time."

Edward stood and held out his arms. Mary happily rose and embraced her brother while the court applauded.

The public duty done, Edward exhaled and smiled. "It is good to have you here," he said in a normal tone. "I hope you will grace us with a long visit. Elizabeth has promised to stay for at least a month."

Mary broke out in a broad smile. "I would be honored." She turned to Somerset, Anne, and Elizabeth, and curtsied. "But greetings must come before talk of remaining."

Somerset bowed to her, not quite as low as he used to, but she would not fault him for that. Anne gave a shorter curtsy than Elizabeth and quickly extended her arms. "Mary, dearest."

Mary's face relaxed into a happy smile. "Anne."

They kissed cheeks and Mary turned to Elizabeth. "How tall you are," she said. "You have grown, my Lady."

Elizabeth blushed. "Thank you, sister."

Mary turned back. "And with my greetings done, I can offer my sincere congratulations to you, my Lord Protector, for your great gains in Scotland. I understand you commanded our army during the Battle of Pinkie Cleugh and brought our enemy to its knees."

"God was on our side," Somerset said.

"Praise Him," Anne said. "For the victory, and for returning my husband to London. The Lord Protector's place is here, with the King."

"The Lord Protector's place is where he can do the most good for the realm," Somerset said. "With this decisive victory, Scotland has no choice but to agree to our terms."

Mary pretended not to notice the sharp look in Somerset's eye or the barb in his voice. Something must have happened during his absence; she would ask the Spanish Ambassador later.

"That will be a great day for England."

"Thank you," Somerset said. "We will celebrate their submission for months."

Conversation faltered and Somerset started to look around the room. Mary jolted at this sure sign of her diminished importance.

She glanced at her brother and noticed his gaze on her rosary. "Why do you wear those beads?" he asked.

Mary glanced at Somerset, who had promulgated the ridiculous decision to outlaw what reformists called idolatry. "To pray for our father's soul."

Edward sniffed. "He doesn't need prayers – there is no purgatory to keep souls from heaven."

The religious chasm yawned between them. It was her duty to educate him. She was his godmother, after all. Mary infused all the gentleness she could into her voice. "There is for me, Sire. And he asked for our prayers."

Edward narrowed his eyes. "You didn't wear beads during my father's reign."

"I would have, but they were my mother's. Our father did not appreciate such…reminders."

Edward glanced at Somerset, who jumped in.

"I am confident your sister means no disrespect. This is a tribute to a beloved parent."

The rap of a stave on the floor precluded further talk. "The Queen Dowager and Baron Seymour, the Lord High Admiral," announced the page.

Mary stiffened at the thought of having to pretend affection for her former stepmother, affection once real but now gone.

They all turned to the front of the room to welcome the new arrivals. Mary thought she heard Anne snort; the sound gave Mary comfort that she was not alone in resenting the new couple. Mary smoothed the front of her gown and placed a cool smile on her face.

Katherine Parr shimmered in a gown of golden damask and wore a radiant smile. Mary flushed. How dare the woman cut short her widowhood after only four months – and to marry Tom Seymour, of all people? How could the woman have let herself be taken in by such a strutting peacock?

Oh yes, Mary had heard the rumors that the two had almost married before Katherine wed the King, that Tom Seymour had been sent from court to eliminate a rival. People excused the haste of this marriage, calling it love reunited. But that only worsened the insult.

Mary gritted her teeth during the greetings, trying to quell the disdain rising in her throat.

"Dearest Mary," Katherine said, "it has been too long since I saw you last."

Her eyes sparkled, and her face looked less lined. She had never seemed so content.

Mary opened her mouth to respond, but she didn't get a chance.

"Brother, you need to move over for my wife," Tom said to Somerset. "It is her place to stand next to the King."

Somerset's eyes narrowed; Anne's popped. "The Lord Protector is the highest man in the land after the King, and I am his wife," Anne said.

Katherine looked annoyed. "We have had this conversation before."

Mary snuck a glance at Somerset. His face was impassive.

"And you have corrected nothing," Anne said. "Nor have you returned the Crown's jewels. I should be the one to wear them."

Katherine gasped as her head jerked back. "I beg your pardon."

"The country's riches should be used for its glory. As the wife of the Protector, I represent England. Especially since you are no longer resident at court."

If Mary hadn't known better she would have sworn that smoke was coming out of the Queen Dowager's ears and nose.

"That would make it look strange when you carried my train," Katherine said between clenched teeth.

"You should be carrying mine," Anne said. "My Lady...*Baroness*."

Mary silently applauded her friend. Indeed, Katherine Parr had forfeited her high status with this marriage.

A quick trumpet blare announced the arrival of the Spanish Ambassador. Mary's heart lifted at the sight of the man who was as staunch a champion of hers as his predecessor, Eustace Chapuys, had once been for her mother. Between Mary's withdrawal from court and his leaving to visit Spain, it had been too long since she'd seen his kind face.

The group turned to watch François van der Delft bow deeply to the King.

"We are glad you could attend our festivities, *señor*," Edward said.

Van der Delft bowed again, not so low but more theatrically. "It was an honor to be included."

"You are always welcome," Somerset said. "England and Spain have always been *especial* friends."

Van der Delft turned to the Protector and bowed low again. "My master bade me to deliver the same message to you."

"*Bienvenidos, amigo*," Mary said.

This time van der Delft smiled widely as he bowed. "*Me alegro ver ustedes*."

"You are certainly more welcome than the French Ambassador," Tom Seymour said.

The breach of protocol irritated Mary, and she found herself clenching her jaw. It was not appropriate for him to speak at a moment of state.

Van der Delft inclined his head. "Ah, but are you?"

Anne's lip twitched in amusement. Tom Seymour's chin rose, the peacock ready to fight.

Katherine Parr placed a hand on Tom's arm while keeping her eyes on van der Delft. "It is hard to resent someone who makes few demands."

Was that earnestness or sarcasm? It was impossible to tell, and despite herself Mary had to admire Katherine's political deftness.

Van der Delft laughed. "Well said."

Just then Warwick approached with the Council. Somerset and Anne joined the King in that conversation, leaving Mary and Elizabeth with Katherine Parr and Tom Seymour. Another sign that Mary's position had shifted.

Katherine Parr quickly took control, monopolizing van der Delft. "You must visit us at Chelsea, señor," she said. "We would love to have you."

"Ah, Lady, I am honored by the invitation, but I plan to visit the Lady Mary first at Kenninghall." He turned to Mary. "If I may."

"Of course," Mary said. "You are always most welcome."

Mary surreptitiously glanced about to see if anyone took offense at the Ambassador calling her Princess. Katherine and Tom either did not notice or chose not to fuss. Elizabeth seemed oblivious to the breach. Luckily for the Ambassador, the others in the room did not hear.

"Ah, but I have an even better plan." A wide smile spread across Katherine's face; she turned to Mary and Elizabeth and grasped their hands. "My fondest wish is for you both to join my household here in London. You could be nearer to court, nearer to your brother, and I would be honored to have you."

Elizabeth's eyes grew wide and she clapped her hands. "That would be wonderful, my dearest Lady mother. Thank you."

Mary did not know what to say. There was no way she would accept the proposal – it would suggest to all the world that she condoned the marriage. She needed to stop Elizabeth as well.

"Your offer is most generous," Mary said. "But it would be difficult for me to leave Kenninghall, and I suspect that when my sister considers the matter, she will find it equally difficult to leave Hatfield."

Elizabeth's eyebrows drew together, but she remained silent.

"Henry Grey has agreed to let your cousin Jane join us. It will be a community of learning, with Robert Ascham teaching us all," Katherine said.

Van der Delft narrowed his eyes. "Lady Jane Grey will not attend the Duchess of Somerset? Her mother has agreed to this?"

"Jane is the great-granddaughter of a king, and the grand-daughter of a queen; it is only fitting she should live with the highest lady of the land," Tom said.

Van der Delft inclined his head but said nothing.

"And with the King's uncle," Tom continued. "Who should have far more power than I do. My brother shares nothing with me, but soon this will change. I will change it."

Mary tried to close her ears to the truculence. She understood very well why Somerset was not giving his irresponsible brother much responsibility or glory. What she didn't understand was why Tom expected any. And why Katherine indulged him.

"His wife is worse."

Mary was shocked. She had never heard Katherine be catty. And judging from van der Delft's blank face, neither had he. "Worse?"

"She claims precedence over me. Says she is the wife of the Lord Protector while I am but the wife of his younger brother. Can you imagine?"

"Bah, she will soon learn," the Admiral said.

Elizabeth's eyes grew wide. *Poor thing,* Mary thought, *she probably doesn't fully understand.*

Katherine Parr patted Elizabeth's hand. "Never you mind,

families quarrel. And they'll put it behind them just as quickly."

"This will not get put behind," Tom said. "I have plans to—"

"I will retire now," van der Delft interrupted, "before you share something you will regret later." He bowed and ran off, and Mary wished he had thought to take her with him.

"Good riddance to a damned Spaniard," Tom said, and loathing rose in Mary's heart.

"I actually had more to say to my old friend," Mary said, stressing the word *friend*. "I will go find him now. Elizabeth, come with me."

Tom looked like he was about to speak, but again Katherine Parr placed her hand on his arm. "We will see you later, at the dinner," she said to Mary. "We can visit more then."

Mary curtsied without answering and pulled Elizabeth away with her. When they were just outside the door, Mary turned to her sister. "You must not accept the offer. You must not join that woman's household."

Elizabeth's eyes opened wide. "Why not?"

"She remarried while the King our father's body was still warm. It dishonored him and us, and your presence would give tacit consent to her shameful behavior."

Elizabeth's face fell. "But I long to be with the Queen, our mother. I long to come to court."

Elizabeth clasped her hands as if in prayer, and Mary's heart melted. Of course Elizabeth was trying to cling to the only real mother she had ever known. She needed family.

"You may come and stay with me."

"But the learning…" Elizabeth's voice trailed off.

Mary was taken aback at the girl's lack of gratitude for the invitation.

"And the excitement…" Elizabeth continued.

"Excitement tainted by sin." Religious zeal rose in Mary's chest. "The Queen Dowager exhibited loose morals when she encouraged the Admiral's suit. There is no excuse but lust for that."

Elizabeth's jaw set and her eyes lidded. She looked sly. "There has been no condemnation from the Council, nor from the King, our brother. Is it for us to point out the beam in her eye rather than seeing to the mote in our own?"

Mary could scarcely believe Elizabeth defended the woman. Of course, Anne Boleyn had also been accused of loose morals; perhaps the apple had not fallen far from the tree. Mary's guidance would be all the more important to keep Elizabeth safe.

"We must guard our reputations. Your own will suffer if you go."

"Yet the Queen has shown me such affection, and done me so many kind offices, that I must use much tact in maneuvering with her, for fear of appearing ungrateful."

"So you accept her insult to our father?"

Elizabeth's sigh sounded theatrical. "We must submit in patience to that which cannot be cured."

Mary opened her mouth to answer, but a whisper of silks announced little Jane Grey appearing before them.

Jane was nine, the eldest of Frances Brandon Grey's three children, all girls, and born the same year as Edward. She had been named after his mother, his father's third wife.

The lack of sons is a Tudor failing, Mary thought savagely. Henry VIII had blamed his failings on Catherine of Aragon and his other wives, but that seemed misplaced.

As always, Mary's conflicted feelings about her father swirled around her and tightened her throat. She pushed them away. "Jane, it is wonderful to see you."

Jane curtsied, a prim motion, then clasped her hands in front of her. She had the reddish hair of the Tudors, as well as the slim build that seemed to stay with them until they turned forty or so, though truthfully only Henry VIII had lived long enough to show them an example.

They curtsied back and exchanged their greetings. The topic of Katherine Parr and her household had to be put aside. This was too public a time to broach it. Mary needed to focus on her role. As the King's eldest sister, she was Princess of England, even if only the Spanish Ambassador formally acknowledged it. It was her duty and her right.

May 20,1548

Barnaby entered Edward's Privy Chamber with careful nonchalance, but raised his eyebrows as he bowed to Edward.

That must mean success.

The court was abuzz with some terrible gossip, but silence descended whenever Edward came near. All anyone would tell him was that Elizabeth had been banished from the Queen Dowager's household, sent to live with Anthony Denny and his wife because of some improprieties. No one would tell Edward the whole story. Somerset would only say between tight lips, "My brother is a foolish man," or "She's better off where she is."

"Ah, Barnaby," Edward said with equally careful nonchalance. "I am glad you are here – I need you to teach me that dance step you promised."

"Happily, Sire," Barnaby said.

"You may leave us," Edward said to the others. "I would prefer to be awkward in private."

"Ah, Your Majesty, you have no need to hide from us," Fowler said.

"It is my preference," Edward said and waited. He had learned the trick of letting his orders sit. Then people had no choice but to follow them. Most people, anyway. And most orders.

Excitement rose in Edward's chest as the men bowed out, but he contained it until the door closed. "Well?" he finally asked.

"I didn't catch the whole story, only part of it," Barnaby said. "I hung about the kitchens as much as I dared, but they chased me away."

Servants always knew everything. His father had warned him, Somerset had warned him. But now Edward had turned it around and figured out how to use that knowledge. With Barnaby. "What did you hear?"

"I heard Tom told your sister to stop wearing black gowns. That they made her look too old."

"But she is in mourning for my father."

"Well, the Queen Dowager abandoned her widow's weeds for gayer attire. Perhaps your uncle didn't want her to feel reproached."

"Perhaps," Edward said. That didn't seem terrible enough for the fuss being made.

"She wore one and he ordered her to take it off, but she must have refused because he and the Queen Dowager ended up chasing her around the garden. When they caught her, the Queen Dowager held her and he took out his knife—"

The word hit Edward with a shock. "His *knife*?"

"He slashed her gown to shreds."

"While she was wearing it? How?"

Barnaby pantomimed coming at him with a knife and an evil smile. The vision made Edward shiver. "My poor sister."

"Apparently they were all three laughing, but when he was done there was no gown left."

"What do you mean, no gown left?"

Barnaby ran a hand through his hair. "They say all her flesh was exposed."

Edward sat back in his chair, stunned. That would explain the term *improprieties*, though not why Elizabeth had been banished. "You say this is only part of the story?"

"There is something about him in her bedchamber, but people were much more guarded when they started talking about that."

"You must go back."

"I have a better idea." Barnaby looked around to confirm they were alone in the room, though he knew they were. "We can wait behind the tapestries in the Great Hall. No one will know we're there."

"We?"

"It is one thing for me to skulk around the kitchens. If I am discovered behind the tapestries, I will be sent away."

"Why would you not be sent away if I went with you?"

Barnaby bit his lip. "If it's just servants, they'll be too scared to report us. If it's someone important, you'll just say right away you ordered me. As long as you are firm, they will only whip me for it."

"Are you sure?"

"That's how they treat your uncle Tom, and they don't even whip him. Surely this isn't as serious."

Edward needed only a moment to consider. "Bring me to the Great Hall."

Barnaby nodded. "You'll have to let me walk ahead to make sure it's safe."

"Of course."

"Not of course," Barnaby said. "That's another thing that will get me whipped unless I am doing it on your specific instruction."

Edward sighed. "I hereby order you to do anything you need to do in this adventure. I trust you and will protect you as best I can."

Barnaby nodded. "Come along then."

Barnaby tiptoed to the back of the room and pushed aside the tapestry to expose the hidden servants' door. He stuck his head out and looked around, then motioned for Edward to follow him. "Remember, keep silent."

At the bottom of the stairs, a small door led into a narrow corridor. Edward looked around at the unadorned walls, curious at the unfamiliar sight and amazed at his own daring. Another door led to a small room, and the door at the other side of that room opened into the back of the Great Hall tapestries.

"Keep your feet sideways," Barnaby whispered. "Follow me."

They snaked their way carefully for a few feet, until they

reached a spot where the stitching on the tapestry was open enough to see through.

"And now we wait," Barnaby said. "It won't be long; they'll be setting up for dinner soon."

Sure enough, a stream of servants arrived to lay the tables. Edward watched their comings and goings in silence until he could no longer hold in his question. "Why do they bow to my empty chair?"

Barnaby shrugged. "You're the King."

No wonder Barnaby had been worried about being whipped for walking before him. The men bowed when they passed in front of Edward's chair, and kissed his napkin when they passed behind. Every time.

A scullery maid passed in front of one of the men. He grabbed her and tickled her, but she stomped on his insole and wriggled out of his grasp. "What the Devil d'ye think ye're doing?" she asked, chest heaving.

"No more than the Admiral did to the Lady Elizabeth," replied the man.

Another servant chimed in. "Less even, for she was naked when he did."

That was all the excuse needed for the group to abandon work to gather round.

"Naked? Nay, it was just her gown that was slit. She still had her shift, I heard," said another page approaching the group, a plate still in his hand.

"No, this was different," someone else said, maybe the first servant. Edward could not keep track of who was speaking, but it didn't matter. He only cared about the flow of information.

"He would also come into her bedroom in the mornings to wake her."

"What man goes to a lady's bedchamber to wake her?"

"He was in his bare feet and she was naked in her bed."

"He would tickle her, and she would squirm and laugh."

This was freedom and informality on a scale utterly foreign

to the boy King. The idea that someone would enter a person's bedchamber uninvited was troubling. That they were undressed was worse – even the gentlemen who slept near him at night kept their nakedness entirely within his rooms. This was sin.

"Where was her governess? Her ladies?" the milkmaid asked with an indignation that matched Edward's own. "Were they not in her rooms?"

"What were they to say to the Lord High Admiral?"

"Her governess would appear when the shrieking started, to put a stop to the antics."

"That was a bit late. She should have been there all night."

"Where was the Queen? Did no one complain to her?"

"The Queen joined in!"

"Impossible."

"She said the Lady Elizabeth was but a child, that she saw nothing wrong in her husband's conduct."

"The Lady Elizabeth is fourteen, old enough to have children of her own already."

"Still, if the Queen was there…"

"Only once or twice, to stop the gossip. This went on for months."

"Months? How late did the Lady Elizabeth remain abed?"

"Late enough to encourage the attention."

"This is getting out of hand," said a deep voice that sounded more authoritative than the others. "I have it on good authority that every day she woke earlier and earlier so she would be dressed when the Admiral came to wake her. He followed her all the way to dawn and then gave up."

"Well, then, maybe it was innocent."

"Then why was she banished from the house?"

Edward leaned forward. This would solve the mystery.

"The Queen was walking in the garden one day and came upon the Admiral on his knees before the Lady, kissing her hand like a suitor."

"Lord have mercy on us."

Edward felt as though he had been kicked in the stomach. What was Tom doing? His wife, Edward's stepmother, was big with child. This was terrible. He pitched forward, violently enough to pop one of the bolts holding the tapestry. A scream erupted from the room.

"Fie on you, what is this?" the scullery maid screeched.

Someone started hitting the tapestry, then more joined in. Barnaby grabbed Edward's arm and tried to pull him back toward the door.

"What are you doing back there?" a man yelled.

"No mischief," Barnaby called out. "It was an accident." The blows stopped, and Barnaby started to explain. His pleading, reasonable tone was at odds with the cunning on his face as he clasped Edward's arm again and slowly pulled him toward the door. "We were coming to bring dishes and didn't want to interrupt. We weren't spying."

One of the men had gone around the other side of the tapestry to trap them. Edward instinctively started to turn around but Barnaby kept pulling him along toward the door in the middle. The other servants resumed the slapping, and in between blows the billowing fabric gave Edward a terrifying view of the approaching opponent's wild eyes and missing front tooth. Just when he seemed close enough to grab them, Barnaby slithered out and yanked Edward along.

Edward's heart was in his mouth as they raced down the hallway. They lost their pursuers definitively by going up the stairs toward Edward's rooms rather than down the stairs to the kitchens, but still Edward's panic did not subside. It remained with him even after they were back in his bedchamber, doubled over to breathe.

Barnaby recovered first and laughed. Edward hit him. "How can you be so calm? We were almost caught."

"Exactly. Almost."

The humor hit Edward and he giggled. The laugh spread deeper and deeper in his belly, and he and Barnaby rolled on the floor in glee until they had spent themselves. Edward couldn't remember feeling so free. Then worry returned.

"I can't ever do this again, you know," he said.

"I can," Barnaby said. "Though I need to wait a few months, or at least for the move to the next castle. Until the incident is gone from people's minds."

Edward nodded. "I will protect you if you get caught."

"I know you will. Like you protect the Admiral."

"I don't know that I can do that anymore. I don't know that I want to."

Edward started to push himself up, and the position brought the story to life for him. "On his knees before her. He can't wed her – he must have meant to dishonor her," he said.

"Many men stray when their wives are with child."

The Queen Dowager was six months pregnant. At thirty-six she was old for a first child, but the Lord moved in mysterious ways.

"Not with my sister."

In one move, Tom Seymour had hurt two of the people who meant the most to Edward. His trust, thin to begin with, dissipated.

"She's better off out of there." Barnaby agreed.

"Far better."

June 16, 1548

Edward stood tall and immobile, his careful pose for the painter Scrots allowing Edward to stare out the window at the Thames. He imagined he could see Chelsea round the bend. It was where his stepmother was, where his uncle was spending more time in order to be the perfect husband. Not enough time, in Edward's opinion. Instead of cowing Tom, the scandal involving Elizabeth had made him bolder in his attacks on Somerset. Not that Tom's complaints weren't justified, but they were exhausting because he kept involving Edward and the Council.

Isolating the movement so as not to disturb his carefully composed posture, Edward readjusted his face to remove any contempt that had crept into it. It would corrupt the image of power he was projecting. He stood with his feet planted widely, the way his father had for Holbein in the portrait that had defined his majesty. Edward had chosen an opulent jewel-studded doublet, with its shoulders padded to give him a similar bulk. Everything in black to add age and *gravitas*. Somerset claimed it was his idea, but that just showed how much he underestimated Edward.

Edward knew the power of a portrait to impress and inspire. He knew how important it was for him to project power and competence. He had been born knowing it. He was his father's son, determined to surpass the master.

Henry VIII had seen the inner rot of the papist system and delivered his people from bondage to the Pharaoh of Rome. But Moses was not allowed to enter the Holy Land. That had to be built by a new generation, one that had never known bondage. It was Edward who would be as Josiah, closing down all the pagan worship sites throughout the land. As Cranmer had said at Edward's coronation, that was his promise.

And this was the first step to define himself for his people.

His internal tirade ended, he mentally checked his posture again. It was still perfect. He'd had a lot of practice, after all. His entire life was a series of people watching him, judging him, alert to any weakness or flaw.

At first, Cheke had suggested they use the endless hours for lessons, but Edward had refused. He liked to read, to be able to see the words on the paper: it helped him understand and learn. Besides, he enjoyed the opportunity to be alone with his thoughts, to ponder without the constant stream of people coming at him. No one would give Edward more privacy; they all wanted something from him.

Somerset had claimed this was why he had refused Edward a purse for so long. That if Edward had nothing to give, the courtiers would be like dogs who knew no treat would be forthcoming. Instead, Edward had now set expectations. And hopes.

Another moment to wipe resentment off his face. The time to have explained this theory would have been the first time the issue arose. That's what a wise counselor did. Edward didn't know if he would have taken the advice – after all, the outcome was inevitable since he would not lack a purse forever – but at least he could have considered it and been prepared.

Again Edward came back to his main conclusion: this situation had grown untenable. Edward needed to start asserting control. Tom was right about that, wrong as he was about so many other things.

The page rapped. Out of the corner of his eye, Edward could see Somerset enter, followed by Cranmer, Paget, and Tom Seymour.

"Gentlemen," Edward said after they had risen from their bows, "you can be sure I am listening, even if I will not look at you for Mr. Scrots' sake."

"We…we have upsetting news for you from Scotland," Somerset said. He shifted from one foot to the other.

The words chilled Edward. He certainly did not want to be posing while he received bad news. "Thank you, Scrots," he said, waving the artist away. Edward maintained his stance though, just turned his head.

Somerset waited until Scrots had left to continue. Edward forced himself to remain immobile, as if his insides were not roiling.

"The French have come to reinforce the Scottish forces," Somerset finally said. "Warwick was not able to defend our positions. All our gains have been lost."

It was more than just gains lost. The Scots had gone running to the French, resurrecting the Auld Alliance that drove dread into English souls. Still, there was one glimmer of hope.

"You have always said the ultimate success of our work was

possession of the Scottish queen," Edward said. "Do we have her?"

"That is the worst part," Somerset said. "They have smuggled her out of the country to France. She is to wed the Dauphin."

That possibility had never occurred to Edward. "But he is only six."

"She will be brought up at the French court, and they will wed when they are both of an age."

"They refused such a proposal from my father," Edward said. "They thought it vital she be brought up in Scotland, to truly know her country."

"They are lying traitors, Sire," Somerset said. "They never meant to let her wed you."

Again, Edward was struck by Somerset acting like he had known this all along, annoyed he had not shared any of his opinions before the outcome had been decided. Then Edward could have considered things – at least he would not have been surprised by them. But that didn't matter now. "Can we get her back somehow?"

"No, Sire."

Edward would not unite the countries. Scotland would be an offshoot province of France instead of a beautiful part of a wholly English island. Melancholy swirled around him. He had let the realm down.

No, Somerset had let the realm down.

Edward fingered the jeweled dagger at his waist. "So what now?"

"We make other arrangements," Somerset said.

"We pray," Cranmer said.

"We set the blame where it belongs," Tom said. "Somerset was wrong to hound the Scots as he did, to destroy them so utterly that they had no choice."

Somerset bowed his head and turned to Edward in a show of submission. "That was your father's strategy. It never occurred to me that it might be wrong to follow it. It never occurred to any of us that it might be wrong to follow it."

Cranmer and Paget looked down at the floor. Tom raised a single eyebrow. "I remember efforts to dissuade you. You make many decisions against the Council's advice."

Somerset bristled. "I make the hard choices, like with the coinage. These things are painful, but they must be done."

The coinage had been debased to stabilize it, Somerset had explained to Edward, though the other lords disagreed.

"Painful? You mean disastrous." Tom nearly spat as the words fired from his lips. "Like your policy on the enclosures – everything you do takes fortunes from the hands of your friends."

"Do you not read the experts?" Somerset looked around, seeking some hint of support. "John Hales explains how all the realm's problems stem from greedy landlords enclosing their land. We can solve poverty and hunger by undoing this mistake."

Tom threw up his hands. "We are the 'greedy landlords' of whom you and Hales speak," he yelled. "The King-that-was would never have allowed such terrible wrongs to his most trusted servants."

"Every day I spend hours listening to pleas from the people," Somerset said. "I hear the harm they suffer when land is used to raise sheep bred for wool instead of growing crops or grazing cattle who can at least provide milk and cheese."

"You listen to commoners and not to your peers," Tom said.

Paget nodded vigorously but maintained his silence. Cranmer kept his eyes downcast, revealing nothing.

Edward sighed. Somerset's policies had made him beloved by the people but hated by the lords of the Council. Even Edward did not know what to think, since the Crown's revenues had suffered most of all from the changes. Worse, the peasants seemed no happier – indeed, the concessions had made them angrier than ever. Edward was not confident Somerset was right.

"The old King's mind was open to new thoughts," Somerset

said. "He loved his subjects dearly and would have wanted to ease their burdens."

Tom shook his head violently. "He gave properties to his friends, or sold them to us, because our wealth strengthens the kingdom. He wanted us to prosper, and instead you try to make paupers of us while your wealth is untouched." Eyes wild, Tom pointed an accusing finger at Somerset. "Are you doing this just to boost your own power? Don't you have enough?"

Somerset's face twisted like he smelled rotten meat. "This is not about me, this is about the realm."

"Unfence your own lands first, then, and see if it works. Or halt your plans for your lavish Somerset Place – stop bleeding the country for it."

"I take only the revenues of my offices."

"Then you have too many offices, and you are failing in all of them. You lost us Scotland forever."

Tom's savage attack hit its mark, and Somerset hung his head. Paget stopped nodding and looked at both brothers appraisingly.

It made Edward feel the way he did when he was a child and one of his toys frayed. It made him just a little sadder, a little less safe than the moment before.

September 5, 1548

Shielding her eyes from the midafternoon sun streaming in through the windowpanes, Mary peered at the lone rider and assessed the facts again. He was coming to the castle's main entrance, so he was coming to visit her. His livery was not red, so it was not a message from the King, Somerset, or the Council. That was a relief – lately Cranmer had been pushing her brother further away from the true Church. They had already tried to take away her beads, not to mention the miracle of communion, and make her worship God in a bare, whitewashed room instead of surrounded by glorious art that sprang from divine offerings.

Mary wanted no new messages stripping away another beloved ritual.

She could not yet make out any heraldry that would signal the man's identity, but she suspected it was the Spanish Ambassador. Her friends had dwindled since her fall from favor, which made this likeliest possibility also the most welcome.

Sure enough, a cheery "*Hola*" greeted her when the rider passed the gatehouse. She immediately recognized van der Delft's voice, even if her eyes still blurred the lines of his face. It made her happy about her decision to come greet him in the courtyard.

The tall man demonstrated an easy grace when he dismounted and started toward her. When his face came into view, his brow was furrowed and his lips thin and pressed. Mary was about to ask what was wrong, but he put a finger to his mouth and lifted his chin toward the house.

Mary grabbed his arm and led him in, offering inconsequential greetings that, were they overheard and repeated, would have no ill effects. Her mind roiled, and her entire body itched to get into the library.

In this country castle, the library was an interior room. All four walls were covered in dark wood paneling or heavy leather books, giving it a masculine strength counterbalanced by the more feminine white plaster of the coffered ceiling that took to its bosom the sound of secrets told.

The second the door closed behind them, the words burst from her lips. "What is it?"

"Terrible news," he said. "Scandalous."

Scandalous? That meant it involved Elizabeth. Was she pregnant by the Admiral? Is that what got her banished from the Queen Dowager's house? Oh, why had the poor girl not heeded Mary's advice and avoided temptation?

Mary staggered to a chair and collapsed into it. Van der Delft knelt and took one of her hands, like a suitor. It seemed odd, and she gave him a puzzled look.

"The Queen Dowager sleeps with the Lord. She took a fever after giving birth to a baby girl and died a few days afterwards."

The world dimmed. All Mary's anger over Katherine Parr's hasty remarriage dissipated and only the love remained. The Queen had been so kind to her. She had created the family that only Mary's own mother and Jane Seymour had offered.

Again loneliness crowded in on Mary. Another mother gone. Another dear friend gone.

Too many women lost to childbirth; the older ones had the most to fear. Mary brought a hand to her stomach. She was thirty-two and her own time was running out.

A thought broke through the darkness. "You said scandal?"

Van der Delft rose and took two steps back. In this posture he was more advisor than close friend. "During the days before her death, she accused her husband of shrewd taunts. She publicly regretted not letting her doctor examine her right after the birth."

"What are you saying?"

The Ambassador raised a single eyebrow and his face became as catty as any gossip's. "She clearly feared her husband had poisoned her. I fear the same."

The thought hit Mary hard, and her own insides roiled in sympathy. "Poison?" That was a nasty game. "Why would he do such a thing?"

"Ambition." Van der Delft shrugged. "To free himself to marry the Lady Elizabeth. Given her recent conduct, he is assured of her affection."

Mary wondered how much of that was true. There were no facts, only conjectures. Van der Delft disliked Elizabeth for being the living symbol of Mary's ouster from heirdom. That hatred colored his opinions and analyses.

"I can scarcely believe it, even of the Admiral," Mary said.

"Women's hearts are more charitable than men's," van der Delft said. "You and the Queen Dowager both hesitate to accuse him of such foul actions."

"But you said she did."

"Only at the height of her fever. When it broke, she recanted everything. She even made out her last will and testament, leaving everything to him and wishing it was more."

Mary nodded. "A woman could never believe such evil of her husband."

"The important thing is action, not belief," van der Delft said. "Your mother never reproached your father, but she knew what he was."

Mary's mother had displayed only respect and love for Henry VIII, even in her last words to him: *And lastly, I make this vow, that mine eyes desire you above all things.*

Mary sat back in her chair and let her mind rove over her memories, the many smiles from her time in Katherine Parr's household. Van der Delft clasped his hands behind his back and cast down his eyes to signal his patience. Happy images soon ceded to twisted imaginings.

"Her women. What do her women believe? Lady Tyrwhitt was never a friend to the Admiral; what does she say?"

"Lady Tyrwhitt agrees the Admiral was quite loving. That he even lay with the Queen on her bed to hold and comfort her and ease her path to eternity. But that could have been his guilty conscience prompting him."

Mary thought hard. In her soul she did not believe Thomas Seymour had poisoned Katherine Parr. She had seen too many women succumb to childbed fever, too many women gripped by fevers; she knew how the mind imagined specters at such a time. It was almost certain this was the explanation here.

"I can't believe there is foul play," Mary said firmly, then sighed. "Well, the investigation will reveal all."

"There is not to be an investigation."

Mary gasped. "No investigation?" This was her father's widow; surely her premature death warranted some sort of inquiry.

"The autopsy revealed nothing sinister. There is nothing more to be done."

That decision seemed wrong, though an autopsy was probably investigation enough. "Was this a case of the Lord Protector protecting his brother and not the realm?"

The Ambassador laughed. "Somerset would be a fool to do that. His brother harries him every day, challenging him for power. You would think Somerset would thank God to find evidence against such a scourge."

"My Lord of Somerset is a good man."

Mary turned away. In all the time she had known him, Somerset had been patient for the success he knew would follow. He had gradually assumed power and responsibility, slowly at first and then faster when his power grew and his momentum became unstoppable. His younger brother had only ever been impatient and rash, and therefore he was untrusted and untested.

Van der Delft leaned forward. "The Admiral is up to something, you mark my words."

"What do you mean?"

"I hear he is protecting pirates, taking bribes to look the other way when they attack our merchants. And he might even be coining his own crowns, though no one will tell me anything beyond this. What mischief is he planning for this pile of riches? I say it is an army to challenge his brother."

Mary thought a moment. "He has made it clear he resents Somerset taking all the authority for himself, that he wants to be responsible for the King's person."

"He wants to be responsible for far more. He wants to lead the Council, the government."

"He is a fool," Mary said.

"Well, with the Queen Dowager dead, much of his power is gone."

"There you go." Mary wagged a finger at van der Delft. "That more than anything else reassures me that he didn't poison his wife."

"You assume he is smart enough to see that. I don't. It won't be long before we hear he has carted the girl off."

Mary nodded. With Katherine dead, there was nothing to temper his designs on Elizabeth. Thomas Seymour would never give up: he was not only as stupid as a dog but also as stubborn.

"I need to help her."

Van der Delft sniffed. "You don't know that she wants help. You need to help yourself. The Council is running headlong toward the Lutheran heresies, trying to make it illegal to worship properly. They questioned the Bishop of Winchester in Fleet Prison after he spoke out against their atrocities."

The Bishop of Winchester, Stephen Gardiner. A man who had helped Mary's father divorce Catherine of Aragon but who in recent years had returned to a truer fold. "I applaud his courage in speaking his conscience. I only wish more men would join him, so the Council could come to true enlightenment and turn from their darkness."

"I care only for your own rights, my Lady Princess." Van der Delft bowed his head after speaking the title the law refused her. "The Council has threatened to forbid you the Mass."

Mary shook her head. "Somerset would never do that to me."

"It is the King who insists."

"My brother is a boy. His views may change with age. Somerset knows this."

"The King maintains his heart is constant. But rather than argue with him, I simply made it clear that England's friendship with Spain will be utterly destroyed if you are not allowed to take communion."

"Well, that must have settled the matter," Mary said. England was at war with France and Scotland right now; the realm could not risk another enemy. "Somerset will surely explain to him how deeply England needs Spain's friendship."

"I agree this is the logical outcome. But just as I have a bad feeling about Thomas Seymour, I see something in the King's eyes that worries me. He is resolute. You may be safe right now, but I worry for the future."

"Our Lord pointed to the birds of the air, who neither sow

nor reap nor gather into barns yet are fed by our heavenly Father. I trust in the Lord," Mary said. "And in my cousin Charles," she added, her eyes twinkling. "Who has always been my staunch friend."

Van der Delft laughed. "And who will continue to be. You are right to feel safe with him."

"And with you," Mary said. "May I offer you refreshment after your long journey? Or perhaps a Mass?"

"A Mass would be the best way to exorcise such a conversation," van der Delft said. "I thank you for the offer."

Mary smiled and summoned her Chaplain. She would always remain firm. Please God, her brother would come to see the truth.

December 13, 1548

A log shifted, spraying sparks onto the marble hearth. Edward considered sending for more wood, but the fireplace still warmed the room nicely. No need to disrupt the servants' routines. Edward had learned they often read into his requests more than he intended. If he called for them now, they would take it as reproach and henceforth would add logs way too often.

The afternoon sun cast a soft glow in the room. *Carpe diem,* it cried, *while the season's sparse light lingers.* Edward reminded himself he had already spent time outdoors today, marvelous hawking that had lifted his soul. To shirk his work in pursuit of more pastime would be to commit the sin of greed.

He looked down again at the blank page in front of him and blew a stray bit of lint off the corner.

Barnaby Fitzpatrick sat across from him, laboriously copying over Latin declensions. He looked up and laughed. "You look satisfied but confused."

"I am indeed both," Edward said. "I have decided to start my treatise refuting the papal supremacy."

"The one Somerset suggested you take on, since that's all you talk about?"

Edward lifted his chin. "The very same."

It was likely Somerset only wanted to keep him occupied, but this was all the opening Edward needed to begin to inhabit his role. This treatise would establish him as an authority when he explained things to his people, helped them see their personal path to God. It would dissolve another obstacle in the path to Edward's true rule.

Barnaby laughed. "Well, it will be good for you to corral your thoughts onto paper. What does Cheke say?"

Edward grinned. "Cheke convinced me to write it in French to practice the language. He says it is less prideful to show my intellect if I am working to sharpen it."

The sound of the door opening drew their attention. Somerset walked in, offering his standard "Greetings, Sire." It was what he did in lieu of being announced.

It occurred to Edward that Somerset always seemed to know what room to come to. He never acted surprised, never looked confused or hesitant. Was that just an affectation ? Or did he have advance knowledge? And if he did, how did he get it?

"Your Majesty wanted to see the Gift Roll," Somerset said, placing before Edward a sheet of paper with a long list of names and symbols.

The Gift Roll. The annual holiday ritual. Each year, loyal subjects would offer a gift to their sovereign to show their loyalty – and receive a gift in return that reflected their political and personal importance. Last year Edward had been caught unawares when the entire court had lined up for the exchange. He had felt ashamed to be as surprised as the recipients at the gifts he handed to them.

"Thank you," Edward said, glad Somerset had honored his request to be more involved in the process. "But what does all this mean? What are the letters and numbers?"

"You are giving cups, plates or bowls – *C*, *P*, or *B*. Gold or silver – *G* or *S*. The numbers show the weight, which hints at the size. The notations are where the workmanship is particularly fine."

Edward looked at the list, overwhelmed. He wanted to check it all. It was his duty to review it, his privilege. But this was intimidating. "When do you need this?"

"Now. Just sign it."

Edward was aghast. "Without reading it?"

Somerset laughed. "It has been very carefully assembled. You do not need to read it."

Edward's teeth clenched. This was all a sham. Form instead of substance: his opinions were still unimportant. "I want to."

Before Somerset could respond, a page opened the door and rapped his stave. "Archbishop Cranmer. He is expected."

"Have him enter," Edward said.

As Cranmer entered the room, Tom's voice called from the hall. "And the Lord High Admiral, who is not."

Somerset waved Cranmer in as he called back to his brother. "You have come during His Majesty's lesson time. The King is occupied."

Tom stuck his face through the doorway. "And yet you are here," he said and strode in. He stood next to Cranmer and bowed to Edward. "His Majesty needs a diversion from your dour presence."

"Diversions are a reward," Somerset said. "Like dessert after a dinner. You always make them the main course."

"I do not parade my toils before others, like a miser advertising a gift of a small coin," Tom said. "But that is a different matter. What is so important to make you and Cranmer deliver the King's lessons?"

As always, the animosity between his two uncles wore on Edward. They constantly bickered, constantly cut each other down. Barnaby had tried to reassure Edward that all families fought, but Edward found it harder and harder to believe. As much as he understood his royal life was different, he knew it wasn't this different.

"The Archbishop has come to discuss Scripture with me for a treatise I am writing on the papal supremacy," Edward said.

"Impressive," Tom said. "But what of my brother?"

"I have brought the Gift Roll for His Majesty's approval."

"Ah, the Gift Roll," Tom said. "What size cup am I put down for this year? Truly, brother, you need to work harder at that. People are tired of your unimaginative formula." He turned to Edward. "Your Majesty should check his work carefully, though it will bore you to tears."

"The late King, his father, approved this system to prevent jealousy and bickering. It assures appropriate treatment."

"Appropriate in your eyes and for your purposes." Tom turned to Edward and winked elaborately. "Just don't let him choose your gifts to the ladies. Those can help you make conquests, like your friend Barnaby here."

Edward blushed and saw his friend do the same. They were still too young for that, though Barnaby had persuaded a serving girl to let him touch her breast. Much as Edward disapproved in principle, he needed to hear the stories. It was the only way he would find out about such things. When he'd asked Somerset, back when Edward was preparing to wed the Queen of Scots, the Duke had laughed and told him he wouldn't need to know for years, since even if the marriage was celebrated, it wouldn't be consummated before he turned sixteen.

"Enough." Somerset's voice was a cross between a scream and a growl, and Edward was relieved his annoyance with Tom had shielded Barnaby's misdeeds.

Tom bowed sarcastically to his brother and waited.

Edward broke the silence. "I will look over the list this evening and sign it for you tomorrow," he told Somerset. A compromise. He would look at some of the entries. And he resolved to change at least one.

Somerset opened his mouth as if he were about to argue but

closed it. "Thank you, Your Majesty," he said. "My brother and I will leave you now."

"I will come back later," Tom said with another elaborate wink. "I know what will do you good, and it's not something I can give you now. I will say, though, it's more than the last time."

Edward suspected he meant another purse, and the idea made him feel dirty. The coins had ceased after that last uncomfortable episode, as had the attempted blackmail, but now it sounded like another plot was brewing. Barnaby had overheard a disturbing conversation about Tom once again hoping to take over the Council. To hear tell, Tom was amassing a fortune, taking bribes from pirates to let them ply their trade so he could in turn bribe the Lords of the Council. And now Edward.

That was too crazy to be true. Even if the impossible piece about his uncle cavorting with criminals was true, the Council would never allow Tom Seymour near a position of real power.

As they bowed out, Edward realized he had been holding his breath. He took a deep one to make up, but it was cut short when a new danger emerged.

"Master Barnaby," Cranmer said, "I hope you are not imperiling your soul with false promises. And I am disappointed in your evil tongue that spreads stories better left untold."

Barnaby's eyes widened. "Your Grace?"

"The Lord High Admiral mentioned a girl. You should not be parading your sin by telling others of your conquests."

"I told no one, Your Grace," Barnaby said.

"No one?"

"None but His Majesty," Barnaby said. "I would never lie to the King."

Cranmer turned to Edward. "Your Majesty, I am quite sad to learn the gossip emerged from your tongue."

Panic gripped Edward's throat. "I said nothing at all."

"So we are back to Barnaby," Cranmer said.

"No, Your Grace, I swear, I said nothing." Barnaby said. "It's the Admiral. He knows everything, always. They say he has keys to all the rooms in the palace and uses them when no one is there. He—" Barnaby snapped his mouth shut and looked down. Cranmer's eyes narrowed and he waited in silence. When Barnaby did not continue, Cranmer shrugged. "The Admiral has been complaining to the Council that security is lax. Perhaps this came from his investigations." The Archbishop pointed an accusing finger at Barnaby. "But you see how sin can be seen even when it is carefully hidden. Go and pray for forgiveness."

Barnaby bowed and made his way over to the *prie-dieu*. Cranmer waited until Barnaby had knelt and crossed himself, and then the Archbishop turned to Edward. "I was going to suggest we move on to our discussion now, Sire, but perhaps after such excitement our constitutions would be better served by walking while we speak?"

"I would enjoy that," Edward said.

"Excellent," Cranmer said. "Allow me just a moment to send for our cloaks."

The second he was out the door, Barnaby's head rose and turned to Edward. "Sorry," he whispered.

"It wasn't your fault." Edward said. "What did you hold back just before?"

"I thought maybe he got the keys as part of his plotting, that he was planning to use them to trap Somerset in his rooms so the Lords could vote."

That had been another disturbing piece from the conversation Barnaby had overheard. The conclusion that the Admiral intended to dedicate his ill-gotten fortune to turning the Council against Somerset over Scotland, the enclosures – anything to spark a vote to allow Tom to replace his brother as Protector.

"That's just crazy talk," Edward said. No one trusted Tom Seymour, he could never wrest power. He would have to be an idiot to actively pursue such a plan.

"Especially since I was being scolded for gossiping."

Edward laughed. "Quite right."

Barnaby turned back to the wall and his prayers, and Edward turned back toward the door to wait in silence for Cranmer's return.

Behind his serene smile, Edward prayed. *Please, God, let it all be the talk of a madman.* Edward did not want England to be governed by such a rash fool. He did not want himself to be governed by such a rash fool, either.

Edward wondered whether there was anything he should do to warn Somerset. He could not do so without revealing his knowledge – which would ruin his chances of getting it in the future. And surely Somerset did not need Edward's help. The Council would do the right thing.

Please, God.

January 16, 1549

Quiet clinking on the other side of the bedchamber's back door slowly penetrated Edward's consciousness. The hair on his neck twitched, and he opened his eyes into the near dark. Only the one candle remained at the far end of the room, and it trembled low in its sconce, casting ghostly shadows around it. Wind whined at the windows. Danger hovered over the room. Had he returned from a nightmare? One he couldn't remember?

Edward stirred and felt Argos laying over his leg. The movement woke the dog, who crawled up to lick Edward's cheek. The giggle dissipated Edward's lingering tension.

"Stop, stop."

With some pushing, Argos receded back down to Edward's stomach. Edward nestled around the dog's curled-up body and relaxed back into the fluff of his pillows. He pulled the soft blanket closer around his chin against the lingering chill.

He worried the nightmare would return even though he could not remember it. He tried to remember happy times from the day before, particular translations he had come up with, something to refocus his mind.

The hair on his neck stood again when he heard the slow, metallic scrape of the lock cylinder turning. Why would anyone be coming into his room in the middle of the night? More important, why would anyone be *sneaking* into his room in the middle of the night?

Argos tensed. The scraping stopped.

The wind outside picked up again, wailing now. Edward held his breath. The heavy air in the room suffocated all sounds except his heart beating in his ears.

The loud silence dragged on, long enough for Edward to take twenty-three breaths. Nothing further. It must have been his imagination.

Edward settled back into his bed, but every muscle tensed at the quiet creak of the hinge. His door was opening. Should he call out? This could not be danger. He was the King. He had guards. This had to be one of his men.

Suddenly Argos started yapping loudly and launched himself off the bed. He scrambled toward the back door and was through it before the intruder could close it. A muffled curse and scuffling added to the commotion, then the sound of a sword being drawn. The barking stopped mid-snarl and a deathly quiet descended.

Edward felt nauseous from fear, desperately wondering what he should do, where he could run, when he was reassured by the sound of heavily clanking boots.

"Halt!" came the cry. "Who goes there?"

"It is nothing." The voice was Tom Seymour's. How was that possible?

"Your Majesty, are you harmed?" a guard called. It must be safe to come out.

Edward drew himself up to his full height and slowly left the bed to walk toward the antechamber. Just beyond the doorway stood his uncle, his sword dripping blood. Edward's beloved puppy lay splayed on the floor, sliced almost in half. Edward's stomach turned over and a chill gripped his bones.

"I wanted to speak with His Majesty; I had urgent business to discuss with him," the Admiral said to the guard before turning to Edward. "I am sorry about the dog. When it attacked, my mind left me. I thought there might be some danger to you."

Blood flooded Edward's face and pounded in his ears at the sight of the half-smile on his uncle's face. The man was not apologizing, he was trying to justify the unforgivable. The cold-blooded murder of Edward's best friend in this world. "Argos," he said. "His name is Argos."

Somerset came racing in. He stopped, appalled, at the sight of the dead dog. "What the hell is going on?"

"I thought to speak to His Majesty and—"

"You did this?"

"It was an accident. I was testing His Majesty's security and—"

Somerset gave his brother a violent shove that silenced him. "You idiot!" Somerset yelled, his face red. "You dare to challenge me?"

"It was an accident."

"Get out!"

The commotion brought two dozen men running. Edward's attendants, Warwick, some of the other lords with apartments nearby – all undressed, all open-mouthed. The size of the crowd reassured Edward; their silence heightened the horror of the scene.

The Admiral turned toward Edward, eyebrows melting down the sides of his wide eyes. His hands raised as if in prayer. "Your Majesty!"

Edward recoiled and turned himself around, away from the sight of his uncle, away from the sight of his dead dog. It was the only way to stay strong and not cry.

He heard scuffling, he heard Somerset shout again, and he heard the Admiral *harumph* and stomp off. The fading of the footfalls was reassuring. Edward felt safer with the brute gone. In truth, he never wanted to see Tom Seymour's face again.

The Admiral's departure pushed the crowd into his bedchamber. "Are you hurt?" Warwick asked with a hand on Edward's shoulder. Edward shook his head.

Somerset stormed into the room to berate the guards who were cowering by the door and close to tears themselves. "Where were you that this could happen?" he asked, still raging.

"We...we were right outside the apartments. He must have entered through the Queen's rooms. Her private corridor was never sealed after the old King's death."

"All his doors should have been guarded, you fools. How could you fail at this?"

The men dropped to their knees and lowered their heads.

"What the Devil happened?" Warwick yelled.

Somerset ignored him and turned to the attendants. "Where were you all?" he continued. "Why were you not with His Majesty?"

Michael Stanhope froze in his tracks. "Those were your orders, my Lord. You wanted him to sleep alone."

Somerset whirled on him. "Never again. He must never be alone again."

Edward opened his mouth to disagree. He didn't like having people near him all the time. His father had planted the idea in his head many years ago that privacy was a gift, and the seed had sprouted full force. "I like my privacy."

Somerset waved a finger. "Privacy is for ordinary men. You are the King. I will go fetch more of your men."

With him gone, the energy in the room deflated. "What happened?" Warwick asked again. "Where is the intruder?"

"It was the Lord High Admiral," Edward said through clenched teeth. "Come to test my security."

Warwick's eyes widened and his brows raised high on his forehead. The same expression spread to them all.

Warwick shot him a look. "Why was he allowed to leave?"

"The Duke sent him away."

Warwick's face twisted. "We will revisit this with the Council tomorrow. He should be arrested."

The words chilled Edward. Warwick was right. How could any man think to enter the King's bedchamber secretly, in the middle of the night? And if Tom Seymour was testing his security, he should have been happy to have Argos sound the alarm like that. Instead he silenced Edward's only protection.

Forever.

Silence reigned as one of the guards picked up the mangled carcass and carried it away. "Wait," Edward called, thinking to caress Argos one last time and thank him for his loyal service. But a glance at the half-severed head hanging limply over the side of the guard's arm changed his mind. "Take good care of him," was all he said as he made the sign of the cross.

"Grab your pallets, you will all sleep in here tonight," Warwick said to Edward's attendants.

Edward opened his mouth to object again but realized he didn't want to. Not with Argos gone. Edward liked his privacy, but he was not ready to be alone again tonight.

"Shall we stay as well?" asked Sir Anthony Denny. "To be sure?"

"I think it would be best to return to normalcy," Warwick said. "Or at least, the normalcy that will prevail from now on."

The lords nodded and bowed and slowly filed out.

Edward stood in silence as his men took up places around his bedchamber. His body felt hollow around him. Finally, Warwick put a hand on his shoulder a second time. "We will fix this, Your Majesty. Sleep for now."

Edward nodded. He climbed back into his bed and closed the curtains around him as if the flimsy cloth would protect him.

January 17, 1549

Hushed noises jolted Edward from sleep. It was still dark behind his bed-curtains, but there were slits of light at the seams.

A fart, then a whispered scolding. "Fie, this is the King's room."

"It escaped before I was awake. It won't happen again."

Edward relaxed. Of course there were noises. There were twelve men packed in there. There would always be twelve men packed in with him. From now on, thin fabric would provide only a veneer of privacy.

Edward heard the door open.

"Yes?" Fowler asked, his voice a whisper.

"John Cheke is in the antechamber, as he is every morning. But with the new change..."

Edward could hear the slight crack in the page's voice when he continued.

"I need to be instructed as to the protocol for him."

Tears rose to Edward's eyes. He crawled to the front of the bed and parted the curtain. "I should like to see Master Cheke."

The men sprang from their pallets and dragged them to the room's perimeter to make a path for the tutor. Cheke walked in, oblivious to the commotion, his eyes fixed on Edward. "My heart aches for you, Sire," he said, kneading the band of the hat he held in his hand. "And I render thanks to God for the dog who gave his life to save yours."

Edward held out his arms. He hadn't cared until now that no one had hugged him since his stepmother had died. No one but Argos, and now Argos was dead too.

He clasped Cheke hard. Unbidden sobs racked Edward's body, and the twelve men in the room stared in utter silence. Their stricken looks brought Edward back to himself. He should not show such weakness in front of others. It made him less a king, less a man.

He sniffed and wiped his nose. "He was worthy of his name."

Cheke smiled wryly. "As fine as when Odysseus left for Troy." Edward's attendants exchanged puzzled glances, and Cheke explained. "We will study the passage later. When

Odysseus left for Troy, 'there was not a wild beast in the forest that could get away from Argos when he was on its tracks.'"

Edward ignored the nods and grim smiles and locked eyes with his tutor. "So you agree my uncle intended me ill."

Cheke seemed to shrink into himself. He even sighed before answering. "One way or another, yes, though there is debate over the degree."

At Edward's puzzled look, he continued. "Somerset says his plan was to gain possession of your person and thereby control the realm."

Edward took a deep breath. "Where is the debate?"

Cheke looked down and picked lint off his coat. "Warwick says his plan was to kill you and take your throne by marrying Elizabeth and ruling through her."

Edward shivered. This was what his father had meant, all those years ago. The day the Abraham tapestries arrived, the ones his father had commissioned to celebrate Edward's birth.

Men and women who harbor greed and vice, who would sell their souls for the riches that come with a crown. They all have it, everyone around you, and you must learn to recognize it. The second they act on their evil thoughts, you must cut them out of your life. Out of life itself.

There had been many people who betrayed his father, people close to him. Even two wives. Now it was Edward's turn.

A question pierced his fatalistic calm and he asked it. "Rule through Elizabeth?"

Cheke looked down. "They say he had a priest waiting. It is not clear whether you were to be married to Lady Jane Grey, or he to Elizabeth, or both."

The words made no sense. "What?"

"He bought her wardship after the death of the Queen Dowager. It is said Grey sold it because your uncle promised to make her Queen."

Edward's mind wandered over old conversations with his uncle about his cousin Jane. Tom Seymour knew Edward admired the girl, had often said they would make a fine couple. *I would see you married and jousting and enjoying life. I would make you a true king.*

Before Edward could say anything, the page entered the room to announce the Council. Edward felt a tinge of regret that he wasn't dressed to receive them, but decided that disarray lent greater authority. The men were here at his convenience, after all.

Somerset entered first, Warwick on his heels. They both startled at the men lined against the walls still holding their pallets. Edward, too, was still getting used to the sight.

The two men quickly recovered and returned their focus to Edward, keeping their eyes on him while the other Council members took their places.

"Good morning, Sire," Somerset finally said.

"No thanks to you," Warwick grumbled.

Somerset stopped in his tracks and turned toward the Earl. "How dare you say that."

Warwick was not cowed. "How dare you complain. Tell the King why we have come to see him."

Somerset blushed and turned to Edward. "We need to talk further about my brother and his actions of last night." He turned toward the men and waved an angry arm. "You may leave us. Get yourselves dressed so you can prepare His Majesty for the day."

Resentment flared in Edward from Somerset's peremptory show of authority. "Master Cheke, you stay," Edward said.

Somerset opened his mouth as if to argue but stopped himself and kept silent while Edward's attendants filed out.

It took them an eternity to leave. Edward could not contain himself. "Well, how does my uncle explain himself?"

Somerset glanced over and waited until the door had closed behind the last man before responding. "I…er…I summoned him to come before us to answer our questions, but he has not come."

Warwick stepped forward. His eyes were wild and bore into

Edward. "Thomas Seymour ignored the summons of Your Majesty's Council."

"He did not understand," Somerset said. "He thinks to thwart me, not the Council."

Warwick drew himself up and looked down his nose at Somerset. "I don't care whom he thinks to thwart. No man is allowed to refuse the Council's summons."

"I have sent guards to arrest him."

"Why were they not sent with the summons? Why was he not detained last night?" Warwick put his fists on his hips, and the gesture reminded Edward of his father in one of his rages. "He controls almost ten thousand men – and you gave him a chance to escape. What if he rouses his army to threaten the King?"

Somerset sniffed. "He is not threatening the King, he is threatening me. He is no less a traitor for that, but the King is not in danger."

"His Majesty's dog knew otherwise."

Visions of Argos dead on the floor filled Edward's thoughts. He didn't think his mind would ever release that image, or his body the terror that had gripped his bowels.

"We are not sure of the extent of his plan," Somerset said. "He claims, convincingly, that his purpose was merely to gain control of the King, not to kill him."

"He tried to take control of the King's person for his own ends. He put the King in danger. What more treason do you need?" Warwick threw his hands in the air. "Why in God's name is he not in the Tower right now?"

"I did not want to overreact to a quarrel with me."

Somerset's words infuriated Edward, as much as the carelessness they evidenced. "Quarrel with you?" he yelled. "It was my life in danger when his bloodlust exploded in my bedchamber."

Even then, Somerset persisted. "Bloodlust is perhaps a strong word, Your—"

"Did you see my dog dead on the floor? The Admiral ran through him with his sword for the crime of trying to protect me."

Somerset dropped his eyes. Edward raised his.

"I was alone, without guards. How can you defend him?" Hot tears stung his cheeks and he brushed them away, embarrassed.

Warwick stepped up and put a hand on Edward's shoulder. "The Admiral should be taken to the Tower immediately. I take it all who love you here agree." He looked around and a chorus of *ayes* filled the room. Even Somerset nodded, lips tight, and Edward felt warm gratitude for Warwick – the one person who was truly defending him.

"We shall investigate all his dealings to unearth the details of his plot," Warwick continued. "The pirates who bribed him, the men who gave him the keys to your chamber, the priest he had waiting for him. And we shall investigate his dealings with the Lady Elizabeth. Whether he had any reason to believe his suit would be met with her approval."

Elizabeth. Had she betrayed him too? Tom Seymour had tried to wed her before he turned his eyes to Katherine Parr. And then scandal had driven Elizabeth from his home. Were they lovers? Was she a part of this? His heart was heavy at the thought that his sister could have supported Tom Seymour over him. He prayed it was not true.

"Thank you," he said to Warwick. "Thank you."

Somerset opened his mouth as if to speak but thankfully thought better of it. Edward did not want to hear any more pathetic justifications. What did it matter that this quarrel was born between them when it had grown to endanger Edward? How presumptuous of Somerset to insert his own interests into this matter at all.

"We will not rest until we have answers," Warwick said.

Edward nodded, relieved. Warwick would take care of it.

February 21, 1549

Edward squirmed in his chair. He didn't like Westminster as much as some of his other palaces, but Warwick wanted to stress Edward's authority. Westminster and the Tower were the ultimate symbols of royal strength. Built by William the Conqueror during the twelfth century, they defined the north and south ends of the City. Right now, with Edward at Westminster and Thomas Seymour lodged in the Tower, the two palaces also defined good and evil. And were connected by blood as much as by the River Thames.

Edward looked down his nose at the men of the Council who stood before him looking grim. He still didn't attend their meetings, but they took him more seriously now: Somerset brought one or two of them to his apartments almost every day to keep him apprised of their actions and decisions. This was an unexpected gift his uncle Tom's treachery had given him, and Edward hoped it would last.

"The investigation has concluded, Your Majesty," said John Gage, Constable of the Tower and one of the day's two guests, Warwick being the other. "We identified thirty-three counts of treason against the Lord High Admiral."

Thirty-three. The sheer magnitude was chilling. With such a number, they clearly did nòt doubt his guilt. Edward took a deep breath.

"And, Sire," Gage continued, "I am pleased to tell you that your sister is innocent in the matter."

The words changed the air in the chamber. Edward could feel the relief but pressed anyway. "She had not agreed to marry the Admiral?"

"No, no, Sire," Gage said. "We questioned her servants to make sure. There was little more they could tell us beyond the sordid details of the early morning romps at Sudeley Castle."

"The ones the Queen condoned? Or were there others?"

"No others."

Somerset stepped forward. "But we should honor her request for a proclamation of her innocence."

Edward thought a moment. "Why does she want a proclamation?"

Somerset pursed his lips. "When Elizabeth was banished from the house, there were rumors she was with child by the Admiral, and now with him arrested, the rumors are afield again. She fears for her reputation, which she says is her greatest asset and comfort."

Edward's heart went out to his sister: he too would have been horrified to have people wrongfully believe ill of him. But he brought himself back. He was not a child anymore, to be led by emotions. He had to focus on facts. His mind raced over the speech again and, like his favorite peregrine, homed in on the words that wiggled.

"You said there was 'little more' they could tell us. That would imply there *was* more."

Somerset pursed his lips like a guilty man caught. "Gage?" he said, waving the Constable on.

"The Admiral had several conversations with Elizabeth's cofferer, Tom Parry, about her holdings. He wanted her to exchange some of her lands for others closer to his to make them easier to administer if he were to marry her."

"This would suggest an agreement between them," Edward said. "Why is this the first I am hearing of it?"

"Perhaps the Duke is protecting his brother rather than you," Warwick said.

Somerset flashed angry eyes at the Earl before responding to Edward with a blank face. "I am certain I told you."

The tone in his voice angered Edward. "I am certain you did not."

"Well, then, perhaps I chose not to burden you with disproven theories," Somerset said. "There was no agreement. When Parry related the conversation to the Lady Elizabeth, she rebuked him. Said there should be no talk of her marriage unless that talk came straight from the Council."

Edward nodded and waved Gage on, but Warwick stepped forward.

"Your Majesty should be aware the Admiral did not confine his efforts to Elizabeth's Secretary. He also spoke to Elizabeth's governess, Kat Ashley, to ask her to encourage Elizabeth to consider his suit. Mistress Ashley went even further, encouraging the Lady towards the match."

Somerset's eyes narrowed. "Stop your rabble-rousing," he said. "Mistress Ashley has been shown to be unreliable. She is the one who is taken with my brother, far more than Elizabeth."

"I do not mean to incite suspicion, my Lord." There was a gleam in Warwick's eye that Edward did not fully understand. "I mean only to make sure the King has all the information that was given to us. Am I wrong in thinking he deserves this courtesy?"

"I thought the facts too inflammatory to repeat," Somerset said. "It is not meet that—"

"Am I a child then, to be spared scary stories?" Edward's indignation could not be contained.

"There was also the salacious nature of some of these claims, and Your Majesty—"

"Have you shared these events with all of the Council?" Edward asked, shaking with resentment at this added insult to his age. "With Archbishop Cranmer and Bishop Turnstall here, for whom salaciousness is sin?"

"Yes, but…" Somerset's voice trailed off.

"You shall not keep these things from me any longer," Edward said, gratified at the strength behind his words. "When there is treason about me, or investigations that may pertain to treason, I must be fully informed."

Somerset slumped his shoulders. "You are right, of course." He paused. "But, Sire, Elizabeth is innocent."

The Lords nodded in agreement. Shakily, but they nodded. Even Warwick, though his eyes were narrowed. Edward's burning gaze cooled and his fists unclenched. But before anyone could respond, Somerset fell to his knees and spread his arms wide. "I am sorry, Sire. Earlier on, I hoped to find a way to save my brother. I was convinced he was attacking me and did not think it was fair to punish him for that. But the findings prove his actions treasonable and must be judged as such."

Edward softened at the unusual show of submission coupled with Somerset's apology. Finally, the Lord Protector was actually protecting him. "Thank you."

"There is more." Somerset slowly pushed himself to standing, though his face hung down from a back curved like a shepherd's crook. "Gage, tell His Majesty what you discovered this morning."

Edward took a sharp breath in. *What was this?* He looked at Gage, who looked equally guilty. "Well?"

"One of his guards noticed a rustling sound when the Admiral was pacing in his cell. It turns out he had letters sewn between the soles of his velvet shoes."

"Letters?" Edward sighed. He was only a boy, yet he knew more than these men about managing prisoners. "Why was he given pen and paper?"

"He wasn't." Gage shifted from foot to foot. "He made a pen from the aglet of a point he plucked from his hose. God only knows where he got the paper."

"Were these honest confessions or just pleas for mercy?" Edward asked. Regret and annoyance mingled in his chest and weighed heavily. His uncle Tom was such a child. Maybe Somerset was right. Maybe he could just be banished from court with a sharp rebuke.

"Neither, Your Majesty. They were letters to Mary and Elizabeth, urging them to rise in his defense."

Edward's insides turned to ice. He shot Somerset a murderous look.

Warwick stepped forward and plunged to his knees. "I know he is your uncle, but this is inexcusable. You must weigh allegiance more than blood. We must be allowed to proceed against him properly."

Somerset followed him down, shoulders slumped. "Sire, the Earl is right. This is just so heavy and lamentable for me."

Silence descended on the room. They all looked at Edward with expectant looks that squeezed the breath from his body. Despite all the talk of treason, Edward found himself unprepared for this moment. The men were actually looking to him to decide this matter of great importance – men who barely allowed him to pick what clothes he wore on any given day.

Cranmer stepped forward and put a hand on the Protector's shoulder. Edward wished someone would think to do that for him. All he could do was rub his aching forehead. "We do perceive that there are grave things laid to my uncle, the Admiral," he said.

The men waited. Mere acknowledgement would clearly not be enough for them: they needed permission to proceed. Tom Seymour's face loomed before his eyes, and Edward shut his heart to the ghostly plea. If Tom was innocent, he would be released; no one deserved any more. "Do what you must."

The quiet words slashed the air, breaking the spell. Warwick rose, his features a picture of grim determination. "We will take this matter to its conclusion without troubling Your Majesty or the Lord Protector any further."

Edward nodded, unable to voice even a simple thank you.

March 17, 1549

The leaden gray of the day matched the color of Edward's soul. He finally understood Somerset a little better, finally understood his reluctance to condemn his reckless brother.

The Council had done their best to shield the King and the Protector from their terrible duty and the thousands of details of Tom's case. An Act of Attainder had been presented to both houses of Parliament; the Lords and Commons had weighed the facts and condemned Thomas Seymour, sentencing him to death. The Bishop of Ely had attended the wretch, instructing him in the things that related to another life, and preparing him to take patiently his inevitable end. But once the Council had drawn up the death warrant, the law of the land brought the final decision home to the Crown.

Edward looked out the window at the Thames, at the gray current that flowed from Westminster to the Tower. The lapping waves reminded him of wretches pleading, and he cringed. He glanced over at Somerset, who was too mesmerized by the fire to notice.

The two of them sat at the table in Edward's library, alone in the room. The warrant lay between them, a mute reminder of the next step required.

It was such a small thing, to sign a piece of paper. But that tiny mark would blacken Edward's soul. He was not yet ready to act as God. He felt too young to take an action with such permanence.

"My brother has made certain requests," Somerset said.

Of course he has. A pardon and freedom were likely near the top of the list. "Oh?"

"He wants Mr. Latimer to be with him at the last, and certain of his servants as well."

Hugh Latimer, an outspoken reformer, was once Edward's own Chaplain. A true man of God. "But my Lord Latimer has long been one of his most outspoken critics."

Somerset sighed. "When we were younger – Tom and I and your mother – we would always run to confess our sins to our mother before our father." He smiled ruefully. "That was because we knew our mother would forgive our trespasses far more readily than our father would, even intercede for us when she told him."

"I don't understand."

Somerset reached forward. "Because our mother's forgiveness was more assured, we valued it less – and trusted less the penance she imposed. After all, we answer for all our sins either here or beyond, so it is far better to know we are truly forgiven now, that our sins need no longer weigh on us. Compassion from a man like Latimer will bring my brother closer to true peace."

Edward nodded at the deep truth of the statement. Then he remembered a question he had to Somerset's original statement. "Which servants?"

"Does it matter?"

Edward shook his head, not wanting to admit to morbid curiosity. He wondered who he himself might choose for such a moment, and was curious as to how his uncle Tom had made his decision. Not that Tom would have been able to articulate a particular scale; the man acted only by instinct.

"He also asks that his infant daughter be brought up with the Dowager Duchess of Suffolk."

Tom's infant daughter, Edward's cousin. Actually, since Katherine Parr had been married to his father, little Mary Seymour was more like Edward's half-sister. A half-sister he was about to make an orphan.

Edward took a deep breath to slough off the panic that threatened to break through defenses barely stronger than an eggshell. He needed to stay with the question at hand. "Not Frances Grey?" Frances was the daughter of Mary Tudor, so the daughter of a queen would raise the daughter of a queen.

"The Duchess was a better friend to Katherine Parr," Somerset said. "She will take good care of the young girl."

Edward bit his lip, afraid to ask the question but needing to. "Shouldn't it count for something that he chose heart over prestige?"

Somerset sighed. "Normally I would agree, but in this case, Henry Grey might have been viewed as a co-conspirator. Asking him would have made things look much worse."

Edward wondered again about his uncle's plan to marry him to Jane Grey. Tom knew Edward liked her, had seen him blush at her touch. Was he trying to buy Edward's support, or bribe Henry Grey to support an attempted coup?

Jane would have made a welcome bride. But it was Edward's duty to marry a foreign princess, someone who would bring a huge dowry and a powerful alliance.

That still, small voice reminded him of his father's inability to consummate his marriage to Anne of Cleves. What if something like that happened to Edward? He would never recover from the shame.

Like the evil serpent that tempted Adam and Eve, the voice rose like a cobra to spread its hood and hiss at him. *What if your Councilors choose your bride unwisely, as Cromwell did? How can you trust them with this decision?* The snake bobbed with mockery. *Your uncle chose a woman who would have made you happy and you will let him die for it?*

The only way to silence that terrible voice was to conjure Argos against it. That always worked. Even Edward's inner snake could not prevail against the face of that innocent blood.

"Sire?" Somerset said, a sharp edge to his voice. He was leaning forward. He must have asked a question.

"Sorry?"

Somerset sighed. "May I have the Council see to fulfilling those wishes?"

"Of course."

"Good."

Their glances fell on the warrant between them. Somerset reached out and pushed it toward Edward. "You must sign."

"Yes," Edward said but, try as he might, he could not get his hand to reach for the paper. "I hate that I need to do this."

"I am angry about that too," Somerset said. "I knew my brother was threatening me, but I never thought he might wish you harm."

You never thought of me at all. The words leaped to Edward's lips but he bit them back, unwilling to get drawn into recriminations, unable to voice his shameful hurt.

"My father told me I would have to do things like this," Edward said instead. "He taught me how kings were obligated to execute traitors. 'God's anointed is the law and the land and the church and no one can be allowed to commit treason and live.'"

Somerset sat back and nodded ruefully, scratching his beard. "I remember when he said that. The three of us were standing before the Abraham tapestries. *The Binding of Isaac.* I also remember talking about it afterwards, you and I."

"We did." Edward could not help but chuckle. "I was glad for that talk – so calming after the fright of his speech. Even now I can close my eyes and conjure the crooked finger he pointed in my face, forcing me to cross my eyes at it. It was only when you explained it to me that I understood."

They had talked about Catherine Howard and adultery, a long list of other treasons and traitors, what it meant to trust, and how it felt to find that trust was misplaced. It still made Edward nauseous to think of it all.

"I knew it didn't make much sense to you then," Somerset said, "but you needed the knowledge. You needed the rules before betrayal happened, so you could judge and guide your own reactions."

"But it's not helping," Edward said. "I know the rules. I know my uncle must die, but I still don't want to sign the warrant."

Somerset shook his head. "Of course you don't. Your father never wanted to sign any of the warrants he did – but he couldn't allow that to stop him."

"He said that, too," Edward said. "That there could be no exceptions, no matter how close. But why? The Lord forgives sinners all the time."

"Men can never forget their own treachery, and the only way they can live with such shame is to cling tight to the hatred that led them to it. And often try again."

Edward pondered. Yes, the Lord could forgive where Edward could not.

"This death is for England," Somerset said. "Much as it hurts to say it."

"England asks much of me."

"You are her king."

Edward sighed and Somerset followed. They both stared at the table for a time. Edward's anguish rose in him and finally burst out. "I know treason can slither from under any rock, but this is not fair. My first death warrant should not bear my uncle's name."

Somerset sighed. "You have a point," he said. "You should not have to sign this. Not at your age. And not for my mistake."

He pulled the warrant over to him and took a quill from the holder. He pointed it at Edward for emphasis. "The next time you are presented with a death warrant, you will sign it yourself."

Edward nodded.

"Promise me," Somerset continued, the quill still pointed at Edward like his father's finger had been so many years ago. Edward knew the right thing to do would be to change his mind and sign now, act like the man and king he knew himself to be. But he couldn't.

Next time he would. Next time he would do what his Council and the law required and spill the blood of a traitor lawfully convicted. But not this time. "I promise."

Somerset nodded, satisfied, and turned his attention to the document. Edward held his breath as his uncle sighed and dipped the nib in the ink. The scratching of the tip sent shivers down Edward's spine.

The ink glistened in the light for a moment until it dried like blood on the block. The signature, so shaky as to be almost illegible, mutely reproached them both.

So perish all traitors.

PART TWO

JUNE 9, 1549

*E*ven on an overcast day, Beaulieu's bow windows captured the reflection of its red bricks, lending a glow that never failed to lift Mary's soul. Her apartments were arranged so each of her main rooms had its own bay, and here in her Presence Chamber her chair of estate was carefully positioned to surround her in a rosy celebration of God's handiwork. The practice was especially helpful at times like this, when she had to receive unwelcome news.

Mary sat back in her chair and fingered the heavy silver rosary attached to her belt. She kept vague interest on her face while William Paulet, Lord Treasurer of the Council, spoke down his nose to her. He had come to inform her of new religious rules he pompously claimed "would govern worship throughout the land." His eyes keep flickering to the beads, so she exaggerated her motion to goad his mounting confusion.

Weariness sagged her jowls. There had been so many of these notices, so many unwelcome messages to tell her what she should believe and how she should worship. Especially now that the Council was able to focus on serious matters rather than slog through the political quagmire that Thomas Seymour had created.

"These are the prayers you will say every day," Paulet said. "These and no others. It's all in here." He held out the oversized presentation copy.

She had no choice but to accept the heavy leather-bound volume. She opened it to the title page, which she scanned with pretended interest. *The Book of the Common Prayer and Administration of the Sacraments and other Rites and Ceremonies of the Church: After the Use of the Church of England.* She turned the thick vellum page to the index and made a show of running her finger down the entries. Baptism, Confirmation, and Marriage were there, but the Viaticum had been omitted, as if the dying needed no final comfort. Prayers, too, had been streamlined. Morning and Evening Prayers were set, along with the Litany and Holy Communion. But Matins, Lauds, and Vespers were gone. This was ridiculous.

"Thank you," she said as she handed off the book to Eleanor Kempe. Eleanor took the book with the respect owed to any of her mistress's belongings, though her tightly pressed lips hinted at contempt. She curtsied and walked over to place it on the table against the wall, just underneath the portrait of Henry VIII, whose fierce gaze suggested his own displeasure with the new formula.

Paulet lifted his eyebrows as if he were about to say something, but Mary turned away to watch Eleanor return to her post. There was something deeply reassuring about having her lady at her side. And the delay offered the added benefit of discomfiting the envoy.

"Have you any other message from my good brother?" Mary asked.

"No, my Lady," Paulet answered.

Mary kept her gaze steady. Once again the reminder she was but Lady Mary, not Princess Mary. The lack of recognition still rankled. She was next in line to the throne until her brother sired an heir. The least people could do was give her the title she deserved.

But right now, that was far less important than the fact that the Council had sent Mary orders they knew she could not accept, without even a kind message to soften the blow. Her Spanish hackles rose, and her mother's blood tingled in her veins. Catherine of Aragon had taught by example the art of gentle resistance, and her daughter ached to follow her lead.

Mary forced her lips into a serene smile. "Did the Duke of Somerset send his own greetings when he bade you come to me?" *Did this rudeness stem from a friend, or an enemy?*

Paulet shifted his weight and straightened the collar of the fur-lined box coat he wore over his jerkin. "It was the Archbishop of Canterbury who sent me," he said. "For the Council. And the Church."

Cranmer. Of course. The heretic whose reforms had destroyed her mother's marriage. Not satisfied with raping and closing the monasteries, now he took prayer away from the masses even as he pretended to place it in their hands. Cranmer would not have thought to send her a kind word, nor would she have trusted it.

"I know the Archbishop has worked hard on this formulary," Mary said noncommittally. "Have I been honored with the first copy or is this to be shared more widely?"

Paulet bit his lip. "I…I don't know whether you are the first, but I do know the Earl of Warwick dispatched an army of messengers to spread the good word throughout the realm."

Warwick. That name was standing out more and more. The man rumored to have driven the wedge between the Seymour brothers. A reformist who was said to be pushing for friendship with France. If he was behind this, his rising power might mean real trouble for Mary.

She would get the real story from van der Delft. He still came to see her regularly; praise God for friends.

"Of course, my household will pray as I do," she said with careful ambiguity. "Please send my love to my dear brother and my prayer that his Progress might take him to Beaulieu this summer."

Most every summer since Mary could remember, the court would leave London's heat and stench while the King traveled around the countryside with a small contingent of courtiers. Until now, Edward had not ventured far beyond his own castles; this year he hoped to greet more subjects and win their hearts.

Paulet bowed. "I don't know that this will be possible; the *geist* for the Progress has already been prepared and the route set."

Mary twisted her face in pretended regret. She knew that, of course. She also knew her brother would not venture into Mary's part of the country, where people held to the true religion. The Council would never let him see that kind of dissent. "I understand, but that does not change my message."

Paulet opened his mouth as if to argue further, so she waved her hand in dismissal. When he hesitated, she rose and left the room. Eleanor fell in behind without a word. At the doorway she paused to glance at the giant volume on the table where Eleanor had laid it, then continued on without signaling her to bring it.

Her heart raced and her face burned. Every step tolled anger and fear over the thought of the Council, the lack of respect they'd shown her, and the position in which they'd placed her. By the time she reached the door to her bedchamber, she was fuming.

"I need to pray," she said between clenched teeth. "Come find me in an hour."

Eleanor's forehead wrinkled. "Would you like your Chaplain to join you?"

Mary shook her head. "Thank you, no. I just need to calm myself."

After carefully closing the door behind her, Mary made her way over to her *prie-dieu* and closed her eyes to summon the words from the thirty-fifth Psalm. *Let them not rejoice over me who are wrongfully my enemies; Nor let them wink with the eye who hate me without a cause. For they do not speak peace, but devise deceitful matters against the quiet ones in the land.*

She waited for the familiar warmth to envelop her, but nothing happened. She tried reciting the words again, but nothing. She was too agitated to pray, there was too much fight in her breast. There was only one thing to do.

She walked over to her chest and pressed the hidden button to open the secret compartment that housed the short stack of cherished letters from her sainted mother. The mother who had trod a similar path so long ago.

The papers were thin and brittle, the ink faded. For their own protection, Mary handled them as little as possible. But she needed their strength now.

Her fingers went straight to the letter that contained her roadmap, the advice her mother had repeated in various forms throughout her fight.

And if this lady do come to you as it is spoken, if she do bring you a letter from the King, I am sure in the self same letter you shall be commanded what you shall do. Answer with few words, obeying the King, your father, in everything, save only that you will not offend God and lose your own soul; and go no further with learning and disputation in the matter. And wheresoever, and in whatsoever company you shall come, observe the King's commandments. Speak you few words and meddle nothing.

Thankfully, her brother was too young to be as ruthless as her father had been. But it was still wise advice. Her mother had kept her soul throughout the process, supported by her nephew Charles. That nephew had grown into a great King and Emperor.

It was time for Mary to write for his help.

August 27, 1549

Edward looked around his Presence Chamber at the hastily assembled crowd. The young messenger knelt before him, a smile on his face.

The lad's arrival this morning had caused a flurry of excitement. He had originally gone to deliver his news to the Council, but the Lords had decided he should speak before everyone. Edward wasn't sure why – or what the message would be. Nor did he know whether the boy had delivered his news already. All Edward knew was that Somerset had summoned the entire court for the event – without giving Edward any chance to prepare himself. Edward was glad that he was wearing the black doublet with the purple slashing, and his diamond knife. The outfit made him feel more authoritative, even if all he would be doing was listening.

Upon a quick signal from Somerset, Edward nodded at the messenger. "We are ready to hear your news."

"The Earl of Warwick has defeated the traitor Kett. More than three thousand rebels died in battle, against fewer than five hundred of our soldiers."

Everyone in the room inhaled together and applauded. Kett's Rebellion was a massive protest in Norfolk, a bastion of popish superstition. The rebels had challenged both political and religious issues: enclosures and reforms. The Council had sent a massive force to destroy them utterly for their treachery and to serve as an example to others who would defy the laws.

"We are all glad to hear this," Somerset said. His formality told Edward that his uncle had already heard the news.

"Another three hundred were hanged for their treachery," the messenger continued.

"May the Lord have mercy on all their souls," Cranmer said.

Somerset spread his arms. "The realm is safe now. We can all breathe easier and begin to heal." He turned to Edward. "We should issue a royal pardon—"

"No, wait," the messenger said.

The entire room turned to stare at the lad, who shifted from foot to foot.

"Begging pardon, sir, it's the part you didn't let me get to before. The Earl was insistent this is not over, that he continues to confiscate extensive lands and properties for the Crown."

"May He further strengthen the Earl of Warwick to deliver His justice," Cranmer said.

"Justice?" Somerset sounded indignant. "It is not always easy to determine which men are loyal to the Crown and which are not. Especially not in the heat of battle. I hope Warwick is up to the task."

William Paget stepped forward. "If they were with Kett, they were disloyal," he said. "Seeking to dictate policy to the Crown is the very essence of treason."

Edward agreed with Paget and was glad to see other heads in the room nod as well.

"In the leaders, yes," Somerset said. "But the followers are starving. Landlords across the country have enclosed their holdings, forcing peasants off land they have worked for generations."

"That is no excuse for rebellion," Paget said.

"No, but it is a reason to show mercy now," Somerset said. "To at least give them the right of a trial before they are executed, or before their property is confiscated."

"They don't deserve that," Paget said. "You speaking like this makes them think they do."

Somerset flushed. Edward could feel anger oozing from him.

"And you speaking like *that* makes me think you blame me for the uprisings," Somerset said.

"Many believe Kett and his followers thought to carry out your will," Paget said.

Somerset had issued a proclamation that landowners found guilty of enclosing would be punished. It was said the commoners thought this gave them the right to pluck down fences themselves.

"Only fools could think that," Somerset said.

Paget lifted his chin and continued. "Yet you waited months to show the military resolve to disabuse them of the notion."

"I had no military." Somerset threw up his hands. "It should have fallen to the Duke of Norfolk to repress such a rebellion – but the attainted Thomas Howard sits in the Tower. Now there's a man who shares the rebels' views."

"Only the religious ones," Paget spat back. "And there are other lords controlling the area who would have done more if you'd been more forceful."

Again, Edward was struck by the depth of opposition to his uncle's belief that the common man deserved a better life. It sounded like a Godly position, but God decided a person's lot in life, and perhaps it was sinful to seek more.

"Force must be backed up by troops, or it is little more than hot air," Somerset said. "We had to wait for the German mercenaries to arrive. Surely you don't blame me for that delay."

Paget rolled his eyes, and Somerset flushed with anger.

"Have you any more news?" Somerset asked the messenger – but didn't wait for a reply before waving a hand to the rest of the room. "Leave us, all of you, so the King's Council may discuss matters."

Edward pretended not to notice the glances exchanged between the Council members. They were as afraid of Somerset's rages as Edward was.

When the courtiers were gone and the door closed behind them, Somerset whirled around on his heels. "Never shame me in public again," he snarled at Paget.

"The Lords of the Council are united against your policy," Paget said. "You need to know this."

"Then the Lords are united against the Gospel," Somerset said. "Godly men should be ready to forego the tiny increase in revenues they earn from enclosing their land to give England's people the ability to support themselves. Whatsoever we do to the least of our brothers, that we do unto Christ himself."

As always, the tempting argument tugged at Edward's heartstrings. Especially now, when Warwick was away – the Earl was singularly effective at opposing Somerset's arguments, which he did all the time now. It was as if Warwick had taken over Tom Seymour's old hobby of challenging the Protector – though Warwick did it with greater integrity than Tom had ever shown.

Paget lifted his chin, defiant. "It is interesting you invoke the Lord to defend the rebels' treason, because the truth is their complaints relate far more to religious reforms than any economic difficulties. The Northerners cling to papist superstition. They have since the time of the King-that-was."

"I know," Somerset said dryly. "I counseled the King-that-was during the Pilgrimage of Grace. And I take instruction from the lessons I learned from him then."

"Then how can you counsel understanding and patience?" Paget asked. "The King-that-was showed no mercy to the pilgrims."

"He listened to their complaints. He received their leader, Robert Aske, at court. He sought understanding."

Edward found himself annoyed by Somerset's reply, which omitted the crux of the story: yes, Aske was received at court, but then he was executed. "Warwick says understanding is overrated. That subjugation is all that matters." The words were out before Edward could consider them, and Somerset whirled on him, eyes blazing.

"Warwick is a fool," Somerset hissed. "You need to keep all your subjects in mind, always."

Edward tried to keep his anger in check. His uncle was being too sympathetic lately to the wrong people and for the wrong reasons. "Like my sister Mary?"

The name calmed Somerset's rage. His tight brow eased and his eyes softened. "Yes, like Mary. I know you want to force her to reform her ways, but you need to tread carefully."

Another area in which Somerset's counsel was vastly inferior to Warwick's. Somerset was too permissive with Mary; he loved her too well and feared her powerful Spanish cousin. Warwick understood she needed to be coerced for the good of the realm.

"I don't see why I need to tread carefully with any subject. Especially one who likely inspired the rebellion."

"She had nothing to do with Kett," Somerset said.

Again, Edward found himself irked by his uncle's sanctimonious certainty. "She is a symbol. She gives hope to all the conservatives. Now more than ever, we need to bring her to heel."

"You think putting down Kett and his rebels was costly? Try war with Spain. Especially when much of your country still cleaves to the old ways. I beg you, do not press the issue. We must not move against Mary until we are ready."

Edward pounded a clenched fist on his chair's armrest. "I am ready now."

"You are not," Somerset said forcefully. "The Treasury has no money for this war."

Paget snorted. "This is why none of us dares to speak what he thinks."

Somerset's eyes widened and his mouth dropped open. Edward was glad someone else was voicing his opinions, though he was careful to keep any triumph off his face.

"Explain yourself!" Somerset said, a hand on his sword hilt.

"Your voice is as sharp with the King as it often is with me," Paget said.

"Nonsense," Somerset said.

"Not at all." Paget said. "You sometimes nip me so sharply that if I did not know you well and were not assured of your favor, I might often have blanched for speaking frankly. If other honest men, not so well acquainted with your nature, say their opinions honestly and are snapped at, God knows what you shall lose."

"And so you rebuked me before the entire court, as would an enemy, instead of advising me privately, like a friend." Somerset's pressed lips rose with his jutting chin.

"A King who discourages men from saying their opinions frankly imperils the realm. A subject in great authority as you are, doing so, is likely to endanger himself as well as the commonwealth."

"Enough!" Somerset's roar sliced the air, and the Lords bowed as they would have to Edward's father. Edward himself might well have knelt if he had been standing.

After surveying the obedience, Somerset turned to Edward as if nothing had happened. "The Treasury has no money for this war," he repeated.

The vast sums Somerset was spending on war with Scotland brought caustic responses about black pots and kettles to Edward's tongue, but he bit them back. "The Treasury never has enough money for anything until a decision is made."

Somerset shrugged.

"Don't you agree?" Edward asked, allowing an edge to creep into his voice.

"I agree we had no choice but to put down the rebellion," Somerset said. "There is never any excuse for insurgency. But it took Warwick too long to do so, and now we need to avoid the expense of further carnage."

Edward cast about for an appropriate response, but Somerset had already moved on. "Sire, it is time for your lessons. I will retire with the Lords and come wait upon you later."

Edward's eyes couldn't help but widen as the Council filed out in silence, leaving him alone in his chair. His trembling hands made him glad the episode was over. He found himself wishing Warwick were back, to act as more of a voice for reason.

What did this mean for his future – the loss of trust in the man who governed his kingdom? The news was good now, but how much longer would it stay that way? Especially if they turned from doing God's will and let Mary continue her papist nonsense. How could Somerset not see that?

Edward needed to take charge. He needed to be older, but that was one of the few things he could not change. He could only wait. And pray.

"Thy will, not mine, be done," he intoned. Over and over.

August 31, 1549

Whitehall Palace was hot in summer; even Edward's large and windowed library felt oppressive. The court should have gone on a Progress to breathe the cooler air of the countryside, but the rebellions had inserted fear into his Councilors' hearts. Stuck in London, they worked all the harder as if to justify their existence.

Edward leaned forward in his chair to dip the quill in the inkwell one last time. The feather trembled as he finished the final sentence.

Since we see, then, that the reign of Antichrist shall not last forever, we must wait for the destruction of Babylon, and submit ourselves to the will of the Lord.

The final words in a long and carefully constructed argument. It had taken him a year and a half to arrange the four sections in his treatise against the papacy. He first had confuted all the papist reasons for declaring Saint Peter primate of the church, then proved there was no evidence substantiating Peter at Rome. Edward illustrated how popes had actually admitted they did not deserve the primacy, then exposed them as the very sons of the Devil, Antichrists. He concluded with a prayer that the Lord would show light unto those who sat in darkness that shrouded this truth from them.

He blew again to dry the ink and, with a triumphant smile, set the vellum page atop the thick pile in front of him.

God resisteth the proud, the Gospel of James quickly reminded him, and his shoulders slumped a bit. *The King is God's representative on earth and must be better than all men in all things,* his father's ghost countered. It was a difficult line to walk.

Edward flipped through the sheets covered in his fine Italianate script, gratified by a job well done and terrified that others would not see the genius he hoped was in there. Random sentences rose from the pages and ignited a glow within. And just as quickly he caught himself and apologized to the Lord. But his work was inspired, he knew it was. He hoped it was.

He straightened the pages and held them close before remembering that Thomas Cranmer was standing just beside his chair. The Archbishop had been waiting there in silence for hours just in case a question arose. Edward pushed aside his fleeting embarrassment and, using both hands, handed the stack of papers to his godfather.

Cranmer sighed loudly and made a great show of wiping a tear from one eye. "How like your father you are," he said. "Learned and careful. He would be so proud of his Josiah."

Cranmer still called Edward that. Accepting such high praise felt wrong when he had not been able to stop Mary's Mass, but Cranmer refused to stop.

"Thank you," Edward said.

Cranmer placed the papers down on the desk and folded his hands into his sleeves. He took a deep breath. "The Earl of Warwick asked me about your progress. When I told him how far you had come, he begged me to request permission for him to visit and speak of your conclusions."

Warwick. Warwick had spent so much time with him early on, debating the different arguments. He had been absent for a long time, doing good things for the realm. The main reason Edward had not allowed himself to feel hurt over the change.

"Of course," Edward said. He turned again to his treatise, but a lingering question brought him back to Cranmer. "Why does he need to ask you?"

"Everyone needs permission to visit you. If they have not been summoned, by you or the Protector, they are turned away."

Edward bristled that Cranmer was treating him like a fool who knew nothing. Edward had used that rule to avoid private audiences with his evil uncle. "But Warwick is on the Council; he sees me all the time."

"It is not just the visit itself that requires approval, but the topics to be discussed as well." Cranmer looked down as if he were searching for the right words, refolding his hands. Finally, he spoke. "It would assume a great deal of familiarity to broach topics unrelated to the governance of the realm. The...er...incidents involving the Admiral – not just the final offense but all his overreaching – led the Protector to insist your privacy be more protected."

Edward supposed he felt grateful for the protection, but really he felt foolish for not having realized how closely Somerset controlled his life. "Well, I invite the Earl of Warwick to discuss my treatise."

Cranmer raised his hand to the page and nodded. The page bowed and announced the Earl, who was already waiting in the hallway. The insight that this exchange had been planned spread across Edward's chest like a cold wind. Did everyone around him manipulate him?

Warwick entered, bowing at the door, then again in front of Edward's chair. The Earl made no concessions to the hot weather: he wore the richest clothes he was allowed, a velvet doublet under a coat with a sable collar. Yet the luxurious fabrics were plain, almost as plain as Cranmer's simple black cassock. It made Warwick look earnest.

"Thank you for allowing me to see your work and discuss it with you," Warwick said with a bow.

Cranmer's face broke into a broad smile. "You shall be the first to test his arguments as the King has just now completed the treatise."

"I congratulate you on your feat, Sire." Warwick's smile spread even wider than Cranmer's. "And I appreciate your generosity at letting me share in this moment. His Grace the Archbishop was commending your work, and my soul soared with hope for the future you are creating for your people. I hope you will excuse my forwardness in asking him to request a chance for me to express this to you."

"Why did you ask my godfather, and not my uncle, for permission to speak with me?"

Warwick looked surprised at the question, but not defensive. "Why, I believe I mentioned something of the sort to the Duke. But this was a private, religious matter, not a political one, so the Archbishop seemed the right person to intercede for me. Do you disagree?"

Cranmer stepped forward, eyes wide. "Warwick and I chanced to meet in the hall. I have not hidden this from the Protector in any way."

The tightness in Edward's chest relaxed a bit. There may have been manipulation, but it was not malicious.

"Do you want to bring this kind of interaction within your uncle's purview?" Warwick quickly added. "We could withdraw immediately."

"No, no," Edward said. "I was just...curious."

Tom Seymour's voice boomed in Edward's head as if the man were there in the room, fists on his hips. *Good choice. I always said you must take upon yourself to rule more.*

Edward swallowed and tried to banish the ghost, though his uncle had been right on that point. Self-interested, but right nonetheless.

Warwick broke the silence and the spell. "May I?" he asked, eying the manuscript.

Relieved, Edward handed him the sheets. Warwick paused perceptibly at the first pages, the extended dedication to Somerset.

Considering then by your life and actions, that you have a great affection to the divine word, and the sincere Religion; I dedicate the present work to you, praying you to take it in good part. God give you His perpetual grace, and show His benignity upon you forever.

Warwick flipped through the remaining pages, his silence leaving Edward free to reminisce about the dedication, the very first thing he'd written of the piece. Back then, Somerset seemed much more inspiring. His feet of clay had not yet emerged.

Edward found himself wondering whether he would still

make the same dedication today. Perhaps he should have given more credit to some of the other people who'd guided him, even Warwick. Or he could have included an exhortation to take this further.

He pulled himself back. This was the first of many treatises that Edward would surely write, each one a step further in the march to reform. The time for exhortations was later. And Somerset had inspired the very first step, and so deserved this homage.

This time.

September 19, 1549

Edward had come to cherish the occasional midafternoon nap. Especially those days when the hunting or hawking began at dawn. Those were the days when Edward's eyes grew heavy during afternoon prayers, and he would crawl into his bed and close his curtains after him for delicious rest.

Muffled yelling from far away penetrated his consciousness. His eyes flew open and his heart raced. A threat? Again? He took a deep breath to control his ragged breathing.

He reminded himself there were now guards posted outside every door of his room to protect him. Besides, yelling meant men were not trying to hide – it was whispers that were dangerous. And nighttime.

Edward sat up in bed and leaned over to open the curtain at the side. His room was still empty; that told him he had slept for less than an hour or his men would be back already. With the curtains open it was easier to follow the source of the sound. It was coming from behind the wall to his right.

The yelling was from the Council chamber.

Edward hopped out of bed and tiptoed toward the door that separated the two rooms. Leaning close, he could make out Warwick's voice, and Somerset's. The others were softer, less distinct, their words barely hums.

Edward looked down at the inch of space at the threshold. He crouched, putting his cheek to the cold parquet floor, and looked underneath the door. He saw the legs of the table and two pairs of feet in front of it. A pair of black leather knee-high boots with a middling heel. That would be Warwick, practical and dangerous. Facing them, a heavily jeweled pair of white lambskin shoes, also middling heel. That would be Somerset.

To their right, plain black slippers under a black cassock. Cranmer. Behind them all, behind the table, a jumble of indistinguishable legs and feet.

"How dare you blame me for the Crown's financial ruin?" Warwick's boots were planted wide apart. His voice was a snarl. "I defended us from attacks."

Somerset's slippers moved forward. "With more troops and pomp than you needed." His voice was also a snarl. His shoes retreated, then started small-scale pacing.

No movement from Warwick's boots. "Ah, but far fewer men than you used in Scotland – where you spent three times the Crown's annual revenue to win nothing. Now you've even lost Haddington."

Edward jolted. They had lost Haddington, their last toehold in the North? How? Had fighting resumed?

"Bah," Somerset said. "What need did we have of it?"

"And yet you paid such a high price to get it."

The slippers paused. "It was too much to defend, and for what?"

"I would say exactly that about your entire foray in the land."

Utter silence descended on the room, and the jeweled slippers stopped their pacing. The black leather boots took a step forward.

"Your war was disastrous," Warwick said, still snarling. "It destroyed an alliance, lost us a queen, and emptied our treasury."

Somerset's feet froze, then they shuffled a little, like a child caught doing wrong. "It was the old King's policy. You cannot blame me for it. But now I have ended it."

"You would have done better never to start. We might not have had to debase the coinage so badly if you had not. That is another reason why the people turned to rebellion."

Somerset's feet took a single step back but only to brace themselves. "We had no choice with the currency – we needed the money."

"And yet you continue to pay yourself a ridiculous salary. You enrich yourself unjustly while—"

"I take no more than what is due to me." Somerset's voice was firm.

"You think too highly of yourself, my Lord," Warwick said. "You are building a palace richer than a king's. The last man to do that was Wolsey; look how he ended."

Edward was glad to hear his secret feelings voiced. It was true. The lavish display of wealth that was Somerset Place was unsuitable.

"How dare you speak to me like that? I have planned this palace for more than a decade, on lands and from annuities I have long held. I am uncle to this King, I was brother to the last. I deserve to live well."

"Opulence during lean times?" Warwick snorted. "You want to know the cause of the people rebelling? Look no further."

"The rebellions are not over my policies, but yours. You are the one who wants to keep lands enclosed, who wants—"

"Enough." The black boots stood frozen, fending off the attack. "They rebelled because they knew you support them. And because they thought you were too weak to fight back. All our problems stem from your weakness."

Edward's breath caught in his chest. At first he panicked that the men might have heard him, but he realized they had all inhaled sharply as well.

"I have had enough of your insolence," Somerset said. "Until the King comes of age, I rule in his name."

"You do that because we, the King's Council, put you in that position," Warwick said. "Yet you pay no heed to our advice."

"I owe you only listening," Somerset said. "Gentlemen, this meeting is over."

And with that, the jeweled slippers strode out of the room.

Edward scrambled to his feet. His eyes went wildly to the main door of his bedchamber, but his ears told him Somerset had not circled back through his anteroom. Edward was safe from discovery.

Shuffling in the Council chamber captured his attention. He crouched again.

Cranmer sighed as his black shoes approached the Council table. The other legs and feet did not move. Warwick's black leather boots remained planted in their wide stance.

"Let us continue," Warwick said.

Behind the table, black shoes with a silver buckle planted themselves on the floor. "But the Lord Protector is gone," said Paget's voice. "The head of the Council must be present for the Council to meet."

"You have your head up your ass, to look to the Lord Protector in all matters," Warwick said. "He should not be followed when he is wrong."

Edward froze. His father had drummed it into him that such contempt was dangerous. If a man could so forget himself, his heart lacked the respect and loyalty of a true subject.

But the advice assumed the monarch's presence. Edward was not there. Neither was Somerset. Did that make a difference?

"My head is on my shoulders, where I want it to stay," Paget said. "This is dangerous."

"We are all friends here," Warwick said. "And we are entitled to debate over policy. Indeed, as the King's Council it is our duty to do so."

"Well, I have been rebuked for making that same argument," Paget said. "Though I never considered the debate could take place outside of the presence of the Lord Protector."

"We still have a quorum, do we not?" Warwick asked.

There was a brief silence. "We do indeed," Paget said.

"Though we have completed the items on our agenda for the day."

"We are entitled to discuss new business that arises," Warwick said. "And what has arisen is the need to discuss that the Lord Protector has gone too far."

"This is not the time," Paget said.

"This is precisely the time," Warwick said. "Our late King contemplated a Council, not a single man, to govern the country. He wanted his son to benefit from all our wisdom."

"Our late King failed to take into account how unwieldy such a Council would be," Paget said. "We had no choice but to appoint a Lord Protector."

"Exactly." Warwick pounded a fist on the table. "We created the Lord Protector. We gave him the power. And we can take it away."

Edward felt as much as heard footsteps in the antechamber and scrambled to his desk. When his men entered, he was sitting, a book in his hands, trying to calm his ragged breathing.

Ned Seymour approached him, concern on his face. "Were you not able to sleep, Sire?"

Edward was not yet ready for a conversation, certainly not with Ned. The best he could manage was to wave his hand and croak. "Give me a moment."

The men bowed and went about their business, tidying or whatever. Edward stared at the pages without seeing them.

What was he supposed to do?

Tell Somerset? Michael Stanhope? Ned? He would have to admit he'd been spying.

He took a deep breath. There was nothing he could do. This was between Somerset and Warwick, and between Somerset and the Council. This was not treachery, this was policy.

Wasn't it?

Where was the line between challenge and debate? Might he ask Cheke? Or would speaking it aloud make it real?

Edward startled when a hand reached out to touch his shoulder. Barnaby's hand.

"You seem quite upset. Is there anything I can do?"

Edward patted his friend's fingers. "No, I am fine. I just wish I were older. This in-between is frustrating."

Barnaby nodded knowingly.

Edward dropped his voice. "You would be proud of me. I just overheard we are out of Scotland."

Barnaby looked at the door to the Council chamber and smirked. "Well, hallelujah," he said. "My cousin is engaged to a man who was up there defending the city. Now he'll be coming back, and she can marry her lover."

This was a new viewpoint. Again, Edward marveled over the way people valued different things. All Barnaby considered was his cousin and her life; he cared nothing for conquest or legacy.

The thought made Edward feel older. That made him proud but a bit sad. "Warwick sounded so angry," he said.

"Warwick is never happy with anything Somerset does," Barnaby said. "And the Council seems to be listening to him more. If I were Somerset, I would be nervous."

Edward tried to consider what that would mean. He had no idea. He had to start conversations with Somerset, to get him to answer some questions without suspecting anything. This would be a weighty problem, like a good translation.

September 28, 1549

Mary looked down at her hands, clasped prayer-like in her lap. Hunsdon House's wood-paneled library with its chair of estate had been a good choice for this meeting. She was glad to be seated, and in a setting that stressed her rank. Van der Delft had been right: the Council planned mischief and would try to embroil Mary in their schemes. This meeting was proof of that. But forewarned was forearmed, and again she thanked the Lord for the powerful friends He had sent her.

Before her stood William Paulet on another errand from the Council. These visits seemed always to devolve to him, poor man, yet he was a good choice for them: quiet and serious, even if not too smart. Mary had always thought him a friend to Somerset. Now rumor said differently.

She glanced at the wall next to her. Michael Sittow had used Catherine of Aragon's face for his painting of the Magdalene, and Mary now looked to the portrait to draw private comfort and courage.

So different from the other portraits in the room, used mainly for show – like the portrait of her father in his prime that dominated the eastern wall – and to illustrate Mary's lineage. Or the portrait of her brother painted right after his accession and hung in the place of honor in the overmantel above the fireplace, to show Mary's loyalty. That one also evoked sympathy: Edward had not yet been ready to let his eyes be plumbed to his soul: his profile stared off toward a bright future he hoped to deserve.

Finally she nodded, and Paulet began.

"The Council needs your help."

Mary composed her face into a mask of disingenuous friendliness. "Does my Lord of Somerset send you?"

"I come from the Council." Paulet wrinkled his nose. "The Lord Protector does not think he needs help, from you or anyone."

"Surely this is not true."

Paulet raised an eyebrow. "Your own friend van der Delft describes him as dry, sour, and opinionated. Surely this is no surprise to you."

Mary laughed. "He has his soft side."

"He has become brusque in his old age. Harsh, abrasive. He does not heed the Council in making decisions. This is a real mistake, as we all have wisdom to share."

You are overvaluing your wisdom, Mary thought. "That is surprising, as I have often heard him speak of your excellent advice."

Paulet's momentary surprise ceded to a stubborn frown. "He barely tolerates dissent. That is one of the reasons things have come to this point."

"This point?"

"Somerset is destroying the realm. His ill-conceived policies have caused uprisings." Paulet's voice rose and his arms waved. "Bankrupted the Treasury, debased the coinage almost beyond salvation."

Mary took a deep breath. "You paint a bleak picture," she said, careful not to acknowledge the truth of the statements. "But why come to me?"

"We hope to change things."

"How?"

"The Protector's time is done."

The words landed with a heavy thud. This was what van der Delft had warned her about. Mary had to be careful not to signal support. "It is treason to say so."

Paulet ignored the loaded word and pressed on. "The only person he listens to now is his wife, and she is too haughty. She makes him cruel."

Mary's thoughts went to the formidable Duchess of Somerset. Yes, Anne could be sharp, but never without cause. She did not tolerate fools.

"I have never known the Duchess to meddle in politics."

"She fought with the Queen Dowager over precedence and the royal jewels. She nearly started a war by pushing her husband to refer to the French king as 'brother.' Now she is pushing him to build that ridiculous Somerset Place."

Secretly Mary agreed that only a monarch should build such a palace. But she also knew there was nothing sinister involved. "It is Somerset, not the Treasury, paying for it."

"With funds that originated from Treasury grants. As Warwick says, even the reminder stirs up resentment."

That confirmed it: Warwick was behind this plot. "Warwick hates Somerset."

"Many men do."

"I hear Warwick's hatred stems from Somerset enforcing the statutes against him and ploughing his hedges," Mary said. "Or is this because Somerset took back two minor posts from Warwick's son? Is this all about the enclosures and the financial difficulties caused by opening fields?"

"Certainly not," Paulet said. "Somerset's tack was certainly not the most courteous approach, but Warwick would not be swayed by personal gain or loss. None of us would."

His nose rose in the air and he sniffed. Mary had never seen such an example of hypocrisy.

"I must be mistaken," she said.

"It is Somerset making mistake after mistake, each more serious than the last. And still he refuses to listen to reason or advice. He forgets he owes his position to the Council."

"What does he say to this? I take it you have discussed it?"

"It is of no use. We plan to rise up against Somerset's protectorate."

Again, Mary hastened to distance herself from their plans. "This is treason."

"Our loyalty to the King is unquestioned. This is about our loyalty to a man who tricked the lords into entrusting him with a position your father never meant for him to hold."

"Why do you come to me?"

Paulet's eyes narrowed and this made him look sly. "Warwick suggested you might be Regent for your brother."

The word hit her hard and she straightened her already rigid posture. Regent. That would ensure England would not succumb to the Lutheran heresies. It was quite a temptation, like Christ in the desert. But she was too smart to engage. Still, she had to test their offer. "You are not worried I would bring England back towards the traditions of my father?"

"It is understood you would."

The thought filled her lungs. Van der Delft had told Mary that Warwick was courting the traditionalists, but she had not expected them to offer so much. Still, she shook her head. Only a fool agreed to the first offer. "Much as I welcome that news, I cannot help but think it would be better for you to come to agreement with the Protector."

"Somerset is too proud, too arrogant. He is incapable of taking the Council's advice, and he is saddled with a vision of society that is shared by no one at court. This is not effective power and he must be stopped."

"He will not see it that way. Nor will the King."

"He will have no choice," Paulet said, his forehead shining. "He will know that when you agree to serve as Regent."

Of course. The cowards hoped to hide their treason behind her skirts until they were sure of victory.

Mary's stomach told her it was a lie. Warwick had no love for traditional ways, and he would never make her Regent. Warwick was rising in Edward's favor because he was more extreme than Somerset. This was a trick, an offer dangled before her like a carrot to a horse. Warwick was not her friend; Somerset was. Mary shook her head. "I am sorry, but I cannot lend my name to a Council faction. I am merely the Lady Mary, with nothing to do with governance. I obey the Council; I do not seek to head it."

"But will you give us your support?"

Did he think her stupid? Support was equally treason, offering all the risk and none of the reward. "If Somerset agrees to step aside, I will consider your offer. But not now. It is not my place to intervene in government affairs."

October 6, 1549

All thoughts of lessons had faded, and Edward stared out the leaded glass of the Hampton Court Palace windows. His library looked out over the Thames – so much calmer here than in London – framed by the forest that ringed the fields beyond. The red and yellow of the leaves was mesmerizing. It was much easier to indulge the slight fever he'd woken up with this morning than try to force his mind to work.

Especially since he was trying not to think about the danger that might be surrounding him.

He startled when his uncle swept into the room. Edward guiltily looked back down at the books and papers before him on the desk.

"I was right," Somerset said, his face grim.

"What?"

"The Council's treachery has been confirmed. They are resolved to eliminate me and raise Warwick to supreme power."

"Would such a vote be legal?" Edward tried to keep the tremor from his voice.

"They intend more than a mere vote," Somerset said. "Warwick never dismissed his soldiers after he put down the uprisings."

It occurred to Edward that Somerset should have kept better track of the soldiers earlier, but this was not the time for reproach. "Didn't you ask him to send the men to other places where they were needed?"

Somerset sidestepped the question. "We have reports of considerable military movement these past few days, especially horses, so we know he brought them all to London. We also know Southampton and Arundel have been meeting with him at his home."

Clandestine meetings with the two key conservative voices in the court, and an army preparing to strike? Even Edward in his youth could recognize a treasonous coup. Ice crawled up his spine.

"The problem is, we are defenseless," Somerset continued. "When they come after us, they will too easily be able to seize your person."

Seize his person. Edward hated the idea that controlling him meant controlling the realm. "I feel like little more than a living version of the royal regalia."

Somerset ignored his complaint. "Your father feared a stunt like this from Norfolk or Surrey – they had the bloodline and the money. None of us thought a knave like Warwick would be such a danger."

Visions of Warwick in his anger flooded Edward's mind, though so did memories of the man kneeling in perfect devotion. How could people be so duplicitous? "What now?"

"We call for the country to come to your defense."

Edward fingered a corner of one of the papers in front of him. "Will they?"

"Aye, if we're loud enough. They have great love for you."

Much as Edward hated that his throne was in danger, he was glad to be in the middle of things. It occurred to him that this was the first time Somerset was sharing everything with him. Edward sat taller. "Then when do we make this call?"

"I have been working on it. And right now, I have the courtiers assembled for you to add your personal plea. Shall we?"

Edward had barely started nodding when Somerset spun on his heels and took off. Edward had to trot to keep up.

"What shall I say to them?" he asked, panting. "I want to do this right."

"There's no way to do it wrong," Somerset said.

They passed quickly through his apartments, past the empty Watching Room to the massive Great Hall packed with lords and ladies looking bewildered. Instead of stopping at the door, Somerset passed through the crowd that parted for them in a wave of bows and curtsies. He made straight for the far wall, stopping in front of the tapestry titled *The Expulsion of Hagar*, and Edward wondered whether he intended to call for Warwick to be cast out of England.

"My lords," Somerset began, looking around the room as if to check who was there, "I have learned that Warwick and certain others are resolved to throw me down. This cannot happen. Not because I seek power for my own glory, but because

I care for His Majesty. Make no mistake, this insurrection threatens the King more than it does me. The days of Richard III are not so far gone that we can forget what can happen to a young monarch."

Edward pretended not to notice all eyes snapping to him; he kept his face impassive against the twinge of fear that gripped it.

"I hereby pledge my life to the King's defense." Somerset's tone had turned to encouragement. "I myself will be one of the first that will die at the gate if Warwick's men come in by any forcible manner into the court."

Murmurs ran through the room. Edward was heartened by the calls of "God save the King" but his head hurt terribly and his tongue was thick and fumbling, even before being called upon.

Movement from outside the windows caught his eye. Approaching peasants, some with longbows but most just carrying pitchforks or tools, a fearful display of rudimentary weapons. Were they attacking?

"Praise God," Somerset said.

"Father?" Ned asked, his face mirroring the confusion Edward felt.

"I had the King's plight bruited in the village," Somerset answered his son. Turning back to the assembly, he continued. "People are arriving, though we need many more. Now is the time for you to show your loyalty, for you to call your own men to add to the royal forces. Your king needs you. Your country needs you. Justice needs you."

Somerset's rising tone was met by rising excitement in the room that burst into a round of cheers. He closed his eyes and bowed his head in a display of emotion, then raised a hand. "Go now," he said, and the men and women spun around to leave.

Edward's confusion grew as the crowd dwindled. When all the people were gone, he turned to Somerset. "What about my own plea? Was that not why you brought me here?"

Somerset had the grace to look abashed. "I was going to have you speak, but then it all came together so well. I didn't want to lose the momentum, especially since you were nervous about speaking to begin with. You were there, they saw you. That's the important part."

Edward clenched his jaw so tightly he could hardly pry the words out. "We should go, too."

Somerset bowed his head and immediately took off. He had to keep stopping to let Edward catch up, for Edward's feet dragged as much from resentment as from his fever. Once again he had been trotted out as a symbol, like the scepter and the orb at his coronation. Holy but useless.

His sulk increased when they reached his room and only the younger men awaited him. The older ones were presumably doing more important things.

"I shall leave you now," Somerset said. "I need to start to organize the peasants into some semblance of an army."

Edward just waved a hand to dismiss him. Anger had fed the fogginess of his fever, and all he wanted to do now was rest. "Remove my doublet, gentlemen, I am getting into bed."

"What is happening?" they chorused as soon as Somerset was gone.

"Warwick is determined to take over the government. Somerset is calling for my people to come to my aid. I need to clear my head and gain strength for it all."

Barnaby stepped forward, a sly look on his face. "I shall fetch you some mead from the kitchens. My grandmother always says that is best for a fever. You can call for it when you wake… or I can attend you on my return?"

Barnaby didn't wink, but Edward knew the posset was not the only thing Barnaby intended to bring back from the kitchens. "Open my bed-curtains to check on me, but do it quietly."

Edward's limbs ached as he climbed into bed and closed his eyes. Disappointment weighed on him over not speaking out at this somber and desperate time. And anger gnawed at him over the hint of relief that he'd avoided the test. Anything less than a shout would have been like blanketing the crowd's fire with water.

It seemed only seconds later that Edward opened his eyes, but the room was dark. "Barnaby?" he called. "Has Barnaby returned?"

"Right here, Sire," Barnaby said.

A minute later Barnaby was inside the curtains and handing Edward a cup. The golden liquid was thicker than usual, which meant it was sweeter.

"I had them use honey from apple blossoms," Barnaby said. "And lots of it. My grandmother's recipe."

Edward took a sip. He smiled and settled back into the pillows. "Thank you."

"Are you feeling better?"

Edward felt his head to gauge his fever. "How long was I asleep?"

"About three hours. Much has happened."

"Oh?" Edward sat up in bed. "Tell me."

"Warwick's group is calling itself The Council in London and has issued proclamations claiming you are in danger."

"Yet I am," Edward said, almost sputtering. "From *them*."

"They're telling people just the opposite. They say it is Somerset who threatens you and they who want to save you."

"Preposterous!"

Barnaby shook his head. "Aye, but repeat a lie enough, and it is believed. They say men are no longer sure which army to join."

Edward's head started to hurt again. "The danger is worse than I thought."

"It may be worse still," Barnaby said. "Somerset sent his wife away. I just saw her leave in tears."

"What?"

"They say it is because he cannot defend the palace properly."

Somerset was worried about his wife but not his nephew? Edward's smoldering anger flared.

Right then, Somerset was at the door. "Your Majesty?" Edward scrambled to sit up and lifted his chin to indicate the curtains. Barnaby opened them and stepped aside.

"Uncle?" Edward said.

"We are leaving here immediately," Somerset said, his face grim. "Please prepare to go."

"But it is ten o'clock at night."

"Exactly. We'll ride under cover of darkness, for safety."

"What is going on?"

"The London Lords are coming. They say it is to interview me, but they do not come in peaceable array. We are not safe here."

Edward's insides tightened. "So we go to the Tower?"

"No. To Windsor Castle."

"Why not the Tower?" The Tower was the castle of choice when a King of England needed to defend himself, the ultimate symbol of royal rule. Why was this not the chosen destination?

"Paulet controls it, and he is with Warwick. Windsor is a better choice. Closer, too, so you'll spend less time in the open."

Dear God, Warwick controlled the Tower. "You think Warwick will attack?"

"Yes, I do. And Hampton Court is built for pleasure, not defense. There are too many doors and windows where treachery can happen. I would never forgive myself if something happened to you."

Mollified, Edward nodded. "Then let us go." He looked around at his men. Some were still scrambling to their feet, but Barnaby was already approaching with Edward's clothes.

They dressed him quickly while Somerset paced the room in his impatience, tossing books and papers into a bag. The silence was thick, but no one wanted to chance Somerset's temper by breaking it.

When they had come to the last few buttons of his doublet, Somerset roughly pushed the young men aside. "Let us make haste," he said to Edward. "The rest of you, grab his things and follow us."

"Wait." Edward walked toward the clothes room. "I want my dagger," he said. "The one my father gave me. The one with the rubies."

Somerset opened his mouth but quickly shut it and said nothing. The men thrust the jeweled weapon into Edward's hand and he attached it to his belt. He felt better armed.

As they left his apartments, they were greeted by a brace of guards waiting just outside the door. Somerset did not bother introducing them or even mentioning them, even when they wordlessly fell in behind.

The two made it quickly to the Base Court, where Cranmer, Paget and Cecil awaited them. A dozen muscled destriers were saddled and waiting, and a large crowd had amassed behind. Somerset nodded, and two trumpeters and six Yeomen of the Guard walked out first to announce the King's presence. The crowd cheered and Edward's heart swelled. His people would protect him. And now he had a chance to rally them to do so.

"Good people," he called. "I pray you be good to us – and to our uncle."

More cheering. Somerset stepped forward and held Edward's hand high. The crowd roared, and their enthusiasm chased away his fear. Finally, the noise faded enough for Somerset to drop their hands.

"I shall not fall alone," Somerset declared in a vast, sonorous voice. "If I am destroyed, the King will be destroyed. Mark my words: kingdom, commonwealth – all will be destroyed together."

Edward cringed, and right then Somerset whirled around to point at him.

"It is not me whom they threaten," he said, eyes wild. He pushed Edward forward. "This is the mark they shoot at."

Loud boos and shouts of "Never!" rang out, and the peasants

hefted their implements and weapons, ready to use them against whichever foe arrived.

Edward froze. He could only stare, wide-eyed and mute, at the surging crowd. Somerset turned and pulled him along to the horses, which had been brought close behind them.

Somerset helped Edward mount and then quickly took his own place while the guards gathered round. They walked their horses carefully through the crowd, who called out blessings that fueled Edward's courage. He unsheathed his dagger and raised it high for all to see it. "Will ye help me against those who would kill me?" he shouted.

The crowd ignited. They pumped fists and roared back at him: "We will die for you" and "God save Your Graces." Edward's heart swelled.

He lowered his arm to ride away, then walked his horse several paces before sheathing his dagger. Somerset nodded at him.

"Well done, Your Majesty. Your father would have been proud."

Somerset let the words fade then clucked at his horse to start them off. The riding was hard from the start, and Edward's head ached from his fever and fear. He had never liked Windsor Castle: his mother was buried in Saint George's Chapel there, his father beside her. Edward had always associated it with deep sadness.

Still, by the end of the road's fourteen miles, he had come to terms with the choice of Windsor over the Tower, indeed, to prefer it. Other princes had been killed in the Tower. As Somerset had said, the crimes of Richard III were too new to be easily forgotten.

Please God, Edward thought. *Please God let me live through this.*

October 8, 1549

Surrounded by a steep hill and shielded by two baileys and several moats, Windsor castle was as impregnable as the Tower. It was also as gloomy, thanks to thick stone walls that grayed the light from the windows. Or maybe that was just Edward's mood.

Usually the King's quarters were magnificent, but since their visit was unexpected, the rooms contained only the bare minimum, the furnishings left in a palace when the royal court was elsewhere. Their arrival the other night had required Edward's own attendants to hurriedly remove the protective sheets covering the furniture and brush away the dust.

Ned peeked his head around the door. "Sire, are you awake?"

Edward sat up in bed. "Aye."

"My father has sent me to bring you to the Council Chamber."

Edward sniffled. His head still hurt; he was still in pain. He was also still scared. "Any word from Russell or Herbert?"

Edward had written to the two men the day before, asking them to raise all the forces they could to rescue him from the conspirators. Somerset had dictated the letter.

Ned's smile did not reach his eyes. "I don't know. My father's face was grim, but it always is. He did not say anything to me."

Edward threw off the fur coverlet and rose from the bed.

Ned laughed and looked around at Edward's attendants. "I wondered why no one jumped to help you dress, but I see you don't need it."

"I just lay on top of the spread and pulled the corner over me. I didn't want to feel…unready."

Unready. That was a more manly way of putting it. The vulnerability of the other night, the unprotected dash to safety, still haunted him.

They walked in silence to the Council Chamber, where Somerset was sitting at the head of the massive oak table, Paget and Cranmer along one side. They all stood and bowed and waited for Edward to take his place.

Edward glanced at his chair of estate, forlorn in the corner without any arras over it.

He took a seat at the other head of the table.

"Any word from Russell or Herbert?" he asked again.

"No."

"How far away are they, that they have not replied to my letter?"

"They are only forty miles away, in Andover. With their men."

Their men. The single strongest military entity in the west.

"The silence tells us all we need to know," Paget said. "Theirs is not a friendly force."

Edward's bowels iced.

Somerset massaged his temples.

"You should not have denounced them as overly cautious, nor castigated their inertia during the Western Rising," Paget said. "This is their way of proving you wrong."

Edward found himself irritated by Paget's challenging tone. This was not the time for dissent. There was an army in position to attack. They were close to war.

Edward placed a hand over his heart, as if that could stop its racing. How could this have happened? This was exactly what his father had feared. Usurpers.

"What now?" Edward asked. *Will we die?*

"We have petitioned the Common Council for a thousand men to repress the conspiracy," Somerset said.

"Aye, and Warwick has petitioned the Common Council for two thousand men to keep order in the City," Paget said.

Somerset's hands shifted to cover his face. "If we had more men—"

"We won't get more men," Paget said. "We would have seen people by now if they were going to come."

"We must keep faith," Somerset said. Edward could hear the plea in his voice.

Paget looked down, and Somerset turned to Cranmer. "Archbishop, you agree with me, do you not?"

Cranmer's eyes steeled. Edward held his breath.

"Faith is powerless when the Council is denouncing you twice a day in every public square in the land," Cranmer said. "They tell the crowds you overturned the late King's will to seize power, that you enriched yourself while the rest of the country staggered under the foolish wars you initiated. They claim that when they sought to persuade you to rule with their advice, you reacted by levying force and spreading rumors of treason."

Edward stifled a gasp.

Somerset leaped to his feet as if preparing to avenge an insult. "Rumors of treason? I revealed their evil plans."

Cranmer slowly pushed himself up and let loose his pulpit voice, the voice that carried to every corner of a cathedral to the glory of God. "And to buttress these designs, you used the King wrongfully." At Somerset's shocked stare, he softened. "That is what they say."

Edward froze at hearing the Lords' arguments presented so forcefully – and so believably. No wonder men were unsure – Edward knew the truth and still *he* felt somewhat conflicted.

Somerset shook his head. "I am doing my duty to my royal brother-in-law, protecting his son from men who would abuse his youth. I ask nothing more of God than to turn over the kingdom entrusted to me, the day the King comes to manhood. You know this of me."

"I know your utter loyalty. It is why I am here." Cranmer glanced at Paget. "Why we are here."

Somerset sat back down. Cranmer did the same.

"To attack the King is treason," Somerset said.

"To free him from an evil plot is not," Cranmer said.

"To attack me, the Lord Protector, is treason."

"Not when seventeen of the twenty-five Councilors are sided against you. Then it becomes state policy."

Paget leaned forward. "And instead makes your continued resistance treason."

Edward could see some logic in the argument. But it went against justice. Didn't it?

Somerset's shoulders slumped. "They threaten us with armies – they are ready to risk bringing harm to the King. That proves me right."

"They claim they are loyal."

"Traitors always do."

"Seizing the King is legitimate cause for concern," Cranmer said. "As when your brother tried to do so."

Somerset threw his arms in the air. "I brought the King to safety."

"They say you endangered him by riding him out into a crowd of thousands and then riling them up."

Edward flashed back to the night they escaped, to the crowds and the torches and pitchforks they'd brought. The sight was terrifying, yes, but he'd felt safer with them than alone on the road.

"I appealed to their loyalty," Somerset said. "The King appealed to their loyalty. Of all the kingdom, these were the men who love His Majesty."

"You were raising an army."

"Given Russell and Herbert, I'd say I was right to think I needed one," Somerset said.

Cranmer sat back. They all sat back in their chairs. Edward's eyes darted, as if the movement would help him figure out what was about to happen.

"If I give in now, they will have me tried and executed," Somerset finally said.

"They say they will be reasonable, if only you will cede," Cranmer said.

"I don't believe them."

"You have no choice. If you continue to hold out, and to hold the King hostage, the only verdict can be guilt."

Somerset raised his arms. "By the Mass," he wailed, "the King is not hostage; he is under my protection."

"You have lost, my Lord," Paget said. "It is just a matter of time. Removing the King from Hampton Court allowed them to call you a traitor."

"They were going to attack. The King and I rode together," Somerset said.

"The difference is that now their attack is justified."

Somerset drummed his fingers on the table then turned to face Edward.

"You need to write another letter," Somerset said. "To denounce their behavior and again demand their loyalty."

He raised a finger. A servant brought paper and ink to the table and set them in front of Edward.

"Write first your greetings," Somerset said.

Edward took a deep breath and picked up the quill. Somerset had dictated every word of the last letter he had sent. Did this mean Edward would have more freedom to compose his own words this time?

"My lords," Somerset said, clearly dictating. Edward sighed. Did Somerset not appreciate how well Edward had rallied his people the other night? Did he think that an isolated talent? Why would he never give Edward the chance?

Somerset jumped up and began to pace, barking out sentences in the cadence of his footfalls. Edward's hand cramped with the speed of his writing. *He means us no harm...He is our uncle, whom you know we love...Proceed not to extremities against him.*

Finally, Edward was no longer racing to keep up. Somerset was looking out the window. When he realized Edward's eyes were upon him, he shook his head.

"Sorry," Somerset said as he came over to stand behind

Edward and read over his shoulder. He nodded. "You can sign it now."

"This still gets us nowhere," Paget said.

"It reminds them of the law," Somerset said. "And I will write a private one to Warwick. Assuring him I will not risk His Majesty's life and I don't expect him to, either."

The silence weighed on Edward's shoulders, and yet he breathed more easily at the idea that violence might be averted.

"Cranmer and I should be the ones to bring the letters," Paget said.

Somerset arched an eyebrow. "Are you leaving me, then?"

"Not at all," Paget said. "Words on a page will not be enough. You need someone arguing on your behalf, answering immediately. You need me and Cranmer."

Somerset clearly didn't like it, but even Edward could see the wisdom of Paget's plan.

"Fine," Somerset grudgingly conceded. "And while you are there, you can perhaps get a better idea whether all this is pretense."

Before anyone moved, Edward sneezed, sending pain through his body.

"God bless you," they said.

When Edward opened his eyes, everyone was looking at him. All he could think was his body ached. He was tired of sitting in the room, tired of the general air of defeat. He needed fresh air. "May I go now as well?"

"Yes, but not too far," Somerset said.

Edward swallowed his annoyance. How far could he go?

~

AFTER A NAP AND A FEW HALF-HEARTED ROUNDS OF CARDS IN which he lost all his meager pocket money, Edward dismissed his gentlemen to take a walk along the windswept battlements.

Although he was grudgingly aware he was drowning himself in further suffering, he felt compelled to do it anyway.

The aimless wandering soon grated on him, and Edward paused to stick his head through one of the gaps. Before him were the distant fields and forests. Below him were the rampart's slick walls, and he thanked God he was not a soldier ordered to try to scale them.

Although the lofty view went on forever, Edward still felt imprisoned. Much as it felt safe knowing no one could get in, the fact was that no one could get out either. And there were no amusements, nothing to pass the time besides one deck of cards. None of his papers, left at Hampton Court in the rush.

Edward's attention was drawn by a barge making its quick way down the river. The oarsmen all wore his livery. This would be a reply from the London Lords.

Edward made his way back to the main part of the castle. He wanted to be there when the letter was first read. Turning a corner, he almost barreled into Ned, who was coming to find him.

"Thank goodness," his cousin said, panting. "Come with me."

They raced to the Council Chamber where Somerset was directing the installation of the arras over Edward's chair of estate. They had found the stock in storage, and Somerset had chosen one that featured the Battle of Bosworth, the event that had launched the Tudor dynasty.

"Good, you are here. You can sit at the desk until we are ready. Or, even better, check out the window to see whether the boat has docked."

"It has," Edward said. "And the messenger is already entering the gate."

"Good," Somerset said. "Your seat is ready, so you can receive him properly. You should prepare yourself."

Edward sat. He squirmed imperceptibly to improve his posture, then shifted his dagger and laid a casual hand over its hilt. The other arm he draped over the chair's *manchette*. "I'm ready."

Somerset came and stood beside him. He, too, placed a hand on his hilt.

The messenger entered, a large basket in his hand. He held it out to one side as he bowed deeply at the door, but when he made his deep reverence directly before Edward's throne, he held it up as an offering.

"The Council was most troubled to learn Your Majesty had been taken to Windsor without food. They have chosen these provisions with the most inestimable care. More chests have been taken directly to the kitchens."

Somerset looked as if he wanted to swat the basket away. "Did they consider that His Majesty would have had food aplenty if they had not forced us here?"

The messenger ignored the comment, as he probably had been instructed to do. He stood and faced Somerset. "The rest of the message is directed at you."

"Why do you bring it, and not Paget or Cranmer?"

"They are still dealing with the Lords. Nothing has been decided yet."

"Then what have you to say to me?"

The messenger swallowed, clearly nervous. Somerset's temper was well-known. "My masters beg the Lord Protector not to frighten his nephew."

Somerset crossed his arms and pressed his lips together. Edward himself was not sure how to react: the request seemed insolent, but the basket of food lent it sincerity.

"I also am ordered to inform you that after your actions, there can be no question of allowing you to remain in your post. But that no matter what happens, you will be dealt with fairly."

Edward found himself holding his breath. Would Somerset agree?

Somerset raised his chin high. "I trust the Lords will not require with blood that which they could obtain with persuasion and honor. But I repeat that any resolution will require that my nephew and I be treated with courtesy."

The messenger bowed. "Shall I take them that reply?"

"I will write it."

The man looked relieved. *With good reason,* Edward thought, *given how ambiguous that answer was.*

"I will also have a second letter, a private note to Warwick. Will you take that, too?"

"Of course."

"Come back in an hour." Somerset waved the lad out and walked over to the table to begin the letter. Edward watched, fidgeting, but Somerset paid him no attention. Finally, Edward could hold back no longer.

"But you already wrote a private note to Warwick."

Somerset looked up, his eyes rimmed red. "That was to pray him to bring things to moderation. This is to remind him of our long friendship, from childhood. And all I did to advance him." Somerset hung his head and let his shoulders slump. "I cannot believe it has come to this."

Edward had no words. His powerful uncle sat before him, broken. Edward's stomach roiled and he felt near to tears.

October 9, 1549

As before, Edward hurried to the Council Chamber at the first sign of the royal barge. When he got there, Somerset was staring out the window, a desultory look on his face. He barely greeted Edward.

Edward quickly joined Somerset at the window and saw Cranmer and Paget walking toward the castle. Their blank faces quickened his already racing heart.

To calm down, he installed himself on his chair of estate to wait. Somerset followed but avoided his gaze. That did not bode well, and Edward steeled himself to receive bad news.

When Cranmer and Paget entered the Council Chamber, their

faces gave nothing away. After they bowed, Cranmer made the sign of the cross over Edward and the room. "I am glad to see you in good spirits," he said.

Somerset's hoarse voice cut off Edward's answer. "Well?"

Paget put a wide smile on his face, his cheeks plumping. "The situation is not as dire as you think," he said. "The Lords say violence will only come from you. That is the focus of the message they charged us with."

"Oh?"

Paget's cheeks deflated as his smile sank into a frown. Even his skin sagged. It seemed as if he was using his face in a grotesque comedy, one Edward could not understand. "They beg you to not let your quarrel with them go to battle. They know once the bloodletting begins, it will never stop. They have no wish for anarchy."

"I have always said I would not be the cause of bloodletting." Somerset's voice was soft. "I have only ever sought to defend the King against any violence that might be attempted against him."

The happy face returned. "They say if this is true, then there is no quarrel."

"So they don't intend to try me for treason?"

Paget cringed and stepped back, glancing at Cranmer.

Cranmer took a step forward. "The Lord Protector must be above reproach in all things," he said. "To seize the King as you did is a serious harm, and there must be an inquiry."

"How is that different from a trial?"

"Justice requires an inquiry." Cranmer's voice was as soothing as a melody. "How else could you be removed?"

Somerset almost spat. "Do they think me such a fool as to not know how easily justice can be subverted?"

Cranmer kept his tone as even as before. "They say the King will be the ultimate arbiter, after the facts have been laid before him."

Somerset's eyes snapped to Edward. Their intensity dried Edward's mouth.

"If that is so, then I am safe," Somerset said. "Your Majesty has seen all. I have nothing to hide."

Edward was afraid to look away; he felt held as surely as if he were on a leash. But he also could not bring himself to hold Somerset's gaze, twitching to Somerset's lips or his cheeks.

Paget broke the silence. "They said they would deal with you fairly."

Finally, Somerset turned his eyes away and Edward could breathe again.

Somerset sighed. "That will have to be enough. I have no other choice, not without risking harm to the King."

Cranmer closed his eyes. A sad smile appeared on his face. "They require your complete submission, but they swear you will be deprived of neither honor nor property."

Complete submission. It was unsettling to try to imagine his uncle completely submitting. Even Somerset's deference toward Henry VIII was dim and hazy in Edward's mind, replaced by the tight and total control the Protector exercised now.

Somerset's face twisted, but the look of contempt did not reach his voice. "I am His Majesty's most ardent supporter. You may give your friends my assurances that I will yield my office on honorable terms."

"We don't need to give the assurances; we will stay here with you. The message is a simple one to write. Once you've sent it, they will come."

Yes they will, Edward thought. They would come to wrest power for themselves, these men he barely knew. Edward would be unable to do anything but pray his realm would be there for him when he finally came into his power.

Somerset closed his eyes. "Aye." He took a deep breath and opened his eyes again, then looked around the room as if seeing it for the first time. Then he bit his lip and slowly nodded. "I shall retire to write the letter."

"While you do that, I will sit with His Majesty and pray.

Give thanks to the Lord that this situation shall be concluded in peace."

What a lovely way of putting it. Edward did love his godfather. Gratitude was so much more virtuous than petitioning the Lord with prayer.

As Somerset and Paget bowed out of the room, Edward closed his eyes to quiet his mind. It was important to approach the Lord with the proper reverence. He was startled when Cranmer placed a piece of parchment into his hands.

"A letter from the Council," Cranmer said calmly. "Explaining their actions."

Edward took it. It weighed heavily. "You did not present this to me when my uncle was with us."

"I was asked to give it to you alone."

"Why is that?"

Cranmer sighed. "Your Lords deserve the chance to persuade you of their honesty. From now on, they will speak with you directly, and you need to trust them. For the good of the realm."

Edward looked down at the sheet. "You say they acted honorably?"

Cranmer sighed again. "I only say you need to read this, and judge for yourself whether Somerset was the one to instigate this struggle."

"But he wasn't."

Cranmer smiled. "Your Majesty's wonderful religious mind thinks in terms of good and evil, but there are many shades of gray between those two extremes. The question to consider is whether the London Lords acted in good faith."

"But they didn't."

"War was averted, was it not?"

The notion puzzled Edward. "You have ever been Somerset's friend, but you seem to be pushing me towards the Lords' side now. What has changed?"

"I love your uncle, but I love you more," Cranmer said.

Edward looked down and picked out random words from the

letter, but the immediacy closed in on him. He didn't have the strength for the effort that would be needed to separate flattery from truth in the words coming from men he didn't believe. He just wanted to be told the facts by someone he trusted. And he trusted his godfather.

Infusing his eyes with all the pleading he could, Edward looked at Cranmer. "Tell me what you think this says. I will read it fully later to see if I agree. But I want to dispute with you now, and we don't have much time."

Cranmer nodded. "I am proud of you. You are quite right," he said, then gestured at the table in the corner. "Let us sit."

Edward sat in the taller chair and held himself straight.

"Their principal grievance is that Somerset severed them from your presence. That through his tenure he violated the terms of your father's will, which established power in the whole body of the Council and not in him alone."

"But my father changed his mind at the last, when he was too feeble to sign. He wanted my uncle to guide me. There were many who knew this."

"Still, there are those who think your uncle should have kept them more a part of the policies, more a part of the governing. There is a difference between having a chief among equals and having an absolute ruler. Somerset acted as the latter."

"Like Warwick, who wants his power."

"Warwick does want power, Your Majesty, but there are many that think he would use it better than Somerset."

"So, Somerset will never be Lord Protector again, no matter what happens."

Cranmer thought a moment, but Edward could not tell whether that indicated doubt or just a failure to find the right words. "Somerset's rule is over. Now it is time for yours."

Edward bit back the retort that sprang to his lips. He was still too young to rule. This change meant only that he would be controlled by men he did not know or trust.

As if reading his mind, Cranmer patted his knee. "Your lords say they want to look to you for decisions. They say they don't believe Somerset did enough of that."

Edward's heart thudded. "And you believe them?"

"I do," Cranmer said.

"What will happen to my uncle?"

"He will be questioned to prove his honesty and loyalty."

"Will he return to the Council?"

Cranmer shook his head. "They have always resented that Somerset ignored their advice, and now they will not chance his resuming power over them – or you."

Edward took a deep breath. "They were quite vehement in that demand. Surely there was a less drastic way."

"Yes, they went quite far," Cranmer said. "But they accuse Somerset of the same crime. Either way, I don't believe anyone ever meant you ill."

The words were cold comfort in the face of all the upheaval of the past week, and Edward found himself shaking his head.

"Sit quietly, with the letter. Pray. The answers will come to you." Cranmer rose and then bowed to him formally before making the sign of the cross over him and leaving.

Alone in the room, Edward looked back down at the letter. Rebels had prevailed against lawful authority, and now they sought to justify their actions. That had to be bad.

Hadn't it?

October 14, 1549

Edward opened his eyes and for a moment did not remember where he was. Then he recognized the bed-curtains. Richmond. It was here the delegation had taken him after they'd come to Windsor.

They had planned to take him to Hampton Court, but Edward was not ready to return there. Richmond, that safe palace where his father grew up, was a better place to awaken to a new day. Especially since it was his birthday.

He hopped out of bed, not even bothering to open the curtains. His men were scattered about, amusing themselves while they waited.

A slight breeze chilled the back of his neck. "Where is my doublet?" he asked, looking around the room. The sight made him smile in spite of himself: despite the lack of warning they'd had, the Council had Edward's bedchamber turned into a woodland with giant arrangements of colorful autumn-hued branches, the standard decoration for his birthday each year.

"Here you go, Sire," Thomas Wroth said, holding the sleeves for him.

Edward slipped it on then turned and waved Wroth off so as to button it himself. Looking down, he picked off a stray piece of fuzz. Black velvet tended to attract lint, and yet the choice made him look older. Maturity always won out in his sartorial choices.

He glanced at his reflection in the mirror, and the sight made him turn sideways and hold up a pretend sword. "They still won't let me joust," he said over a shoulder to his attendants, trying to keep his tone light instead of wistful.

Henry Neville looked up from the game of tables he was playing in the corner with Philip Hoby. "We will joust for Your Majesty," he said as he shook his dice cup. "Ha! Four," he said as he picked up his opponent's blot and put it on the bar.

Hoby threw a seven on his turn and reentered his piece. "We would even wear your colors, if we could," he joked.

"Has there been a tournament announced?" Edward asked. That would be a welcome celebration.

His men looked at each other and shrugged. Edward bit back his disappointment.

"You may leave me," he said, just as the page at the door announced Cranmer and Warwick. Edward banished his melancholy. He needed his wits for this meeting.

Warwick entered first, bowed first, and spoke first, clearly claiming precedence over the highest prelate in the land.

"Sire, we are proud to bring you the agenda for the first

meeting of your new Council, constituted more in accordance with your late father's will. We are committed to giving you our hearts and advice so your wisdom can lift the land."

"Thank you," Edward said, taking the paper Warwick extended.

"Reaffirm solemn oaths of loyalty" was the first item. It would remain to be seen how well they would follow through, but so far Edward supposed they had acted loyally. They certainly had treated him with respect – more than Somerset ever had – even if they weren't very caring.

He scanned the rest of the paper. "When will they elect you Lord Protector? I don't see an item for that."

Warwick bowed. "As I said, Sire, we intend to follow your late father's wishes. There will be no Lord Protector."

The idea made no sense. "But I thought it was important to have one person for the world to look to, one person to speak for the group."

Warwick smiled. "That person should be you, Your Majesty. We intend to involve you fully in the process."

Edward's heart leaped: this was what he had always wanted. Then it plummeted: what if he was not adequate to the task?

Before Edward could say anything further, a page entered.

"Your aunt begs leave to wait upon Your Majesty."

"Of course," Edward said.

Warwick turned away but his face was reflected in the bedchamber's mirror, and Edward saw the Earl's twisted expression.

It occurred to Edward that he, too, was still in front of his mirror. He walked over to sit in his chair.

Warwick and Cranmer followed him and stood to his right as if it were the most natural thing in the world.

Anne Stanhope Somerset paused at the door before rushing in to throw herself to her knees before him. She wore a panicked look on her usually proud face, and tears flooded her eyes. "Pardon my husband, Sire. Spare his life, I beg you."

What was the woman talking about? "His life?"

"He is held prisoner in the Tower," Anne said. "And if Your Majesty doth not pardon him, the Council will kill him."

"Jesu!" Edward said, and no one scolded him for his misuse of the Lord's name. "They told me the Duke was ill – why have they taken him prisoner?"

Warwick and Cranmer each looked at the floor, probably waiting for the other to explain. Edward turned to Cranmer. "Godfather, what hath become of my uncle?"

"He is a prisoner in the Tower," Cranmer said, his voice tight.

Edward bit back his annoyance. He knew that part. "What evil has he done that he should be lodged in such a place? Only vile traitors are sent there."

Cranmer turned to Warwick. So did Anne.

"There are twelve charges, Your Majesty." Warwick was using his calming voice, like a priest urging Christ-like acceptance of one's cross.

Edward took a deep breath. "Twelve? Tell me them."

"Yes, tell him them," Anne said as she rose from her knees.

Warwick held up a hand. "Ambition, vainglory," he counted off on his fingers. "Entering into rash wars in your youth, negligent looking on in Newhaven, enriching himself of your treasure." He held up his other hand. "Following his own opinion, doing all by his own authority..." His voice trailed off and he shrugged. "And others."

Edward bit the inside of his lip. He knew these had been the Lords' complaints, he just hadn't considered they were crimes. "None of this seems treasonous," he said.

"These are of course auxiliary to the main crime of removing you for evil purpose," Warwick said. "But this is not the time to be thinking of this. Your Majesty will have ample time to consider the facts, as will we all."

"There was no evil purpose," Anne said. "My husband is as true a man to the King as any here. Truer."

Warwick looked down, and Anne lifted her nose still higher.

"I was there when the Mayor escorted him to the Tower," she continued. "I saw the crowds that gathered to cheer him. It seemed like all London came to wish him well. Loudly. He could easily have rallied them to a frenzy against the men who entrapped him, but he didn't."

Warwick's silence intensified the tension until Edward could stand it no longer.

"If he went willingly to the Tower, it is a sign that he be not guilty," Edward said.

Warwick stepped forward. "May it please Your Majesty," he said. "If God had not helped us, the country would have been ruined, for the lords were all up in arms. The conflict might have killed you."

"The Duke never did me any harm," Edward said.

"Your Majesty does not know all," Warwick said.

Anne hissed. "Change with the wind, Warwick, like Judas with Christ. You were once my husband's friend, a good enough one to know his motives true, and yet you turn on him. And you, Archbishop, you know his motives were true."

Cranmer sighed. "There are men who believe your husband acted treasonably, and events lend credence to their concern. It is the Council's duty to examine the evidence. This was a serious matter, and it must be handled seriously."

"You could have handled it seriously without taking him to the Tower," Anne said. "This proves your bad intentions."

Edward agreed it seemed excessive. "I would see my uncle."

"Your Majesty may do so," Cranmer said. "His fate is in your hands."

Anne sank back to her knees. "I beg you, Sire, spare his life. Show him the mercy he deserves."

Edward bit his lip. "I shall pardon him, I promise."

She closed her eyes and let the tears wash down her cheeks. "Thank you, Your Majesty. Thank you."

Edward's nod led Warwick to nod. Two pages approached to

help the Duchess up and escort her out of the room before any more conversation could be had.

He wondered what they were trying to avoid. He thought about asking but decided it wasn't worth it. They'd never tell him the truth.

"Your Majesty, you will have the chance to discuss your uncle's case at the next Council Meeting," Warwick said. "I will put it on the agenda."

"Thank you," Edward said, mollified.

"There is one other task that should be completed before then, Sire. We should consider reordering your household, changing the gentlemen of your Privy Chamber to be more conformable with your person."

"Oh?" Edward kept his face impassive. The last time his Privy Chamber had been rearranged was right after Thomas Seymour's treason, to replace Tom's friends with Somerset's.

"I was hoping to appoint Sir John Gates to Michael Stanhope's place," Warwick said. "Gates is loyal and trustworthy, more than anyone else you have."

And Michael Stanhope is Somerset's brother-in-law, Edward thought. He vaguely remembered the older man with the kind face who always had sweetmeats at the ready. "Sir John served in my father's Privy Chamber, did he not?"

"Yes, Sire." Warwick bowed. "And very ably, may I add."

That was a better trade than he'd expected. Edward nodded. "I accept him."

"And then we could restore Sir Nicholas Throckmorton in lieu of Ned Somerset. He was always a favorite."

Indeed. Throckmorton was the attendant Edward missed most from the Tom days. Edward had given Nicholas his knighthood on a crazy whim. It was the day when Edward had knighted some seven men chosen by the City and had the Sword of State in his hand. Nick had feared the others would be jealous and had tried to decline, but madness had gripped Edward and he had chased Nick through the halls, whooping and yelling, brandishing the sacred sword high before him until he got close enough to give the magic tap on Nicholas's shoulder. Edward still blushed now to remember how completely he had lost his reason, but he was still glad he had done it. And relieved he hadn't sliced his friend in his enthusiasm.

"I do love Throckmorton, but I also love Ned," Edward said.

"He may remain at court," Warwick said. "Just not in your household."

"Fine."

"And I think it might also be a fine time to make some changes in the grooms of your Privy Chamber as well."

Edward's interest was piqued. Grooms were junior, more general attendants. They were not around the King as much, though there was some access. Warwick was being more thorough than Somerset had been.

"I think it might be time to give a chance to men closer to your own age," Warwick said. "Men whom you already love. Sir Henry Sidney. My son Robert. And Barnaby Fitzpatrick."

Henry, Robin, and Barnaby? How much nicer life would be if those three friends could be around his Privy Chamber more.

Edward had always been delighted to have Henry Sidney and Robin Dudley around because they were old enough to be the dashing young men he wanted himself to be. And Barnaby! His friend and closest confidant would no longer be kept from him when their school time was over. Edward tried to contain the smile that threatened to explode his face – only a child showed such glee. "They are certainly welcome."

Warwick smiled and bowed. "I am glad you are pleased."

"Yes, very." Edward sat back. His entire body felt strangely relaxed. He felt cared for, safe. If Warwick was planning evil, he was hiding it well.

Cranmer's brows knit. "Barnaby seems a bit young for such responsibility."

"He shares the King's lessons and has the King's trust,"

Warwick said. "But if His Majesty shares your concern, I will not press."

"No, I am not concerned at all," Edward was quick to add.

"Well, then, it is not my place to grumble," Cranmer said.

Edward paused a moment. He wanted this so badly he was afraid to celebrate it before it was certain. "When does this begin?"

Warwick shrugged. "Gates, Robin and Barnaby are in London; they may begin immediately. I will send word today for Throckmorton and Sidney, who should be here in two or three days."

"Excellent," Edward said with as much calm as he could muster. He raised his chin, hoping to end this audience at such a peak, before anyone could go back on their promises.

"Also, Your Majesty, one other change I would like to propose." Warwick bowed.

Edward's spirit plunged. Here it was. The price to pay.

"Your uncle was always...careful with you," Warwick said. "When you were first come to the throne, of course, that might have been appropriate. But he kept you...young...shielded, longer than he should have."

Edward braced himself.

"You are twelve now, old enough to begin the military training that is fundamental to a ruler. You should arm and tilt and manage horses. You need to be able to handle weapons while you ride."

Edward's heart soared and his eyes saw only light. He had dreamed for so long of being man enough to do such things well. Now it was coming true.

"And not only that, Sire." Dudley took a step forward. "You should be outside more even when you're not riding or hunting. You deserve every sort of exercise: drawing the bow, playing rackets..."

"Such pleasures were always curtailed so I would not miss

my lessons," Edward said. "To make sure I am ready to fill my role when my time comes."

"Lessons and pleasures can coexist." Warwick gave a quick laugh. "Perhaps we should make your tutor another one of your gentlemen? Though I worry that he may take it upon himself to advise you about matters he knows nothing about."

Edward's eyes widened. "I will not let that happen," he said, praying Warwick would accept the promise. Anything to bring Cheke closer like that.

"I trust your discretion." Warwick bowed. "We will retire now, if it pleases you."

"Thank you," Edward said, his voice barely a whisper.

Warwick smiled and bowed again, as did Cranmer, and they both left.

Frozen in place, Edward stared at the closed door for a long time.

November 28, 1549

Beaulieu's somnolent red bricks hid a hive of activity, very different from the usual contemplative days Mary imposed.

Two days earlier, Lady Frances Grey had come with her daughters for a short stay. This was the first time she had visited Mary, likely because she had only recently taken up residence nearby. The family was at Tilty in Essex, rather than at the family seat of Bradgate Manor in Leicestershire, because of how close the rebels had come earlier in the year.

Mary closed her eyes to shake off fear of the uprisings. Van der Delft had just arrived and would give her the facts. Ostensibly this was just an ordinary visit, but Mary knew it would finally allow him to explain the situation at court without putting pen to paper.

With only Eleanor in the corner, Mary and the Ambassador could speak safely.

"Lady Frances was quick to tell me that the King has become

a wise ruler now that he has been liberated," Mary said. "She also says the 'traitor' Somerset is sure to be punished for his arrogance." Mary straightened the rosary that hung from the pearled belt at her waist and smoothed a non-existent wrinkle in her wine-red kirtle. Having gathered her strength, she looked him square in the eyes. "What is the truth?"

Van der Delft checked behind him.

"She is resting upstairs with her daughters," Mary assured him. "And the door is closed. When they come to join us, we will have warning."

Van der Delft nodded and bent his head closer so he could lower his voice. "Warwick has assumed power, although he pretends otherwise."

"I should have taken his offer," Mary said.

Van der Delft grimaced. "He was never going to accept conservative rule."

Mary exhaled. "So Somerset sits lodged in the Tower with twelve treasonous charges against him."

"Twenty-nine."

"Twenty-nine?" Surely no man could escape from such a burden. Mary said a quick *Ave Maria* for her friend.

"More were added when the King indicated his inclination to mercy." Van der Delft snorted. "They have basically found fault with every action he has taken as Lord Protector – as well as for taking the title of Lord Protector to begin with."

"A title they were only too keen to give him," Mary said.

Van der Delft shrugged. "They faulted every exercise of power. And every penny that passed through his fingers."

"Was it really so much?"

"The Lords of the Council are making hay of everything," van der Delft sneered. "They even claim he stole a purse of gold crowns that the City gave the King at his coronation."

"The one that was too heavy for my brother to hold?"

"The very same."

Mary squinted. "That seems wrong. And petty."

"It makes for good theater."

The air around her thickened and she cringed. "Will he die for such crimes?"

Van der Delft raised his hands as if in prayer. "They can't kill him. He is too popular with the people."

The thought was comforting but not fully convincing. "And yet they didn't rise for him."

"Ah, but they will defend him."

The words conjured crowds of peasants brandishing weapons, and Mary took a deep breath to clear a mind racing with fear and violence. "God willing."

Van der Delft crossed himself. "Hopefully they will defend you as well."

Hairs rose on Mary's arms. "Do I need defending?"

"The new Council's policies are veering more to reform than the old one's. The court is no longer a place where it is safe to revere and worship the sacrament."

Mary's knees trembled. The land's golden capital hid a rotten core, and Mary couldn't see how she could ever return. "Already?"

"Are you surprised?" Van der Delft waved a dismissive hand. "Warwick is thinking only to ingratiate himself with a boy who does not yet know his right mind."

Mary felt for her rosary. Just the motion of fingering the beads could calm her, even without saying the prayers. "Where do you worship?"

"I don't." Van der Delft sighed. "Ever since the Emperor forbade the heretical reform service for the English Ambassador in Spain, they have forbidden me the Mass."

Mary toyed with one of the large beads of her rosary's decades. "You can hear Mass with me while you are here. Praise God for my cousin Charles."

"The Emperor will do all in his power to help you," van der Delft said. "But Warwick is making overtures to France, favoring French requests."

Mary flushed. "The Council lets him do this?"

"Lets him? The Council pushes him in that direction. Anything to distance the country from Somerset's policies."

Mary's stomach turned. "Warwick is the most unstable man in England. This conspiracy against Somerset was driven by envy and ambition, and we will suffer for it now."

The creak of the opening door forestalled any further conversation.

"The Marchioness of Dorset, Lady Frances Grey, accompanied by her daughters, Lady Jane Grey, Lady Catherine Grey, and Lady Mary Grey," announced the page.

"They are welcome," Mary said, her voice as light as she could make it.

Frances entered first, of course, and bowed. She wore a highly ornamented purple dress to advertise her rank. Her three girls fanned out behind her and sank as well. They wore plain black. Reformist garb.

"Greetings, cousin," Frances said, rising. "And greetings to you, Ambassador. I had not thought to see you here."

"The Emperor, my master, has great affection for his dearest cousin," van der Delft said. "And in truth I do as well. I visit as often as I am able."

Frances smiled. "What is the news from court? It has been some weeks since I was there."

"News that congratulations are in order, my Lady." Van der Delft bowed. "I understand your husband is to be named a member of the Privy Council."

The smile widened. "Yes, he is. Thank you."

Her total lack of surprise made it clear she expected this news. Henry Grey must have supported Warwick's coup. Not that Mary would have expected anything different – Grey hated Somerset.

"Congratulations, Frances," Mary said. "You must be so proud. And your girls as well."

Nine-year-old Catherine giggled in response but stopped

when her mother swatted her cheek. "Yes, very," the girl said instead.

"When you come to court at Christmas," Frances said, "you may congratulate him yourself."

The thought of congratulating Henry Grey for helping to raise a snake like Warwick made Mary's stomach flip again. The thought of congratulating Warwick himself made her feel even worse. She shot a look at van der Delft. "I do not plan to come to court this season," she said. "So your own voice will have to carry my message."

Frances's eyes widened and her mouth made a circle. "What? This cannot be! The Council will insist."

Mary's lips pressed together. They only wanted her there as a visible symbol of submission. Not only would she be deprived of her Mass, she might even be forced to accompany her brother to the Lutheran travesties. "The Council will understand," she said. "There will be many, many people celebrating. I will not be missed."

"Not be missed?" Frances shook her head. "You and Elizabeth are the highest ladies in the land. Your presence is essential."

Mary took a step back. "The travel would not be good for my health," she said, praying that would dissuade her cousin. Everyone knew Mary was often ill.

"They have already vowed these would be the finest tournaments and celebrations the country has ever seen," Frances continued, "to praise the Lord for the deliverance He sent."

"Ah, these celebrations are best for the young," Mary said, seizing the chance to veer from the topic. "Jane, for example. Jane will enjoy them far more than I."

Mary smiled at Jane, but all she found was a sullen face. Catherine and little Mary were dimpling, but Jane was clearly not happy with the prospect.

"Won't you, Jane?" Mary asked.

"I am still too young for most," the girl answered.

"She means she prefers her studies," Catherine said.

Mary pretended not to notice Jane's sharp intake of breath as Frances pinched the girl's neck.

"You prefer what your father and I tell you," Frances said in a whispered hiss.

"Yes, Mother," Jane said and curtsied.

"But study is good," Catherine said, a puzzled expression on her face.

"In its place," Frances replied smugly. Then she looked at Mary as though nothing were amiss. "Children these days need correction so much more than we did."

Mary had to agree this was true, and yet she was still grateful her own mother had been softer. Mary often wondered how harshly she would treat her own children when she had them. Obedience was important, but it didn't seem Jane had done anything worthy of censure.

Mary considered this might be Frances's way of discouraging the girl's heavily reformist tendencies, but the woman had slapped Catherine over a giggle, so the violence was more likely just a bad habit. Hopefully it was not more outrageous in private.

"Children today love luxury," van der Delft said. "They have bad manners, contempt for authority; they show disrespect for elders and love chatter in place of exercise."

Frances lifted her chin, glad to find her views championed. "Amen."

Mary stifled a smile. She could see Jane do the same.

"Children are now tyrants, not the servants of their households," van der Delft continued. "They no longer rise when elders enter the room. They contradict their parents, chatter before company, gobble dainties at the table, cross their legs, and tyrannize their teachers."

"Is it thus in Spain as well as England?" Frances asked.

Van der Delft laughed. "In Greece, too. I was quoting Socrates."

Frances pressed her lips together and looked around the room, searching faces to see who else had caught the joke.

"And then they become adults, and their youthful mistakes fade into the distance," Mary said to defuse the situation.

"As long as those mistakes have been properly corrected," Frances said, still sulking.

"But of course," van der Delft said, bowing elaborately.

Frances squared her shoulders as if mollified, and Mary relaxed. Her cousin's bad humors were famous, but usually they passed quickly.

"Your thoughts echo my own, my Lady," van der Delft continued. "For some time now I have argued that children change when they come of age, enough that we cannot pay them too much mind before then."

Frances narrowed her eyes. Mary guessed that the Marchioness, too, understood the Ambassador's real meaning. The girls clearly did not, as they blushed with embarrassment as if he were talking about them and not the King.

"Oh?" Frances said.

"The King wishes to change the religious laws, to force his countrymen to abandon the Mass," said van der Delft. "But it would be a mistake to proceed too far in this matter before he is fully adult and ready to make these decisions." He paused, then smiled as if to gentle the tension his words had provoked. "Just like we cannot trust little Jane's decisions about what pastimes she would prefer to undertake."

Frances waved her hand as if she had not a care in the world, but her face was blank. "I pay no attention to religion. I leave that to the men. Politics, too."

The denial made Mary wonder what the woman's real purpose was for this visit. It had originally seemed as if she merely wanted to rekindle their former closeness, or perhaps to remind the world of her royal blood. But maybe her husband had sent her, to encourage Mary over to the Warwick fold? If so, Frances wasn't a true friend.

With Somerset gone, Mary didn't have many of those left.

February 2, 1550

Edward looked up from his writing, his pen hovering over the paper. Was that a noise? All he could see were shadows in the room lit only by the fire and the four candles in the stand next to the desk.

He was in his new Withdrawing Chamber, the room he had insisted they create right off his bedchamber. Wood-paneled and cozy, it was where he wrote in his journal late at night, without his men. He loved his attendants – they were also his friends – but there was a part of Edward that only felt fully free in private, and so he retired to this special room to think and write.

And to meet with Warwick.

Another quiet knock.

Edward set his quill down. "Come in," he whispered softly so his men in the next room would not hear.

Warwick entered and shut the door behind him. For these nightly visits he wore only a shirt over his hose, as did Edward himself. It was a working uniform for a working team, and Edward gloried in the feeling of power it gave him.

Tonight's was a special meeting. After three months of trying to work without a titular head of state – a single person who had the power to speak for the underage King – the Council had given up and asked Edward to allow Warwick to take control.

With Edward's blessing, Warwick had been voted President of the Council and Lord Great Master. He would not hold the same power as Somerset once had, of course, but he would have authority to act alone on Edward's behalf.

Now in Edward's chamber, Warwick bowed deeply. "Sire, thank you again. I am deeply humbled by this honor."

"It is nothing more than you deserve," Edward said. It was the truth. His father had long ago taught Edward that men who did not seek reward were the ones who deserved it most. And

Warwick did not seek reward: he had tried to refuse the new post until persuaded it was necessary.

Warwick bowed again. "Your Majesty, I promise to discharge my duties to the best of my ability. And to serve you as best I can."

Edward basked in the respect with which Warwick treated him. A respect that had not wavered since that very first day after the horrible time at Windsor.

The truth was, Edward felt more capable with Warwick than he had with his uncle. Perhaps that was due to Warwick's confidence. Somerset had been too afraid of things, too afraid of people – even as he disdained them outwardly. And so he had held tight to the reins of government and insisted on getting credit for every decision. Not Warwick.

Warwick didn't need other people to think him smart or to give him credit for policies. He was happy to advise Edward behind the scenes, so Edward could act learned and confident before the Council and the world. Warwick was wonderful.

And yet, his uncle was family, family who had done the best he could. His political failures were due to honest mistakes. Stupid mistakes, perhaps, but honest ones.

"There is one thing you can do to thank me," Edward said.

Warwick bowed a third time. "Anything, my liege. Anything."

"Release my uncle."

Warwick's eyes widened but the rest of him froze. "You wish my first act as President of the Council to sharply contravene the wishes of that Council? It is the complaint we had against Somerset, that he exceeded his authority."

Fear rose in Edward's throat. He hadn't thought of it that way. And yet it was not unreasonable. "I ask it of you."

Warwick shook his head. "I cannot restore a traitor against the Council's wishes, even for you, Sire. If that makes me a traitor myself, I understand. But I love you too much to put you in danger."

"Not restore, just release. The Council will understand, especially since it would be at my heartfelt request."

"I don't know if Quintilian himself could persuade them." Warwick scratched his beard. "Somerset confessed to twenty-nine counts of treason. He is lucky to be alive."

"And yet he meant no harm," Edward said. "He believed every one of those acts to be in the best interests of the country. It is not treason to bungle things."

"Some would say it was."

Edward narrowed his eyes and opened his mouth to reply, but Warwick was already continuing. "I bear him no malice, Your Majesty. My problems with him stem from the harm I perceive he did to you."

"He did me no harm," Edward said. "Truly I would appreciate it if you would reconcile to each other. He always told me how you two had been friends from youth."

"We were indeed," said Warwick. "And if you command it, we shall be dear friends again. Like Ruth swore to Naomi, your people shall be my people."

Edward smiled.

"I must say, though, his absence has helped greatly with the topic I wanted to discuss tonight," Warwick said.

Edward was vaguely frustrated that he could not imagine what that would be. "Oh?"

Warwick clapped his hands on his knees. "France." He stood and walked over to the fireplace, grabbed a poker and stabbed at the logs. Embers flew and a wave of warmth rippled through the room. He strode back to his chair. "Our friendship with them has flourished now that the Protector no longer sours it by favoring Spain. That has opened the possibility they might ask to ransom Boulogne from us. What do you think about that?"

Warwick had been seeking Edward's reaction early and often. At first it had frightened Edward to be put on the spot. But now Edward appreciated it for the practice it gave him. It propelled him into the middle of the conversation and led to understandings harder to reach on his own.

"I would think it a sad thing to lose a city my father conquered so gloriously."

"Exactly!" Warwick's smile was wide. "That reluctance is natural, and will guarantee a fair price. That should be your public stance always." Warwick glanced at the door, as if to make sure they were alone. "Now what are your private thoughts?"

Apparently, he expected Edward to be amenable to the idea, but Edward did not understand why. Instead of answering, he used his favorite new trick: turning things around. "I would want to know why they want this, and what it is worth to them. Also why we would prefer the money to the city."

"Your Majesty has developed a keen wit for politics. Those were precisely the questions to ask in this situation."

Edward sat up straighter in his chair.

Warwick placed Edward's quill in the center of the desk. "This is the English coast." He set the inkwell in front of it, then removed the stopper and placed it a few inches to the left. "This is Calais," he said, pointing to the inkwell. "And this is Boulogne," pointing to the stopper. "Calais has been in English hands for two hundred years; she is a thriving city, and her villagers are English to the bone. Boulogne has been ours for less than ten years. She is much smaller now that she is no longer an important French port, and her people are still French. The only Englishmen there are the soldiers we pay."

The scene before him seemed clear. Boulogne was an afterthought, unnecessary. And yet it had been so important at one time. "Why did my father spend so much energy to take it?"

"It was supposed to be the first step to taking Paris. But Charles V signed a treaty that left England in the cold."

"He has always been perfidious," Edward said. "And he is rude to me now, in threatening England over my sister's Mass. I know we need a friend. I know—"

"That is another reason to accommodate the French." Warwick finished his interruption with eyes intensely wide. "Think about it. Step by step, as is your strength."

Edward took a deep breath. "You think the French might be a friend? How could we trust them after they stole Scotland from us?"

"We precipitated the theft. The former Lord Protector did not endear himself to the Scottish lords or their people."

England's military incursions had indeed destroyed her relationship with Scotland. But still Edward shook his head. It was hard to think of France as an ally, even though it would solve so many problems.

"Nor did Somerset endear himself to the French," Warwick continued. "The Duke always prioritized our alliance with Spain. But a friendship with the Emperor should not prevent a friendship with France. Indeed, since they are enemies, they each need us. But because of bad politics we have not taken advantage of this position – and so the Emperor thinks he can dictate policy to us."

It was the right move. Edward knew it. "I agree."

"I'm not asking you to decide now," Warwick said. "I mean only to present the possibilities so you may choose wisely when the time comes. I am glad you are prepared to do so."

Edward nodded. "Then what happens tomorrow?"

"I will inform you and the Council of the rumors I have heard about the ransoming of Boulogne. Arundel will respond first with scorn – the religious traditionalists are all pro-Spain. That would be a good place for you to agree with him, to express doubt they will value it highly enough."

"But won't that end a discussion we want to open?"

"Just the opposite. Your agreement will disarm his suspicion and give me the opening to quantify the enormous expense of maintaining that city. The number is sure to give men pause and move them to consider the opportunity before us."

Edward weighed the information. "But you do not mean for that to happen tomorrow, do you?"

Warwick smiled. "Ah, Sire, your natural instincts are a joy to see. No, indeed, such a major change must happen slowly. Think of it as the seduction of a virtuous young woman: if you come at her too quickly, she will shy away. Every step must be but a small increment from the last."

"What will be the next increment, then?"

Warwick scratched his beard, as he often did when deep in thought. "You are right we could set that up tomorrow. Once I finish my arguments, you can pretend to interrupt me, you can call me to heel. You should insist that none of this be agreed while France is still our enemy. You can even mock me – yes, you *should* mock me – and tell me to first come to you with a treaty. That will free me to pursue our goal."

Edward nodded, reviewing the steps in his mind. "Wait – how will I know you have finished your arguments? I don't want to begin too soon."

Warwick pursed his lips. "Perhaps I could run my fingers through my hair."

"Scratch your beard," Edward said. "It won't seem out of place."

"Thank you, Sire," Warwick said. "Do we have our plan?"

"We do indeed."

"Then I will bid you a good night," Warwick said. "And thank you again for the great honor you do me, in allowing me to counsel you and in advancing me as you have done."

Edward nodded. "As I said earlier, it is nothing more than you deserve."

Another bow, and Warwick was gone. The room felt empty.

Sweet fatigue enveloped Edward. He would return to his bedchamber now, with such good work accomplished. Tomorrow he would look regal in front of his Councilors, adding to their growing respect for him.

Somerset had meant well, but he was never this skillful.

Henry VIII had chosen loyalty over ability when he chose Somerset to be Lord Protector. Assuming he had – some of the Councilors claimed this was a false claim by Somerset to seize power. Edward didn't quite believe it, though it didn't matter: Somerset's rule was ended now.

Edward's had begun.

April 9, 1550

Edward breathed deeply, glorying in the faint whiff of the hyacinth blooms peeking through the heavy odor of moist earth.

"Take heed and beware of covetousness," intoned Hugh Latimer from the lectern.

Latimer had earned his role as outstanding reformist by being one of the most inspiring speakers in the land. Today he was preaching the day's sermon in the new open-air pulpit in Whitehall's enormous Privy Garden. Edward's three-hundred-foot-long Privy Gallery formed one of the walls of the enclosed space, and tall brick walls supplied the others. Flowery beds and statuary lined the perimeter and the inner aisles, reminding congregants of God's glory; the giant sundial in the center aisle reminded them of His permanence. Edward surveyed the crowd, exulting that this venue offered such a holy opportunity for so many.

The garden had long been used for sermons during Lent: there had always been more men who wanted to share the King's service than could fit in the Chapel Royal. Edward had decided to extend the practice through the summer, to allow more of his people to hear the Gospel preached by the most learned men in the world.

Some in his Council – the traditionalists – had been skeptical when he first proposed the change: they worried about the animal baiting and wrestling matches held there during the week. But Warwick had expected this objection, so Edward was prepared when Arundel raised the issue.

"It would be too disheartening when the space was not filled every Sunday," Arundel had sniffed, his nose in the air. "And it would anger your people that their pastimes were interrupted or curtailed, as must surely happen if the garden must be reconfigured each week."

"Why, rearranging the seating is a particular skill of my royal servants," Edward calmly remarked. "They do it for jousts and tournaments, and this is not such a different task."

"Yes, but…well—" Arundel sputtered.

Edward cut him off with an airy wave. "Surely they will happily help me fulfill my role not only as England's king but as the head of its Church." Then as his lords started to nod, Edward leaned in for the kill. "I consider this an imperative, my Lords, as I am sure you must, too."

Cranmer had pounded on the table. "Hear, hear." The others had followed with a round of applause and approval that still made Edward smile, even now. Especially now.

Next to him, Somerset shifted in his seat to sit even taller. Another reason to exult.

Thanks to Edward's influence, Somerset had been released from the Tower. Again an example of Edward's will starting to guide his Council and his country.

Latimer's raised index finger jolted Edward back to the scene, and he reined in his inattention.

"And here I would say a thing to Your Majesty: for God's love, beware where you marry; choose your wife in a faithful stock. Beware of worldly policy; marry in God, not for the great respect of alliance. For thereof cometh all these evils of breaking of wedlock, which is among princes and noblemen. For the love of God, take an order for marriages here in England. For here is marriage for pleasure and voluptuousness, and for goods so they may join land to land, and possessions to possessions; they care for no more here in England. And that is the cause of so much adultery, and of so much breach of wedlock in the noblemen and gentlemen, and so much divorcing."

Edward looked down, wondering who, exactly, Latimer was

referring to. Was this just general advice? Had he heard that Edward was looking to France for a potential bride? Or was he referring to the way Warwick and Somerset had cemented their renewed friendship by betrothing their children?

Somerset leaned over. "My Anne will be a good wife to John Dudley," he whispered.

Obviously his thoughts were running along the same lines.

"I thank you for turning Warwick's heart," Somerset continued. "In that matter and in all others. I take it you are the one who suggested I might be returned to Council?"

Edward nodded. It had indeed been his idea, though this was not the time to discuss it.

"I had not hoped so high, and I do promise—"

"Shh," Edward interrupted. "This is holy time."

Somerset laughed.

"Ah, Sire, I apologize. Your father loved to discuss important matters during the Mass, and such a habit is hard to break."

Edward's first reaction was indignation on his father's behalf, but he had heard this fact from others. Still, that was the Mass; some self-righteousness was permitted Edward now. "Never during the sermons," he said. "And not when he sat among his subjects."

Somerset sat back, properly chastened, and focused on the Lord. Edward allowed himself to exult yet again over how far he had come in three years. From a tiny boy terrified to misstep, to a confident young ruler ready to prove he could handle all the responsibility they gave him.

His moving the sermons to the Privy Garden was the perfect example. This gesture represented an important arrow in his quiver to expand religious reforms. What better way to spread the Word than to inspire people through powerful sermons? And with the French and Spanish Ambassadors attending on occasion, it might even lead to better worship throughout the world. How better to do God's will?

At the pulpit, Latimer banged his fist on the lectern. "Sin

must be rebuked; sin must be plainly spoken against. Was this a time well chosen and discreetly taken of Jonah, to come and reprove Nineveh of their sin; to declare unto them the threatenings of God; and to say plainly unto them, that unless they repented and amended their evil living, they and their city should be destroyed of God's hand within forty days?"

The message punched Edward in the stomach with its import. Edward was failing in his duty to rebuke sin. Mary still practiced idolatry and superstition, and her example encouraged his people to turn from God's will. Edward needed to utterly reject his Council's argument that this was not a "time well chosen" to rebuke Mary. He needed to step in. Firmly. Immediately. Warwick would help him.

The scent of the hyacinths wafted over him again. It was a sign. Edward looked at the sky and thanked the Lord for the blessing of such clear instructions.

May 28, 1550

The darkly paneled walls of the library at Hunsdon House were more somber than usual; even the white ceiling registered a sad gray. Mary stood as her dearest friend and best ally entered the room with the newly appointed Spanish Ambassador who would replace him. Her ladies leaped to copy her, their sewing hoops still in their hands.

The tears filling Mary's nearsighted eyes made it even harder to see the new man's face, but there would be time enough for that when he drew closer. "I am so glad you came to see me," she said, her voice creaking through her tight throat.

François van der Delft clasped his hands together as if in prayer. "I would never leave England without paying my respects. Or without seeing for myself that you were in good hands."

The two turned to Jean Scheyfve, Seigneur de Rode-Saint-Agathe. He was a tall man, about Mary's own age, with kind eyes and a Gallic nose that dominated his face and overshadowed a gentle smile. The lace ruffs at his neck and wrists were small, and his shirt was not pulled through the slashing in his doublet, a restraint that suggested earnestness. Mary felt immediately comfortable with him, even as she wished she didn't have to.

"Welcome," she simply said to him.

Scheyfve knelt and kissed her hand. "I promise to further your cause with all the fervor you have come to expect. You deserve no less, Your Highness."

His accent puzzled Mary and she squinted in spite of herself. "You are French?"

He laughed as he stood, shaking his head. "Thankfully, no. I grew up right outside Brussels."

"But the sound of his voice will stand him in good stead at court, where Warwick kisses the feet of the French bastards," van der Delft said.

Mary wondered idly whether resentment over Warwick's rise had something to do with van der Delft's decision to retire, or whether it was truly all about age as he claimed.

"And the fact that I was raised so far north will help me appreciate the beautiful English gardens, God's reward for harsh winters," Scheyfve said. "My colleague has sung the praises of the ones you have here. Perhaps we could take a stroll now?"

Mary smiled. This new man's youth did not make him naïve: a garden walk was the ultimate trick to avoid spies. Indoors, every word could be overheard by a person truly intent on the practice.

"I would be proud to do so. I only hope they do not disappoint."

At her words, her ladies started to fold the large cloth they were working on, so they could join in. Van der Delft shot Mary a look, though she did not need the warning.

"Ladies, I will pray you to remain here and continue with your sewing. I have mentioned this altar cloth to Bishop

Gardiner, and he is anxious to use it." Not the most skillful excuse, but on short notice it would have to do.

They walked past the walled garden to the knot garden, where the plants were low enough that no one could sneak up and overhear their conversation. Its beauty momentarily caused Mary to forget the danger that had brought them out there. The irises were past their prime, but that only intensified the utter abandon with which they grew. Enough that the just-unfurling roses were imbued with even more charm as the three allies walked through.

Mary waited for van der Delft or Scheyfve to broach the topic that had brought them there. She had learned long ago never to hasten to bad news. She did not have long to wait.

"The Council is determined to impose its will on England," Scheyfve said. "They are insisting *The Book· of the Common Prayer* be the sole basis for religious worship throughout the land and are threatening dire punishments to those who do not comply."

Mary shot a look at van der Delft, but his face was impassive. "May the Lord have mercy to those forced to submit. Have you read that drivel?" Mary sniffed. "My household continues to hear the Mass as it was intended to be heard."

"You should be more discreet, Your Highness," Scheyfve said. "To give them less cause to meddle with you."

Her throat clenched. Her new representative needed to show more courage, or she would be lost among the wolves at court. "I am the King's sister and the Emperor's cousin. They have promised to leave me be."

"The Duke of Somerset promised to leave you be. The Earl of Warwick claims to know nothing of this."

Mary bit back angry words and turned to van der Delft for assistance. "Surely you can intercede to place things on the right track before you leave."

Van der Delft rubbed the back of his neck. "I will certainly try, Your Highness, but I cannot be sure of success."

The reality of her situation dawned on Mary like fire lit under a martyr's feet. "Surely the King must allow me to worship as our father did."

"Unfortunately, he says that, as his sister, you are a prime example to the people," Scheyfve said. "He is more insistent about your conformity than anyone else's."

"But the King is a child," she cried, her voice sharper than she intended. "He cannot make such an important decision yet; he must wait until he is of age. They agreed to that."

"Again, Your Highness, Somerset agreed, not Warwick," Scheyfve said.

Van der Delft crossed his arms in front of him and lowered his eyes with a heavy sigh.

Foreboding weighted her shoulders, and Mary locked eyes with Scheyfve. "So what am I to do?"

Scheyfve bit his lip and looked down.

Van der Delft stepped forward, a wild look in his eyes. "Escape."

Escape? Mary stopped in her tracks and looked around to confirm once again that there was no one near them who could have heard those remarks. "How?"

"The Emperor will help you," van der Delft continued. "I saw which way the wind was blowing, and I secured his agreement to send a ship to take you to Spain. You will be safe there, lodged at a court that will be happy to welcome you."

Mary's heart burst from her and roamed the far-off hills like a falcon flying free. She let it continue for a bit, relishing the promise in the thoughts, then brought her thoughts back to earth.

"This is treason if I am caught."

Van der Delft took her by the shoulders and locked his eyes on her. Mary froze at their intensity and utter sincerity. "You will not be caught."

The idea wrapped around her like a soft blanket. She imagined this was what seduction felt like, and her resistance shielded an invitation. "How do you know? A ship will be seen. One pair of eyes will doom me."

"But thousands will save you." Van der Delft drew back. He smiled and raised an eyebrow. "Scottish pirates have been raiding our ships. I have complained of this, but the Council will not intervene for fear of angering France, and because half of them are English anyway. The Emperor has decided that our fleet shall accompany our trading ships, to be ready to defend them. In that confusion, in that great proliferation, is your opportunity. A trading ship will be able to easily deliver you to our glorious army, right offshore."

She could feel herself melting. Still, she resisted. "They will never let me leave."

Van der Delft whispered like a lover. "They will never know."

Mary's mind filled with visions of all the ways the plan could fail, all the danger she would risk…but the sharp edges of those fears softened from the smoke of the incense that burned in the Church of her heart. Scheyfve was still staring at the ground, lips pressed together. "You do not seem to approve," she said.

He shook his head. "I merely dislike the urgency. I don't see them refusing you the Mass without Parliament's consent, which won't be until Michaelmas at the earliest."

"Which is only four months away," van der Delft said.

"Ah, but there is also talk of Somerset regaining influence. He may be able to turn things around."

Van der Delft put a hand on Scheyfve's shoulder. "This stems from the King. I am not suggesting we rush things, but we must begin the process." He turned to Mary and took another step forward, edging Scheyfve out. "You should move your household to Framlingham – it is closer to the sea. Unless you've only just arrived? I would not want to arouse suspicion."

"We have been here two months already."

"That should be enough," van der Delft said. "The court moved more frequently than that in your father's day."

Mary shook her head. The royal court moved locations because of the burden it placed on the surrounding countryside; but here, most of Mary's household needs were supplied by her own gardens and lands. "There has been some contagion reported in the village. It would be easy to blame that," she said.

Van der Delft nodded. "Better. Also, I will need to communicate with a member of your household. Is there someone you trust?"

"I trust them all. None of them has accepted this new *Common Prayer* abomination."

"That is actually dangerous," Scheyfve said. "Those of your servants who refused will be targeted. Still, a maid or a groom would be a better choice than an officer."

The advice was sound. "Eleanor Kempe," Mary said. "Or my Comptroller, Robert Rochester, if you need a man. But why is it less dangerous to speak to them than to me?"

Scheyfve raked a hand through his hair. "I cannot believe you have ensnared me in this plot," he said to van der Delft.

"She is far better off away from here, and it will be easier sooner than later."

Scheyfve turned to Mary. "I do not intend to speak to them," he said. "That can only be trouble. I want them as a way to get you letters so I don't have to visit. A servant can go to the weekly market and buy fish or spices on a specific corner, without awakening suspicion."

Mary smiled wryly at the young man's initiative. "You will be arranging this escape?"

Scheyfve bowed. "Van der Delft will see to the main arrangements the second he leaves England. I will fulfill his instructions here."

"The plans are not in place?"

"They will be soon," Scheyfve said. "And when they are, I will find a trustworthy merchant to pass on the information."

"This still sounds dangerous. What if the chosen corner is not available?"

"Have your maid introduce herself. That will not be suspicious. Doesn't she always tell people at the market that their products are for you? They will give their own names back – a woman will be named Maria, a man, Felipe."

"Those are common names."

"Corazon, then, for a woman, or Truylo for a man."

They walked in silence for a bit, Mary trying to imagine what her life would be like in the land her mother had loved and revered.

"Shall I be a pensioner all my life, living off the Emperor's charity?" she asked.

"He will marry you to someone he esteems. You will finally have the life you deserve."

Deserve? Mary certainly thought so, but it was hard to say this was the case when she craved it so desperately. For God to deny it, He must have a good reason. Mary just could not think of what that would be.

Mary was thirty-five now, old to marry and have children for the first time. Look at what had happened to Katherine Parr, dead from childbed fever at age thirty-six. Though she had been happy for a time, thanks to eyes that were blind to her husband's faults.

Mary should be so lucky.

June 3, 1550

Edward looked around at the banqueting house whose wavy walls revealed it was built from longbows. The ephemeral space was a magical place, built for this particular occasion. Edward loved the practice, popularized by his father, a reminder to seize pleasure before it passed.

The guests around him wore happy faces, and Edward knew his own expression must show equal or greater bliss. Every day should be as wonderful as this, with masques and banquets and tilting. Though of course, he corrected himself, that would leave no way to celebrate truly special days. Which is what this was: his cousin Anne, Somerset's eldest daughter, was marrying Warwick's son and heir.

Men on horses, with red or green ribbons decorating their jousting armor, emerged at the far end of the field, elaborate plumes dancing atop their helmets. Just then, Robin Dudley, somehow not in armor, appeared before Edward wearing a wide smile. Robin knelt immediately, proffering a heavily embroidered handkerchief. "I have been sent to make sure you have this, so you can open the games."

Edward smiled. "I have the handkerchief you gave me this morning. Why another one?"

Robin laughed. "You might have used it since then, Sire. And this way you will not be without one."

Edward's grin widened. "Thank you."

The contestants lined up into two rows of six gentlemen each and rode up the field toward the chambers. Ned Seymour led the red-ribboned riders, Henry Sidney the green.

"They're starting," Robin said, lifting his chin. "I am told they will run courses first, then fight at tourney."

Edward bit back his deep desire to participate. He was not quite ready, what with less than a year of preparation. Tilting at the ring alone took mastery of so many things at once. You needed to drive a long lance into a small circle just slightly larger than its point. You had to hold the shaft high, which tired your arm. Then if your aim was not dead-on, or if your angle was off even the slightest, you would send the ring flying. Tilting was hard enough to do just standing in front of the ring, let alone riding at it full tilt down a long field.

And then once you got good at that, they sent you at an actual opponent. Turn your lance on another man, not to hit him but to hit his buckle. This was far more dangerous than the ring, sometimes deadly. If you did it right, you'd shatter your lance and win. If you did it wrong, you could get unhorsed, and some men died. Edward's father had stopped jousting after a fall left him unconscious for two hours. Edward was glad in his heart they forbade him from this one.

But Robin was a different story. Robin was a third son, given much more freedom than an heir. He'd become a horseman early and now, at eighteen, had the kind of easy nonchalance Edward kept trying to emulate. Just as he emulated Cheke's academics, Warwick's political astuteness, Cranmer's religious lore, and so on. It was like an apprenticeship.

"Why are you not with them?" Edward asked.

Robin rolled his eyes. "At the last, Amy's father asked me to sit out today's exertions, for fear I would injure myself before I could speak my vows tomorrow. I think he worries I will change my mind."

The Dudley family was celebrating another wedding the following day, a much quieter affair. Unlike his eldest brother, Robin was marrying for love. Well, mostly. His bride's family was well landed, and she was their heir. But Robin was fore-going political advantage, and Warwick was letting him. It showed Edward that Warwick was not a striver, not swayed by status.

Edward gave his friend a big smile. "I would ask you if I were in his place. I think any father would."

"You do me great honor," Robin said. "Thank you."

Edward shrugged off the thanks. His peers needed to show such submission, but he didn't need to dwell on it. "Two weddings right after the other...your family is blessed. Where is your father, that I may congratulate him?"

The look on Dudley's face changed. His eyes shifted from side to side. "He is not here, Sire."

Robin's eyes inspired even more fear in Edward than his words. Warwick had been sick, but it must be serious for him to have missed his eldest son's wedding. "Not here? Is he in danger?"

"He has no fear of assassins," Robin hastened to reassure.

Warwick was afraid of assassins? Yes, weddings were the

classic choice for an element of surprise, but who would want him dead? Only Somerset came to mind. Edward had heard that the peace between the two men, including the wedding, had been brokered between their wives, not themselves…still, that could not be. This must be a joke. "Ha! No, I was referring to his health."

Robin flushed. "Of course. He is improving. He just did not want to risk the health of Your Majesty or the people around you."

Thankfully Seymour and Sidney rode up then, and stymied further conversation. Their followers fanned out around them to form a half circle before Edward, then they all raised their swords to yell "God save the King."

The full gathering echoed their shouts, and Edward stood to acknowledge the tribute. "Thank you, my good men," he said to the riders. And, as Warwick had taught him, he lifted his glass and waved it in a circle before him. "And thank you as well, my good men and ladies," he said to the other guests. "May we all display in our lives the valor these men are about to display on the field." After the applause died down, he turned back to the contestants. "May the best man win," he said and dropped the handkerchief.

When the first edge hit the floor, the riders scattered, racing back to their starting points. The contest had begun.

"With your leave, Sire, I will see if I can be of service on the field," Robin said.

"Of course," Edward said, not taking his eyes from the action. He wanted to experience all the details of how they conducted themselves, athletically and socially. This was the kind of information no one would ever know to tell him.

Out of the corner of his eye, Edward noticed a young page race out to retrieve the handkerchief and scuttle back. It was the first time he had ever considered that part of the ritual.

"Thank you again, Sire," said a voice behind him. Somerset.

"It is I who thank you," Edward said. "Congratulations."

"My daughter tells me you gave her a beautiful ring as a present. I know she thanked you herself, but I want to add my own voice to the honor you show us. Allowing us to hold the wedding here and gracing us with your presence was already generous."

The Palace of Richmond was a royal residence, much more suited to such a celebration than Somerset's Syon House. Of course, once Somerset Place was finished it would dwarf Richmond. But Edward put his resentment aside. "She is my beloved cousin. How could I do any less?"

Somerset closed his eyes and bowed his head, hand on his heart. "She will treasure it forever."

Anyone would treasure a ring worth at least forty pounds sterling, but Edward's real goal with the present was to reassure Somerset, who still felt diminished by the loss of his former position. Though given Robin's reaction from just before, perhaps it was not Somerset who needed the reassurance. Warwick afraid of assassins? Edward did not know what to think about that.

Nor did Edward know what he would do with this information, but he was glad to have it. That's what mattered.

Discernment.

That would be his goal from now on.

July 2, 1550

Seeing Eleanor enter the library with a quick step and a sharp look in her eyes, Mary knew something was afoot. She had to force herself to avoid glancing at her ladies to see if they'd noticed.

"Look," Eleanor said, showing a pomegranate from her basket. "I was able to buy five of these from Corazon at the market just now."

Corazon. Mary could barely breathe at the name, but she

forced herself to act normal. "Pomegranates! We shall feast tonight."

"We should make a special *salcero* with them, like your mother used to love," Eleanor said.

Mary found herself transported in spite of herself. "Do we have partridges, perchance?"

Eleanor nodded. "Mabel, will you take charge of things in the kitchen? Bring the others." When Mabel hesitated, Eleanor continued. "If not partridges, hens would be ideal, but chickens will do. The Princess and I are going in search of herbs."

Mabel opened her mouth and Mary worried she would try to object, but all Mabel said was, "Please make sure to gather some mint for sweetmeats. No feast would be complete without treats. Come, ladies."

The women filed out, leaving Mary and Eleanor alone in the room.

"What happened?" Mary asked, but Eleanor shook her head and grabbed her by the hand. The two quickly made their way to the kitchen garden, where Robert Rochester was waiting for them. Eleanor made a big show of bending over and picking mint leaves. "It is tonight," she said with a quiet hiss. "They want you to leave tonight."

"There will be a ship ready to whisk you off," Rochester said, fingering one of the leaves. "It will be there at two in the morning, when the tide is favorable."

Mary picked at a cuticle, ignoring the sting that meant she had drawn blood. The plans had come to fruition. It felt eerie, wrong. Pain gripped her stomach, though in truth it had not left since this adventure had been suggested. "How could I be ready this quickly?"

"Easily," Rochester said. "You have a chance to strike, and you take it. The boat will carry you to safety. Forever."

Mary shook her head. "It is too quick. How will I pack all my things? I had thought to use long hopsacks, so they won't look as if they contain anything heavy, but I don't have enough right now."

Rochester shifted, and Mary could tell he was trying not to stamp his foot. "At two of the morning, it does not matter what the sacks look like. But more importantly, there is little need for you to pack. Leave it all. Once you cross the water, you will lack for nothing."

Rebellion rose in Mary's throat. She could not bear the idea of her treasures being lost to her forever.

"Once you cross the water," Eleanor repeated, emphasizing the words. "It is the attempt that is perilous. There is a watch posted every night at all of the passages. It will be impossible for us to bring you to the water side without running grave risks."

"A watch? Here?" Mary's stomach turned over. "Have we been betrayed?"

"Corazon could not swear there were no rumors of your plans," Eleanor said.

Rochester gave a dismissive wave. "No one can prove a negative. The watch is focused on the Spanish fleet, not small merchant ships delivering their goods."

Despite this tiny reassurance, Mary recoiled. Her lips pressed tightly together and she started to walk along the path, pulling herbs here and there with enough force to take their roots with them. Eleanor followed behind her, also picking choice plants. Rochester walked beside with the basket.

"Is it wrong for me to think of leaving?" It was the first time Mary had so doubted her success. Even she could hear the plaintive note in her voice, as if begging them to stop her. "I am the rare voice speaking for God. The people in the North are rising again. How can I leave those good Christians? In my absence, they may become lost sheep, and even follow these new opinions. Thus might I incur God's censure, which would be a heavy grief to me." She turned to face them.

Rochester shook his head. "They rebel more for their purses than their souls. They resent the enclosures and the currency and the famine. Yes, they want to hear Mass each day, but they want to know they will fill their bellies when it's done. You can leave them without guilt."

"What about my household? How can I abandon them?"

Rochester sniffed. "Not all of your household are as loyal as you think. Many harbor suspicions as to your plans. What if they betrayed you to the Council?"

Mary glanced around her to check again they were safe from prying ears.

"If she does not act, there is nothing to betray," Eleanor said to him. She turned to Mary. "They set watches for a reason. It is too much a risk to leave right now. Let them get bored of watching the ships and waiting for something to happen."

Hot tears stung Mary's eyes. "I feel like an ignorant girl. I care neither for my goods nor for the world, but only for God's service and my conscience. There is peril in going and peril in staying. I must choose the lesser of two evils, but I don't know which one that is."

"Given what the Spanish Ambassadors have consistently reported, and what you have seen yourself, you must accept that the Council will eventually forbid you the Mass." Robert's voice was firm. "You must go."

"And yet she is still as free to live as she likes as she has ever been. Her situation may never change if Somerset regains influence. She need not go tonight."

"When, then?" Rochester asked, exasperation obvious in his raised voice. "How long would you have her wait?"

"Van der Delft said we have until at least September," Eleanor said. "That would give us time to see if they get bored and stop the watches."

"I am just so uncertain," Mary said. "And worried I will offend the Emperor if I turn down the chance to leave now, after I have so often importuned His Majesty on the subject."

"If you are satisfied then the Emperor will also be content. He wants only to see you happy and safe."

Mary drew a deep breath. "This is so hard."

Rochester swallowed. "I know, my Lady. I want you safely away and settled, but I do understand the desire to delay. You must decide."

"Thank you," Mary said. She looked at the basket in Rochester's hands. "You two take the herbs to the kitchen. I will pray on the matter."

She watched them retreat after their uncertain reverences, then turned her face to the sun. Its rays heated her cheeks and also her body, almost uncomfortably so. It would be this hot – hotter actually – in Spain.

Such a strange thought, that she might leave this land of her birth. Never to see it again. Never to rule.

Mary would lose all hope of the succession if she left. If anything happened to Edward, Elizabeth would reign, another Protestant. Even if nothing happened to him, how could Mary abandon her post as the one Catholic voice near her brother? Surely God would want her to stay where He had placed her, like Moses, to speak to the existing power structure. Assuming, of course, He had not made her as Noah, who saved humanity by saving himself and his family.

It was so hard to discern God's true purpose, especially when her reluctance sprang mainly from fear and not from the single-minded pursuit of His will. Would she be punished for that? She did not know.

What she did know was she could not face the prospect of leaving tonight. That was too soon. Eleanor spoke true: Mary had time before her situation became impossible. And it was possible God would see it never would.

She walked slowly back to the house, marveling at its appearance. It was more than just the reddish hues of sunset, it was the tinge of destiny shining around it. She was meant to stay here for now, meant to weather whatever storm the Lord might send to buffet her. As her mother before her had dug in to accept her lot in life. Mary's lot was in England. She was sure of it.

She would stay. At least for now.

Rochester was at the door as soon as she walked in, trying to look patient but with curiosity painted all over his face.

"I cannot leave tonight," she said softly. "Will you let them know this, on my behalf?"

Rochester nodded and walked away. As she gazed after him, her eyes fell on the portrait of her sainted mother hanging in its place on the wall. Mary could never leave that behind.

She must have made the right choice.

October 18, 1550

The shadows from the *torchère* next to his desk danced on the walls as Edward shifted in his chair and pulled the blanket around his shoulders against the nighttime chill. It was like this every year: after celebrating his birthday in the brisk autumn air, winter would descend within a few days and chase away frivolity.

The thought of his birthday changed things. He straightened his back, determined to be impervious to the cold. To welcome the chill. Now he was thirteen, he should be stronger. Force of will was all it would take.

He slumped again. He could also order a better fire in his Withdrawing Chamber at night. There was no reason why it should not be at least as warm in here as in his bedchamber. There was no shame in that; he just needed to assert himself. He straightened again.

He looked down at his Chronicle, open before him. He had written the date and nothing more. He thought a moment, trying to decide what deserved most to be recorded. He stared up at a dark corner of the ceiling, brushing the plume of the quill back and forth across his chin. A thought squeezed through and he leaned forward to capture the sentence.

Prices were set by proclamation for all kinds of grain, butter, cheese, and poultry.

Edward was about to elaborate about changes to the currency, but his ears picked up the muffled sound of velvet-slippered feet approaching the private door. The sound was reassuring, not terrifying, and Edward thanked God for the wonderful changes He had wrought in the land. He shut his Chronicle and pushed it away.

Warwick opened the door and bowed. When he held the pose for longer than usual, Edward knew something was wrong.

"Is it bad news?"

Warwick rose and sighed. "Ah, Sire, your powers of observation are wonderfully keen." He slowly approached the desk, a pout on his lips, then lowered himself into his chair, again slowly. He sighed. "I am sorry to tell you this, but your grandmother has remitted her soul to God."

Edward heard the words but felt nothing. He didn't really know the woman: age and frailty had kept her from court, so she had never been a part of his life. He couldn't remember the last time he had seen her. "I am sorry for it."

"I am sorry for you, Sire," Warwick said. "Especially since the Duke, your uncle, is being difficult."

"Difficult?"

"He seems to think this is an occasion that merits a state funeral and court mourning. Can you believe it?"

Actually, Edward could. It was his grandmother, after all. Surely this occasion should be marked. But before he could express himself, Warwick slapped his hand on the desk.

"He expects an extravagant, papist demonstration," Warwick said with a sneer. "So inappropriate."

That was a point that had not occurred to Edward. Yet surely those obstacles could be overcome. "I am sure Cranmer could conduct a proper ceremony. And perhaps the expense could be minimized by limiting the guests?"

Warwick shook his head. "There are ways to get around the principal difficulties, but this is a private matter. Private men should reserve their private sorrow to their own houses, and not diminish the presence of their prince with doleful token."

Edward considered the advice. That didn't seem wholly right. "She is the last living matriarch of my family. An official display of grief would not be uncalled for."

"The woman was never a part of court life." There was spittle at the corners of Warwick's mouth. "She lived quietly in the country. And she was your grandmother, not your mother. It is entirely different."

Edward looked down, unsure what to say. It felt wrong somehow not to mark the passing of this life. "But it would mean so much to my uncle."

Warwick's face darkened like an approaching storm. The sight sent a chill down Edward's spine.

"Has he spoken to you about this?" Warwick asked, his bulging eyes taking on a red glow.

Even Somerset's worst rages had not felt this ominous. For the first time in a long time, Edward felt vulnerable and alone. He was once again a child, powerless to control the smallest details of his life.

"N-n-no," Edward stammered. "You brought me the first news of it. Remember?"

"It would be completely inappropriate for him to sue directly to you," Warwick snarled. "He does not deserve this honor. He is no longer Lord Protector, no longer free to try to impose his will."

It occurred to Edward that the only person trying to impose his will right now was Warwick, but he kept that observation to himself. "He – he has not done any such thing."

"It is time he understands his place. This will make it clear."

Edward nodded. The rest of him remained frozen.

"And if he comes to you," Warwick continued, "you should tell him not even to wear *deuil* himself; it would be unseemly." Warwick raked a hand through his hair and sighed like a dog shaking off a fit. "Remind him such frippery would serve as pomp rather than edification and merely distress you."

Edward's icy fear began to thaw, leaving room for anger to seep in. Warwick was not any better than Somerset – he was equally Edward's master, just better at hiding the leash. "I don't think he will come to me, but if he does, I will do as you command."

Warwick must have heard the sarcasm in his voice because he winced and shook his head forcefully. "Nay, nay, Sire. I did not mean to command. I was merely angry over Somerset's ill-use of his power. This was advice, my own and that of your Council. I was wrong to deliver it as I did."

The apology was sincere and tugged at Edward's heart. In all, Warwick had been much more respectful than Somerset; that had to mean something. "Thank you for the apology."

"Of course, Your Majesty. I shall leave you now." Warwick stood and took a step toward the door, then turned back and threw himself to his knees. "Thank you for understanding this old soldier. I wish only to make things perfect for you."

Edward reached an affectionate hand to Warwick's shoulder. "I know. Thank you."

Warwick smiled weakly and rose. This time he left.

After the door closed, Edward pulled his Chronicle back and opened it. He could remember his grandmother on his own. He dipped his quill in the ink and held it over the paper. His fingers trembled and the words didn't come. He put the pen down, shut the book, and pulled the blanket around his shoulders again.

December 22, 1550

Once again, Edward gloated to himself over having successfully insisted the court repair to Greenwich Palace for the Christmas festivities. He knew his Councilors preferred the convenience of London – he had seen them try to avoid rolling their eyes – but there was something special and holy about being able to hunt and hawk for hours each day in the vast countryside.

And it wasn't as if Edward's request was unheard-of. Somerset had always said Greenwich was Henry VIII's favorite palace in his youth, that it was only in later years Henry had come to prefer Hampton Court. Admittedly, Hampton had an amazing bath, a miraculous contraption with actual faucets, one for hot water and one for cold. But the bath in Greenwich was equally warm, it just meant more work for the servants and they didn't mind.

From his chair of estate atop its dais, Edward looked out over the Great Hall. He had grown tall enough that even seated he could survey the crowd, the thousand courtiers gathered in small glittering circles, like raindrops on a window that merged into or split off from each other.

Elizabeth was with him, her chair a special height just below his, a mark of how close they had become. His sweet sister had been given place of honor despite her inferiority, a signal to the world that good living was rewarded. He smiled down at her, and caught her own happy response before he turned back to stare through the crowds to watch the door.

They were waiting for Mary, who had agreed to celebrate Christmas at court this year. She had tried to refuse again, but his Council had insisted. The entire country believed she had been spirited away to Spain, and they needed to dispel that belief. Despite the emphatic denials from the Spanish Ambassador, Edward knew in his bones that such persistent rumors could not have been total inventions.

Warwick entered from the side door and approached quickly, ignoring everyone but Edward. He bowed before the throne then leaned in to avoid being overheard. "The Lady Mary is proceeding from her apartments and will be here soon to bow to you."

Elizabeth looked at Warwick, a patient smile on her face.

"Greetings, my Lady," Warwick said, unabashed. "I trust you are well?"

"Wonderful, thank you. How could I be anything but? I am by the side of my dearest brother."

"If there is anything you require, anything at all, you have only to ask and I will see to it," Warwick said.

Somerset slipped into the room by the same side door and joined the group on the dais. He gave a deep bow to Edward, a quick bow to Elizabeth, and a nod of his head to Warwick. "The Lady Mary approaches," he said.

"Thank you," Edward said.

"The Spanish Ambassador is not with her, but I would still counsel you not to rebuke her."

Edward's fists balled.

"The Spanish Ambassador was not invited," Warwick said laconically.

Somerset's eyes widened and he looked back to survey the room. His eyes stopped at the French Ambassador, who bowed to him with a smile that lifted only one side of his mouth. Elizabeth looked down at her hands, as if fascinated by something in her lap.

Edward felt strange speaking of Mary in front of Elizabeth, though he was about to do worse in front of a large crowd. This autumn they had arrested Mary's almoner for saying Mass before members of her household. After his release he had continued to celebrate the services according to the papist traditions, speaking Latin rather than the King's English and sanctifying the Host as if it were the true body of Christ. Even a visit by the Lord Chancellor to take him back into custody had not convinced Mary they were serious about her compliance. She had questioned Baron Rich as if she did not understand why such a course had been adopted, adamant that the Council must not have ordered such a thing. She acted as if she had full permission to worship in darkness.

Edward intended to teach her she did not.

"You want me to pretend all is well?" he said. "Would it not be best to first resolve this issue that is destroying our amity?"

Somerset glanced at Warwick, who shook his head. Somerset raised his chin and continued anyway. "A public shaming would be cruel and would provoke Spain needlessly."

"You fear their power far too much," Edward said.

"I do not advise you to stand down, only to treat her well in public. At least until the French alliance is certain."

Warwick's plan for a sweeping alliance with the French, cemented by Edward marrying the French king's daughter Elisabeth, was proving a difficult thing to arrange. With Edward excommunicated, England and France were at a temporary stalemate, trying to avoid the possibility that the Bishop of Rome might require a concession England was not prepared to make.

It still irked Edward that he could not simply marry the Scottish queen and unite the two countries. Warwick was still working mischief there, providing support to the Scottish nobles – good Protestants for the most part, working to counteract the influence of young Mary's mother, a Catholic Regent. The lords might well overthrow their queen and declare for Edward, though admittedly that was unlikely. But Edward could be patient.

"I will try," he said. "But if she raises the matter, my temper may well get away from me."

"That is all I ask, Sire." Somerset bowed. "Reasonable generosity."

Warwick rolled his eyes and Somerset cringed.

Before the discussion could continue, Mary appeared at the door, clad in a rich gown of burgundy velvet. Relief flooded Edward when he saw a purse, not a rosary, hung from her belt.

After a pause that allowed all eyes in the room to focus on her, Mary curtsied deeply. She rose and approached, eyes locked on his. She stopped just before the dais and curtsied again.

"Dear sister," Edward said, surprised how much joy he felt

seeing her face. She had always brought him such comfort. "It does me good to see you."

"And I, you," Mary said. "I am glad to see Your Majesty looking so well, and I thank God for the grace of being together." She crossed herself.

The gesture stirred the anger that was never far from Edward's surface. "Unfortunately, you thank God contrary to the laws of the land. I understand you still hear Mass in your chapel."

Mary drew herself back and all expression disappeared from her face. "I do indeed follow our father's ways, Your Majesty. I have been permitted to do so by your Council."

Out of the corner of his eyes, Edward could see Somerset redden and Warwick shrug. Edward stood to assert himself and signal he would brook no interference. "You were permitted to do so when our laws were first promulgated; now you should do out of love for us what the rest of the country does out of duty." He was proud of his matter-of-fact tone, happy with the threat it conveyed.

"My understanding was that I would be permitted to worship in accordance with my faith for as long as Your Majesty was still a child."

The word *child* landed like a slap. "The Scriptures abound in instances to prove that the best-ordered church of the people of Israel was instituted and upheld by kings younger in years than we."

Her eyes flickered. "You are too young in years as yet to weigh the arguments."

He made his own eyes glower, like their father used to. He wanted to cow her. He was not a child, and this was not a whim. His very bones felt the sanctity of proper observance and shuddered over the insult to the Lord of men setting priests as their conduits to divinity. "In truth, sister, our youth is an advantage, for perhaps the evil has endured in you so long that it is more strongly rooted than we supposed."

228 | JANET WERTMAN

She cringed a little, but held it like a drawn bow.

Good.

"Your Majesty, praise God, is indeed gifted with understanding far beyond that possessed by others at your age." She spread her arms. "But consider that both sides of the question are not brought before you. The people who advise you all think the same way; there is no one but me to argue the other side." She clasped her hands as if in prayer; they trembled violently enough that it looked like she was shaking them at him. "Therefore, I beseech Your Majesty to suspend your judgment on spiritual matters until you reach riper and fuller years. Then with better knowledge and understanding Your Majesty will exercise your freedom to decide according to your pleasure."

She was doing worse than ignoring his power: she was placing herself before him. Disloyalty was treason, whatever form it took. His own uncle had proven that to the world. And suffered the consequences.

He infused his voice with all the icy self-righteousness he could muster. "Truly we do not wish to presume beyond what our age concedes; that is to say, in matters yet doubtful we place no reliance in our own wisdom; but in those things which are plain we believe there is no difference between us and older men. This is plain."

Mary drew herself up. She peered out of the lower left corners of her eyes, as if trying to gauge the crowd behind her. Edward had almost forgotten about the huge group, so focused he was from anger. They were frozen and silent, more like a painting than real people.

"My faith and my religion," she said loudly, "are those held by the whole of Christendom, formerly confessed by this kingdom under the late King, my father, until your Council altered them with new laws."

Edward noticed this time she had said "my father," not "our father." She was no longer appealing to family, she was claiming a right. His breathing quickened and the whole room dimmed.

She bowed her head briefly. "I hope God and nature will so work in Your Majesty that when you reach years of greater understanding, you will not be wroth against me, who live and am your poor suppliant. I pray you consent to no changes in religion until Your Majesty has reached the age to judge for yourself."

"If our father was building a ship and died before it could be finished, would you suggest I leave it until I was grown? How is it different with religion, where he brought us only so far down the path? If I give you leave to follow your conscience, I have to allow others to violate my laws. You ask too much."

Mary's face twisted. "It is just my household. More specifically, me and my Chaplain, who has been taken away from me for questioning. It seems to me not suitable that he should be robbed of freedom by laws and statutes on spiritual matters passed during your minority. No such thing has ever been seen in any Christian kingdom; and God knows whether Your Majesty may not take it amiss in time to come."

Edward's face burned from her intransigence – and her continued insistence on his youth. He needed to stop her from repeating that charge, repeating it before the entire court as if they would agree with her. His voice emerged from his chest more shrill than he expected. "If you intend to govern your faith according to the practices of what you refer to as Christendom, and not according to the Anglican Church of which you are a member, you err on several heads, such as our father would not have permitted to pass."

Her eyes opened wide, but instead of apologizing and backing down, she began to weep.

For a moment, Edward exulted in his victory and the murmurs of the crowd. But the sad wail in her tone tore at his heart. Gone was the rebellious subject; all that was left was the loving sister of his youth. The one who kept away the monsters when he had nightmares, who nursed him patiently when he was sick, who rode out with him to hunt and hawk when he was barely off a pony. Tears mounted in Edward's own eyes.

"Dry your tears, sister," he said with a catch in his throat. "I think no harm of you."

Mary sniffled and wiped her nose with her hand.

"My Lady," Somerset said, "I am sure the King had no other thought except to inquire and know all things."

She smiled ruefully and nodded. "Thank you, dearest uncle. I appreciate the care you take of me and the love you show me."

Edward froze. The political Mary was back.

"Perhaps you would like to retire for a bit, to compose yourself," Somerset said. "You could wait on the King tomorrow, without all this formality."

That had been Somerset's suggestion earlier, Edward remembered. It irked him for some reason, but he let it pass.

Mary looked Edward deep in the eyes. "I would appreciate that greatly."

Edward sniffed. He meant it as annoyance, but her smile told him she took it as weakness.

"Thank you," she said.

She offered a slow, formal curtsy and walked off with her head held high through the silent crowd. Edward stared after her.

"So, nothing has changed," he said quietly when she had disappeared.

"We will continue to discuss this with her," Warwick said. "I am confident she will come to submit, and no further action will be needed."

Somerset shook his head. "She will never submit, like her mother never did. We did offer her – and Spain – assurances we must honor if we will avoid war."

Again, Somerset wanted them to back down. Edward was glad the Duke no longer controlled the Council. His advice on this issue was one of the things that had clouded this entire proceeding.

"The Council offered assurances, not the King," Warwick

said. "And they did so before His Majesty's personal convictions and decision were made known to them. This is the first time His Majesty has directly intervened in this matter, the first time he has made his personal position clear. We will move forward from here."

"But Spain—" Somerset began.

"Is at war with our friend France," Warwick responded. "And less likely to intervene than they have been in the past."

Somerset opened his mouth as if to argue but snapped it shut. His bow was jerky, angry. He disappeared as quickly as he had arrived.

The room was utterly silent. Every face stared at the floor. Everyone but the French Ambassador.

"Ah, Monsieur de Noailles," Warwick called out, as if to reward his courage, "have you greeted the King yet?"

The Ambassador stepped forward, a wide smile on his face.

March 16, 1551

Mary smiled and waved at the hundreds of commoners lining the road along the Strand, calling to her and her formal state procession in an outpouring of love that made her heart sing. Fifty knights and gentlemen in velvet coats and chains of gold preceded her, heralding her arrival with banners and trumpets. Fourscore more gentlemen and ladies followed her. Every one of them wore black rosary beads at their waists.

She was coming to visit her brother at Westminster, summoned to answer his increasing anger over her religious practices. He had hardened his stance since Christmas time, reaching ever higher with arrests of notables who failed to renounce the Mass – all the way up to Stephen Gardiner, the rightful Bishop of Winchester, who had been stripped of his offices and lodged in the Tower. The two sides were now implacable, the battle lines clearly drawn. Mary would not back down; she was on a crusade.

She had chosen a busy route, riding through Fleet Street to garner as much attention as possible. The people thronged the streets, cheering and waving and tossing flowers, and Mary smiled and waved back heartily to encourage them to even louder demonstrations. Surely the cries would be heard through every room in the palace; her brother could not fail to hear them. And unless every curtain was drawn, he would see the solid mass of heads that stretched all around him.

Indeed, by the time she arrived at Westminster, a delegation was waiting for her at the gate. Sir Richard Wingfield, the King's Comptroller of the Household, surrounded by many lords and knights, their long faces pretending to smile as if they were delighted with the situation.

"Greetings, my Lady," Wingfield said, bowing. The crowd cheered and the lords and knights looked like they had smelled something bad.

"I am honored to visit my good brother," Mary announced to even louder applause from the crowd and more intense face twisting from the lords and knights. She turned to face the people; this was for them, after all. "Thank you, my good men and women, for the love you show. To me and to our king."

Shouts of "God save Your Grace" and "God save the King" echoed in equal measure, wrapping Mary in a soft confidence that the country was with her. God, too, though she had never doubted Him.

Wingfield's smile dimmed as they entered the palace and his face could no longer be seen. He guided her to a private gallery where Edward was already ensconced on a chair of estate. As at Christmas, the platform had been raised high enough that she had to look up at him. Back then it had felt like a sweet attempt to overcome his slight frame and the innocence in his eyes; now it felt like a deliberate attempt to intimidate her. And the private audience deprived her of supporters, so she also knew herself to be entirely alone. It gave the room a chill she felt to her bones.

She bowed and commended her soul to God.

"Dearest brother, I am delighted to gaze upon your face."
Edward nodded and muttered some words of greeting before
anger gushed out. "I have long suffered you hearing Mass
against my will. But now I perceive by your letters that there is
no hope of a reconciliation between us, and I cannot bear it."

Mary swallowed her dismay over his quick turn to anger. "I
merely answer the Council in the same tone they use to write
to me."

Edward's eyes narrowed. "I am the one writing to you, not
my Council."

"Your letters are always enclosed with theirs. If you did not
know this, Sire, it tells me I am right to resist, that it was not you
but rather the men around you who drew up the ordinances of the
new religion."

Warwick stepped forward. "Sire, we have on occasion
included our warnings along with your own. So your sister could
have no doubt as to what learned men consider the law of the
land."

Edward's eyes widened and he bit his lip. He looked lost, or
perhaps surprised, to find he'd been used.

Oh Warwick, Mary thought, *you do such harm to my brother
and to England.*

"I do not know what to say," Edward finally said.

Warwick stepped forward and effectively took over the
conversation while the rest of the Council looked sheepishly
down at their hands. "Your letters keep referencing an alleged
promise made to the Emperor that you would be allowed to
continue to practice your religion during the King's minority."

His arrogance made it clear he dominated the Council.
Arundel and Scheyfve believed Somerset was regaining control,
but seeing him here now, Mary knew they were wrong.

She lifted her chin toward Edward Seymour. "My Lord of
Somerset, when he was Lord Protector, assured me this was the
case."

Silently she apologized to Somerset for placing him in this

difficult position. He shrugged as if to signal he understood – or that his word mattered for little; she was not sure which.

Now it was Warwick wrinkling his nose at an imagined odor, like the nobles who had greeted her.

"My Lord of Somerset is no longer Lord Protector, and the King has rejected any compromise that would allow you to hear Mass." He took a sniff of the clove-infused orange he carried with him.

Such a pompous fool, Mary thought.

"Has he?" she said. "Or do you put words in his mouth?"

Warwick waved the orange in the King's direction. "His Majesty is the one to remind us of the grave troubles that might arise if you, his sister and heiress to the Crown, observed the old religion."

Mary forced herself to tear her attention away from Warwick and look around at the other faces. Most were still looking down, afraid to take a side. That was a good sign; it fueled her bravery.

"I do not ask to be allowed public observance, just to follow my conscience in my own home. As I have been permitted to do since my father's reign."

"Your exemption from *this* King's laws was always meant to be limited, and subject to the King's good pleasure."

"I urge you to discuss this with the Spanish Ambassador, as I understand the Emperor shares my recollection rather than yours," Mary replied to Warwick. She turned to her brother. "I have always prayed for your prosperity and the realm's peace," she said, deliberately softer. "But I still believe riper age and experience will teach you more."

Edward's lip trembled like it used to when he was a boy, frustrated over being refused something he could not have. But his eyes were hard and his face as aloof as a hawk's.

"You too might have something to learn," he said. "No one is too old for that."

"You are right." Mary nodded for only a moment before shaking her head. "But given my age – and my inclinations and devotion – it would be very hard to change my religion, in which the King, our father, had bred me and left me at his death."

"The late King changed several points before his death," Warwick said, again inserting himself between them. "And if he had lived longer, he would certainly have drawn up rules like those now in force."

Mary was quite sure her father would not have done anything of the sort. But that fight was not worth her breath. "I cannot dispute that point. All I can do is wish for everything to remain as he left them."

"Things have already changed," Warwick said. "And the late King's will requires you to obey ordinances and submit to the Council's instructions."

Mary worked hard to keep the confidence on her face from slipping into gloating. "I have read that document carefully," she said. "It binds me to obedience only on the point of my marriage, and I have not been disobedient there." She clasped her hands before her in the classic pose of a master schooling a student. "It further orders two Masses be said for his soul every day, and four obsequies every year. You have refused to observe those ceremonies on your side. Who is more disobedient?"

She could not stop the corner of her mouth from turning up when Warwick started to sputter.

"How now?" he said. "It seems your Ladyship is trying to show us in a hateful light."

"I did not come hither to do so," Mary said. "But since you broached the matter and pressed me so hard, I cannot hide or dissemble the truth."

"The truth as you see it."

She shook her head. This was going nowhere. They thought they could bully her into submitting; they were wrong. She had submitted once before, to her father. She was still ashamed of admitting her mother's marriage invalid and herself a bastard, but it had freed her to be in this place, at this time, when her resistance would actually mean something.

She lifted her chin, ready to follow Christ's path if that was His will. "I would have hoped that as the King's sister I would have been shown more respect. In the end, though, there are only two things: soul and body. My soul I offer to God, and my body to His Majesty's service. I will submit to death rather than abandon the true religion taken from me."

The room gasped at the stakes she had just set.

"I ask for no such sacrifice," Edward said quickly.

She gave him a rueful smile. *Poor thing.* She was sure Warwick encouraged these ridiculous religious policies just to worm his way into the King's affection. "It does my heart good to hear it, for the love I bear to you."

Warwick shifted as if he was about to argue further. Mary refused to give him that satisfaction. She dropped to her knees. "I humbly pray Your Majesty to excuse me from court, as I am ill. I have no wish to fight you, and I do not want to draw more attention to my religious practices by being here, near to you."

"But nothing has been resolved," Edward said.

"But it has all been said," Mary said. "I beg you, dear brother, give no credit to any person who might desire to make you believe ill of me, whether about religion or anything else. I will always remain Your Majesty's humble, obedient, and unworthy sister."

Edward bit his lip and looked at the floor. "You may go," he said without looking up.

March 19, 1551

Edward watched out his window as Mary's retinue, which now included the Spanish Ambassador, slowly made its way down the road out of Whitehall into the maw of the London streets. They were not thronged as they had been the other day – arrivals to court always received more attention than departures – but he could still see people streaming out of their houses to greet his Catholic sister.

He turned back around to the Council table. As he did so, his glance fell on the handkerchief-covered mound on the small table next to him. *Not yet,* he told himself.

He looked around the table at his Councilors. They did not have the benefit of a platform, and they were lifting slightly out of their chairs and craning their heads so they, too, could watch the cortege. Their narrowed eyes made it clear they were also monitoring the size of the crowds.

Edward looked at the ceiling of the Council chamber as if a solution would be found among the prancing horses and Tudor roses in the plaster's embossed pattern. "We should not have let her go," he said with all the force he could muster, as if he had shared in the choice.

Edward had wanted her to stay. *Proximity bred obedience.* His father had taught him that long ago, and this morning his spirit had reminded Edward of that lesson. Mary knew it too.

Warwick sighed loudly, like a minstrel performing for his audience. "She did not want to further anger Your Majesty. She knew her presence would cause you displeasure."

Edward's face heated again with the anger that had consumed him for the past week. Even Warwick had betrayed him, urging mercy for Mary's continued intransigence. Edward clipped his words to stress the correction. "She wanted to get back home so she could hear Mass."

The Councilors froze as if waiting for the words to dissipate into the room, like smoke. Instead, Edward puffed more after them. "Should she not be punished for putting her false beliefs above me?"

Warwick slammed his hand on the desk, and Edward jumped as much from the shock as from the noise. Then he caught sight of Warwick's eyes, wide and fixed on him as if their power alone could control Edward.

"Your view is understandable, Sire," Warwick said in a soft, precise voice. "But there is another." He leaned forward. As his face loomed closer, Edward felt like Warwick's eyes were reaching out to shake him. This was intimidation worse than what Somerset once inflicted. Edward shivered.

"She made her first concession to you," Warwick said, "by honoring your right to ban the Mass from being said at court. This is the first restriction she has been willing to recognize on her right to worship. In her own mind, she is above reproach and expects you to recognize this as a mark of respect. I beg you to concede the issue right now. For now."

Edward felt like his father must have, back when England was still Catholic and the Bishop of Rome barred the path God had so clearly indicated. It was the same thing now: Edward's Councilors barring the path of righteousness.

His father had waited seven long years before finally taking matters into his own hands. The Council expected Edward to wait the full seven years until his majority. Until now Warwick had managed to make it easier. But even that had changed.

How dare they emasculate Edward by not letting his letters stand on their own? What had the lords really said? Could he trust Warwick? Could he trust anyone?

No one, his father would have said. *Trust no one.*

It was a lesson that had been proven to Edward. Multiple times.

He brought himself back to the room, back to the important task at hand. "She deliberately challenged our authority by riding in as she did and then taunted us for our cowardice, daring us to test whether she is indeed ready to die for her faith. We are like dogs whose noses are being rubbed in their own filth."

Somerset extended his hand across the table, a signal he wanted the chance to speak. Edward nodded his permission, just in time, because Somerset might not have waited.

"She will not back down," Somerset said, pleading in his voice. "And any assault on the Lady Mary will be considered an assault on the Emperor. The Spanish Ambassador insists it would not be tolerated."

Instead of moving Edward as Somerset surely meant to do,

his little speech enveloped Edward in detachment, even resentment, that his sister had real supporters while he did not. "She will not be assaulted, only forbidden an illegal act."

Somerset opened his mouth to reply, but Warwick waved his hand. Edward felt embarrassed for Somerset by the disrespect inherent in the dismissal. Warwick hadn't even looked in Somerset's direction; his eyes were only for Edward.

"She will not allow the ultimate punishment to stop her," Warwick said, "As the most experienced general in the land, I will tell you: if we are not prepared to impose our force, its show has the sound of ridicule."

Somerset flushed. There was a time when he considered himself to be the most experienced general in the land. Again, Edward felt bad for him but stopped himself. His uncle's reputation was not Edward's problem. Especially not now. *This was the time,* he told himself.

Edward took a deep breath and dramatically pulled off the handkerchief that covered the mound next to him, revealing a dead falcon. The poor thing had been killed in the field that morning, and Edward had insisted on bringing it back with them, thinking to honor it somehow. Then, as they were dismounting, the keeper had thrown one of the dead rabbits to reward the dogs. The sight of the dogs viciously tearing the carcass apart had stirred a visceral memory of his father's genius for keeping the world in line. Fear bred obedience as much as proximity, and words induced less fear than action.

Holding the bird in his lap, he started to pluck its feathers. One at a time, slowly, without even looking at it but instead staring at each of his Councilors in turn. "Am I to live in fear of the Emperor, then? Am I not king in my own realm?"

His Councilors stared at the bird with nauseated fascination.

Warwick pressed his lips together as if this would counteract his widened eyes. "This is a delicate matter, Sire," he said. "I suggest we allow her to continue to hear Mass as we have always done—"

"Her and the hordes who join in her superstition?"

"Your Majesty is of course right that others must be stopped," Warwick said.

Edward's grim satisfaction over the concession only fueled his anger. "I have asked for so little during my reign. Just this one thing, one thing only, in four years. And even this is too much for you?"

"We have no choice right now," Warwick said smoothly. "But only her. No one else in her household."

"Other than her Chaplain. And whoever else will try to circumvent the rule by listening at the door." Edward infused all the sarcasm he could into his voice and plucked harder. "So, two religions would be practiced in the same house?"

"The true religion for all, and popish superstition for her alone."

"It is the popish superstition that is the problem," Edward said.

"May I remind Your Majesty that your ambassadors are now permitted to celebrate the Anglican service in the Emperor's dominions?" Warwick said.

"My ambassadors are not subjects of the Emperor. My sister is fully English, whatever Charles may think."

"I beg you, Your Majesty, calm yourself. It is only for a short time. Your uncle Somerset had previously counseled that we delay provocation until the treaty is signed with France. I think his advice is sound. Rash action might discourage your prospective father-in-law. This is the right approach."

"I am disgusted by your fear." Edward was embarrassed by the stridency in his voice, the stridency of a child. He lowered his tone. "Are we to set aside what we know to be right? Will we deny Christ and His sacrifice because we are too afraid to follow Him?"

"This is different. This is a temporary concession," Warwick said.

Warwick seemed to roll his eyes. The look disappeared, if it ever existed, but Edward's anger swelled. "This is an insult."

"We cannot allow your sister to martyr herself."

The anger expanded until it almost stopped Edward from breathing. It was time to make the point he had prepared. "I feel like this falcon, plucked by all of you." He looked down at the bird and ripped off one leg, helped by the careful slices he had placed in the joint earlier. He heard sixteen sharp intakes of breath as sixteen men finally understood he was prepared to indulge in violence.

Like his father.

He ripped off the other leg and mouths dropped open. "But in time I will pluck you too. And tear you apart."

Beads of sweat appeared on every forehead. *Good.* Hopefully they understood now. There would be consequences for failing him in this matter.

"S-Sire, this is but temporary," Warwick said. "Our counsel is that you not assail your sister. Orders prohibiting her the Mass—"

"I understand that," Edward said. "But I also understand her Chaplain is an English subject. Why can we not stop him from performing the Mass for her?"

"We can stop him, but what of the others who will come to take his place?"

"At some point, they will stop coming." Edward said. "And if not, then we are picking off our enemies one at a time."

Warwick narrowed his eyes. Somerset and the other Councilors did the same. Warwick shook his head. "We started to discuss this long ago, then abandoned the idea somehow. But it would be a more natural way to proceed. Let us debate among ourselves, Sire, then return to propose a solution that will satisfy you."

Edward nodded. "Good. You may leave me."

They filed out in silence, like dogs after a scolding.

After they were gone, and the door closed behind them,

Edward giggled. Then he looked at the poor dismembered falcon and slowly picked up the pieces. He looked at the pile, blessed it, then put it down while he took his kerchief out of his pocket. He wrapped the carcass carefully and patted it when he was done.

"Guard!" he called.

Two liveried men were instantly in the room, spears raised but ready. He walked over and handed the package to one of them. "I want this bird buried properly, not just thrown on the trash heap."

"As you wish, Sire," the lad said, bowing.

Edward turned and went back to the window, at the empty space where he had last seen Mary's caravan and the crowds it incited.

"Just wait," he said.

April 30, 1551

Mary fingered her beads to calm herself as Scheyfve bowed before her. She had sent an urgent – yet discreet – message begging him to come visit her. God bless the man, he had come within two days. She could not have stood the suspense much longer.

She didn't even want to squander the minutes it would take him to reach her apartments. She had come to greet him in the entry.

He rose and she began straight away, minimizing the friendly greetings. She knew he would understand.

"Thank you for coming, it is a great comfort to me. Tell me, what news of my Chaplain?"

Francis Mallet had been seized for questioning by the Council again. More than a week had gone by with no news.

Scheyfve bowed a second time. "He is in the Tower, Your Highness."

Mary's knees buckled, enough that the Ambassador grabbed the chair behind her and helped her into it.

"The Tower," she said, somehow breathless. Her worst fears confirmed. A fearsome place that few left alive.

"I am sorry to be the one to bring such tidings," Scheyfve said.

Mary's mind raced. "But he was questioned once before and released. What is this new treatment?"

Scheyfve shook his head. "He continued to offend after being forgiven. And, from what I hear, he would not promise to stop."

"How could he stop? He is my Chaplain."

Scheyfve looked from side to side, then held out a hand to lead her outside.

By the time they reached the garden, Mary's heart had slowed to a normal pace.

"You must do your duty," Scheyfve said, "and continue to reply with moderation to the King, your brother. You cannot expect great liberty in the use of Catholic ceremonies."

Mary raised a suspicious eyebrow. "What is this change, this caution? Where is the man who swore my cousin's army would rescue me if need be?"

"They tried and you refused." Scheyfve ran a hand through his hair. "When I spoke with the Council on your behalf, they informed me many of your neighbors come here, especially on holidays, to hear Mass with you. Worse, they come even when you are not here."

The scolding tone slapped her face like a winter wind. "I thought you knew." Her voice was small. "Van der Delft knew."

"Well, he didn't tell me. I would have told you to stop, to give the Council less cause to act against you."

Mary's face burned. How could she be in the wrong when God was on her side? "It is not so many people. Surely you exaggerate."

Scheyfve's eyes narrowed. "When you are not even here," he repeated.

"Can I really close my doors to the faithful? This will be the ruination of their holy souls."

"I cannot help English souls. I can only hope to help yours."

Mary looked deep into Scheyfve's blue eyes, and their earnestness pulled her to reason. "What would you have me do?"

"What you should have been doing all along. Hear Mass with your doors locked and no strangers admitted."

Loss weighed heavily on Mary's shoulders, hollowing out her heart. She felt twenty-one again, powerless to stop the nightmare of her father destroying her life.

How could Scheyfve not have known? More important, how could she have misjudged such an important detail? What else had she misjudged?

Once again, the decision to remain in England weighed like iron in her stomach. Resolutely, she pushed the trepidation aside. "And you think this will save me from persecution?"

"It must. I cannot believe they would be so wretched and insensate as to take the Mass away from you altogether."

"And if they do?"

Scheyfve sighed. "Then you will have to submit, as to something you can in no way avoid. You must do your best to dispel all cause for sinister suspicions from the Council's minds, for otherwise you will entirely alienate them and cause them to withdraw all permission whatsoever."

Mary's stomach plummeted over this sudden reversal of fortunes. "I don't understand," she said. "Your threats worked so well until now. What has changed?"

Scheyfve reddened. "England and France are soon to be allies. Spain cannot fight them both."

Mary waved her hand dismissively. "Warwick has been making overtures to France for some time, trying to overcome generations of enmity."

"Well, now it is in France's interest to do so, and a French contingent is on its way to formalize and celebrate their deep and abiding love for England."

"You cannot believe this will last," Mary said.

His eyes implored her to understand. "It will not last forever, but it will last long enough that you need to take care. Our army is thinly spread among the French, the Ottomans, and the Lutheran princes. The Council knows it and discounts our threats accordingly."

Mary straightened her back. "So I am on my own."

"No, but you need to take care." Scheyfve shrugged. "Until we are in a better position to make demands."

Her being felt hollow. "No Masses?"

His eyes hardened. "The Mass is a comfort to our soul, not a precondition to our salvation. As long as you remain constant, and do not allow yourself to be led away from the true faith, all will be well with you."

Regret reared again, clawing at her heart. She should have left England when she had had the chance. God had sent a means for her rescue, and she had refused it. Now there were fewer choices for her salvation.

"Well, thankfully you speak the truth, for without my Chaplain they have taken away the Mass already."

"Surely there is someone else who can say it for you. I do not want to make too many requests, lest they deny the most important one."

The tone in his voice made Mary realize she sounded ungrateful. The truth was that without Spain's intervention, she would have been deprived of her religion long ago. She needed to thank them now, remind Charles how important he was to her.

"You are right. Let them think they have scored a great victory. Then maybe they will cease to bother me."

"Exactly. And I will continue to remind them of their promises which now will seem smaller."

She set her face in a brave smile and straightened her already rigid spine. "Please tell your master I could never render thanks enough to God for His benign mercy in so inspiring His Majesty, my Spanish cousin. I feel more and more bound to him as time goes on, and will remain his humble servant as long as God shall give me life. I will pray for the success of his holy projects, for it is in him, after God, that I put my chief hope and trust. Without his intervention, I would have been forced long ago into death, for no consideration could ever make me conform to their sacrilege."

Scheyfve nodded. "I will tell him."

Although he sounded sincere, Mary continued. All she could offer was gratitude, and she had to make sure she did that completely so Charles would continue to meddle to her benefit. "God the rewarder of all virtue will surely recompense the Emperor for his affection, and I shall continually pray our Creator to crown all His Majesty's desires."

Scheyfve bowed abjectly, giving Mary confidence her message was understood.

But she still felt hollow.

May 3, 1551

Edward shifted in his saddle. His horse stomped nervously from the noise and bustle, and Edward patted the side of her neck. "There, there," he said softly. "You must be patient and calm, as I must be."

He looked around the massive pavilion tent, fifteen meters by six meters, which held the thirty-odd contestants on their horses, with ample room to spare.

Edward looked at the ceiling and allowed himself to be awed by the golden suns painted around each of the soaring masts, the fleecy white clouds floating on the light blue background of the canvas. They had built the tent to impress the representatives of the French king. This would surely do that.

Edward bit his lip. But would he be as worthy of admiration? This would be his first tournament, and he would be both running at the ring and tilting at the buckle. His teachers swore he was ready for this.

When Warwick entered on foot, the sea of people and horses milling about parted for his impatient strides. He stopped just to

Edward's right and took gentle hold of the horse's bridle to stroke its muzzle. The animal whinnied in pleasure.

"He's in fine shape for you, Sire," Warwick said. "How are you feeling?"

Edward swallowed to relieve his dry mouth. "Good." Much as he had craved this day, he was terrified of failing in front of this crowd. He hadn't expected to feel such trepidation – after all, he was used to people judging his every move. But this was different. He was claiming manhood. What if he failed?

Warwick leaned in and lowered his voice. "Fear is a good thing, your first time. Only a fool is overconfident."

Edward nodded, not wanting to admit to more.

"Remember," Warwick said, "we talked about this. About how this is a good chance for you to get your footing, get the feel of a tournament before the full French deputation arrives this summer."

That part raised the stakes even further on Edward's performance. As part of the historic rapprochement with France, each sovereign was bestowing his country's highest chivalric honors on the other. Henri would be invested with the Order of the Garter, and Edward would be invested with the Order of Saint Michael. The English deputation had already been chosen; it included the Bishop of Ely, the Marquess of Northampton, the Earl of Rutland, Warwick's eldest son, and many more. They would be leaving soon, as would the French deputation, so the two ceremonies could take place on the same day. This was part of the send-off.

Despite the reminder of the even more terrifying trial to come, or perhaps because of it, Warwick's calm voice lulled Edward back into confidence, soothing him the way the man's touch had soothed his horse. Edward nodded again.

"The French Ambassador has taken his seat," Warwick said. "He has had nothing but compliments for us all."

Edward fought the chill that whispered between his shoulders. "I pray he has as many after the tourneys."

Warwick laughed as though he had heard nothing so witty in weeks and then stopped abruptly to get serious. "I know your riding, Your Majesty, and your tilting. Your skill is far beyond your age, and that will be apparent no matter what. Remember, this is not about winning. The courage is in the attempt."

The patronizing platitude broke the spell. "You have said that before, but I want—"

"But nothing."

The sharp interruption, a major breach of protocol, stunned Edward into silence.

Warwick leaned in even further, squinting. "You are not even fourteen and this is your first tournament. You are competing against men twice your age, some of whom have honed their skills on the battlefield. You owe no more than your best attempt. If you can't do that, then dismount now and we will invent some excuse."

Warwick's calm cruelty made Edward feel as if he had been knocked from his horse. The overwhelming feeling of distance calmed Edward where coddling had failed. "There will be no need for that," he said, tightening his hold on the reins.

Warwick relaxed. "It is a glorious day for this loyal subject, Your Majesty. I see in you now the resolve I have seen in my best soldiers right before a battle. Go do us proud, just by trying."

Edward nodded his promise.

"Get into place and I'll inform Herbert," Warwick said. He raised an arm and looked around the tent. "Prepare yourselves," he called out.

Edward guided his horse to the entrance and stared out at the field beyond, deliberately oblivious to the controlled chaos behind him as the others took their places. The sudden blare of the trumpets made him jump, but he took a deep breath and did his best to consider his racing heartbeat as a sign of opportunity rather than fear.

William Herbert, the Master of the Horse, nodded to him. It was starting.

Edward looked down at his black silk coat, pulled out with white taffeta, and took another deep breath. He glanced behind at his newly formed retinue and stepped his horse forward. His ten horsemen followed, all dressed like him, as well as sixteen footmen in white fustian pulled out with blue taffeta.

When the King's party was arranged on the field like warriors ready for battle, the other side joined them, creating their own phalanx. They all wore yellow taffeta so the teams could be easily distinguished.

Another round of trumpet blasts commanded the attention the audience had already freely given. When they stopped, Herbert stepped into the head of the lane. Behind him, Edward could see the small ring already suspended from its cord, a tiny speck in the distance. He swallowed.

"The King shall tilt first, then my Lord Hertford from the yellow team after him," Herbert announced. "The other riders will continue alternating."

Teddy Seymour stepped his horse forward and smiled at Edward, apology in his eyes. No one liked to challenge a king.

Edward tried to listen to the rest of the instructions, but the rush in his ears drowned out all other sound. And he knew the rules anyway.

All too quickly, Herbert was stepping away. One of Edward's footmen appeared next to his horse and handed him a lance. Edward hefted it into position as he had done so many times before. The feel of the wood steadied him, and the cheers from the crowd inspired him. He could do this.

He looked down the lane at the ring again, squinting to hold it in his sights. Without taking his eyes from it, he lifted his lance and spurred his horse forward. It lurched into a gallop, and he urged it even faster, keeping his weapon straight despite the animal's gentle rolling, the point aimed squarely at the tiny hole.

And then he was upon it, and it felt like victory was his –

until the ring went flying. He heard a sigh spread through the audience and his face flamed.

He pretended nothing was wrong as he slowed and turned his horse to yield the field.

A page quickly brought a stool and steadied the ring for the next rider. Edward paused while Teddy tried his own hand, the thunder of hooves escalating the tension until he, too, sent the ring flying.

Teddy's failure comforted Edward slightly, much as his confessor would condemn such an uncharitable impulse. The next few failures felt even better, especially when he allowed himself to notice the crowd's cheers for the attempts. It reminded him of his own admiration for the men who were skilled enough simply to be on the field, reassured him that he was entitled to be here, that he was good enough to be here.

By the time his next turn came around and no one had yet pierced the ring, he was truly calm. And determined.

Again, he lifted his lance and aimed it squarely at the tiny empty space. He kept his legs tighter around his mount, determined to be the first...until he wasn't. But this time the failure did not sting as much. At least not until Throckmorton lanced the ring, and even then the slight jealousy dissipated quickly.

In the one hundred twenty courses, five by each rider, the yellow team took the ring twice and Edward's not at all. But the loss did not feel terrible – indeed, it felt just fine. The world felt different actually. They were all men, warriors. They all deserved to be here.

"Prizes for the winners," Warwick called. "And who better to award them than the man who knows the effort it took?" He swept his arm toward Edward, and the yellow team turned to him expectantly.

Edward had not considered this part of the tournament, but before he could even think of panicking, a page was next to him holding up a silver tray piled with eleven velvet pouches filled with coins. Edward smiled and one by one tossed the purses at the winners, his sense of power increasing with each pitch. He felt like his father. He felt like a king.

"You are lucky," Somerset said to his son, "for the King outrode you. You see the importance of choosing a team wisely." Edward felt slightly guilty for such praise after he hadn't even noticed his uncle was there, and decided to hide embarrassment behind humility. "We are all on Team England."

Somerset beamed. "May we all continue to prosper. And may our new allies help."

The words puzzled Edward, until he remembered that Somerset was trying to establish the manufacture of serge in a little town of his and had sent to the French town of Hainault for workers. That would be a wonderful source of new jobs, and a welcome new outlet for English wool. Another reason the English people loved Somerset as much as they did. If only the Duke were as skilled with politics. Or administration. Not that Edward wanted him back; Warwick's regime was far preferable.

With the prizes awarded, the audience crowded the field to congratulate the winners and commiserate with the losers. An army of servants milled about, offering goblets of wine and marzipan subtleties. Edward took some gladly, proud of his thirst and hunger.

Warwick approached, the French Ambassador right behind him. Both wore large smiles. "Monsieur de Noailles wishes to congratulate you, Sire," Warwick said. "He was just telling me how impressed he was at your dexterity."

"I was indeed," de Noailles said. "You bore yourself right well; it was a wonderfully fair display. It even made up for me missing the jousts and revels that my own master commissioned for his court to celebrate this new unity."

Edward stood up straighter, happy that the right answer came to him instinctively. "This was a small beginning. As time passes, I hope to do my duty better."

The pride on Warwick's face felt as good as the inner warmth that came from a job well done. Edward closed his eyes, trying to etch the day in his memory so he could conjure it again when things looked less rosy.

May 8, 1551

Edward's thoughts had admittedly been wandering, though in his own defense the Council had merely been approving land grants that Warwick had already listed during their secret sessions. But now Edward's attention had been commanded by Somerset standing and whirling to place a booted foot on his former seat. He looked like a mummer ready to tell a story. Edward shifted in his throne and shook the cobwebs out of his head.

"You are going too far with the deprecation of the currency," Somerset said, raising a finger to point at Warwick. "The people are grumbling."

Edward had long noticed his uncle often acted as if his moves were being watched by the entire court, even when he was in a small group. It was an important skill, yes, but one Somerset overplayed. Warwick had noticed as well; it had caused much merriment late one private night. Mocking Somerset felt a little disloyal to Edward, but the Duke did deserve it.

Warwick waved his hand as if he would wave away the melodrama. "Of course, you always make a big show of caring for the people and pandering to their love," he said. "But the people are not much affected, only the merchants. So don't blame me that your overdone palace is costing more than you expected."

Somerset's foot came off the chair. The Council members exchanged discreet glances. Edward pretended not to notice and looked down at his hands.

"How, pray tell, can you argue the people are not much affected?" Somerset asked, a hint of triumph in his voice.

Warwick grimaced as if he were scolding a naughty child. "The people are worse affected by coins they cannot trust." He raised one finger. "The pound weight of silver, three ounces fine and nine ounces alloy, will be coined into seventy-two shillings at twelve pence apiece. That will restore their confidence, but the measure needs to be paid for." He paused and lifted a second finger. "We have all agreed to pay a merchant, for every ounce of fine silver that he brings to the mint, ten shillings of our money at ten pence apiece instead of the twelve we offered in the past. This is not such a terrible change, especially since we might have gone further. We must fix the problem once and for all."

Warwick turned to Edward. "Don't you agree, Your Majesty?"

Edward's stomach did a quick flip, and he took a deep breath to summon his confidence. They had discussed this, Warwick and him. Somerset was overreacting and Edward nodded. "A two-shilling change does not seem so high. Surely the merchants can accept that, especially for such an important cause."

Still, a worry nagged at him. Why was Somerset acting like he was winning?

"Ah, but it is not two shillings, Sire, and it is not just the merchants," Somerset said. "The problem is that the old coins do not contain the amount of fine metal they should, so an old shilling will be exchanged for only nine pence. And before you say this is only three shillings more, I beg you to consider this is a one-fourth reduction in wealth that will affect everyone in the land."

That was information Warwick had not shared. How could he have held it back? Had he not realized it? Or had he hoped to hide it? Edward was not sure which was worse. "That is quite high."

Somerset's face spread into a broad smile. "Outrageously high."

Warwick snorted. "It is what is needed to stabilize the currency."

Memories of past discussions replayed themselves in Edward's mind, discussions that contradicted what Warwick was saying now. "But I thought the ransoming of Boulogne would fix all this?"

"That was a start, Your Majesty, but the coins were quite debased. Many were further clipped and sheared."

More arguments leaped to Edward's mind. "But I still thought we fixed the worst of the clipping when I first came to the throne. I remember Somerset calling in the old coins from my father's time to do that very thing."

"Many were hoarded and not turned in. And that measure did not address the other problems with the coinage, specifically the large number of counterfeits."

"Why so many?"

"Because of the baseness of the coins. It becomes too much of a temptation, especially abroad," Warwick said. "Not to mention the fact that these too were clipped and sheared as if they were pure – no matter how many men we hang or threaten to hang." He looked down and fiddled with the hilt of his knife. "Your Majesty should also know we were not able to bring the legal coins of the realm to the purity they deserved – we only improved the worst problems. Which is why these measures are needed now."

Again, Edward felt hurt that Warwick had not shared this information with him before. "Well, as long as this fixes it," Edward said, trying to keep the grumble from his voice.

Warwick pursed his lips. "It is part of a larger plan. In March, we decreed that commissions across the land would take unto your hands such church plate as remains. That will all be coined as well."

That was not terribly reassuring. Edward knew his father had been quite careful when he dissolved the monasteries, seizing not just their plate but even the lead from their roofs and the copper from their spouts. It was doubtful there was much left. "But will that be enough then?"

"When we sign the treaty with France, you will be paid Madame Elisabeth's dowry."

"But—" Edward stopped himself and bit his lip. He had almost mentioned something Warwick had told him to keep secret, that there was talk of further strengthening the alliance by having his sister Elizabeth marry a French nobleman. He reformulated the question. "But if my sisters should marry, we would need to provide dowries for them."

"Your sisters' dowries will be smaller, though still honorable."

Somerset's boot went back up on his chair. "I would expect many will try to avoid this new rate, and there may be Englishmen who will help them do it for a price."

"We have forbidden anyone to make any exchanges other than at these levels, or to carry out gold or silver from the realm."

"Good luck," Somerset said.

"Have you another solution to the problem?" Warwick asked.

The foot came down and Somerset shook his head. "It just hurts to see such pain inflicted on so many."

Warwick sniffed. "It is particularly hurtful to me that people blame me for this, for I was most careful and vigilant in my solicitude for the country's welfare."

"Sins of the father…" Somerset said with a wink.

Warwick's father had been one of Henry VII's most trusted ministers – but hated by the people because he was the man who had suggested, imposed, and collected heavy taxes. When Henry VIII had come to the throne, he had Edmund Dudley charged with constructive treason for such excess. Dudley had been executed and the people pacified without any reduction in the tax rate.

Warwick's face hardened. "They do me a grave injustice."

Somerset nodded, more conciliatory now. "It's just very quick," he said.

"We must address it before the French arrive in earnest," Warwick said. "This cannot be done in front of them."

"How do you plan to do that?"

"I want the Council to agree today to issue express orders to the Mayor and sheriffs of London to call together the people of this great city and explain to them that these measures were dictated by zeal for the public good. We only want to place the currency on the old footing. Surely if they understand, they will stop their grumbling."

Arundel banged his fist on the Council table. "I say we try it."

The others nodded and a round of "Hear, hear" broke out.

Edward relaxed and sat back in his chair while the Council discussed the particulars. It was a relief to once again trust Warwick's advice, even if he should have shared his strategy in full with Edward. And even if the strategy might seem hurtful to some people, it would all be sorted out.

And if not, you have your scapegoat, a voice in his head soothed him.

Edward flushed and looked around, nervous that his thoughts might be guessed.

This was not the time to think of such things.

May 18, 1551

Ignoring the crowd around him, Edward lifted his nose toward the prow and let the air splash his face like the waves were splashing the ship. For now, the French delegation would come second.

Edward loved the royal barge, one of the greatest things his father had designed and built. He could sit outside to enjoy the wind and wave at the people lining the shores, or he could sink into a comfortable cushion in the saloon, cocooned by windows and arrases of blue and gold thread. And he could have any whim indulged, since half the ship's seventy-five-foot length was devoted to the workers who contributed to the magic: the crew who divined his needs before he had them, the musicians who soothed with their melodies, and the eighteen rowers whose strength propelled them forward at mighty speeds. *"Aussi beau que notre Seine,"* said Rene de Laval-Bois-Dauphin, the Master of the Household to Henri II. "As lovely as our Seine."

Antoine de Noailles, the French Ambassador, had explained at the start of the trip that the translations would help all the courtiers, both English and French, to understand all that was said. Of course, the truth was he was afraid Edward would not understand, but was just too polite to say so.

"I would love to see it one day," Edward said with a relaxed smile, as if he had not expected this compliment and practiced his answer carefully. *"J'aimerais bien le voir un jour."*

As always he exulted in the Gallic smiles that met his fluency, proud to be what Warwick called a "natural master" at diplomacy.

"I hope to join you on that trip," Somerset said, detaching himself from the crowd to join the main discussion. Not that this was a major feat: only thirty-four courtiers were on the barge. Smaller boats surrounded them, packed with people of lesser importance. And behind trailed the huge French sailing ships that carried vast stores of the personal possessions the French nobles could not live without during their visit.

"Vous seriez bienvenu, welcome," said Louis de Lansac, the late Francis I's natural son by his mistress Jacquette de Lansac, and half-brother to the current French king.

It was interesting how Somerset had become more central to the visit than Warwick. Edward felt a little guilty about that, though he could not imagine how he could be to blame.

Warwick had been the one to formally greet the hundred or so French visitors on their arrival. He had brought several Councilors with him to the mouth of the Thames, then his ships had conducted their galleys up the river. Along the way, they had been saluted by peals of ordnance from the shores – pageantry that shielded a subtle reminder of England's might.

The French had treated Warwick with full respect until they reached Sheen Palace, where Edward and Somerset awaited them. Somerset had prepared a fair *souper*, which somehow the French took as a sign of greater power and influence. Or at least they must have, because when Warwick invited the group to return to their barges to watch the spectacles he had arranged – wildfire cast from boats and other pretty conceits – Lansac had lifted a single eyebrow until Somerset assured him this was England's invitation and not just the Earl's. De Laval-Bois-Dauphin had flounced over to the royal barge, ignoring the invitation to join Warwick on the *Edouard Grace à Dieu*, the English ship leading the convoy.

Now Lansac's French accent interrupted Edward's thoughts. *"Arrivons-nous à Hampton Court?"* he asked. "Is that Hampton Court?"

Edward looked in the direction he was pointing, where the palace shone as brightly as the sun in the sky. A fitting home to courtiers who also sparkled from rich clothes and lavish jewels – even the servants had been specially outfitted in an effort to have England outdo her guests and dispel all rumors of financial problems. Every royal purveyor had been pressed to send lavish supplies, and the Earls of Rutland, Bath and Worcester had been called upon to repair to the court immediately with their best apparel and furniture to make the place more resolutely gay than Edward had ever seen it.

"It is," Edward said, trying to stop pride from crossing over to smugness.

"Sa renommée la précède, mais la réalité est bien meilleure," Lansac said. "I have heard it highly praised, but that did not do it justice. The woods around it must have excellent hunting."

"Some of the best in the country," Somerset said. "Even better than Savernake Forest, where I grew up."

A thought occurred to Edward about how to bring Warwick honor in French eyes. "What else did Warwick arrange?" Edward asked Somerset.

"A host of amusements." Somerset waved his hand dismissively. "Warwick's specialty."

Lansac tittered.

It was time for Edward himself to counteract Somerset's contempt. "The Earl has seen to it that we will enjoy a grand tournament of tilting at the ring, then we will watch bulls and bears being baited. We were told these activities are as beloved in France as they are here."

"They are indeed, Your Majesty, as in any civilized court," de Laval said. "And may I ask whether you will grace the field? Monsieur de Noailles has greatly praised your skills."

Regret and relief passed through Edward's heart. "Ah, thank you, but I would prefer a wiser use to the time we have together. Our countries are soon to be forever joined by my marriage to your princess, and I would prefer to foster friendship over competition."

It was true, though he wasn't mentioning this wasn't his own idea. After his strong showing on the field, Warwick had suggested he no longer needed to prove himself to the French, that practicing his diplomatic skills would be better than showing off. In truth, Edward had welcomed the reprieve.

"Your Majesty is wise beyond his years."

"I am happy to give my friends the chance to participate. This will be the first course run by Henry Brandon, the Duke of Suffolk. And Lord Lisle, Warwick's son. I look forward to cheering them on."

Somerset sniffed. Ned and Teddy were not participating either. They had probably been sent off to *fête* the Spanish Ambassador, to minimize the jealousy – for of course the Spaniards were avoiding court right now while the French and English celebrated their great friendship.

This was a new era. The time of Henry VIII and Francis I was over, their enmity buried with their corpses. And the French were probably a little nervous about Warwick. He had, after all, been Lord High Admiral during the Battle of the Solent, when the French had sent an invasion fleet to attack. Warwick had shown them they were fools to think they could conquer England.

Edward paused to ponder that point. Showing power was the path to respect, but too much could dampen friendship. This was the morass he was swimming through with Mary, trying to move her from love to obedience. He might not be able to have both. And if not, he had to choose obedience.

"Have you changed your mind, Sire?" Somerset's voice was low, for Edward alone.

"What?"

"You seem angry."

Edward forced a smile. "No, no, not at all. I was just…" His voice trailed off as he could not come up with an excuse. "Music!" he called out. "We should have music to celebrate."

This was not the time to think about Mary. This was the time to enjoy his political triumph.

Life was good.

July 30, 1551

The Great Hall at Beaulieu seemed to beg for purification the way churches beg for incense. Mary added water to the large bowl of parsley placed carefully on the small table at the center of the room so its magic could radiate on all sides. The herb offered a sure remedy against the plague, sweetening the air to stop the sickness from spreading. Hopefully it would also work against this latest outbreak of the sweating sickness. The disease was far more deadly than in years past: people were dropping quickly across every city.

Also standing around the table with her were the Earl and Countess of Arundel, who had come to visit her on the way to their own estates now that they had retired from court for the summer. Arundel crossed himself as Mary fluffed the branchlets.

"The country is so much more healthy for a person," she

said. "I am glad you left London, and only wish my brother would do the same."

"He is at Richmond right now with a small number of men, which should be quite safe. But they will be venturing farther next month. Hopefully the sickness will have abated by then."

"Please, God, let it be so," Mary said. Richmond was outside of London, yes, but it was still large enough that it required more people than was prudent.

"At least it has stopped the uprisings."

Mary's eyes darted to Arundel's face. His eyes were sad, not uncaring, so his words must have been sincere. She reminded herself he was a man and therefore had to be practical in every assessment. "There is such suffering among the English people," she said noncommittally.

Arundel shrugged. "What a terrible time, when people can suddenly lose their friends to the sweat and their fortunes to the Royal Mint."

The Council had issued a second proclamation concerning the currency because of the terrible price increases caused by their first. Now the new coins bought only half of what the old coins did. Half the nation's wealth gone. It would have been so much easier to tax the people, but instead they did it this way.

"Warwick did this; it's all his fault," said Arundel's wife, Katherine, her face red. "The Good Duke would not have hurt us this way."

In no position to scold one of her few friends, Mary bit her lip to hide her bitterness over hearing Katherine refer to Somerset as the Good Duke, the name the people had given him because of his great heart. Arundel had opposed his policies and supported Warwick's coup. Now that Warwick had turned his face from the conservatives, Somerset was again the Good Duke.

"He tried, my dear, but his methods did not work," Arundel said. "If this measure succeeds, we will all be better off."

"Unfortunately," Mary added, "the Good Duke is no longer listened to as much." She turned to Arundel. "Am I right about this? You have said in the past that he has been scoring points with the Lords. I just don't want to cling to false hope."

Arundel looked around to make sure they were alone and leaned in over the table. "Warwick continues to have the King's full support, and that makes things difficult. You know, the two meet at night, privately, before important votes of the Council so His Majesty knows what to say."

"Who told you that?" she asked.

"The Spanish Ambassador," Arundel said.

"Anyone else?"

"No."

Mary sat quietly with the news, weighing its believability. Finally she spoke. "I would not trust quite everything he hears, not if he is the only person reporting this."

Arundel laughed. "He was right about the latest currency changes. Thanks to him, I was forewarned and made shifts before the rules were imposed."

Mary could not doubt it, though she did not know what to say. She swallowed her hurt over not having been one of those forewarned. Not that she had any idea what she would have done if she had.

"He also knew about the seriousness of the sweat," Arundel said. "Though his warning could not help us there."

"Other than to push you to leave London," Mary said. "They say a hundred men die each day in the city." Mary crossed herself at the terrible number.

Katherine sniffed. "And they die within three hours – unless they sleep as they are desirous to do. Then they rave, and will die raving." Katherine shook her head. "We should have left weeks ago."

Mary fluffed the parsley again. "I pray the Lord will keep our households safe."

"And all righteous people," Arundel said.

Mary was about to offer a sincere *Amen*, but stopped herself. A spy might misconstrue their words as applauding the Lord's judgment on the Protestants. She needed to take care, do absolutely nothing that could earn her censure. "Most especially the King," she said.

Again, she found herself wondering whether this plague was meant to tell them something, like the locusts and snakes sent to warn Pharaoh in Egypt. She prayed the Council would wonder the same thing and turn from their plans to meddle further with Mary and destroy the true religion.

"I pray the Lord will keep him safe," Mary repeated firmly.

August 15, 1551

The Council and the Dudley family surrounded Edward in the Royal Oratory in Richmond Palace, which had been scrubbed of all papist symbols. Despite the close quarters, Edward preferred it to the Chapel Royal, whose stone walls still exuded the remnants of hundreds of years of incense.

Edward put aside his annoyance over misguided popish traditions and allowed his heart to swell. His Privy Chamber was being made over. Finally, he had been given more choice over his Gentlemen, even his Principal Gentlemen. The Council had always placed their allies in these influential positions; now Edward would have his own friends. Robin Dudley and Barnaby Fitzpatrick were about to be sworn to their positions.

"I thank Your Majesty for this trust," Robin said, as much for Edward as for the people gathered around. "I know I am young yet, but I promise to make up in energy what I lack in experience."

A female voice breathed "Amen." Edward smiled at Jane Dudley, Warwick's wife. She blushed and smiled back.

"I promise too," said Barnaby.

Edward smiled again. "I could say the same about myself. Let the older, sober men adorn my Council – in my privy moments I would prefer to be surrounded by my peers."

Of course, Robin was nineteen and Barnaby seventeen while

Edward had not quite turned fourteen. But Edward had always felt older than boys his own age. Or at least wanted to.

"Shall we begin?" Edward asked Warwick, who was picking an invisible speck of lint off his son's shoulder.

"Yes, Sire," Warwick answered, his chest puffing with pride. He nodded to the Lord Chamberlain, who would preside over the ceremony.

Thomas Darcy, Baron Darcy of Chiche, was one of Edward's cousins through Henry Wentworth, Edward's great-grandfather. Somerset had arranged for Darcy to take over after Thomas Wentworth, another distant cousin, died. Warwick had wrinkled his nose but said nothing.

Darcy stepped forward and bowed to Edward before turning and pointing to the ground before the lads. "Kneel."

The two friends dropped to their knees and put their right hands over their hearts.

"Because of the King's age, the Council was asked to consent to your appointment. That consent has been awarded, conditional on your vows and the King's final decision." Darcy paused and bowed again to Edward before continuing.

"On your souls, do you promise to defend and protect the King against all enemies, give him good and sober advice when he asks, fulfill your duties honestly and carefully, and keep his secrets?"

"I promise," each said.

Darcy turned to Edward. "Do you accept their service, Your Majesty?"

"Gladly," Edward said.

Another bow and Darcy turned back to the boys. "Rise, then, and keep your holy vows ever before your eyes."

With that, the magic was done. Edward walked over to be the first to embrace his new Gentlemen. After him came a dizzying series of handshakes and bows and hugs as the room celebrated the new era.

"I am thankful for this honor, even though it will mean I will be banished quite soon," Barnaby said with a smile.

"We will all be banished soon," Robin said. "Our only hosts during the summer's Progress are isolated manors with few residents. After today, we will feel very lonely."

Sins of the papists had brought the sweating sickness back to the country. No one knew how it spread, other than through crowds. Henry and Charles Brandon, horribly, had fallen prey to the disease. Having friends his age dead had sent Edward fleeing to Richmond for safety's sake; now they would be cloistering themselves even more.

"Nay, that's wisdom, not banishment," Barnaby said. "I'm talking about being sent to France to represent the King at the court of Henri II."

The French Ambassador had suggested it, based on Barnaby's closeness with Edward, and Warwick had agreed it would be a masterful touch. And this new honor would make Barnaby even more worthy.

"Never banished," Edward said. "Who would I send but someone I trusted completely?"

"Don't let him fool you, Your Majesty," Robin said. "Any one of us would be thrilled to visit the French court. Their women are marvelously fine."

Jane Dudley rolled her eyes; Warwick patted her hand.

Edward turned to Barnaby. "Ignore him. I expect you to behave yourself honestly, more following the company of gentlemen than pressing into the company of the ladies there."

Barnaby laughed. "You make me think the care you take for me is more fatherly than friendly."

Edward smiled ruefully. "Perhaps it is."

Guilford Dudley approached, his blue eyes shining in his round face. He was exactly Edward's age – but with none of Edward's cares, he seemed far younger.

Guilford clapped his older brother on the back. "Do the Dudleys proud."

Robin smiled and tousled Guilford's hair. "I shall do all in my power to serve the King. And that way you will be allowed to join me when you are old enough."

"He's still a child." Jane Dudley wagged a finger at Robin. "Don't put ideas into his mind."

Guilford flinched at her words and pressed his lips together as if that would stop the tears pooling in his eyes. Edward looked away, embarrassed for him and ashamed for himself.

She was treating an almost fourteen-year-old as a child. The entire situation was deflating. Edward felt wronged, like a horse given a poorly fitting bridle.

He took another breath to force himself to be patient. He leaned over and whispered to his friend. "Mothers are always cautious; if my own mother had lived, she would probably have been equally dismissive and kept me controlled until the day I turned eighteen."

If my own mother had lived.

His heart ached again for the woman who had sacrificed everything for him.

"Your life would have been quite different," Guilford said. "The realm too."

For the first time, Edward found himself wondering whether his mother would have excused or ignored her brother's treason. Edward was sobered by the terrible possibility she might have prevented Warwick from taking over, and the even worse suspicion she might have championed Mary's Masses.

He pushed aside the yearning that had turned into horror, and instead contemplated the present, the life God had chosen for him. Warwick was not Somerset. Warwick believed in Edward and was grooming him to begin his rule early. Had Warwick not proven that time and time again? This very day was proof Edward's wishes increasingly dominated the Council's choices.

Except where it mattered. His Council still would not stop his sister: they were too afraid of her talk about willingly suffering death. But he wasn't asking for that. Surely, they should be able to enforce their rules more gently.

Warwick came over to join them, putting his hands on his son's shoulders and pushing him away. "I don't know what you said to the King to provoke such a look," he said, "but I am stopping it right now."

Guilford scampered away before Edward could reassure Warwick nothing was wrong.

"I apologize for whatever he said, Sire," Warwick said. "He does not have your understanding or experience."

Somewhat mollified, Edward shook his head. "Nay, nay, he actually gave me an important idea. Tonight, when you come to visit, I want to discuss a new way of dealing with my sister."

"Oh?" Warwick looked skeptical.

"I want us to arrest anyone in her household who joined her for Mass. And install an officer to stop people in the future."

Warwick scratched his beard pensively. "That is indeed a practical solution. I am ashamed I did not think of it before this. I will go straightaway to start making notes to implement that brilliant idea."

Warwick's praise soothed Edward's budding anger that no one had advised him until now. "I will write the letter to Mary myself," he said. "Once our plans are firm, of course."

Warwick bowed and left Edward alone with his lingering fear of what might have been. The walls of the already small room closed in on him, and he was filled with a sudden, desperate need to leave.

"Now that you are fully my gentlemen, let us be away," he said to Barnaby and Robin. "I order it."

The Councilors looked puzzled, Jane and Guilford Dudley looked disappointed, but Edward didn't care.

He was the King, after all. He had the right to do this.

August 28, 1551

Through the slit of the drawn curtains, Mary peered out the window at the approaching visitors. Their faces were blurry, but there was no mistaking the glint of their chains of office. This would be an official visit from the King's Council.

"Look at their long faces," Eleanor sniffed. "After they sent their evil minions yesterday."

She referred of course to the royal guards. Sixty of them had arrested six of Mary's household officers, then rounded up her servants to remind them they were forbidden the Mass. Mary was glad to have an opportunity to respond in person to the insult, rather than just send another letter that would go ignored.

She moved to the center of the room, Eleanor right behind her, and faced the door to wait. It did not take long.

"Lord Chancellor Richard Rich, Master Secretary William Petre, and Sir Anthony Wingfield," announced the page.

"Let them enter," Mary said.

Their bows were perfunctory. As they approached, Mary straightened her already rigid back to better look down her nose at them.

"Greetings, gentlemen," she said, her tone icy. "What brings you this far from London?"

Mary had chosen Copped Hall in Essex for the summer, part of her new practice of avoiding the suspicion associated with residences close to the water. Not to mention it had once belonged to the Abbot of Waltham, and Mary could feel the holiness created by centuries of sincere and proper prayers.

"We have a letter for you from the King, your brother," Rich said.

She dropped to her knees to receive it and kissed it reverently. "For the honor of His Majesty's hand, wherewith the letter was signed, I kiss the letter. I do not kiss it for its contents, which I take to proceed not from His Majesty but from his Council."

The men exchanged nervous glances.

"If you will give me a moment, I will read it and then we will speak."

Without waiting for their reply, she strode over to a chair by the window. She deliberately extended no invitation to them, forcing them to remain standing awkwardly in the middle of the room.

It was as she expected: a scolding to accompany the Council's arrests. Here and there, she allowed herself to remark about what she read, taking care to ascribe her scorn to the lower-ranking members of the Council. It was not worth offending more powerful people who might yet come to her defense. "Ah! Good master Cecil took much pains here."

The men shifted their weight from side to side and *tsked* regularly. When their movements quickened enough that she feared they might try to take control of the meeting, she began the difficult part. "I have read the letter. Is there a message to accompany it?"

Rich huffed pompously and began. "The message is the same as in the letter. The King's Majesty has used gentle means and exhortations to move you to abide by the Rites of Religion and Order of Divine Services adopted by the Church of England – yet you have refused to conform, and remain in your former error."

"When the King's Majesty shall come to such years that he may be able to judge these things himself, His Majesty shall find me ready to obey his orders in religion. But now, in these years, although the good sweet King may have more knowledge than any others of his years, it is not possible he can be a judge of these things."

"This attitude will no longer be tolerated." Rich clenched his fists, and Mary could not tell if he was preparing to attack her or stopping himself from doing so.

Mary kept her voice soft. "You have a problem with the truth?"

"His Majesty, together with his Privy Council and other

members of the nobility, has decided you should no longer use the private Mass, nor any other divine service than is set forth by the laws of the realm." Rich started looking around for his pouch. "I am happy to show you the names of all who were present at this resolution."

Mary twisted her face into a frosty smile. "I care nothing for your names."

Rich's eyes widened for a second, and he swallowed before continuing. "His Majesty's pleasure is that we should also give straight charge to your chaplains, that none of them should presume to say any Mass or divine service other than that set forth by the laws of the realm. And like charge to all your servants that none of them should presume to hear Mass or any other divine service than as aforesaid. And—"

"Hear me, my Lord Chancellor," Mary said, angered by the repetition. "I was, am, and ever shall be His Majesty's most humble and most obedient subject and poor sister. I would most willingly obey all his commandments in anything except my conscience. I would willingly and gladly suffer death to do His Majesty good, but I cannot agree to use any other service than was used at the death of the late King, our father."

"You do not have that choice."

"A promise was made to the Emperor that I would."

"That promise does not exist. We have repeatedly told you this, yet you persist in this lie."

Mary looked into Rich's eyes but saw only Warwick's sneer. *What a sad world it is,* she thought, *when men can lie with such unashamed conviction.* "You may deny it now, but the promise was confirmed to me in His Majesty's own presence. I also have the Emperor's letter testifying this promise was made, and I believe that more than I believe you men of the Council. And though you esteem the Emperor little, yet you should show more favor to me for my father's sake, who made most of you almost of nothing. But even if the Emperor were dead, I would say as I do. And if he would give me now other advice, I would not follow it. To be plain with you, his ambassador shall know how I am used at your hands."

"You are not ill-used, Lady. We merely insist your household conform with our instructions. Your servants have manifestly disobeyed His Majesty's Council. They were instructed to see you conform to the law and they did not do so. They have not served you well and—"

"It is not the wisest counsel to expect my servants to control me in my own house. If they refused to fulfill your orders and instruct my chaplains and me as you instructed, then they are honest men who did not speak against their own conscience. For their punishment, you may use them as you think good."

"We have. They have been arrested and we shall give you new servants, including my Lord Rochester, to ensure our orders are followed."

The Bishop of Rochester? That heretic? Anger churned in her, and she lifted her already high chin. "I will appoint my own officers. I have years sufficient for that purpose. If you leave any such man, I will go out of the gates, for I will not share my dwelling with such a one."

"You shall have no choice, my Lady. The King will see his rules followed."

"These are not the King's rules – the King can make no such rules yet. If ships were to be sent to the seas, or any other thing to be done touching the policy and government of the realm, I am sure you would not think His Majesty yet able to consider what were to be done. Much less in these years can he discern what is fit in matters of divinity."

"Say what you will. Only the new service shall be said in your home."

Rich's lips were pinched, his jaw clenched. This was a man who understood little of nuance. A bulldog who understood little beyond direct orders. Mary's lip curled.

"The pain of your laws is imprisonment for a short time," she said. "If my chaplains are too fearful to say Mass, then I can hear none, nor can my poor servants. But none of your new service shall be used in my house, and if any be said in it, I will not tarry here."

"You cannot escape the rules by leaving – they will follow you to any dwelling. Yea, even a barn, if that be your choice. Though such an abode would not be healthy."

"I am sickly but will not die willingly. Yea, I will do the best I can to preserve my life. But if I chance to die, I will protest openly that you of the Council were the cause of my death. You give me fair words but your deeds are always ill toward me."

Rich's mouth opened, but Mary persisted. She dropped to her knees and pried a ring off her finger. The emerald Katherine Parr had given her to match the one that Henry had given Edward. The symbol that Mary was equally Henry's child, the tangible proof of worth that had succored her ever since. Praying her brother would recognize it and understand, she handed it to Rich. Trying to stop her voice from trembling but failing miserably, she told him, "I shall die the King's true subject and sister, obeying his commandments in all things except these matters of religion. He may stop me from hearing Mass, but I will never accept the new service."

She rose and swept from the room into her bedchamber. She glanced behind her to make sure Eleanor had followed her, and after she heard the firm shut of the door, her knees buckled. She heaved herself over to her *prie dieu* in the corner to offer thanks for the strength she had demonstrated in her hour of trial. A vision of her mother filled her mind – the mother who had endured exactly what Mary was being subjected to now. Her loyal servants arrested, her friends kept away. She needed to preserve her mother's example ever before her eyes.

Noise in the courtyard startled her. She jumped and thanked God for the warning against squandering this opportunity. She had more to say to them, to make them understand what their silly games were doing beyond just destroying her peace of mind.

"My Lady?" Eleanor asked. "Would you like me to bring a message?"

"Nay," Mary said. "I want to say this publicly, so my people can hear it from my mouth and theirs. They should know I never forget them – and how cruelly this weighs on me."

She raced to the window and opened it. The retreating figures were silhouetted by the haze of heat hovering over the horizon. Leaning out, she called to them. "Gentlemen, a moment."

The three whirled around and looked up, as did the twenty or so servants milling around the courtyard.

"We shall return to you," Rich said, wiping his brow.

"Nay," Mary said, taking advantage of the window seat to calm her shaking. "I wish only to beg kindness for my servants, who have only followed their consciences. The Tower is a fearsome place and not the proper abode for people who love the King."

"Confession does not shrive us of sins we continue to commit," Rich said.

Mary ignored them. "I pray, my Lords, that the Council at least restore the Comptroller they seized several months ago. For since his departing I have had to take the accounts myself of expenses. As you might guess, my father and mother never brought me up with baking and brewing, and it has taken me some time to learn how many loaves of bread be made of a bushel of wheat. To be plain with you, I am weary of this office, and therefore if my Lords will send my officer home, they shall do me pleasure."

"You should have considered that before you refused the Council's offer to appoint new officers," Rich said. "And as for your Comptroller specifically, I cannot advise you. It may well be they will send him to prison with the others."

Mary's first instinct was to cuttingly ask why they had not done so immediately, but she didn't want to bait them. "Well, if they do, I expect him to go merrily and with goodwill that bespeaks his eventual Divine reward. But I do hope the Council will exercise restraint and mercy in their decisions, remembering always that these poor souls are fully loyal to my brother and my father before him."

"They cannot be fully loyal if they continue to hear Mass," Rich said.

Mary ignored his argument in order to drive home her main point. Rich had been a staunch conservative in earlier days, until he had trimmed his sails to match the new wind. "And I pray God to send you to do well in your souls and bodies too, for some of you have but weak bodies."

September 9, 1551

Edward worked hard to pay attention to the land transfers being ratified by the Council, but last night's discussion weighed him down like chains. He stifled a yawn.

Somerset leaned forward. "May I address an important issue, Your Majesty?"

Out of the corner of his eye, Edward could see surprise registered on Warwick's face. Curious, Edward kept his tone inviting. "Of course."

"Your Majesty needs to act on behalf of the least of your subjects," Somerset said. "We must do more to relieve the great suffering in the land or we will answer for it before God."

Warwick had just raised the same issue the night before. Had they both had the idea independently, or was Somerset trying to steal some of the Earl's thunder – and Edward's – and gain more power in the Council?

"Warwick and I have already started considering measures," Edward said. He turned to Warwick. "Will you explain them, my Lord?"

Warwick bowed his head. "I would be honored if you would do so, Sire."

Edward nodded, happy to have the chance to show off his

grasp of the situation. "We have some further opportunities to amend the coinage. As we have already reduced the testoons to the value of six pennies each, we can mint new coins with ten ounces of silver in each pound without any further great loss."

Somerset cocked his head. "How is that?"

"A pound of testoons six ounces fine, added to another pound of testoons four ounces fine, would together furnish a pound of bullion ten ounces fine."

"Also," Warwick added, "we have some testoons of eight ounces fine. A pound weight of them, together with two ninth parts of a pound weight of those of nine ounces fine, would also furnish a pound of bullion ten ounces fine."

Somerset looked around the table, a small smile on his face. He clearly thought Edward had overlooked the flaw in the plan. Edward hastened to correct him.

"We would still coin the new pennies, halfpennies, and farthings in silver only four ounces in the pound fine, which would yield a profit enough to make good the loss that might arise from the loss upon such of the coins, particularly upon many of those of six ounces fine, as were supposed to have been made baser than their appointed standards."

Edward sat back, trying not to seem smug that his answer sounded natural and unrehearsed. But instead of acquiescing, Somerset shook his head. The Councilors all turned to him, waiting expectantly. Only William Paulet and William Herbert looked skeptical. And of course Warwick, who was staring stonily ahead, clenching and unclenching his hands. The scene jolted Edward into the realization that his uncle had indeed regained tremendous influence. His stomach turned at the idea, and he watched with nauseated fascination as Somerset sat back and steeped his fingers.

"I appreciate Your Majesty's care, but I cannot conceive in what manner the uniting of one pound of silver of six ounces fine with another pound of four ounces fine, can produce a compound of ten ounces fine; by which is meant ten ounces of fine silver and two of alloy. The compound would in fact consist of ten ounces of fine silver and fourteen ounces of alloy; or would, in other words, be silver of five ounces fine only. In like manner, a pound of eight ounces fine, and two ninth parts of a pound of nine ounces fine, would not give a compound of nine ounces fine, but of a quality considerably inferior."

Edward's head ached. He had followed Somerset's argument, and could not reconcile it with his own. There was no way to refute it, try as he might. Was it his youth, his particular inability, or simple fatigue? It didn't matter. He couldn't do it.

"We can go over the details later, in writing," Warwick said quietly. "So we can all agree on the figures."

"Yes, yes," Somerset said with a wave of his hand that made Warwick's nostrils flare. "But far more important," Somerset continued, "is a new approach. The adjustments to the coinage will eventually help, but the people need help now."

"Hear, hear." The Councilors banged on the table. Richard Rich, the Lord Chancellor, even shot a sidelong glance at Warwick, who drummed his fingers on the wood in a gesture Edward took as annoyance.

"What do you propose?"

Somerset paused and bowed before speaking. "To change the prices we have imposed on cattle and various other articles of provision," he said. "Make them more reasonable – not so cheap as when the coin was at the perfectest, but within a fifth part of it, or thereabouts." He swept his arm toward the Council. "I believe these gentlemen will all agree. Indeed, if you were discussing measures to relieve suffering, I am surprised the Earl did not suggest this."

"It is not as easy as you make it sound," Warwick said between clenched teeth. "It requires a careful hand to establish the correct prices."

"And yet I assume you agree this would help the poor, which is close enough to the Gospel to make it imperative that we try."

Warwick stood, rolling his eyes. "It would be the kind thing to do, Your Majesty."

With no dissenters, it seemed the matter had been agreed. "Let us issue a proclamation to that effect," Edward said. "Uncle, I look to you to see it done."

"It shall be, Your Majesty," Somerset said, his smile wide.

"If we could return to business now," Warwick said, motioning at Somerset's chair. Somerset sat in it, his movements theatrically slow.

"The Spanish Ambassador has again asked that the Lady Mary's chaplains be released," Warwick said. "I handled it in such a way as to send a subtle message, and I am confident I strengthened our position."

"Allow us to be the judge of that," Somerset said pompously. "What did you say?"

Warwick stared at him for what felt like an eternity, though if Edward had counted, he likely would not have made it past ten.

"I repeated what the Council agreed. I told him this would be impossible without His Majesty's" – Warwick broke off and turned to Edward – "Your Majesty's consent, and that you were elsewhere. He tried to argue this was not necessary, but I explained that Your Majesty was so old that you wished to concern yourself with all the matters of the kingdom."

Edward nodded, grateful for Warwick's response and for his reminder that the decision had been ratified by the full Council. God forbid his uncle should use his newfound influence unwisely. "How did Scheyfve respond?"

"We had some discussion about your capacity, and the Lady Mary, during which he kept referring to her as Princess of England and not as Your Majesty's sister. I mentioned that to him, and he defended his speech, saying the King, your father, had so held her."

"My father held her as a princess, but not as Princess of England," Edward said. "To name her such would be to wrong the Lady Elizabeth, who is also my sister."

"I said exactly that," Warwick said.

"This is a minor point," Somerset said. "What did you finally agree about her Mass?"

"There is only one answer to give about her Mass," Warwick said. "And I gave it. The King does not want her to hear it."

Somerset ignored Warwick's smirk. "There is not only one answer. The Council promised. The fair compromise is to limit the privilege to her alone."

Warwick stepped a foot forward. With his wild eyes and raised chin it looked as if he were about to strike the Duke.

"She has failed time and time again to uphold that limitation," Warwick said. "It is time to remove the privilege."

"That is a dangerous choice with the wedding not yet concluded." Somerset puffed out his chest while Edward's tightened.

The treaty with France had been signed and celebrated. Edward was tired of Somerset defending Mary on this point, tired of him derogating Edward's authority. Mounting rage spurred him to his feet. "The Mass is either of God or of the Devil. If it is of God, is it but right that all our people should be allowed to go to it; but if it is not of God as we are taught in the Scriptures, why, then, should not the voice of this fury be proscribed to all?"

Somerset's eyes widened. All the Council drew their heads back and let their jaws drop. Edward sniffed and sat back down. "Gentlemen, this is why you must continue to be firm with my sister. It is the only conclusion to be drawn." He locked eyes with his uncle, modeling his expression on his father in a rage, in the hope of making Somerset back down.

Out of the corner of his eye, he saw the hint of a small smile lift one side of Warwick's mouth. The approval should have made Edward proud, but instead he found himself nervous.

He sat back down and waved them on.

September 27, 1551

The knock on Edward's inner door was softer than usual, and it gave him pause. "Warwick? Is that you?"

The door opened. Warwick entered and bowed, a playful smile on his face. "After your exertions of earlier today, I thought you might be too tired for our meeting tonight."

Edward filled with warmth at the memory. They had bagged six deer and a brace of quails on the hunt, and then he and his men had run at the ring so long as to lather all the horses in the royal stables. "Nay, just the opposite. I find it hard to sleep from all the excitement."

"Ah, it is a fine trait, to be comfortable with effort," Warwick said. "May you continue to use it for good."

Edward had two cherished memories of his father infusing such warmth in his tone. Warwick was even standing like Henry at the height of his strength. "I shall try," Edward said.

"I know you will," Warwick said. "And, in fact, I think you should be given more of a chance to try."

"Oh?" Edward's hopes soared, though he wasn't sure why.

"Right after your birthday, I will suggest that your signature should not need the Council's countersignature to be effective. You will be fourteen; it is time for you to exercise your will."

Edward sat up straight. The thought of holding the power that he had coveted for so long squeezed tears into his eyes.

"Thank you," he said, his voice tight.

"Though you might prefer not using that power with tonight's item."

Edward soured at this retreat, and his annoyance drew his eyebrows into a furrow. Watching Edward's changing expression, Warwick spread his palms wide.

"Forgive me, Sire, but I wanted to discuss the possibility of elevating men to higher stations. If the Council does this, you may avoid dishonest men pressuring you to do something similar for them."

Edward relaxed. "Perhaps. Who?"

"It is not so simple." Warwick set his papers down on the table and settled into his chair. He straightened the pile and moved it to the side, then crossed his hands before him. "Dorset is asking to be recalled from his post of Lord Warden for the Marches of Scotland. He doesn't feel he can serve properly."

Henry Grey, Marquess of Dorset, had been named Lord Warden less than two months before, after the post had gone vacant for fifteen years. It had been done to mark the improved relations with Scotland since the French treaty. And Somerset's fall.

Edward wondered at the change and Dorset's sudden loss of confidence. "Do you think he serves well?"

"Not if he doesn't."

Edward thought. "Well, then, let him be recalled. But that leaves a void in an important position. Who should be Lord Warden in his stead?"

"It needs to be someone of substance," Warwick said. "Which is not easy since the noble houses around you have much decayed from your father's day. There are fewer men of high rank – for goodness' sake, you have only one duke in the land right now."

The thought hadn't occurred to Edward. He remembered his father's will had elevated many men; he assumed that was enough.

"So this brings us to the elevations you mentioned," he said.

"Precisely," Warwick said. "The first correction I would recommend is to honor Dorset with the Dukedom of Suffolk. His wife is the next rightful heir, with Henry and Charles Brandon dead. It is the perfect way to reward his service."

Edward nodded. "You are absolutely right, though that won't help us in Scotland."

"But it is no less my first recommendation." Warwick smiled. "For my second, I was thinking you might like to honor Sir William Herbert. A higher title would be expected for your stepmother's brother-in-law, an honest uncle. And it would certainly be a good way to compensate him for his travails."

Another good idea. "What do you suggest?"

"You could revive his grandfather's Earldom of Pembroke and remove the stain of illegitimacy at the same time."

Herbert's father had been an illegitimate son of the last Earl of Pembroke. Yes, it was time to end that shame. "Could he be sent to Scotland?"

Warwick shook his head. "He's too useful here."

Edward considered the matter. It seemed correct, especially if Warwick thought so. "Fine. But we still need a Lord Warden?"

"Aha – William Paulet. Who also deserves recognition for the job he has done as Lord High Treasurer. You could name him Marquess of Winchester and send him."

"Wasn't he named Earl of Wiltshire last year?"

"A reward long overdue."

Paulet. Well respected, if a bit soft. Too soft, actually.

"And yet he is not a soldier," Edward said. "The Lord Warden should be a soldier."

Warwick took a deep breath. "You are of course correct, Your Majesty." He looked down at his papers then back up at Edward. "But I still think the title would befit him."

"Yes, yes." Edward waved his hand. "But we need someone stronger."

"There are not many of us at court with battle experience, other than Somerset and myself."

The obviousness of the idea struck Edward like a punch to the face. "Of course. You. You would be perfect. You should be Lord Warden."

Warwick's eyes opened wide. "Me? I am honored…but that would not be right. You need someone with lands in the North, a personal stake, to be most effective." He looked down at his papers and traced a finger along an edge. "Of course, most Northerners are papists. Like the former Earl of Northumberland, right before he was attainted and his title removed from him."

Another clear solution. "Which makes it available to be bestowed on you," Edward said.

Warwick's face lit up but quickly dimmed. "You have already honored me with an earldom," he said. "A second one seems redundant. Especially since it's not the usual pattern of advancement."

Of course. New titles were always higher ones. But this was easily solved as well. "Well, then, I could make you *Duke* of Northumberland," Edward said. "That would suit you better."

Warwick opened his mouth as if to argue, then shut it. His eyes glistened. "Are you sure? That was the whim of a single moment, and I will understand if you want to change your mind."

Edward was touched by Warwick's generosity. "I will never see this as anything but the perfect decision."

Warwick pushed his chair away to kneel and swept his cap from his head. "Thank you, Your Majesty, for the honor you show me. I will serve you with all I have."

"I know you will," Edward said, meaning it.

Warwick rose and sat back down in his chair. "And the first part of that service will be to insist this not be the first act you take on your own. This one should be approved by your Councilors, lest they accuse me of ambition I do not have."

Edward hadn't considered that. Yes, some might see this as Warwick pushing when he clearly hadn't. "Then let us plan for these creations to be made Sunday next. The day before my birthday, the day before you speak to the Lords about my new authority." Edward smiled. "Besides, they will be more likely to listen to you, once your stature is increased."

"Perfect, Sire. Though I still worry the Duke of Somerset will be discomfited when he learns of the plan. These gentlemen whom you will honor are all friends of mine, and he is likely to read ill into this. You know how he can be."

Edward did know and was grateful for yet another instance where Warwick's loyalty helped protect the throne. It was wonderful to have someone who cared about him. "Yes, my uncle can be difficult."

Warwick started massaging his temples.

"What is wrong?" Edward asked.

Warwick sighed heavily. "Nothing, Your Majesty. It is nothing."

That was clearly a lie. "Something is weighing on you. I can see it. Tell me."

Warwick shook his head. "I should not. It could just be gossip." He started to rifle through the papers on the table.

"Tell me." The words were barely a croak.

"It is nothing," Warwick said, still rifling.

Something was terribly wrong, and Edward could hardly breathe. He put a hand on top of the pile. "Tell me."

Warwick sighed. "You are too discerning. It is impossible to keep things from you."

He sighed again, clasped his hands in his lap and glanced heavenward as if for strength before beginning. "It is said Somerset is working against your French marriage."

"How is that possible?" Edward asked. Somerset had retired from court two weeks before, right after he lost the argument about Mary. Two of his servants had succumbed to the sweating sickness, and he did not want to risk spreading the disease.

"His health is good," Warwick said. "And the Devil makes work for idle hands to do."

That answered one question, but Edward had another. "Why would he do such a thing?"

"I think perhaps to hurt me," Warwick said. "Though in truth he has always preferred to placate the Spanish. Maybe he wants you to marry a Spanish bride, and that's why he defends Mary so keenly."

Edward shuddered. "I could not stomach a Spanish bride. Or the demands they would place on me to allow her a popish service."

"I agree it is preposterous," Warwick said.

"Besides, rumor says he wants me to wed his third daughter, Lady Jane Seymour."

Warwick pulled back, eyes wide. "Where did you hear that?"

"Your son Robin. My other men all knew of it."

"It is unthinkable this could happen," Warwick said. "Such a move would be tantamount to a claim to his old power."

Edward's eyes narrowed.

"Surely this is no more than idle gossip," Warwick said. "And speaking of the Duke and gossip—" Warwick stopped and banged his hand on the table. "There I go again."

"What is wrong?" Edward asked.

"Nay, nay, this is truly just conjecture."

"You must tell me."

"Well, it does involve religion, and I suppose I must share it." Warwick wagged a finger. "But only because you insist."

He took a deep breath, then shook his head. He sighed a second time and then began. "There is a prophecy, Your Majesty. A woman from Poole, a country village in Dorset, Mrs. Woocock by name, heard a troubling voice that followed her for days. She told her neighbors, who reported it to the local magistrates, who sent her to London to be examined by the Council."

"Is she a papist?" Edward asked. "Is this a dream provoked by an excess of incense?"

"Nay, nay. A good reformist. An honest woman. And this was not a visitation by saints, it was just a single sentence repeated over and over until she had to speak out."

"What did the voice say?"

"He whom the King did best trust will deceive him and work treason against him."

Edward reached for the blanket on his chair and pulled it around his shoulders. "And you think this refers to the Duke of Somerset?"

Warwick shrugged. "I do not know that. I only know you trust him well."

Edward thought about it for a moment. "What did my Lord of Somerset say to this?"

"I have not had the chance to confront him. This happened during his latest absence."

"Ah," Edward said.

"When he returns, I will speak to him straightaway. Though I am sure I will find nothing. I cannot believe an uncle of yours would betray you." Warwick inhaled sharply and his eyes widened. "Not again, anyway."

Edward suddenly felt very, very tired.

October 11, 1551

"I heard them," called Robin Dudley, who had been sent to peer down the hallway. Henry Sidney immediately turned to adjust Edward's long purple train and brush away an invisible speck. Then he joined the other attendants who were arranging themselves beside Robin, still breathless from racing back from his post.

Edward looked around his Presence Chamber, where he was waiting with his men for the procession to arrive so four lords could be elevated. The space felt empty but ready to receive the glory of the approaching procession. The higher the new position, the greater the pageantry; with two dukes and a marquess being made, the ceremonies would contain many of the civil elements of a coronation. Edward looked forward to reliving some of the awe evoked by fulfilling traditions almost six hundred years old. He sighed happily at the tactile details that had already transported him for a brief second back in time, like the iconography that inspired the room's special decorations for the event: tapestries featuring brave knights triumphing in battle, and small laurel wreaths encircling the plaster medallions on the walls.

Edward exulted over being able to share this gift with worthy people.

As was fitting, the day had begun with services. Then the lords had all retired to the King's Closet to don their robes of estate before proceeding on a snaking path through the Great Chamber to arrive into Edward's presence.

The trumpeters closest to the door raised their instruments to their mouths, and the rest followed one at a time, like a wave on the Thames, to begin the elaborate choreography that did not exist a moment ago.

First to enter were the Officers of Arms, in their coats of arms. Next came Sir Gilbert Dethick, the Garter Principal, bearing Warwick's patent upright in his arms. Then Baron Cobham, who was a Knight of the Order of the Garter and who bore upright in his hand a gold verge. The two men had turned the hoods of their robes down about their necks and opened their mantles on the right side to highlight their collars of the Order. They stood before Edward, then turned back to face the entrance. Next came the Earl of Rutland, bearing the cap with its coronet, and the Earl of Bedford with the state sword in its sheath, pommel upward. Dethick and Cobham each moved to the side to allow Rutland and Bedford to mount the dais and stand next to Edward, one on each side. Finally, Warwick entered, between Somerset and Dorset, with all the other Lords of the Council behind.

They made reverent obeisance one at a time, in the same order in which they had entered, then Warwick knelt. The Garter Principal handed the rod of office and the letters patent to Thomas Darcy, the Lord Chamberlain, who inspected them and handed them to Edward. Edward inspected them as well, or at least he pretended to, then handed them to William Cecil, Secretary to the Council, to read the Latin text aloud.

At the words "*gladii cincturam,*" Cecil paused for Bedford to unsheathe the sword of state and hand it to Edward; Warwick bowed his head and Edward touched his shoulders with the blade. At the words "*cape circuli,*" Cecil paused again for Edward to take the cap from Rutland and set it on

Warwick's head. Finally, at the words "*traditionem virge auree*," Cecil handed the letters patent back to Edward, who again pretended to inspect them before delivering them to Warwick along with the rod of office. Warwick held the letters in his right hand and the rod in his left while Archbishop Cranmer said prayers of thanksgiving, and then Warwick stood and bowed and came to stand at Edward's right hand. Another wave of trumpets blared while all the Lords filed out to return to the Closet.

It seemed silly to conduct the full ceremony for each elevation, but every man deserved his personal moment of glory, even if it did add greatly to the length of the day.

"I thank you again, Sire," Warwick – no, Northumberland – said quietly.

"It is no more than you deserve," Edward said.

"Congratulations, father," Robin Dudley said in a loud whisper. Northumberland smiled but shushed him.

After that, there was no question of anyone watching the door while they waited for the men to return again, this time with Dorset in the place of honor next to Somerset, whose stony face could be attributed to the formality of the occasion.

They repeated each step of the ceremony, after which the newly created Duke of Suffolk joined them on the dais. At that point Northumberland and Suffolk held the royal regalia, so the third ceremonial entrance, the one for Paulet, was a little shorter. Still, by the time the Lords had retired to begin the process for Herbert, Edward's feet were hurting. He shifted his weight and bent his toes in their velvet slippers.

Despite Edward's efforts at discretion, Northumberland noticed.

"You should take a seat, Sire. No one will know," he said. He turned to his son. "Robin, go watch the door and tell us when they are near."

Sidney giggled and Edward joined in.

"What?" Northumberland asked.

"We were doing that before you arrived," Edward said. "We thought you would think it childish."

"We used to do that back in your father's day," Dorset – no, Suffolk – said. "There is no reason to suffer."

The respite made a big difference, and again Edward said a quick prayer of thanks for loyal courtiers. When the Lords had left for the last time, but the new honorees remained, Edward turned to Northumberland. "What now?"

"They will remove their robes and then join us for dinner."

"What about you four?" Edward thought back to his own experience after his coronation. "Will you keep your coronets?"

"No, nor our mantles," Northumberland said. "Only our surcoats. Though before we remove them, this would be an excellent opportunity to execute your plan."

Edward stood straighter and turned around to smile at his attendants. "Cecil, Cheke, Sidney, and Neville, come stand before me," he said.

The named men glanced at each other but quickly did as they were told.

Northumberland handed Edward the sword of state.

"Kneel," Edward said, and comprehension flickered over their faces, along with hope they were right and fear they were wrong.

"My Council's concern over the lack of high titles around me alerted me to the fact that lower titles were missing as well. They agreed a new knight might be created for each high office granted today." He took the sword and touched each of their shoulders. "Rise," he said when he was done.

The four men rose, their faces shining.

Edward turned back around. His other attendants were looking down, and their forlorn looks told him Northumberland's warning had been correct. "The rest of you will be rewarded as soon as I am allowed," he said. "I will not forget you."

Northumberland winked. "Now let us repair to the Great Hall, where a feast awaits us," he said.

The trumpets blared with their every move, such was the formality of the day. There were even fanfares to celebrate them taking their seats.

Edward was of course at the head of the main table. To his right sat the newly minted lords: the Duke of Suffolk, then the Duke of Northumberland, thirdly the Marquess of Winchester, and finally the Earl of Pembroke. When the other lords entered, to still more trumpets, they took their places on Edward's left: first the Duke of Somerset, then the Earl of Bedford, thirdly the Marquess of Northampton, then the Earl of Rutland, and finally the Baron Cobham.

After the second course, the herald of arms proclaimed the King's style and the styles of all the newly created lords. The wine was flowing freely, and Edward found his mind slightly clouded behind his wide grin.

"A toast," Somerset said, raising his glass. "To good friends – the new peers who will guard this realm."

But his tone was a strange one. Edward looked at his uncle and saw glassy eyes atop a crooked smile. *Has the man been drinking too much?* Edward wondered.

"After all, they have worked miracles," Somerset continued. He wagged a finger at Northumberland. "Ah, my Lord, do you realize you are the first Duke in history without even a trace of blood connection to the royal family?"

Northumberland's eyes narrowed. "The King knows how to reward loyalty."

"Or the semblance, it seems."

Northumberland's eyes had a hard glint as he brought his cup to his lips. Edward looked away.

Somerset's jealousy was far too apparent in the unseemly display. That woman's prophecy played in Edward's mind: *He whom the King did best trust will deceive him and work treason against him.*

There had been no further word on the outcome of Northumberland's investigation. It must have come to nothing.

It must have.

October 13, 1551

The late afternoon sun tinged the room rose, making the maple of Edward's lute glow with a light that felt divine.

He plucked the notes from the bridge of the piece he had chosen for the upcoming masque. He went slowly, getting comfortable with the progression of notes. Only when his fingers had learned the sequence would he start to go faster. Long experience had taught him this was the best way to learn.

His musical preceptor accompanied him on the virginals, holding the keys to draw out the notes for the pace or repeating them when Edward made a correction. His other men played cards at the table in the corner, wagering even though it was against the law. Now that Edward had more choice over his attendants, he was less subject to rules enacted for ordinary people.

The knock at the door was quiet but insistent. Robin Dudley opened it, "Ah, greetings, Father."

After urgent whispering, he turned to Edward, eyebrows furrowed. "Sire? The Duke of Northumberland asks leave to wait upon you. It is important."

"Have him enter," Edward said.

Northumberland strode into the room, his face twisted as if he were in pain. He stopped and looked around as he bowed, as if startled by the presence of the men. "I would speak with you alone, Sire," he said.

Edward felt the air tighten around him. "Leave me," he said to his men without taking his eyes from the Duke.

When the room was empty, Northumberland swayed a bit and closed his eyes. "May I sit?"

Edward motioned to the chair but said nothing, taking advantage of the shield of protocol to delay this moment he instinctively dreaded. *To share immediately gratifies the teller's needs, not necessarily your own,* his father had told him. But his father had also always insisted his messengers come immediately to the point, and Edward had not understood the distinction. Until now. He took a series of deep breaths, until the thudding of his heart had gentled and slowed. "What is it?"

Northumberland took his own deep breath. "I did not want to say anything until it was more certain. But it seems Somerset has been conspiring against the state for the last six months. Since Saint George's Day."

He whom the King did best trust will deceive him and work treason against him.

"Tell me everything," Edward said.

"He wants to resume his dictatorship as Lord Protector. He planned to enforce his will with two thousand soldiers. Arundel was to hold the Tower while Miles Partridge raised London, seized the Great Seal, and rallied the accomplices. They were going to massacre anyone who did not desert for Somerset and his conspirators."

"How could he think to succeed against the city's militia? Surely we could raise a force larger than that?"

"He planned to begin this evil scheme by removing your staunchest supporters. Suffolk, Northampton, me and several others were to be assassinated at a banquet at his home. His wife was part of the plot."

Edward covered his face with his hands, as if hiding from the terrible news would stop the flow. But Northumberland continued.

"With Arundel, he knew he would have support from all the Catholics hiding around the country. Maybe even Spain."

"Did he not consider France might come to our aid?" Edward asked bitterly.

"He intended to be firmly in charge long before, with you married to his daughter Jane instead of Madame Elisabeth."

Such a comprehensive plan. Somerset had to be guilty. *And yet...*

"Could he really be so evil?" Edward did not try to hide the deep pleading in his voice.

Northumberland sighed. "Remember how violent and tyrannical he can be – remember how he rushed you to Windsor under the pretense you were in danger to save his own rule."

Edward remembered that too well. That was when the mask had been removed from the face of the man he had completely trusted. Who would have guessed there was yet a more terrible mask beneath that one?

And Anne Somerset conspiring with him.

Edward remembered his stepmother's pain over the Duchess claiming precedence. And the royal jewels. *But still...*

"We should remove to Westminster," Northumberland said. "This matter would be more easily and surely dispatched there."

Edward bit his lip. "Whatever you think best."

"I will give the orders to the Lord Chamberlain tomorrow as if nothing is wrong. We will leave in two days' time, and this will be resolved promptly after that."

"Good." Edward felt a little nauseous. Another uncle putting himself before Edward, before the realm, before God.

How cursed Edward was in uncles, if this was true.

Again, his father and his Abraham tapestries loomed before his eyes. *God's anointed is the law and the land and the church, and no one can be allowed to commit treason and live.*

He lowered his head and allowed sobs to rack his body. No one was too old to cry at a moment like this.

October 17, 1551

A gentle hand on his shoulder and a whispered "Your Majesty" finally woke Edward. He turned over. The light was still thin in the chamber.

Henry Sidney towered over his bed. "It's Richard Rich, Sire. He apologizes for the early hour, but he begs an urgent audience. He is most insistent."

The Lord Chancellor? This must be important. Edward sat up and rubbed his eyes to focus. "Have him enter."

The man was beside him in an instant, on his knees with his shoulders hunched in abject pleading. Fear surrounded him like a cloud, and his forehead glistened with sweat. "Sire, I am old and terribly sick," he said, eyes wild. "I can no longer properly perform the duties of my office, and I beg leave to retire."

"Sick?" Edward drew back. Sick people had never been permitted to approach him.

"No, not like that," Rich said. "I am just ailing – dying – and I must go."

Edward relaxed a bit. The man was in his fifties after all, the natural end of life for many. "Of course," Edward said. "Write your letter and I will approve it. The Council will thank you and arrange for—"

"I beg you, Sire, do not make me go through that." Rich clawed a hand through his hair. "I must attend to my devotions and prepare my soul. My tomb as well – say the word and I will be off to my Essex estate."

The urgency troubled Edward. He never liked things to happen so quickly. "I don't know what to say."

"Say yes, then, and give a dying man comfort. Accept my resignation now, instead of waiting. There will be no difference in the end."

Rich spoke true. Today, tomorrow, it made no difference. "Fine," Edward said. "Retire and see to your soul. Godspeed, and we will pray for you."

Rich raised his eyes heavenward in relief before flying from the room as if the Devil were chasing him.

For the first time, Edward noticed the faces of his men, still on their sleeping pallets. Their wide eyes and tight lips showed fear, and he hastened to reassure them. "The poor Lord Chancellor fears for his soul," he explained.

"God only knows what sins lay so heavy on his conscience," Cheke said.

The words set them all to uproarious laughter that freed their bodies and spirits from the tension Rich had left behind. Edward lay back, spent.

"Let me play a soothing tune for you," Throckmorton said. "Perhaps sleep will return."

Edward tried, he really did. Several times he thought he might have succeeded, but always his eyes flew open despite his best efforts. Finally, he conceded that sleep had left him for the day. "What say you to hawking?" he asked the room.

His men leaped up with *whoops* and put away their pallets.

"I'll go give the instructions," Sidney said. "And wake the laggards."

"With that kind of effort ahead of us, we should break our fast first," Robin said.

"I don't want to wait – we can stop along the way. Surely they will have pasties for us."

"I'll make sure," Sidney said and raced away.

Their speed was rewarded with the perfect autumn morning. The fog offered the subdued light that gave the hawks cover when pursuing their prey, so almost every launch succeeded. They returned with a take better than any of them could remember, and Edward had never felt so triumphant and kingly.

They were still exulting loudly as they dismounted in Whitehall's courtyard. Northumberland laughed as he approached the group.

"It warms my heart to see you all so joyous," he said.

"We have returned with food for everyone," Edward said, including Northumberland in the inner circle he referenced: even ten times their catch would not be enough for the thousand mouths the court fed every day.

"Supper is about to be served, but surely these can grace dinner later," Northumberland said. He raised a hand to signal for the panniers to be taken to the kitchens.

Edward handed his reins to the page, who smiled shyly in

thanks. "I hope you will join me, then," he said to Northumberland.

"I would be honored," Northumberland said. "I will even wait until then to tell you of my progress."

"Progress?"

"The witnesses we are questioning. With Somerset arrested, they have been much more forthcoming."

"Why would that be?" Edward asked.

"They no longer fear the Duke might retaliate if he survives this as he has survived previous struggles," Northumberland said. "He was arrested for treason before."

The words felt like a scolding, but Northumberland's raised eyebrows suggested only helpfulness.

Still, Edward waved his men away. "Tell me now," he said. "Walk with me." He pointed at the covered colonnade, which offered a peaceful *allée* with random seats in case he tired. They had, after all, ridden hard.

"What have you learned?" Edward asked.

Northumberland sighed. "Arundel has confirmed that Somerset hoped to reform Your Majesty's administration and spoke to him of a plot to do so. The plot's first move contemplated...apprehending me."

Apprehending. The bright joy of the day dimmed a bit, and Edward shuddered. "So, Arundel admits to being an accomplice to attempted murder?"

"Alas, Sire, it is never so easy. He swears they planned no harm to my body. He also says Somerset decided to take no action."

Edward thought a moment. "Does this exonerate him? And my uncle?"

"Not at all, Sire. Somerset himself has conceded that he did indeed hope for a change in your Council and admitted to several meetings with Arundel – and with others."

"Who are the others?"

"The chief conspirators were Michael Stanhope, Miles

Partridge, and Ralph Vine. They maintain their innocence, but we have statements from Thomas Palmer, William Stanley, and Francis Newdigate. Also Crane, Barvile, and Hamond. The only other person to be questioned is Lord Chancellor Rich."

Edward's remaining shreds of triumph plunged. "You won't find Rich."

"Beg pardon?"

"Master Rich resigned this morning."

Northumberland stopped walking and looked around, as if an answer was hidden in plain sight. "It is still 'this morning,' Your Majesty. When did this occur?"

"He came to my rooms before I was risen."

Comprehension dawned across Northumberland's face. "Did he say anything else?"

"Like?"

"Oh Sire." Northumberland bent over to rest his hands on his knees while his body shook with angry laughter. Finally, he rose and sucked his teeth. "Our friend Rich wrote a letter to the Duke of Somerset warning him what the witnesses were saying and sharing with him my plans for his prosecution."

"How do you know this? Did my uncle show you the letter?"

"Our former Lord Chancellor has never been the most careful of men." Northumberland shook his head, still smiling ruefully. "He addressed the envelope 'to the duke,' forgetting there was a former duke lodged there."

Edward understood immediately. "Norfolk."

Thomas Howard, Third Duke of Norfolk. Imprisoned when Somerset discovered his treasonous plan to wrest the throne, to serve as Regent. To essentially do exactly what Somerset was now accused of doing.

"Norfolk was only too happy to tell me of Rich's perfidy," Northumberland said.

Of course he would be. Norfolk blamed Somerset for his attainder. In truth, the man would be dead now if Somerset hadn't bungled the execution plans.

.

But that was the least of the problems now. Now Edward had to focus on the immediate issue. That's what a grownup would do.

He resumed walking, watching his steps while he pondered the situation. "Why would Rich try to warn Somerset?"

"I don't know. That's why I wanted to question him."

Edward sighed, angry at himself for ignoring his instincts. "I should have known better than to let him leave. But he said he was dying, and I could not think of a reason to refuse him."

Northumberland patted his shoulder. "Of course you could not."

They kept walking.

"It's not an irrevocable mistake," Edward said. "We know where his estates are. You can arrest him there."

"In truth, we don't need him," Northumberland said. "We already have more than enough evidence to bring Somerset to trial. That's what I was coming to tell you."

Edward tried to sound offhand. "He is to be tried?"

"The Duke is much loved by the people," Northumberland said. "They will insist."

The statement confused Edward. Why did Northumberland not assume Edward would insist his uncle be given a chance to refute the charges? "Of course they will, and they are right to do so."

"Of course."

December 1, 1551

"Twelve," Edward announced to reflect his double pair royal.

"Five," Robin said, which meant he had a run of five and could not challenge Edward's hand. Edward added another coin to the pot, and the other players groaned and threw down their cards.

Although Noddy was one of Edward's favorite games, Westminster was one of Edward's least favorite palaces. Like the

Tower, it had been built by William the Conqueror. Also like the Tower, its magnificence felt harsh. Edward much preferred the nearby Whitehall, which offered a much more modern luxury.

But his presence was required here. His people needed to see him close by during Somerset's trial, especially since Northumberland was presiding over it. Otherwise the people would resent the image of the Bad Duke judging the Good Duke, as they had named them.

The trial was underway right now in the Palace Yard. Somerset had been brought in by barge at five in the morning, under cover of darkness. But the crowds had been there anyway. Thousands of commoners thronged the yard and the streets beyond, praying and singing to lend hope to their beloved champion.

Edward looked toward the window, in the direction of the Yard.

"The next messenger should arrive soon," Robin said.

Messengers had come at the hour marks to keep Edward apprised. There had been seven messengers for the trial itself, and five so far for the deliberations.

Edward looked back down at the pile of coins, wishing his victory felt sweeter. As he drew the pot toward him, shouts and cheers erupted from the Yard. The card game forgotten, Edward hurried over to open the window and peer down.

Joyous abandon greeted him, as far as his eyes could see. Men and women danced and embraced and threw caps in the air, cheering and weeping and laughing.

Two guards guided a stone-faced Somerset through the crowd; their blades were turned away. Edward's heart surged at the verdict of innocence this represented.

"I had never believed my uncle could be a traitor," he said aloud to no one and everyone.

The guards led Somerset onto a waiting barge and cast off quickly. Edward found himself compelled to continue watching, as if he could feel the salt air of freedom on his own face. But instead of stopping at Somerset Place, the barge continued on down the Thames.

"Your Majesty," said Northumberland's voice at the door. Edward turned and motioned him in. "Where do they take my uncle?"

Northumberland's face was calm, steady. "The Tower."

"The Tower?" Edward recoiled. "Was he not found innocent of treason?"

"Actually, we did not pursue the case of treason against him."

That explained the axes, but not the rest. "But the messengers...the testimony they described..."

"We tried him for felonious intent. He was found guilty of that."

Edward took a deep breath. This was clearly a longer conversation, involving news he should hear in private. He walked over to a corner chair and motioned to Northumberland to join him.

"Please explain," he said when his heart had stilled to its normal beat.

"Treason is a crime committed against a sovereign. I would not have an attempt on my own life dignified by such a name."

Edward bowed his head to acknowledge the respect contained in that decision. "What is the penalty for felonious intent?"

Northumberland sighed. "Death."

Edward froze. "Did he realize that?"

"Without a doubt. He knelt at the verdict, thanked the court for its trial, and asked mercy for his wife and children."

Edward's throat was too tight to speak. Northumberland continued.

"Ah, Sire, I felt such pity for him at that moment. I spoke to him, before the crowd, as gently as I could."

"What did you say?" The words came out a croak.

"I reminded him he was brought into the utmost danger. That I had once before delivered him from a similar hazard of his life, and that I would not now desist in serving him, howsoever little he may expect it. I said he should appeal to the royal clemency, which I doubted not would be extended to him."

Edward's heart soared with fear and terror. "I may pardon him?"

"Of course you may. It is how he escaped death the last time."

Edward thought back to those dark days. Somerset had not deserved to die for that. If this was not treason, perhaps he should not die for this. "I may do that," he said, firmly this time.

"Ah, Sire, you and I are too generous sometimes," Northumberland said. "I, too, would forgive him for this. I love the man well, much as I deplore how he has treated you."

Edward relaxed a little. "Fine. What happens now?"

"You write out your pardon and send..." Northumberland put his hands over his eyes as his voice trailed off. He heaved a great sigh and then put down his hands. His eyes were red. "Ah, Sire, I hear the voice of your dear departed father. He always said he could never forgive a traitor, because they could never forgive themselves and would inevitably offend again. As Somerset did here."

Northumberland's words awakened a shadowy echo in Edward's mind. He pushed away the thought. "And yet, now as then his crime does not seem so terrible."

"I fully agree with you," Northumberland said. "But mercy may inspire others to betray you as well."

Edward considered the argument. "Perhaps there is some other punishment that could be imposed."

Northumberland nodded thoughtfully. "Perhaps."

"A fearful fine," Edward said. "Or...or...there must be something else."

"There must be. But better heads should be brought into the discussion. It should be the full Council to determine the appropriate punishment."

The advice was sound. And fair. Then why was Edward's heart so heavy?

His anguish must have shown in his face because Northumberland leaned forward and put a hand on Edward's arm.

"Let your Council take this burden from you," Northumberland said. "And to take your mind off this terribly tragedy, this shall be the gayest Christmas you have ever seen. We will even appoint a Lord of Misrule, a practice which languished during the late years of your father's reign. I promise that when we repair to Greenwich for the season, you will see plays and masques and dancing befitting your station. We will summon your sister Elizabeth to preside for the women; I'm sure she will be honored."

Edward nodded. That would help.

January 20, 1552

Edward pulled his furs tighter around him, shivering despite the roaring fire in the hearth. Somerset's death warrant lay on the table before him, awaiting his signature.

Northumberland had brought it to him earlier, tears in his eyes over his failure to move the men of the Council with his impassioned pleas. They had been adamant Somerset must die. And now there was nothing Edward could do to avoid this final, terrible step.

Kneeling before him, Somerset's incarnation pleaded for mercy. In the empty chair across from him, Tom Seymour's ghost dipped a quill in the ink and held it out to him. *The next time you are presented with a death warrant, you will sign it yourself.*

Edward squirmed as he heard his own promise, made two years ago.

This death is for England, the specter said.

Edward wanted to scream, to cry, to pull out his hair. To

refuse. But he could not. It was his duty, his responsibility. Even though so many of his people disagreed.

He shut his eyes tight. But when he opened them, it was his father pointing the quill at him. *It is never an easy thing.*

It is an impossible thing, he wanted to scream.

Now Northumberland's words echoed in the room. *I prayed this cup might pass from your lips. But as Christ's plea went unanswered in Gethsemane, so did mine.*

Edward looked down at the warrant. Such a small paper for such a big deed. It didn't seem right.

Do it quickly, came a whisper. *Be done with it.*

He took a deep breath and held it as he pulled the paper toward him, grabbed a quill, and scrawled his name across the top.

He exhaled, staring at his drying signature. He waited for the ghosts to react, but they were gone.

Edward was all alone. Truly all alone.

January 22, 1551

Edward sat in his chair of estate, gripping the *manchettes* to keep himself from leaping up and running away. *This is your duty,* he repeated to himself over and over. *Your duty.*

Sir Arthur Darcy was reporting on Somerset's execution. And Edward had to listen. And react appropriately, like the monarch he was.

"Proceed," Edward said.

"The crowd was fierce, Your Majesty. Large and fierce," Darcy said.

"But what about our orders?" The Council had Edward issue a proclamation with instructions that all people keep themselves and their families within doors.

"They went unheeded. It felt like all of London was there, and more. They were in the streets, on rooftops, standing on chairs in courtyards." Darcy paused and glanced at Northumberland. "They wanted to hear his last words."

"Yes, yes," Northumberland said, his voice clipped and matter of fact.

That had been a point of contention in the Council. Some of the Lords had wanted to forbid him from speaking, or to have the drums drown out his last words lest they provoke an uprising. Northumberland had refused, saying that the people would think it was a dishonest trick, that they might rise up then and there because of it. He said it wasn't worth it, that Somerset would make a good end, knowing his wife and his children had been spared by the King's mercy. Knowing clemency could be withdrawn.

Edward brought himself back to the moment at hand. "Go on."

"He was fully attired in court dress, with all his orders," Darcy said.

"That should not have been permitted," Northumberland said. "Such grandeur might have been inflammatory."

"Nay, just the opposite. Silence fell when he stepped on the scaffold, except for sniffles from weeping women."

The pathos of the scene clawed at Edward's heart. "So, what did he say?"

Darcy looked down at the paper in his hands. "I wrote down the words, to get them right. Shall I?"

Edward bit back annoyance. He had just asked the man to tell him, why the second question? But then Edward worried this might be a warning. The truth might be more than he could stand. Except he had to. Unable to speak, Edward waved Darcy on.

Darcy nodded. Looking down, he took a deep breath. "Masters and good fellows, I come hither to die, a true and faithful man as any was unto the King's Majesty and his realm. But I am condemned by a law whereunto I am subject, as are we all. And therefore to show obedience, I am content to die."

Edward dug his fingernails into his palms but kept his face impassive.

"For as any man, I have deserved many deaths at God's hand. And whereas He might have taken me suddenly, it has pleased His goodness to call me with this present death as you do see. He has given me time to remember and acknowledge Him, and also to know myself, for which I thank Him heartily. My friends, I say to you that I have always used my authority, to the utmost of my power, to further the glory of God. I am nothing sorry for that; indeed, I do rejoice most gladly that I have done so. And I beseech you all to continue my work, and follow it on still – for if not, there will be a worse plague."

Darcy stopped. He cleared this throat and mopped his brow.

A worse plague. Edward took a deep breath. "Was that all?"

"No, Sire. It's that…it's just that right then there came the noise of marching men."

Edward's eyes opened wide. "Rebellion?"

Darcy shook his head. "It was Sir Anthony Browne arriving with a running body of soldiers. They had sent for extra men in case of unrest, but the people thought it was a reprieve. They started to shout and jostle. They tried to tear Somerset from the scaffold and carry him away."

"We sent no reprieve," Northumberland said.

"Of course, Sire – I mean, Sir," said Darcy, and the mistake made Edward wonder to whom Darcy was telling the story.

"They came only to reinforce their comrades who were having a difficult time holding back the crowds," Darcy continued.

"It was a good thing they did," Northumberland said, and he sniffed.

"Actually, the crowd could have made easy sport of the lot of them. It was only Somerset that saved the day. He knew it was no reprieve and told the people as much. He quieted them down so he could resume."

Hot tears stung Edward's eyes. He pressed his lips together at the image of the loyal uncle of his youth, making one final appearance.

"And did he?" Northumberland asked.

Darcy nodded and resumed his posture. "Dearly beloved friends, there is no such matter here as you so vainly hope or believe. I pray you all to be quiet and contented with my death, which I am most willing to suffer. For I have often looked death in the face, upon great adventures in the field; he is now no stranger to me. And among all the vain mockeries of this world, I repent me of nothing more than in esteeming life more dear than I should."

I repent me of nothing more than in esteeming life more dear than I should. Words to remember.

Darcy shot a glance at Northumberland, then bowed his head and continued. "I have endured the hate of great persons – so much the more dangerous because unjust. I have incurred displeasure from inferiors, for giving way to the faults of others – and now, being constantly resolved, I neither fear to die nor desire to live. Let us now join in prayer to the Lord for the preservation of the King's Majesty, to whose Grace I have always been a faithful, true and most loving subject, desirous always of his most prosperous success in all his affairs, and ever glad to help forward the commonwealth of this realm."

Edward could no longer hold back the tears and they slid silently down his cheeks. The telling of Tom Seymour's death had somehow not been this difficult to hear. Maybe because it hadn't come from Edward's direct order.

"Was that the end?" Northumberland asked. Edward wanted to shush him but didn't.

"Not quite. Shouts of 'Yes, Yes' rang out. They drowned out his voice for most, but I was close enough that I managed to hear. He said, 'If any have been offended and injured by me, I most humbly ask him forgiveness – but especially Almighty God, Whom throughout my life I have most grievously offended.

And all others, whatsoever they may be, I do with my whole heart forgive them.'"

That would be the end, Edward thought. The point at which Somerset would turn and kneel and place his head on the block. "Thank you," Edward said, his voice barely a croak.

"Nay, Sire, there was more. The crowd started shouting against Northumberland and the Council." Darcy kneaded his hat. "Again, the Duke calmed them down. He called for silence and told them, 'I once again require you, dearly beloved in the Lord, that you all keep yourselves quiet and still, lest by your tumult you should trouble me. For albeit the spirit be ready and willing, the flesh is frail and wavering – and through your quietness I shall be much more quieter. I die here in the faith of Jesus Christ – desiring you all to help me with your prayers, that I may persevere constant in the same.'"

Oh Uncle, I pray for you, Edward thought. *The flesh is frail and wavering.*

"Then Doctor Cox gave him a copy of Cranmer's *General Confession*, which he read aloud. He shook hands with the sheriffs and the Lieutenant of the Tower, thanking them for their courtesy and patience. He took off his collar and orders and then his doublet, gave the executioner his fee, and knelt. His face turned crimson and he put his head on the block and called out 'Lord Jesu, receive my soul.'"

Edward closed his eyes and bowed his head, feeling the *whoosh* of the axe's arc.

"The Lord was merciful. His head fell on the first stroke. Many people burst through the ranks of the men-at-arms to dip their handkerchiefs in his blood. New relics, unfortunately."

"Thank you. That is quite enough." Northumberland's face was impassive.

"You may all leave me now. I would like to be alone," Edward said.

Northumberland opened his mouth as if to argue, but Edward

kept his eyes on the floor to block conversation. With no choice, the entire room bowed deeply and left.

When Edward was finally alone, a strange uncertainty gripped him. He looked out the window but nothing caught his attention. He looked around the room for a clue, but everything was flat. He sighed deeply and walked over to sit at his desk.

A stack of returned papers was in front of his Chronicle, and he moved them to the side. He opened the journal to the blank page and stared at it. Thoughts jumbled; he shuffled through the papers looking for something to distract himself. He stopped at the single, unfolded sheet that contained his instructions regarding Somerset. Under the title "Certain Points of Weighty Matters to Be Immediately Concluded by My Council," Edward's usual perfect writing was distorted in one spot. Thick.

It was the fateful sentence, with extra words squeezed in between the lines: "The matter for the Duke of Somerset to be considered, as appertaineth to our surety and quietness of our realm, that by his punishment and execution according to the laws, example may be showed to others."

That wasn't what Edward had written. He had written "that by his punishment, example may be showed to others." Someone had added the reference to execution, making it look like Edward wanted this to be the punishment associated with Somerset's crime.

Panic rose in him.

He crumbled over on himself, hands covering his head. Deep sobs racked his body until exhaustion soothed him. Slowly he lowered his hands and looked back at the paper. The handwriting was meant to look like his own, but it was off slightly. It did not look like Northumberland's hand, thank God. But it was someone who had access to Edward's papers. And those would all be Northumberland's friends.

Edward let his mind roam over the possibilities. They were endless.

His eyes fell on the small stack of coins in the corner. The new ones, just issued in accordance with Edward's instructions. They featured Edward crowned and holding a sword with a lion in the background. Unfortunately, the background was not clear, and a rumor had arisen that the lion was not in fact the lion of England but rather the bear and the ragged staff of the Dudley family. Those who had spread the rumor were arrested and fined, but the common people still believed it.

They loved Somerset; they hated Northumberland. As opposed to the nobility, who were educated enough to understand Somerset's policies would bankrupt the country. Whoever had done this evil likely thought the end justified the means, but Edward was devastated that he had been so easily played.

Edward looked back down at the paper, at the added words. Northumberland must have known of the dirty trick. Was he more involved than that?

This was the world in which Edward lived. He had to be more careful. Edward had always thought his father's behavior too guarded, even a bit extreme. But he had been right. A king needed to be more careful.

What that meant for now was not clear. And he was too tired to think further about it.

He took out his journal and looked at the blank page. He wrote the date and again looked at the expanse of white before him.

With a trembling hand he wrote a single sentence. *The Duke of Somerset had his head cut off on Tower Hill between eight and nine in the morning.*

He closed the book, pushed it away from him, and rose to leave.

PART THREE

*E*dward opened his eyes and sat up quickly to shake off the disturbing dream he'd just had.

The fabric above him featured the Seymour device of wings. Angel wings. The design had been needlepointed by his mother, and always comforted him. Even now. Especially now.

He carefully felt his face, his new obsession. The pustules were smaller, dryer. He was sure of it, though the difference was imperceptible from the last time he'd checked, about an hour ago.

Two weeks ago he had fallen sick with measles or smallpox or both, and was quickly covered with giant white blobs so many and so large that almost no part of his skin was unaffected. But after a difficult time, he was feeling better. Prayer had caused the fevers to recede.

"Are you awake then, Sire?" The whisper was Robin's.

Edward considered his answer. Yes, he was fully refreshed from his nap. More than that, he was eager to rise and celebrate. The Lord had succored Edward past the danger point. It was time for Edward to act on his gratitude.

"I am, thank you. And ready to make plans."

He pulled a corner of the curtain open, and at that signal his men opened them all.

"Excellent," Robin said. "I hope we can serve your pleasure in these."

"I was thinking I would like to have Archbishop Cranmer wait on me tomorrow morning, so I can speak with him about his *Book of Common Prayer*," Edward said.

"I heard he was just about done with his final changes," Cheke said.

"Aye," Edward said. "And that is why I want to push him to publish it. It is time the people start to worship properly, without the terrible superstitions that have held them enslaved. I have been patient long enough."

Somerset had urged leniency for the people who were slow to accept. But now Somerset was gone.

As always, the memory of his uncle hurt Edward's heart, the third death he had caused through no real fault of this own. He had slain his mother at his birth, then left two of her brothers to their fates.

Waste not fresh tears over old griefs, he reminded himself. *You learned important lessons.*

"I'll go give the orders," Robin said.

"Would you like to prepare in some way for the meeting?" Cheke asked.

Edward considered the question. In truth, he was tired of spending all his time locked in his own mind, and he didn't need to consider anything further before the conversation. Indeed, it was the physical side he longed to indulge. To feel the force of his muscles, the cool air on his face. "I would go riding."

Cheke shook his head. "I fear your Council will insist you forbear just a little while longer, not to overexert yourself."

Resentment washed over Edward. That was Northumberland's doing. It wasn't fair.

"Archery!" called Sidney, throwing his arms in the air.

Archery. Edward's father had so valued skill with the bow that he had commanded that every Englishman practice weekly, even the old and infirm. "That is a pastime my Council cannot refuse," Edward said. "Especially if we invite them to enjoy it with me."

Cheke chuckled. "That will certainly be most persuasive."

"I shall make sure they are ready for you," Sidney said, racing from the room.

Cheke sighed, but it was a happy sigh more than a sad one. "And I will inform the Council you will shortly be at the butts."

"Shortly? I am leaving now."

Edward strode out of his room, knowing his attendants would fall in quickly behind him. Just outside his Presence Chamber, a group of women sat with their sewing hoops. His cousin, Frances Grey, newly Duchess of Suffolk, was in the center chair as the highest-ranking female at court right now. Her daughters were with her, and Jane looked up at Edward. A smile broke over her face as comprehension spread.

"We are on our way to the archery field to celebrate the King's recovery," Robin announced. "You are welcome to join us."

Edward felt a twinge at the hubris of announcing a recovery. But the evil eye was superstition, like popery, and should be ignored. "We would love to have you."

Frances rose and put down her sewing with a flourish. "Then have us you will." She turned to the women. "Come, ladies, our calm heads shall judge whatever competition may arise."

As they progressed down the palace hallways, Edward was struck by the people milling about aimlessly until they saw him. Then they jumped to attention and bowed and smiled and clucked over how well he looked and praised God for his delivery and fell in enthusiastically behind the growing crowd, as if they were rats and he the Pied Piper.

"Are people so desperate for amusements?" he asked Robin in a low voice. "Were there none during my illness?" The court was supposed to be a gay place, to serve as a figurehead for the realm.

"Well, Sire, it is Lent. So there was no reason to take a chance you might be bothered."

The thought troubled Edward. His father had always insisted traditions be fulfilled, even those he did not attend himself. "But surely my presence is not required all the time. Surely there were others who could have presided in my stead."

Robin looked away but his words came through clearly. "Somerset used to do that."

The name swayed in the air like a hanging corpse, commanding silence.

The silence held across the lawn. Edward gradually forgot about it as his heart soared from from the fresh breeze on his face and the Master of Revels approached them with a giant smile on his face and longbows in his hands.

"I thank God to see you looking so well, Sire," said Thomas Cawarden, who had held his post for some eight years, a reward for keeping Henry VIII amused and happy during the siege of Boulogne. "I know – I pray – this will be the perfect activity to help regain your strength."

The crowd forgotten, Edward turned and squinted at the target in the distance. He walked over and placed his toes just behind the shooting line. He spread his feet to shoulder width and turned them until they were ninety degrees to the target. He turned his bow to horizontal and held out his hand for the page to hand him an arrow that he placed on the arrow rest before lifting the bow.

He squinted again and closed one eye. He held the bow steady as he drew back the string far enough to brush his lips, exulting in the growing strength across his back. He checked his aim one last time and released his fingers, the only two muscles that moved.

The arrow landed perfectly in the yellow center, and Edward whooped loudly. It was only when he quieted that he realized there was loud applause from everywhere. He looked back and marveled at the two hundred courtiers who were somehow all watching, eying him up and down with calculating smiles on their faces. They must have been more worried about his health than anyone had let on. The day's warmth dimmed.

Now his Council was arriving, with Northumberland ten paces ahead and lengthening his lead with every stride. His smile was threatening, or perhaps fearful, and Edward took a deep breath to dispel his sudden resentment.

"Master Cheke has conveyed your welcome invitation to join the first outing of your recovery," Northumberland said. "I am happy to accept, despite the commanding lead you have just established."

The applause that greeted Northumberland's statement revealed that people were as eager to court Northumberland's goodwill as they were Edward's. Thankfully he had already taken his shot, for he could feel his hands shaking a bit.

"Jane shall shoot next, then Robin. You may shoot after him," Edward said nonchalantly.

He tried to keep his mind focused on the game, but his thoughts kept wandering to replay Northumberland's old accusation against Somerset. *He cares more about his own reputation than yours.*

The applause broke out again when Northumberland approached the shooting line. Edward pressed his fingernails into his palm to quiet himself.

Northumberland took aim and squinted, pulling his bow taut and letting the arrow fly. It went wide, landing in the white background.

The crowd groaned good-naturedly, and the sycophancy grated.

"You aimed better when you cut off the head of my uncle Somerset," Edward said.

Shocked silence spread as surely as the laughter had only a moment ago.

"Your turn, Sir Henry," Edward said, addressing Northumberland's closest ally. "See if you can do better."

That will show them, Edward thought.

Yet pride turned to dismay at Northumberland's stricken look. Edward realized he was more tired than he'd thought. What was done was done; he needed to release his anger.

But first, one thing.

He motioned Northumberland over and waved away the immediate abject apology that came out of the Duke's mouth.

"It seems I have displeased you, that—"

"It was but a jest," Edward said. "A poor one."

It was the pattern his father had used, saying something provocative and then backing off immediately so his courtiers did not know whether he had been serious or joking. The smart ones knew he was both.

"But there is one favor you could do for me," Edward continued.

"Name it."

"Is Ned still imprisoned in the Tower?"

Northumberland looked away, and his voice took on a guarded tone. "He is still detained, yes. There were several—" He stopped and swallowed. "He is still detained."

"I want him released, and with his father's properties restored to him."

"It shall be done, Sire," Northumberland said. "Without delay."

As he strode off, it occurred to Edward that he had not asked about the other people included in Northumberland's "several." He resolved to follow up later.

Once his headache went away.

May 30, 1552

Edward grasped the pen carefully. This would be the first warrant for payment signed by his own hand instead of the collective signatures of the Council, and he wanted to savor the moment. He bit back the thought that Somerset's death warrant had been a far more momentous document. That was an aberration.

He focused on how far he'd come since his accession. He'd been so young then, little more than a pawn.

Another thought of Somerset. He had to stop doing this to himself.

Instead, he put all his attention on the details, the scratching of the quill and the gleam of the ink. After he finished, he looked again at the paper with pleasure and, with all the nonchalance he could muster, handed it to William Cecil.

"Well, that concludes our regular business," Northumberland said. "Does anyone have anything to add before we adjourn?"

"I do," Edward said. "I should like to go on a true Progress this year. I think it a fine year to begin."

His father had always told him how important this tradition was – the practice of traveling through the country to see his people and be seen by them. It was a way of building loyalty, cementing rule, but so far Edward had never strayed far from London.

Northumberland's eyes narrowed. "I worry about your safety, Sire."

Edward shrugged. "I am fully recovered from the pox and there is no new contagion about."

"The unrest seems to have calmed as well," Suffolk said. "Even the furor over the coinage has died down. More evidence Somerset was stirring up trouble."

Edward ignored the dig at Somerset. Even after his death the Council continued to blame him for all the country's ills – even more so after his death, in fact. As if they were trying to make up for the fact that the common people were turning him into a saint.

Northumberland sighed. "This is all true. Perhaps I am overly cautious. It would be a fine thing for you to go south, to visit Portsmouth and see the naval defenses you have been funding."

Portsmouth – the very name conjured heaven: Edward had long been fascinated by waterways and could recite the names of every port, haven, and creek, not only in England but in Scotland and France as well. Still, it went against Edward's original thought and plan. The Progress was not about pleasure, it was to copy the deliberately long Progress his father had arranged to persuade people to come around to his early religious changes. "I was thinking north to calm the papists and bring them the new *Book of Common Prayer*."

Northumberland and the other Councilors exchanged glances. Finally Northumberland cleared his throat and spoke. "I would counsel you to wait for a time yet before traveling to that hotbed. We cannot risk your person."

Edward could only imagine what a hotbed would look like. He had never gone much farther into the country. They said the rest of it looked different, and Edward wanted to see it all. His current ignorance felt like a jacket become too small, and Edward itched to go beyond.

Especially since Barnaby had been writing to him from France, where he had met with wonderful success as Edward's ambassador. Henri II liked him well enough that he had quickly appointed him a Gentleman of the Chamber, and then had brought him along to the battlefield to war against the Spaniards. Barnaby represented the goodwill of England, which had helped Henri secure the support of the German Protestants. He had turned into a valued counselor, and Edward was proud of his friend.

And a little jealous. The cliffs, the sea voyages, the battles – everything his friend had seen for himself that Edward could only picture. This trip would give him some of that: the sea, the shipyards…

"Portsmouth sounds like a fine idea."

Northumberland let out another sigh and put a hand on his stomach. "This trip will be good for you. And many of the Council have homes between here and there. They will be able not only to host you but also to prepare your way. Make sure you meet with all the important local personages."

Sir Anthony Browne bowed. "I pray you will come to my home in Cowdray. I promise you good hunting and good cheer if you do."

"I would be honored to welcome you in Wilton, as well," said Pembroke, Edward's quiet uncle. "Though it's not so fine as Cowdray."

Cowdray was reputed to be one of the most splendid private homes in England. Browne had taken care to build a house, not a palace, so he'd never drawn resentment, even from Edward's father.

Edward sighed. "I will be pleased to visit you all. Your companionship will compensate for the fact that I will not be going north."

Northumberland stood. "May I make a request, Sire?"

"Ye-es," Edward said, unsure.

"The pains in my stomach are making me melancholy. While you are on Progress, I ask your blessing to retire to my estates in Northumberland. While there, I will do my best to answer questions and create support for your religious reforms."

Again, Edward felt guilty for the rift that had arisen between him and Northumberland. The Somerset incident hung over him as well; it wasn't fair to pile on. "Of course."

Relief flooded the Councilors' faces. Northumberland was not very popular, and his presence might have dampened the enthusiasm that was expected to greet Edward.

"I am not sure you are the right person to create support for religious reforms," Pembroke said. "Perhaps I will join you and together we can visit the local landowners. If they show us enough love, then maybe next year the King can get his wish."

Edward smiled. Everything was arranging itself in accordance with his fervent wishes. And His fervent wishes.

Life was good.

July 19, 1552

This Progress was shaping up to change Edward's relationship with the members of his Council and of his court in general. An interesting group would be traveling with him, a combination of men in powerful positions like the Lord Privy Seal, Lord Treasurer, and Lord Chamberlain, or men with high titles like the Duke of Suffolk, and men who could teach them the important things, like Baron Cobham, Lord Warden of the Cinque Ports, who would impart the military understanding Edward coveted. All surrounded by days of freedom that would little resemble the more formal atmosphere of the regular year.

Edward stepped through the front door and took a deep breath of the fresh air. He was glad to be at Oatlands. The palace had always been his favorite way to experience the country, largely thanks to the ornate pearled bed his father had commissioned, the ultimate in luxury amid the rustic setting. Now Edward was about to experience new places and new wonders. His heart fluttered.

His cousin Henry Grey, Duke of Suffolk, breathed deeply next to him. "Ah, such clean air. And this is just the beginning," he said. "It will get cleaner still, as we get closer to the sea."

He looked around the courtyard to make sure the pages were waiting with their horses, and waved Edward on.

Edward descended the stairs eagerly, ready for the adventure to begin. "What are the stops after this?" he asked. The names all rolled into one.

"Guildeforde, then Petworth, then Cowdray."

"What about Waltham?"

Suffolk shook his head. "That's the last stop before Portsmouth. Halfeneker is just before it."

"It's after Portsmouth that the real fun starts," said Cobham, a reformist after Edward's own heart.

After Portsmouth, the plan was to continue as far as Salisbury and Wilton. A little farther than Northumberland had wanted, but he had agreed these traditionalist enclaves would be good places for Edward to practice convincing his people.

Edward held out his hand to the page for the carrot to give his horse, a trick he had practiced from the very first time he rode. Somerset had taught it to him.

His jaw set, Edward swung his leg over the back of his horse to mount it. He settled into his saddle, and the pages checked his straps to be sure all was secure. He took the reins into one hand and looked around the courtyard. The riders chattered atop their horses, ready for the order to leave. The mood shined like the morning sun.

Northumberland stepped from the shadows, a sad look on his face. Although he would eschew the Progress itself, he had come to Oatlands as if he feared being left out. "I will take my leave of you, then, and wish you Godspeed," he said.

"I shall return soon," Edward said, "and my absence will give you time to recover. You carry a heavy burden when you serve me."

Doctors had been giving Northumberland restoratives to stop his inward bleeding and restore his corrupted humors. The pain in his stomach made him sad all the time, and Edward resolved again to show him more kindness.

"I thank you for your caring concern," Northumberland said. "But my joy is in watching you excel. Like the way you dealt with the Spanish Ambassador the other day. Your Majesty has my sincerest admiration for that."

Suffolk guffawed. "That was rich, Sire. I was fit to burst when I heard the story."

"Oh?" Robin Dudley said. "What happened?"

Edward blushed. "He asked me for military support against France, based on the treaty he signed with my father ten years ago. I referred him to the Council."

"Your Majesty is far too modest," Suffolk said. He turned to Robin. "Spain has argued for years the King is too young to make key decisions for England. It took all I had to hold my face straight when he said, 'Your master should be happy I am finally heeding his counsel.'"

"And then he told Scheyfve that he had since himself sworn amity with the French king which he could not break, and offered to broker a peace between them," Northumberland said. "It was a masterful suggestion."

Edward thrust out his chest over the way he had controlled that conversation. "The offer was genuine; I would hope to see them friends. But I admit I was annoyed the Emperor was once again presuming on our relationship."

Northumberland laughed. "That was a politic way of putting it, Your Majesty." He turned to his son. "The Emperor has long acted as if he held all the power, not only now but also all the times he meddled over Mary. This will hopefully teach him he needs to earn England's friendship."

"I think it may have, as he mentioned he would love to join the Progress at some point," Edward said. "Or perhaps he was just jealous at hearing the French Ambassador will ride with us for a time. I referred him to you for the dates, by the way. I leave it to you whether their visits overlap."

All the men laughed at that one. Edward tried not to feel smug.

"I thank you for giving me the chance to play the two men against each other," Northumberland said. "The laughter will be a sure remedy against my stomach ails."

With that, Northumberland slapped the horse's rump and nodded at the trumpeters. They fumbled briefly, waiting for Edward's confirming signal that he was ready as well, then they started off the line.

Edward's chest tightened with excitement as they left the courtyard and headed southwest to new territory. New horizons. What a metaphor for his life, growing larger than it had ever been.

It was good he was patient. His governess had taught him long ago that better things came when he waited. She had taught him with wafers, giving him the choice between having a single one right away or two if he waited for the shadow to reach the next notch on the sundial. He had given in to temptation only once and had taken his mistake to heart. Over time, he had learned to love duty; the talent had served him well.

Somerset used to tell him his mother was like that.

Somerset.

His mother.

Edward sighed and put aside the past. Again.

He was getting more skilled with the practice.

July 31, 1552

Edward sat at the high table in Waltham Palace and surveyed the Great Hall before him, marveling over its lack of religious icons despite having belonged to Stephen Gardiner and all the Bishops of Winchester before him. Gardiner had surrendered it to Edward when he was arrested and stripped of his See. Edward had then awarded it to William Paulet, who had shown his worthiness by carefully eliminating all evidence of its having ever been an episcopal residence. Edward thought the fair old manor house must secretly thank him for that fact.

Because of the rain, they were all dawdling over supper, indulging in drink.

"To His Majesty and his hospitality," the French Ambassador said, raising his glass.

After the room had taken a sip, Edward raised his own glass in response and glanced at his left and right to bring them all into the toast before he faced the Ambassador. "To welcome friends. I wish only you could stay with us longer."

That was a lie, of course. De Noailles had been told he would not be welcome at Portsmouth. Edward would be inspecting his shipyard, and a foreign agent should not be there in case anything went amiss.

"I should have joined you sooner," de Noailles said, "though then I might have been sent home with the others."

Edward found himself irked by the words, but decided to accept them as a lighthearted joke and act as if they hadn't been said. De Noailles was after all correct that two-thirds of the people on the Progress had been dismissed: Edward had left Oatlands with a crowd of four hundred and fifty-four. Their train of horses alone had eaten up the country, leaving little meadow or hay for the peasants. Now they were down to a more manageable one hundred fifty, enough for pomp but more cognizant of limitations. Edward was being more careful of his people than himself, as a good leader should be.

"And to King Henri and the hospitality he is extending to my friends," Edward said.

The thought saddened him a little. Right now, Barnaby was with France's army, not its king. This was not needed for diplomacy; this was not needed for anything. It was a kind gesture with no reward.

"Though I think it is high time Barnaby return to England," Edward said. "It has been almost a year, long enough to overstay a welcome."

"Not at all, especially since I hear he is proving himself on the battlefield. It will be a difficult thing to pull him away from this campaign."

Another argument. When Edward had first started to miss Barnaby and had hinted at recalling him, the conclusion had been that it would be better to pull him away from success than before success had been achieved. Barnaby had said so in his letters, back when he had first received his commission and before he had been put into the field: he thought it would not look well if he were to leave. He feared to appear lazy, or even afraid.

"How long is the campaign expected to continue?"

"They'll likely keep the fighting going through the autumn, but by December things will quiet for a time."

"Then I will write to Henri asking him to release Barnaby for the winter," Edward said. He felt better. He would see his friend soon.

"My master is always happy to have a letter from your hand," the Ambassador replied.

Further conversation was curtailed by the arrival of pages with trays of venison, the very deer they had killed that morning. The room exploded into gossip and laughter over stories of the hunt. Edward thrilled to this new life. A manly life, in which he felt truly a king, a real king solving real problems better than anyone else in the land.

"May I say what a joy it is to see Your Majesty so relaxed, and how honored I am to participate in this your first Progress and to see how beloved you are of your people."

"It's my father's absence that relaxes him," Robin Dudley said. "No stern taskmaster."

"The Duke values excellence," Cecil said. "We all try to live up to his hopes."

It was true this mood had come upon Edward only in Northumberland's absence.

The thought made Edward feel like time was standing still, like there was a great truth hovering before him to be deciphered. This sense was not about freedom from work. It was about freedom from oversight. When Northumberland was around, he was the ultimate arbiter, however much he tried to pretend otherwise. Edward never acted in a way that Northumberland would disapprove; or, rather, he was always conscious of what Northumberland's reaction might be. On this Progress, when he was free to relax and consider what he truly wanted, what he truly thought, exuberance had emerged. And Edward had become more…more what his father must have been like as a young king.

Was it a failing of Northumberland's that Edward had not had this experience before? Perhaps, though he was not yet of age, like his father had been. And it was ungrateful to complain when Somerset had held the reins much tighter still.

"That is an important quality in a leader," the Ambassador said.

"My father learned it from Great Harry," Robin said. "From our earliest days, we were taught you needed to be perfect to serve a king, especially one so great as that." He turned to Edward. "It is why I am grateful for Your Majesty's kindness to me. I am always terrified I will be found wanting."

That was Edward's greatest fear as well; it was interesting Robin shared it. He didn't even seem unmanly because of it.

Edward felt something shift inside. Understanding he need never fear Northumberland again, that he should fully accept the service that had matured him so effectively. Where would Edward be without loyalty like that?

"The only thing wanting now is more wine," Edward said as he lifted a finger to signal the page.

Robin smiled broadly. The entire room applauded the joke, whose deep emotion was wrapped in a nonchalant touch, and Edward's back straightened still further.

Not even his father could have done better.

December 10, 1552

Edward sat down heavily in a chair and wiped his brow. His heart was full.

He and his men were preparing for the Christmas revels, which would be as lavish as the ones from last year. George Ferrers had been appointed Lord of Misrule again, and he had promised to recreate his controversial procession of mock priests and bishops parading through the court with a representation of the holy sacrament in its monstrance, wetted and perfumed in a most strange fashion.

For now, they danced. Barnaby was back from France. He was mature, manly and suave, but still Barnaby underneath. Edward felt that must be true of himself as well and felt comforted.

Barnaby had insisted on teaching them the new French galliard, exhausting everyone with the impossibly high leap after the four hopping steps. They needed a nice, slow pavane again to rest.

"You were supposed to be learning how to be a soldier," Edward said, only half-joking. He always felt guilty enjoying himself too much, a virtue he expected those around him to emulate.

Barnaby laughed. "The French set much more store on the gentler pursuits. King Henri insisted his gentlemen excel above all others."

"I am still sorry you will not have the chance to do that this year," Edward said. Barnaby's father was dying: his affairs in Ireland needed settling.

"As am I," Barnaby said.

"If only you could shirk your duties for a short time," Edward said. Again, he hid a real plea behind a joke.

"Ah, Sire," Barnaby said, "you taught me too well that duty comes first in life. I even put duty before the French ladies."

Amid the general merriment, the words triggered a thought in Edward's mind. Elisabeth of France. Barnaby could give him a better description of her than the fawning praise supplied by the French Ambassador. Edward turned to his men.

"You should practice now, since you know the steps," he said. "I want to talk with Barnaby."

He stood and walked to his bedchamber, knowing Barnaby would follow. Once the door was closed, Edward wasted no time. "I want to know more about the character and beauty of my proposed bride."

Barnaby looked embarrassed. "She is a sweet child but still only seven, Sire."

The caution was worrisome. "Is there some problem she needs to grow out of? Or virtue she needs to grow into?"

Barnaby shook his head. "No, no, not at all. She is lovely. A little shy and timid, but that is a fine thing in a woman."

"I prefer timid to...to brash." Edward said. "They say the Queen of Scots is cocky."

"She is the highest-ranking lady at court after Queen Catherine. They say that is the source of her considerable pride."

"That and the beauty they claim she has." Edward tried not to sound snide. He was still angry she was to marry someone else. *Forgive me my pride, Lord,* he prayed.

"Madame Elisabeth is still young yet," Barnaby said. "She will clearly become even more beautiful than she is now."

The thought captivated Edward, and he sat at his desk to muse. Barnaby came to stand closer to him but kept a respectful silence.

When Edward was ready to speak again, he noticed Barnaby reading the book that lay open before him. Edward's Chronicle.

Barnaby jumped when he realized Edward noticed him. "Sorry, I didn't mean to pry," he said. "I just..."

Edward looked down and saw the entry he had finished earlier, about the fine Paget was to pay for supporting Somerset. "I keep a diary of things that happen, to remind myself of events. Cheke suggested it, long ago."

"And that is yet another reason I would make a terrible sovereign," Barnaby said. "There are too many things I would prefer to forget. But of course, that's just me."

Edward picked up the diary and flipped through its thick pages. The early entries seemed so childish to him, and then his heart stopped when he came across that horrible sentence he had written just about a year ago: *The Duke of Somerset had his head cut off at Tower Hill between eight and nine in the morning.*

Barnaby was right. Did Edward really need to write down all these things? He had started the journal as a way to remember the wonder of the new days of his reign, and instead he wrote only of punishments and fines and problems. It gave him no joy, only a sense of grudging duty.

He closed the book. "You're right. In truth, the Council

records are all I need." He smiled at his friend. "You might not make a wonderful sovereign, but you are a good advisor."

Barnaby smiled back. "Thank you, Sire."

Edward filed the book on the shelf. Maybe he'd feel differently in a decade.

He turned back around and sneezed three times quickly. His eyes widened when he couldn't catch a breath, but then his chest relaxed, and he was fine.

March 1, 1553

"The King prays you be seated, my Lords," the Lord Chancellor announced. The room quickly obeyed, and Sir Thomas Goodrich began the brief speech that would open Parliament.

Edward coughed into his hand, hoping to stifle the sound and not let it amplify and echo like the last one. He didn't want to interrupt, didn't want to call attention to himself. Not this way.

The ceremony was being kept a low-key affair because Edward had been ill. Not terribly, he kept assuring them, just another of those winter illnesses that left a person coughing and weak for weeks. But men had always cringed when he exhibited any weakness, and the virulence and length of this cough made them cringe even more. They had forced Edward to agree to forego the formal procession to and from Westminster that normally would bookend the royal appearance.

Instead, Parliament had come to Edward at Whitehall, to the Great Hall where the bishops and lords now sat on separate sides. Edward had received them in his ceremonial robes, wearing the Crown of State and holding his scepter, and now he sat under a cloth of estate to preside over the session. It was enough pomp to honor the occasion, and Northumberland swore to him that his father had done it this way several times. Given the fire that raged now in Edward's chest, he was glad his exertions had been curtailed.

The Chancellor finished the overview of the Council's priorities for the coming year and closed his speech to polite applause. Edward adjusted his mantle slightly, careful not to disturb the twelve-foot train so carefully arranged around him. Strong rumors warned that Edward would ask to accelerate his majority. He pretended not to notice the sighs of relief that flooded the hall when the overview omitted any mention of such a request.

Northumberland had explained that the subterfuge was necessary. *The change must not be seen as coming from you,* he had said. And of course, Northumberland had already gotten each Councilor to secretly agree that Edward would assume control at sixteen. They did not need to tip their hands to anyone, in case ignorant men should object before it was a done thing. It was proper caution and a fair compromise.

Another cough racked his body, hard enough that a headache sprang up in its wake. Again, Edward pretended it was nothing. Northumberland shot him a questioning look, and Edward shook his head in a way he hoped would reassure.

He settled into his seat as the assembly began to debate the issues the Chancellor had raised. He forced an attentive look on his face, though in truth he could barely concentrate. His body sighed with exhaustion, and he suspected his fever might be returning. All he wanted to do was go back to his rooms and rest.

But only a boy would do that. Instead, he would stay and fulfill his duty. He would sign every single one of the seventeen acts they planned to put before him so they could become the law of the land.

If he wanted to be treated as a king, he needed to act as a king. However weak he felt.

March 17, 1553

"He has too much black bile. He needs more rhubarb."

"He's getting the same dosage we once gave his father, and he's nowhere near as large. We need to treat other symptoms – starting with nettles, to clean his blood."

Edward lay in bed, propped up on his pillows and trying not to seem annoyed at the doctors arguing in front of him. They had been far more cautious after this last illness than they had ever been.

He had not relapsed after opening Parliament, though he had continued to be sick enough not to care that he was confined to his apartments. But lately he had been having better days. And it was long past time to feel the sun on his face. Bright warmth that would plump his skin and promise him all would be fine.

He slapped the covers next to him. "A walk, doctors – can I not even take a walk?" The emotion in his voice tickled his throat, triggering a series of coughs. After the spasms passed, he collapsed back into the cushions. The episode was unlikely to persuade them. "I don't want to go far."

Doctor James Curthorp pulled at his scraggly beard with his bony claws. He glanced at Northumberland, who watched from the foot of the bed, before answering. "We are afraid even that change in your environment would place your life at risk. We cannot chance it."

Place your life at risk. Edward shivered with annoyance. All his life, the world had worried overmuch about his health. And had stopped him from living a normal life because of it.

He shouldn't be holding back, he should be pressing on. He was strong, after all, always had been. He had shaken off smallpox and measles a year ago. And he had survived the height of this fever. So what if it lingered after the danger had passed? Why could they not see?

A memory came to him, an argument to use. "What about in one of my father's wheeling chairs, as a compromise?" he said, as if it would be a concession to them and not his own fear to walk far.

"We think not, Your Majesty. Not until we understand the mystery of your sputum."

"Why do you call it a mystery?" Edward asked.

Again, Curthorp glanced at Northumberland before speaking.

"Because we would expect Your Majesty's sputum to vary with your fevers, but they don't. Whether you expel pink, green, yellow or black has no correlation to other symptoms, including the color and taste of your urine. We have tried so many remedies, for everything we could, but nothing is working to rebalance your humors."

Northumberland took a deep breath and squared his shoulders. "Your Majesty, I think we need to abandon plans for any Garter celebrations this year."

Visions of the sea of velvet mantles and ostrich feathers filled Edward's eyes, and regret filled his heart. "The whole court looks forward to the ceremony. And all I have to do is sit there. Surely I can manage that."

"You would not be able to do that now," Northumberland said.

Edward bristled. "We have only one holy day left in *The Book of Common Prayer* – that of Saint George. It must be celebrated."

"Celebrated, yes, but the manner is malleable. We can honor England's patron saint without the Garter ceremony. It is not worth straining your health."

"But I am feeling better," he said.

Northumberland shook his head. "I thank God for that, but you cannot ask this of us."

Edward clenched his fists. It wasn't fair he was sick. And he'd been sick for far too long. What was wrong with these doctors? His father never would have put up with this incompetence.

"I am feeling better," he repeated. "And all I ask is to sit there to preside over the ceremonies." Edward felt the tears mount to his eyes and prayed they would not spew out.

"I know it seems like a small thing," Northumberland said. "But we were so worried for you. We do not want to overturn your recovery."

Edward shook his head. "You act like the frightened women

of my youth, who cosseted me overmuch. It was wrong then, and it is wrong now."

A screech burst from Northumberland. "We don't want you to die."

The doctors turned to face Edward and sank to their knees, head bowed. Northumberland followed slowly before continuing in a firm voice. "Not when your successor would return England to papacy and superstition."

Stunned into silence, Edward tried to breathe around the constriction in his chest. What a terrible future to threaten him with. It was one thing to fear Edward might die when the fever raged, but there was no reason to worry now that God had spared him. "I am better."

Northumberland looked up at him. His eyes were hard. "Not better enough to take a chance. Not with an uncle and half-brother both dead at fifteen from diseased lungs."

The significance of the sputum washed over Edward. *Of course.*

Arthur Tudor, Henry VII's firstborn son who should have inherited the throne. Henry Fitzroy, Edward's bastard half-brother, considered as an alternative before Edward was born. Fifteen. Lungs.

Numbness invaded, and Edward clenched his fists.

Northumberland cleared his throat. "Now you see our worry. We cannot be left with Mary." He shifted his weight. "Forgive me, Sire, for my treasonous words."

Edward's father had long ago made it fatal to discuss a sovereign's death. He had therefore learned so late of his impending end that he had been unable to speak to confess his sins.

"I appreciate truth," Edward said, his voice croaking from horror.

He shifted for a more comfortable position but knew there was none and settled back. He took several deep breaths to calm his speeding heartbeat. He was not dying, he was recovering. He would not take foolish risks, but he would do as he thought best and push himself in the tiny increments that experience had taught him how to take. "I agree to forego the Garter celebrations, though I would like to be permitted some gentle amusements."

The doctors had stepped back during Northumberland's outburst, but now Thomas Saverson came forward. "We have already seen improvements in your cough and the color of your urine. We just want to make sure these continue before we relax the rules."

Edward nodded. "Leave me," he said. "I would rest a little."

"That is the best thing for you right now," Saverson said.

Edward turned on his side and nestled into his pillows, not even waiting for them to bow out.

He closed his eyes and felt his half-brother and uncle near, coughing and dying. But Edward had passed the danger point. Edward was improving. God had saved him from this curse, just as God had succored him through countless other trials.

He took a breath and a thought seeped into his mind.

His father had died in this room. In this bed.

It was the first time he had thought of it since the earliest days of his reign, when Somerset had insisted he watch it dressed that first time. He had been soothed then that only the frame was the same as the one that had cradled his father's departure.

He shoved the thought away.

Spasms racked his body, and he coughed until they drew blood. The blood always stopped the spasms. That was a pattern the doctors hadn't mentioned. He put the thought away for later.

Edward would rest and do everything they wanted him to do, and he would get out of this castle. Hampton Court Palace was next on the circuit. That was farther out in the country, and he loved it there. It was where he'd been born.

And where his mother had died.

He swallowed.

Greenwich. He would go to Greenwich.

May 7, 1553

Edward raised his face to the warm sunlight. He had recovered enough for the doctors to allow him to remove to Greenwich at the start of April, and the fresh country air had strengthened him for a time. But these past few days the pain was back, enough that he doubted any assurances he would fully recover.

He'd walked all the way to the gardens, the farthest he'd been able to walk lately. After a rest in the chair set with cushions and blankets for him, he'd recover enough to make it back. And enjoy light and freedom in the meantime.

He had dismissed his men. When they were there, he could feel their sidelong glances, their concern and fear. He hated being watched while he relaxed and enjoyed. He could tolerate surreptitious glances during the never-ending cards or board games, but not when there was nothing else to take the focus away from him.

He looked down at the letter he had brought with him to ponder. Mary had written to congratulate him on his recovery from his "rhume cough." That's what people were calling it, to make it sound innocuous.

He had been so touched by her account of how she had prayed to God to give him perfect health and strength. He knew she loved him underneath it all, just sister to brother, person to person. In that spirit, he had sent her a token. He loved her too, even if he was about to hurt her deeply. He had to. She could not inherit. Edward could not appear before God knowing his throne had gone to a woman who would bring back darkness. That was a sin more heinous than any other – especially for England's Josiah.

Cranmer had always called him that, claiming Edward would remove all pagan worship throughout the land. But that wasn't all of Josiah's story. After thirty-one years of God-inspired rule, Josiah had been murdered and all his reforms undone.

Edward could not let that happen to England. He had been forewarned. He would see to it that such a thing never happened.

Even if Edward survived this illness, he had to fix things in case of a future sudden accident. On the scaffold, Somerset had thanked God for the opportunity to cleanse his conscience. This was what Edward needed to do: put his own bill through Parliament to appoint a different successor.

Even Elizabeth had to be sacrificed. Northumberland was right: she had a taint of bastardy, and if people refused to recognize her claim, they might turn to Mary. No, both his sisters had to be excluded. Immediately.

Again, he thought of his mother. All his life he'd felt guilty over causing her death, but now he wondered whether she was showing him the path. Showing him how to leave this earth with dignity by providing for its future. God was merciful to those who did His work.

He stood, swaying a little as he overcame the dizziness. When he was still, he took a deep breath. He slowly put one foot in front of the other, wincing from the vague outline of the gravel under his shoes and the ache in muscles too long unused.

May 13, 1553

Mary clutched the letter from Scheyfve in her hand. Eleanor sewed next to her without looking over, as if she were not avidly curious over what it contained.

"He says the King has deteriorated again," Mary told her. "It is said he will not escape from this illness."

Eleanor looked up, needle poised. "How does he know this?"

"He has a spy in the royal household," Mary said.

Eleanor's face twisted and she went back to her sewing. "Spies everywhere," she said. But in a moment she paused again. "What do they think the illness is?"

Mary scanned the letter. "The hacking cough and high fever suggest a suppurating tumor of his lung."

Eleanor crossed herself. "No wonder the rumors say he has died."

"What rumors?"

"The ones they spread in the marketplace. Quietly of course – those who speak openly find themselves punished. There is a man in town right now with his ear nailed to the pillory for such gossip."

Mary crossed herself and looked back down at the letter.

Deep below the sadness for her brother was a mounting sense of wonder.

She would be Queen of England. God had answered her prayers. Not that she had prayed for harm to her brother, of course. No, she had been honest when she told Edward she prayed for his recovery. But He was delivering her from her trials. He was going to place her on the throne so she could return the country to Him.

Perhaps.

For now, she would kneel and allow indefinite prayers to move her. She was ready to accept whatever He had in store for her, as she always had been.

Thy will, not mine, be done.

May 14, 1553

Edward pulled the blanket farther up his chest. "Are we alone?"

Northumberland looked around again and jerked his chin at someone. The door slammed and Northumberland turned back to face the royal bed. "Now we are."

"I have done what you suggested," Edward said. "I have titled it 'My Devise for the Succession,' and I want to know what you think."

"Sire?"

Edward started to speak but his chest constricted and the cough extended to a paroxysm. Northumberland, bless him, sat patiently. Finally Edward quieted and spat into his handkerchief. He pulled the cloth back to look: black and fetid.

Northumberland bowed. "I am glad you did this. It will ensure your legacy and secure England's future."

Edward waved him on.

Northumberland scanned the document and quickly looked up, eyes blazing. "You would pass the throne to the heirs male of Frances Grey, the Duchess of Suffolk? A woman past child-bearing who has no heirs male?"

"It goes to the sons to be born. See here, I have made provision for twenty lords to act as Regency Council."

Northumberland took a deep breath. "Ah, Sire, your intellect has created an excellent plan." He smiled a crooked smile. "But we require an heir now. The Crown must vest in someone."

"Then Frances Grey. She is the next by blood."

"Mary is the next by blood, Elizabeth is the next by blood, but you are excluding them for the good of your people. You have the right to exclude Frances too, whose religion is somewhat suspect. Let the Crown go to your cousin Jane, whom you trust much more."

Edward sat back. "She is so young."

"She is your age," Northumberland said. "And you have already created a Regency Council. Who is on it?"

Northumberland looked back down and scanned the document. Edward watched the Duke's eyes, trying to gauge his reaction. When none came, the announcement burst from Edward's lips. "I have appointed you Lord President."

Northumberland pulled back and placed his hand melodramatically on his heart. "I am honored by your trust and confidence in me, Sire. I have always been your most ardent and loyal supporter, and I am deeply grateful for this proof that you know it." He straightened and his eyes hardened. "And I am proud of you for understanding I am the key to this scheme. That I am the finest general in the country, and that the duty behind a reward such as this will lead me to crush any rebellion or Spanish invasion to ensure your will is done."

Edward blushed. "You are the only person for the job. I would not trust anyone else."

"Unfortunately, you may have to, and you may not like your choice."

"What do you mean?

"My appointment will deeply offend Henry Grey. As Jane's father, he would expect that post. And I am not willing to create such enmity with a friend, or allow her rule to begin with such a rift."

The man was so honorable. "But you have proven your worth! Surely Suffolk would understand?"

Northumberland snapped his fingers. "Jane could marry my son Guilford. Then Suffolk could not object."

The suggestion was so obvious that Edward wondered why they hadn't thought of it before – but then it hit him that Northumberland likely had. In the flickering light, Edward glimpsed raw ambition in Northumberland's eyes. He would rule England through his daughter-in-law and then grandson. His legacy would be eternal.

The spell passed, and the raw ambition melted into innocent pride. Edward wondered whether that made a difference.

It didn't. Indeed, the ambition would make Northumberland an even better Lord President of the Council. It would assure his full loyalty to the Crown, his own flesh and blood. As Somerset had always been loyal to Edward.

And Northumberland would be an able administrator.

Edward smiled. "Jane and Guilford would make the perfect couple, and your paternal guidance will strengthen the entire realm."

Edward suddenly noticed his head did not hurt. He was not sweating. The Lord might be even now strengthening him after a stern warning.

"And perhaps Lord Henry, the eldest son of the Earl of

Pembroke, should wed Catherine Grey."

Katherine Parr's nephew. That felt right, too, that his stepmother's family should be more closely connected to the throne.
"Excellent."

"I shall make the arrangements immediately. The weddings
can occur at my Durham Place next Sunday."

"Before the Council has acted on my Devise?"

"I don't want to present this to the Council until after the
weddings," Northumberland said. "Otherwise, men may want to
subvert your careful planning with their own suggestions. They
may allow petty jealousies to interfere with their thinking."

It made sense. "Fine. And I should be there." Durham Place
was not terribly far, though it was in London. "Will you persuade
my doctors to allow me to attend? I promise not even to dance,
just sit and watch."

"We can make that decision next week, when we see how
much better Your Majesty feels. I would love to have you there,"
Northumberland said.

Relief flooded the boy. He wanted so much to attend, he
wanted so much to leave his room – even the palace was starting
to close in on him. "And I shall supply the robes for the celebrations as well. This shall be my present to the couples."

Northumberland smiled, but only on one side of his face. "I
know they will be as grateful as I am for that kindness, Sire."

May 21, 1533

Greenwich Palace was quiet, deserted. The entire court was at
Durham Place, celebrating.

Northumberland had been crowing about the wedding all
week, about how magnificent it would be, with jousts and games
and masques. He had invited the French and Venetian Ambassadors, even large numbers of common people. Edward was
devastated he could not attend.

But he had to conserve his strength. His doctors didn't need to tell him that. He knew.

He was dying. After months the pain was mounting, not ebbing.

He accepted that, with Somerset's words as his mantra: *I repent me of nothing more than esteeming life more dear than I should.*

Edward would fulfill his destiny.

He owed it to God, who had entrusted him with removing superstition from his men's prayer. He owed it to his people, as their king.

He had to stay alive until he could push this bill through his Council, until he could make sure he had created the legal framework to enforce his will.

Northumberland would enforce it. He could trust Northumberland. Northumberland had an incentive.

Edward wished he could talk to Cranmer about this. But Northumberland insisted on maintaining secrecy. Too many people might have sympathy for Mary; they could not take any chances.

Edward started coughing again, his chest on fire. When he was done, he reached for his medicine. His doctors warned him he should not have more than twelve grains in a single day, but he needed more than that to survive. He could not sleep for the pain, he could not think for the pain. He was taking the grains every hour at least.

He brushed a hand through his hair and a great clump held to his fingers. This had been going on for several days now; his head was covered with bald spots.

God, deliver me, he thought, drifting into the twilight sleep he seemed to live in now.

The ghost appeared to him again, clad in gossamer white. A veil always covered her face but he knew it was his mother. She too had been sacrificed. Edward had risen like a phoenix from her ashes, and now Jane would rise from his.

Did it hurt you this much too, Mother?

The ghost kept her silence, as she always did, and he answered himself. We all must suffer, even our Lord had to suffer.

I accept what You decree, O God.

June 12, 1533

While Northumberland paced in the Council chamber, Edward sat in his chair, his back as straight as he could manage, which was not much. He was resting from the effort it had taken to get the short distance, grateful for the cushions that kept him upright.

"Are you ready?" Northumberland asked. "If you are to convince them, you must seem strong. Your life and legacy hinge on this moment."

"I know," Edward said.

The Council had agreed to his plan. Not without dissention. Cranmer, in particular, had begged leave to reason with Edward in private. But in the end, they all had agreed. Now they would make it impossible to challenge.

More pacing. "They must believe this comes from you. You understand?"

"I am ready," Edward said.

The Judges of the King's Bench entered, open curiosity on their faces. This was the land's highest court, with jurisdiction over all cases involving the Crown. It would legitimize Edward's plan – and quickly. While its records might be subject to review by Parliament, that wouldn't happen until it was too late for anything to be done about it.

Northumberland had figured that out.

Each judge peered at Edward, then quickly looked away when they saw how he was watching them. Edward knew rumors were flying about his condition; the Council was trying to tell people he was recovering, but more and more people were reporting that he was already dead.

"Good day, gentlemen," Northumberland said when they

were all seated. "The King has asked you here to discuss a matter of vital importance for the realm."

The judges exchanged glances but remained silent.

Northumberland nodded and William Cecil, as Council Secretary, jumped up from his desk in the corner and passed around the copies of Edward's "Devise." When Cecil was done, he returned to his post and picked up his quill.

The judges picked up the document, scanned it, and exchanged more glances.

"The succession needs to be settled," Edward said.

The Lord Chief Justice, Sir Edward Montagu, coughed. Not an indication of illness, but an expression of discomfort. He sat back and stroked his long white beard. "The succession is settled, my Lord. Settled by our late King and Parliament."

"This King wishes to change that," Northumberland said. "This is the framework he wants you to turn into a legal document."

Montagu coughed again. "We will need some time to consult on this. My own opinion is that it would be treason to overturn the existing plan."

"Shall nothing ever change, then?" Edward said. "Must we continue to do things as my father did them, despite all the things we have learned since then? I will not allow Mary to inherit my throne; she will overturn all the progress we have made in matters of religion."

"Perhaps she could be required to promise to make no alteration to religion," Montagu offered.

"Never," Edward said, vehemently enough that a fit of coughing gripped him.

Northumberland slammed his fist on the table. Edward saw the unmistakable sign of one of his rages come over his face. A purple vein throbbed in his forehead, just like a vein used to in Edward's father's forehead. "I will fight in my shirt with any man living before I permit this insult."

The judges cringed, their faces pale. Edward was also

uncomfortable, even knowing the rage was not directed at him – indeed, it was on his behalf.

Montagu, shoulders cowed, tried to respond. "But the treason…"

"My sister Mary would provoke great disturbances and leave no stones unturned in her efforts to gain full control of the throne and its policies," Edward said. "I tell you again, it would be all over for the religion whose fair foundation we have laid together."

"But by what argument do you set her aside?"

"Mary was the daughter of the King by Catherine the Spaniard, who before she was married to my worthy father had been espoused to my father's elder brother, and was therefore for this reason alone divorced by my father."

"Then why do you bypass Elizabeth?"

"It was her fate to have Anne Boleyn for a mother. This woman was cast off by my father because she was more inclined to couple with a number of courtiers rather than reverencing her husband. Thus, in our judgment, neither she nor Mary deserves to be considered among the heirs of the King, our beloved father."

The judges exchanged glances again. Edward was annoyed they were so timid – and enraged they were balking at something that should be clear.

"I demand Jane be made my heir, demand that you draw up the letters patent of my will. You worry it would be treason to ignore the will of my late father, well I say unto you that it is treason to refuse me now."

Northumberland nodded his approval, his mouth set. "What say you, gentlemen?"

Montagu leaned over and spoke in a low voice to the others. Try as Edward might, he could not make out the words. Finally, the man looked back at him. "I beg your pardon, Sire, it was never our intention of displeasing you or refusing to obey your orders. If you will order us in writing – under the Great Seal of

England – to take this action, and issue us a pardon, also under the Great Seal, for having done it, then we will be fully protected against charges of treason."

Edward swallowed, not wanting to give himself over to anger over this excess of caution. An order and an advance pardon for following it? He reminded himself he was getting his way, so it should not matter they were acting like this. It was not an insult to his position, despite how much it felt like it was. He felt the heat in his head and realized a fever was building.

He just didn't have time to deal with all of this. He needed the document drawn up and formalized. His health was deteriorating; this could not wait.

Northumberland pointed at William Cecil. "Do you have all that down?"

"Aye, sir," Cecil said.

"Good," Northumberland said. "And you shall sit with Lord Montagu after the meeting to make sure the documents contain all the language he needs."

Edward took a deep breath. It would happen.

July 4, 1553

Mary calmed her ragged breathing. It had been a lone rider approaching the palace, with a cloak over his face that shielded his identity. It was too large a man to be Scheyfve, that was all she knew. Now she could hear his steps in the hallway.

"The Earl of Arundel," the page announced as the Earl stepped into the room, not waiting for permission.

"Greetings, my Lady," he said, bowing lower than he had ever bowed to her. "The Council will soon be sending a messenger to summon you to London to visit your brother, to bring him comfort by your presence."

Mary's heart went out to her little brother, so very sick. "Of course I will go."

"Nay, my Lady," Arundel said, "you must run away. The

messenger has been instructed to escort you straight to the Tower. They want control over your person."

She raised her chin and narrowed her eyes. "What is this?"

"They have subverted the succession, and plan to pass the Crown to Lady Jane Grey and her husband, Guilford Dudley. Northumberland forced the Council to agree to the scheme, and dozens of noblemen, including myself, have signed the letters patent."

A howl rose in Mary's chest. Northumberland was trying to steal her Crown. And Arundel was helping him. "You betrayed me?"

"I was given no choice; none of us were. I went along with their scheme and snuck out the back to give you this warning. You must run away."

Fear spread through her, but anger followed hot on its heels. "I will not run. I have given in to threats all my life – first a father who mistreated me, and then that silly young boy manipulated by a power-hungry man. No more."

"That power-hungry man has the law on his side for now," Arundel pleaded. "Get out while you can."

"Without Parliament, this mockery is not the law," Mary said, resolve filling her lungs. "I will not run. I will fight for my throne. I am the next Queen."

"Northumberland's army awaits you in London. Think of this as a strategic retreat. You are loved in East Anglia; go among your supporters there and gather yourself an army."

Of course. "They may be there already." East Anglia was the Catholic heart of the country, where Kett's Rebellion had been born. Where Mary had been blessed for sharing her Mass with them. They would stand with her against this treason.

The spirit of her mother hugged her. She felt her grandmother too. Warrior queens. Isabella of Castille had driven the Moors from Spain, Catherine of Aragon had driven off a Scottish attack and killed their king. Now Mary would join their line. With God's help, she would earn her throne.

July 6, 1553

Please, Lord, release me, Edward prayed.

He knew he could not last much longer. His strength was gone; only pain remained. Pain as bad as any martyr ever suffered, pain that surrounded him and crushed the air from his lungs.

"What news of Mary?" he croaked, hoping she had arrived and had been apprehended. Though his "Devise" had been fully legalized, it would be prudent to have her under guard to make sure no one would consider rising for her. If she were free, the Emperor might be tempted to intervene.

"Not yet," Cheke said. "But Northumberland says he expects her any minute."

Northumberland had a thousand men in the field and more in reserve, and he was the greatest general the country had. He would handle the situation, Edward knew.

A wave of pain washed over him, tearing more prayers from his soul. He needed to hear they had Mary in hand. Then he would fear nothing. Then he could die in peace.

Sir Henry Sidney mopped Edward's forehead. His doctors stared at him as if their concentration might offer some solution. There was none, Edward knew. The time was at hand. He had fought this long and hard, only to cede more and more territory to the pain. He had nothing left. He raised his eyes to Heaven and spoke as best he could, in a reedy whisper.

"Lord God, deliver me out of this miserable and wretched life, and take me among thy chosen; howbeit not my will but Thine be done. Lord, I commend my spirit to Thee."

When nothing happened, he wondered again whether this was just a divine test that he was failing through doubt. "O Lord, Thou knowest how happy it were for me to be with Thee; yet for Thy chosen's sake, send me life and health, that I may truly serve Thee. O my Lord God, bless Thy people and save Thine inheritance! O Lord God, save Thy chosen people of England. O my

Lord God, defend this realm from papistry, and maintain Thy true religion, that I and my people may praise Thy holy name, for Thy son Jesus's sake."

Henry Sidney approached again, startling him.

"Are you so near?" Edward asked. "I thought you were farther off."

"We heard you speak to yourself, but what you said we know not."

"I was praying to God."

Edward shivered, and Sidney took him in his arms. The touch exploded but then numbed the agony. Edward closed his eyes. "I am faint," he said. "Lord have mercy upon me and take my spirit."

The ghosts that had been haunting the corners of his room approached the bed, days after Argos had claimed it, curling up at Edward's feet. The sweet puppy had gradually moved up Edward's side to give greater comfort; now he rested his head on Edward's shoulder.

Tom and Somerset were above him, but he wasn't scared: they looked more sad than grave. His father was not with them.

Instead, it was another ghost. A woman.

She had the gentleness of Katherine Parr, but not her face. Her face was Somerset's.

"Mother," he said.

"He's hallucinating again," said a voice around him. One of the doctors. One of the men who did not have his own direct connection to the divine. Poor man.

"The dream is over," the ghost said. "The Seymours are done."

It was a soft voice, borne on the wind.

"He's dead," one of the doctors said.

"Get Jane Grey. We need to proclaim her quickly."

He tried to speak, to croak, to move, to tell them he still lived. But before he could, he realized he was wrong.

EPILOGUE

August 3, 1553

*T*raditionally, a monarch's reign begins with a triumphant entry into London. This one was no exception, but this triumph was true. Thousands lined the road to cheer the new Queen on her way, pressing joyfully to shout blessings on her.

Mary's heart was full to bursting as she waved back at her people from atop her white palfrey. More than eight hundred nobles and gentlemen followed to show their support for the woman that had almost been put aside.

The country had been as outraged as Mary over the attempted theft of her rightful throne. They had rallied for her, flocked to her in numbers great enough to cause Northumberland's supporters to turn tail and flee. Including the Council.

Cries of "Long Live the Queen" rose from every throat; some in the crowd wept with joy as she passed. People threw money from windows, and old men were seen leaping and dancing as though beside themselves.

It had once been forbidden to speak in Mary's favor, under

penalty of death. Now bells pealed and bonfires flared to celebrate her.

Mary had prevailed, and for the first time in years the organs of every church in the land blasted a jubilant *Te Deum*.

In the end, even Northumberland had proclaimed Mary Queen. As his soldiers deserted and Mary's army of peasants surrounded him, he held his arm aloft, waving his white staff of office. Casting off his weapons, he urged others to do the same. With tears in his eyes, he told one observer he believed Mary to be a merciful woman, whom he would sue for pardon.

Mary sniffed. The man was a heretic and a traitor who had dragged people she loved into his horrible schemes. She would show mercy to Jane, even Henry Grey. But Northumberland? Never.

As she approached the City, the streamers hanging from the gates came into focus. The mayor welcomed her there with the royal regalia, kissing the scepter before placing it in her hands.

"Thank you, good sir. The City has always been good to me."

She passed on streets freshly graveled, as trumpets and bells echoed above like thunder. Rich cloths and tapestries hung from buildings. Images of the Virgin Mary and other effigies of saints, proudly restored from their hiding places, peered out from windows. On every crossroad, banners proclaimed the same message: *Vox populi, vox dei* – the voice of the people is the voice of God.

As Mary neared the Tower, another peal of ordnance rang out. She could see the line of prisoners that had been arranged for her, and her heart quickened.

She dismounted at the Tower gate, and the prisoners knelt, waiting for her mercy. They had been carefully chosen – not a one from the recent rebellions. Just four of them. The first was her cousin Edward Courtenay, imprisoned for decades because of his royal blood and only ever discussed in whispers. He should have gone free on Edward's accession – well, he'd go free now.

The other three were Mary's dear friends, imprisoned

because they shared her beliefs or loved her: the Duke of Norfolk, Bishop Stephen Gardiner, and Anne Seymour Somerset. Mary bid them rise and kissed each one. "These are my prisoners," she declared, and with that they were free.

All of them.

She looked at the sky, and the billowing clouds suggested her mother's hair.

You won, Mother.

Your daughter is Queen of England.

AUTHOR'S NOTE

Remember that the story you just read was filtered through the eyes of a boy who wasn't quite sure what was going on (though Mary is also a point-of-view character, and her scenes provide good reality checks). In the interests of that story, I had Edward attend way more Council meetings than he actually did, but there were still things that no one would have told him, so I worked out ways to have him find out on his own. Like hiding behind the tapestries at Hampton Court palace (I have to believe he did that!), or overhearing yelling from a room next door.

Also in the interests of story, I made a few deliberate changes to timing: Cheke actually became a Gentleman of the Privy Chamber on Edward's accession, but it was clearer to keep his role separate until the huge change in attendants that took place after Somerset's (first) fall. Similarly, Warwick became Duke of Northumberland a week before his friends were elevated, but I conflated the ceremonies to occur on the same day. I ignored the reports that had Tom Seymour killing Argos (a name I invented) with a gun rather than a sword - to me, bringing a gun connoted premeditation (the sword made it possible that Tom reacted from instinct and not malice). I fudged a bit on the French ambassadors: there was no official envoy to the English court between

Charles de Marillac, who left in 1543, and Antoine de Noailles, who arrived in 1553, but there were representatives who functioned in that capacity so I referred to them as such. Finally, I know that on September 9, 1551, Somerset may not have been at court (he stayed away from court after a servant caught the sweat, to make sure he did not infect the King). Still, I needed a confrontation so readers could sense the budding plot - and since I could not signal this through Edward (or Mary), I chose to do it this way.

I hope you appreciate the choices I made — and I hope you love the book! Please consider leaving a short review (even just a star rating) on Amazon or Goodreads (or Barnes & Noble, or Kobo, or iBooks – or your library's website!) to help other readers discover it. It really does make a difference and it would mean the world to me!

ALSO BY JANET WERTMAN

The Boy King is the final book in the Seymour Saga trilogy, the tale of the unlikely dynasty that shaped the Tudor era. The series begins in *Jane the Quene* with a 27-year-old Jane who is increasingly desperate for the marriage that will provide her a real place in the world, and continues in *The Path to Somerset*, taking us through Henry's crazy years after Jane's death to show Edward Seymour's rise to become Lord Protector of England and Duke of Somerset.

All three books have won rave reviews, and yes, you can read them out of order, so feel free to circle back to *Jane* or *Somerset* now that you're done with this one! Each book in the series is standalone...though they do play nicely together and will satisfy your Tudor cravings.

While we're on the subject of Tudor cravings, you do subscribe to my blog, don't you? I publish a new post every week or so (though admittedly during the runups to a publication day I rely a little more on the "or so"). It's a great way to get a regular dose of the Tudors in between my book releases! www. janetwertman.com. Hope to see you there!

Made in the USA
Monee, IL
12 October 2022

15715738R00215